LAW

OF THE

LEMHI

PART ONE

SAVAGE LAW: BOOK 1

LAW

OF THE

LEMHI

PART ONE

SAVAGE LAW: BOOK 1

KIRBY JONAS

Cover design by Forrest Design Group

Howling Wolf Publishing
Pocatello, Idaho

Howling Wolf Publishing
1611 City Creek Road
Pocatello ID 83204

For more information about Kirby's books, check out:

www.kirbyjonas.com
Facebook, at KirbyJonasauthor

Or email Kirby at: **kirby@kirbyjonas.com**

Manufactured in the United States of America—*One nation, under God*

Publication date for this edition: December 2016
Jonas, Kirby, 1965—

Savage Law 1: Law of the Lemhi, Part One / by Kirby Jonas.

ISBN: 978-1-891423-26-0
Library of Congress Control Number: 2016906888

To learn more about this book or any other Kirby Jonas book, email Kirby at kirby@kirbyjonas.com

Dedicated to Brad Dennison, without whom
this book would never have been

CHAPTER ONE

♦ *1972* ♦

Tuesday, October 31

Coal Savage had not killed anyone in over six months. And certainly not his own wife. Was Laura dead? Yes. But not by his hand, and *nobody* was going to accuse him of it. At least not to his face.

No, Coal had killed no one in over six months. But perhaps that was all about to change...

There was no doubt which house on Schubert Street belonged to Charles Bryne. The cul-de-sac in the upscale Gray Mockingbird subdivision in Warrenton, Virginia, was lit up like a football stadium, the hit song "Too Late to Turn Back Now" blasting from the open door and the front room window, and the cars there practically stood on top of each other: bright new Lincolns, Mercuries, and Cadillacs, at least one Porsche, a bright red Corvette, and a dozen other cars belonging to, or at least driven by, high school students with foolish parents who made too much money and didn't have sense enough to buy comfortable underwear, much less teach their children the value of a dollar.

In deep shadow down the block, Coal Savage sat musing on the irony of that particular song banging against his eardrums, as he kept watch from his 1970 Buick LeSabre, its midnight blue blending with the night. It was a company car. He should not have taken it. But his pickup, although also dark blue, was *big*. He couldn't afford to stand out, especially not here.

He had attached a Swarovski extendable spotting scope to his partly rolled down window. Unlike the car, the scope *was* his. And if he had a choice, he would have been searching through its lens over some mountain slope in the wilderness back home in Idaho for a trophy bull elk, not spying on his fifteen-year-old daughter, Katie Leigh, and her so-called friends.

But in this particular instance he *had* no choice.

Being her father took all choices away.

When he leaned back from the spotting scope, Coal felt a heavy thump against his chest, and he winced. Not because it was painful, but because the thump reminded him that inside his black leather jacket he was carrying what an old Marty Robbins song called "six ways of dying," and another by that venerated Western singer referred to as a "big iron"—in this case a Model 27 Smith and Wesson revolver with a six and a half-inch barrel and six rounds of .357 magnum ammunition. He had always found the phrase a little silly, since it really wasn't six *ways* of dying; all six bullets offered the exact same way to die. But if even one of those one hundred ten grain bullets hit a man in any one of the places where it surely would if it was coming out of a revolver wielded by Coal Savage, die he surely would. It was a sobering thought, for that revolver had seen blood before. Six months before, to be exact.

A scattering of teenagers came out of the Bryne residence now and then, but ever since nine o'clock that evening, most were staying, not leaving. And Katie Leigh was one of them. Coal had been watching and praying. He would have seen her go.

Coal Savage had to admit to mistake after mistake in his forty-two years of life. The old saying went, "live and learn," but

Coal never seemed to learn. And only by some miracle did he continue to live. His mistakes haunted him. Probably always would. The death of Laura most of all. But the mistake of allowing Katie to stay in the Bryne house on this Halloween night was never going to weigh on his conscience in the future. Who knew what would become of her here? Drug overdose, pregnancy, alcohol poisoning, rape. Even murder. Any and all possibilities had ranged through his mind throughout the evening, ever since learning Katie had dodged his sentence of three weeks' grounding and ducked out the back door to this supposed "freedom."

No, Coal had made a thousand mistakes raising Katie Leigh, but he was not going to allow her to endanger her life tonight. He had already lost so much...

And so he pulled down the spotting scope and set it carefully on the floor, rolled up the passenger window and pushed down the door lock.

And then he took a deep breath, opened the driver's side door.... and prepared to make the next big mistake of his life.

CHAPTER TWO

Coal Savage had walked up on plenty of noisy houses before, in his days as an MP in the Army. And worse, he had participated in quelling a huge riot of Army prisoners in a place dubbed Camp LBJ—standing for Long Binh Jail, but referring derisively to President Lyndon Baines Johnson. Officially, the place was U.S. Army Vietnam Installation Stockade, or USARVIS. It was the ugliest place this Idaho mountain boy had ever seen—a prison not for the housing of Vietcong, but for the worst of his own fellow Americans.

The riots broke out just before midnight on the night of August 29th, 1968, and lasted a week into September. It was the week of hell when Coal learned how ugly a mob of angry colored men could be. He had joined the Marines in forty-eight, just coming out of high school, then, after ten years, taken a one year hiatus before joining up again, this time with the military police division of the Army, in time to fly to Vietnam. Until joining the military, he had never even laid eyes on a colored person, except at the rare movie he was allowed to attend at the Roxy Theater, in downtown Salmon, Idaho. After the Long Binh Jail riot, Coal could have left Vietnam with a hatred of colored men, but he didn't. One of his best friends had stood beside him during the drawn-out days of that riot: Slugger Janx, as dark as any Negro Coal had ever seen, straight out of the swamps of southern-most Louisiana. Another, Tony Nwanzée, was currently his FBI partner in D.C. In Coal's eyes, both of them were brothers, and he would take a bullet in their defense just as he would any other brother.

Now Camp LBJ was long ago, far away. Dark. Dank. The smoke of its riot fires, which were held down low to the ground by stifling humidity, a thing of the distant past. But the filthy rich, privileged white stench of 919 Schubert Street, in the Gray Mockingbird subdivision, was all around him.

The bizarre notes of "Slipping Into Darkness," by a popular rock group with the endearing name of "War," assaulted his eardrums now, seeming to shake the house itself, and again the odd similarity between the title of the song and his current situation did not fail to somehow amuse him, in spite of the tension of the moment. But he did not understand this song, and being an avowed fan of classical music and of cowboy singers like Marty Robbins and The Sons of the Pioneers pre-destined Coal to be severely annoyed by its lyrics, its angry beat and bizarre melody—if such it could be called.

By now, people in the neighboring homes were beginning to part their drapes and look out. That was a bad sign; they might already have summoned the police here. If that were true, it might be a little hard for Coal to explain his presence. His *armed* presence, no less. He had to get Katie Leigh out of this house. He had to find her *now*.

There was no sidewalk here. Coal simply ghosted along the fronts of the yards, over the crisp green grass, stiffened by late autumn, that ran up abruptly against the asphalt of the wide cul-de-sac. Sometimes the great old trees concealed him, the chestnuts, the ashes, the beeches. Although most of their leaves had fallen and been mostly raked away, the trunks themselves were wide enough to provide plenty of cover, when used by a man who had grown up hunting the forests of central Idaho.

In spite of the grating music and lyrics being foisted upon the world through the walls of the Bryne house, this night exuded a certain charm. The old grass and the few decaying leaves that remained lent their autumn aroma to the air, the crispness of the evening braced his skin, made his scalp tingle. Once again, he was stalking his mountains. Once again, he was closing on his prey.

Coal had no intention of using the .357 under his jacket. He wore it habitually because, as an agent of the FBI, it was part of him, although unlike most agents he chose the longer-barreled six and a half inch rather than the snub-nosed version. The other reason he wore it was, frankly, one just never knew. He would rather sit in prison for a few years somewhere than run afoul of some killer and lie asleep forever, either in Arlington Cemetery, or way back home in Idaho. And a man just never knew what he was going to come upon while sneaking around in the dark—even in an upscale neighborhood like the Gray Mockingbird.

In the shadow of a dark Lincoln Continental, Coal paused. He thought of his position at the FBI. He thought of his honorable discharge in November of 1958 from the Marines, and December of 1968 from the Army, and of the medals hanging mounted on green velvet in their frame on his wall. All well-earned. All for honorable service. And then he thought of his little girl, Katie. She was being rebellious—just a stage. He wanted to take her over his knee and teach her some manners. But Katie was his little girl. No matter how she had sassed him, no matter how much disrespect she had fired in his face, as if from the barrel of a howitzer, he could not change that fact. This was the baby girl he had watched, during his time as an MP in Vietnam, growing up in pictures. This was the little girl for whom he was proud to serve his country, no matter the reception he and thousands of other soldiers received upon returning home. There was no way in hell she was staying in this house, unprotected, while vile boys did... whatever they planned to do. This was war. Every bit as compelling as Vietnam.

Taking a deep breath, Coal stepped away from the Lincoln and strode toward the front door.

He came up on the porch, and the music seemed to him like a wave of colored prisoners from Long Binh, pushing him back, spitting at him, urinating in his direction through the chain link fence. It seemed much lighter here, yet in another way much darker, for at Long Binh he had never had so much to lose.

He didn't knock. He simply grasped the doorknob and turned it, shoving the door open wide. It struck someone, and he heard them swear and yell at him to be careful. Then his appearance registered on the young man who was berating him, and he stopped mid-sentence.

"Where's Charles Bryne?"

"Hey, man!" said another high school-age boy on Coal's left. "You ain't supposed to be here. This party's for students!"

Coal exploded into action, his left arm coming up. He planted his forearm across the youth's throat and rushed him the five feet across the entryway to slam hard up against the wall, and against a tall, slender hallway table, in the process knocking a white vase full of fake plants off and shattering it on the ceramic tile floor.

"If you want me to leave, throw me out, you little turd." He shoved harder against the boy's throat, as he sensed the wave of teenagers in crescent shape coming in like a tide around him. "Where is Charles Bryne? And where the hell is Katie Savage?"

"Somebody call the cops!" he heard a plaintive voice in the crowd. As the others in the smoky room crammed with dozens of people dancing and carefully balancing sparkling drinks in their hands began to become aware that an intruder had infiltrated their ranks, there arose a cacophony of curses, gasps, yelps and yells.

Coal shoved up against the mouthy boy's throat once more, then left him and turned. He could feel the anger burning in his eyes, and he saw its reflection in the startled gazes of the crowd who were closest to him.

And then he heard that voice. That voice he had come to hate as bad as almost any of those in Washington, D.C., where for the past four years he had had the dubious pleasure of being employed by the Federal Bureau of Investigations, where he had spent countless hours being forced to listen to the opinions of some of the most pompous judges and politicians in existence, and some of the most vile criminals he had ever imagined.

It was the voice of eighteen-year-old Charles Bryne.

"Get the hell out of this house, Mr. Savage." *Mister.* Still the inevitable signs of high society, even in the face of a confrontation. "I've called the police on you."

"Where is my daughter?" Coal growled even as he whirled into the pathway of young Bryne's alcohol-heavy breath.

"I'm not telling you where she is. You killed your wife—you think I'm going to let you kill your daughter too?"

The words took a moment to register on Coal Savage. All he could see was the face he hated, all he could hear was the voice he despised. And then the words struck him. *Killed your wife.* Killed my wife? A bright flash went before his eyes. Those words were a declaration of war. Coal had been to war. He had fought like the savage of his name, and he had killed. He had killed with a rifle, with a pistol, with a bayonet, and he had killed with his bare hands. But the men he killed were mere faces, if even that. He had not hated them. They were only in his way. An obstruction between him and an assigned objective.

But Charles Bryne he hated. This was the young man who had introduced marijuana to his baby girl. And alcohol. And then, the last three straws—heroine, cocaine, and LSD. Bryne had survived the past week only because the Warrenton police had him locked in jail. This was his first night of freedom. His night to roar. His night to celebrate release.

His night to go to war with Coal Savage—whether he wanted it or not.

Charles Bryne was a linebacker at Warrenton High School. He stood six-foot-three and could bench press two hundred twenty-five pounds ten times without faltering. But his nose was molded from a rotten pear.

At least it seemed like it to Coal, for it squashed and folded beneath the force of his battle-hardened bodybuilder's fist, and Bryne went flying backward into a bookcase—a big, sturdy maple one that hardly even shuddered—and then he slumped to his butt on the hard white tiles and decided to stream blood all over his shirt and on the exquisite floor.

Coal felt a hard hand on his shoulder, and he ducked away and whirled. That move saved him from an incoming swing from another teenager, the teenager who soon blocked a blow from Coal's right fist—with his cheekbone. The boy staggered into the crowd, and two more came in, sloppy with alcohol and brave with drugs. Coal didn't want to hurt his fists anymore, so he used the first one's crotch for a football. Then, when the other one started to turn to his friend, he slapped him with cupped palms over the ears, and the boy fell to his knees, grabbing his head and screwing his eyes shut.

Then Coal heard Don McLean on the phonograph crooning, "Starry, Starry Night," and almost in sync he saw the whirring flash of blue lights skitter across the walls, accompanied by the yelp of sirens.

The place erupted. Athletes scattered like rodents, dashing for any open hole. Band members ducked, cheerleaders screamed and cried out, glass broke, a door slammed, and it sound like someone went through a screen.

Soon, there were left in the room only those too scared to run, those too wounded to care, four agitated policemen, Coal... and Katie Leigh, who stood a room away and stared at her father with a look in her eyes that could only be considered the fire of hatred.

CHAPTER THREE

Two police officers brandished clubs. One had drawn a gun. A third stood there with just a flashlight. All ignored the war zone of the room and the handful of wounded and scared. Without exception, they were watching one person: Coal.

"I know you," said one of the billy club officers, who wore the name of Tarkinton proudly on his name plate.

"Mr. Savage."

It was a different officer, a county deputy, who spoke his name, his face sad, almost scared, as he stared at Coal. He was the one with the flashlight, with the name Williams on his badge. The last time Coal had seen him, they were taking measurements and photos in the grim, cold shadows of the old red barn on the property with the historic farm house Coal and his family called home. An hour or so later, the workers from the funeral home set Laura's body gently on a stretcher and wheeled her out to the dirt drive that led up the hill to the house.

Another officer tromped into the room now, this one short, stocky, with a bristly gray mustache. He wore the three stripes of a sergeant.

He looked straight at Coal and just mumbled, "Oh." Then he looked at the boys, both Charles Bryne, still on the floor, and those standing in various positions of pain and suffering about the room. He glanced at the five other boys who had remained behind, too scared to run, and the three girls, two of them sitting in silent shock on the couch, the other staring her spears of hatred through her father's head.

After a moment, the sergeant waved an annoyed hand at the wreath of marijuana smoke curling before his face. "Damnit. Open some more doors!" he ordered. "Get this stench out of here."

The sergeant, much shorter than Coal, looked up at him and drilled him with steel eyes. "You hardly took time out to mourn."

Coal's immediate reaction was anger, but even as the fire of it leaped into his cheeks, it just as quickly died. He had heard ruder things than that. And this officer had most likely seen worse things and become calloused by time. Maybe he meant nothing by his comment.

"I didn't have a lot of choice. I didn't want to have to mourn the loss of a daughter, too."

The sergeant, whom Coal recalled wore the name of Cussler, and whose badge bore this out, shot Katie Leigh a glance. There was little doubt who the "daughter" was. Not only did she have the black-brown hair that Coal had had as a boy, then grown out of, but she had his eyes of blue steel as well. The only thing those eyes did not have in common was the hate. Coal's showed none, only dying ferocity, and a little hint of the sorrow that slowly seeped in to replace it.

Sergeant Cussler looked around the room, and finally his eyes settled on Charles Bryne, who was holding his face in shame while he sat in the blood pooled in his lap and on the floor.

"I've made a living these past thirty years reading pictures just like this and making them into a story, Mr. Savage. What I see here is something like a book. We'll have our chance to talk elsewhere. That I promise. But before that, I can tell you how this story goes from here. I know your anger. I understand it. But you and me both know this house belongs to Justice Meriwether Bryne, and no matter how much I understand what happened here tonight, no matter how much I would like to let it go, you know what would happen to my job if I did. And those of these other officers. I cannot trifle with the livings of other officers, and I *will* not destroy the retirement with Warrenton I have worked so long to get. Mr. Savage, I have no choice but to place you under arrest. Be it now, or be it tomorrow, you know it's coming." With that, he took a straddled stance, his gun side away from Coal, bracing his hand at his belt, near the Colt revolver on his hip.

Coal was not going to fight the police. A different place and time, maybe. If he had been in the right, then perhaps. But Cussler was right. He had done wrong, in his fury, and Justice Bryne would never let this lie. One way or another, they would come for him.

"What about my daughter?" he asked quietly, suddenly feeling a throbbing in his fists, a throbbing that in intensity came nowhere near the one that had gone on in his chest since he first saw the hating eyes of his daughter land on his own.

"Can we call anyone?" asked Cussler.

Coal shrugged. There was nobody. No relative here. They were all in Idaho or Montana. No real friends here in Virginia or Washington, D.C. He had left the boys with Mrs. Downing, a neighbor. But he couldn't ask that dear old lady to put up with Katie Leigh, too. Right now, only the devil himself deserved that.

"Maybe my partner," he finally said. "Tony Nwanzée. But he lives in Alexandria. He couldn't be here for probably an hour."

"It's all right. We'll take her down to the station with us. She can ride in the back with you."

Katie came suddenly to life across the room. "I'm not riding with him! You put me with somebody else. I hate him!"

Coal had been stabbed once, by a bloody, battered wife who had just learned Coal was arresting her husband—the very Army lieutenant who had just beaten her senseless. That four-inch blade hurt nothing like the figurative one with which his own daughter had just stabbed him in the belly.

*   *   *

Coal rode to the police station in the front passenger seat of Sergeant Cussler's Ford Galaxie. He wore no handcuffs, and the sergeant had never said why. Katie rode with Officer Williams, her face defiant, her voice silent.

The high school boys back at the house had refused any first aid, and the officers had left them alone. They must have figured the destruction to the judge's home was going to bring on enough punishment to make up for anything the courts would do for their drug and alcohol use and disturbing the peace.

Before leaving the Gray Mockingbird subdivision, the police had shuttled Coal's Buick away from its current location, to a far side-street where the boys would probably not think to look for it in the event that they went seeking revenge. They would send someone back later to bring it to the police station.

Coal let his head sink back against the seat. His heart still throbbed, and so did his fists. The palms of his hands stung from slapping the boy on the head.

How far was this thing going to go? he wondered. Justice Bryne was certain to have a lot of power in D.C. But how much was a lot? Who did he know in the FBI? And did it really matter? Coal had gone into a home without being invited, with the express intention of... Well, how could anyone really know why he had gone in that home? For all anyone knew he had gone only to retrieve his daughter. After all, the marijuana smoke could be smelled from the street. And if he had looked through a window he could have seen they were consuming alcohol. What if he just told them he had come to get his daughter, and the boys had attacked him? Who was going to listen to a bunch of drunk and drugged up teenagers over an agent of the FBI? A well-respected one at that.

But that *wasn't* what had happened. At least not at first. He had been the one attacking. And the truth was, he had gone there hoping for a fight. He had wanted nothing more than to flatten Charles Bryne's nose—just exactly as he had.

Since far back in his childhood, Coal Savage had prided himself on telling the truth. Even as the tires hummed on toward the main part of the city, where City Hall and the jail were located, he knew he couldn't lie.

It wasn't Justice Bryne who was going to cost Coal his position with the FBI. It was Coal himself, and his damnable pride.

CHAPTER FOUR

Monday, November 13

Katie Leigh was sullen. She sat in her bedroom alone, staring out at the rolling fields beyond her upstairs window. Her long, dark hair fell down past her shoulders, glistening and lovely in the soft glow from the indirect sunlight coming through the window pane. Tears shone in her eyes, belying the dark, hard line of her lips. She was a beautiful girl, with such dark hair that the same shade had won Coal the peculiar spelling of his name at birth—and the fine, wonderful, model-quality features and build of her mother.

But even for Coal, who stood in the doorway two weeks after the incident at the Bryne house watching her, it was hard to see the beauty. She was his little girl. Once, she had been his angel baby—or so he had called her. Now he didn't even know her. And he guessed she did not know him. And the look on her face now, in spite of her perfect features and the lovely, soft hair, was one of ugliness. Maybe Katie really did hate him. She had maintained that stance now ever since the death of her mother.

Coal looked beyond Katie to the fields that were catching her gaze. Only stubble lingered, short and yellow in the places where grain had been, tall and bent over auburn where the grass grew wild. This place, Roland Farm, it was called, lay in the heart of Civil War country. Manassas, or Bull Run, lay within just a few miles. As a child in Idaho, this land had called his imagination, made him yearn to see the fields where all those scenes had unfolded, where brother had laid down brother with rifle fire, to become a part of this sod forever. In spite of the blood spilled in the past, it was indeed a charming countryside. But it was not home.

"I know you hate me, Katie, and I understand. But there's no place for us here anymore, and I need you to pack."

Even to himself, his voice sounded dull and lifeless. It made him sad to know it was the tone of voice he used now for his own daughter—his *only* daughter. The little girl whose hand he used to hold when they would go walking down to the Lemhi River, whose eyes would light up with delight when he would skip a flat stone across the river, or when she would throw a piece of bread into the water only to watch it be snatched from the exploding surface by a cutthroat trout.

Where had they gone, those days when she would come running to him yelling, "Daddy" at the top of her voice? He could almost have cried. But he was too mad.

Coal went down the hall and looked into the boys' room. Quietly, the way he did most everything, thirteen-year-old Virgil was pushing his rumpled clothing into a slick orange backpack. Of course his drawings would go, too, but they would be last, probably stowed between two big books to keep them safe. Virgil loved his drawings.

Coal smiled when he looked at the twins, Wyatt and Morgan. He had named his sons after the three most famous Earp brothers, who had fought in the infamous Gunfight at the OK Corral, and, like Coal, they had grown up on the lore, books, art, and film of the Old West—along with the stories that Coal himself would tell them on those rare occasions when he would be home and they would still be awake when he came in to see them.

The boys' favorite toys, by far, were made by the Louis Marx Toy Company, who called them Johnny West. They were eleven and a half inches of the toughest little caramel-colored cowboys ever known, along with blue cavalrymen, white and caramel-colored Indians, Johnny's wife, Jane, four children, and even a couple of Vikings and knights—along with a handful of horses. All came fully equipped with tack and any accessory a Western animal or person could ever need.

Right now, instead of packing, Wyatt and Morgan were going through their Johnny West collection—which was extensive. A little too extensive, probably, because Coal had gone out of his way in his excitement every Christmas to make sure the boys had something of everything. He didn't normally like to spoil them, but he had a feeling a toy that built his boys' imaginations like Johnny West and his friends was not going to be around forever.

"Boys, you need to pack that stuff in the boxes. We're leaving in the morning, and whatever you don't have packed is going to get left here."

As he had foreseen, that promise sent the two younger boys scrambling, while Virgil continued on at his silent, steady pace. They would be packed when he got back. About Katie he wasn't so sure.

Coal would have liked to take the boys with him on his last walk of the Roland Farm. But they were busy. Anyway, he was a little afraid of his own emotions. This had been a wonderful home to them all. How did he say goodbye gracefully? And anyway, how could the boys have faced the barn? For that matter, how would Coal?

He slipped out the front door, afraid if the boys heard him go they would be inclined to follow. To get the worst part over first, then hopefully have time to recover, he trudged down the slope to the big old red barn. He had not been inside one time since... that day. For a long time, he stood outside its huge main doors, his heart pounding. It was as if a dark presence were pushing back at him from inside, some kind of alien force field. Finally, he filled his lungs and stepped inside to stand in the silent shadows.

He was immediately surprised that it wasn't the horrible memory of the undertakers carrying Laura away that struck him most about the barn. It was, instead, the good things. The musty smell of old hay and straw filled every corner, and he could even smell oats and liniment, and the molasses in the sweet feed. He fancied detecting the odor of sugar cubes, the ones he and the boys used to feed to the horses they allowed some neighbors to keep here on the farm, although none of them ever got a chance to ride any of them. He thought back over the four years spent here, catching black whip snakes, sitting up in the loft and dreaming, or just brooding in silence after one of his arguments with Laura.

Up in the loft, there were bales of new green hay, smelling sweet and strong. It was an aroma he was going to smell a lot of when they got where they were going. He suddenly realized that to the children, being in this place would be far more traumatic than for him, for they had seen something he had not. They had seen something that would surely scar their little minds forever.

Coal set his hand on the rough wood of one of the old stalls, where the strong teeth of one of the horses had worried at it in its boredom. A sigh escaped him, and along with it there was almost a tear. He looked past the big open doors, where the black mare, Colorado, stood in the pasture across the little lane munching hay, along with Max, the chestnut gelding. A good looking couple of horses—nothing like Jerry, the Shetland whom they had nicknamed Tiger, for his ornery, bellicose nature.

Farther down the lane he trod, over the rocks and down to the bridge that crossed the creek where the trout lurked. He went on to the glassy pond, where now the grass along the banks lay trampled and brown, and the ruby strawberries that once had sparkled in the grass were but a far-off memory of summer, as well as the black tadpoles he and his boys used to sit and observe darting along the bank. In the pond, he could see a bass or a bluegill come to the shallows now and then, but mostly it was just the glass-blue reflection of the sky, and a ways out the protruding heads of a couple of turtles. On the farthest side of the pond, two ducks were swimming and watching him nervously, and ten yards away along the edge of the shore a huge bullfrog looked on with wary eyes.

He would never forget this place, the cottontail rabbits his dog used to catch, the whitetail deer that would come in here, prancing with their tails held straight up behind them like flags of surrender, a stray opossum hissing from the top of a fence post. Myriad birds of all colors—bobolinks, cardinals, blue jays, finches, warblers, grackles, red-winged black birds. The call of the whip-poor-wills in the gloaming of evening. The flicker of fireflies. It had been a good place for his children to spend some of their growing years. But Salmon would be good too.

The investigation by his superiors at the FBI had gone exactly as he had expected. He had sat in a cramped, hot office, surrounded by windows he couldn't see through from his side of the table, with nothing but the long, semi-rectangular table and a dozen chairs, a carafe of coffee and some mugs sitting on a round table to one side.

They fired questions at him, and he told them the truth. They nodded with grudging respect from time to time, but during the remainder of the session they frowned. A good employee had to keep his cool. And a good employee, second of all, did not beat up on minors. Football players aside—Coal Savage was a large and powerful man who spent way too much time lifting weights, a highly trained warrior, retired from the Army as a military policeman, with a sandan, or third degree black belt, in karate, a proficiency in the boxing ring he had earned in school when most of his friends were playing football or basketball, the ability to conquer enemies with sticks, knives or any kind of firearm. He had no business going into what he had known could turn into a fighting situation with young men who, for their misdemeanors, should have been dealing with the local police, not a trained FBI agent who in his high school years was bulldogging four or five hundred pound steers to the ground while those boys he had taken on were only used to tackling other high school students.

Coal admitted that he went to the Bryne residence to confront Charles Bryne. He admitted that he had hoped there would be an altercation. He admitted that he had attacked before being attacked, and that only the last two boys had come at him ready for a physical confrontation.

Coal Savage had four years with investigations, on top of the twenty he had already served in the two branches of the military, leaving with the rank of sergeant from the military police. He was a solid agent. He had graduated near the top of his class. But the one thing that marred his record, the one thing that found him sitting in this room time and time again, was his temper. He did not like to be spoken back to. He liked people to respect him, and when they did not... sometimes it didn't go well for them.

But the most important point of all in this instance was one glaring fact: When he had broken the nose of Charles Bryne, he had been attacking the only son of a federal judge, a judge with twelve years on the bench and a galaxy of favors owed to him by various people throughout the country—some of them being Coal's supervisors. There was no sidestepping that or leaping over the obstacle: It always came down to whom you knew.

The director had a big soft spot for Coal, and he let him go with the almost unheard-of sum of five thousand dollars in his bank account—he called it severance pay. It was within the director's discretion and authority to issue something to prevent legal issues with the *laying off* of an agent, and of this he took full advantage. It was five thousand that would never be missed by the agency, but which would go a long way toward getting Coal and his family settled into their new life—back home in the little town of Salmon.

Other than Tony, his partner, there had been no one to tell goodbye. The neighbors were nice enough people, but Coal had mostly kept to himself here, and there was no one he would miss very much or who would miss him. Well, there was one, but he could not go to her. And he just hoped that she would understand.

And so he lowered himself to the bank of the old pond where he and his sons had fished, and where Wyatt had always insisted they throw back the biggest and most colorful bluegills they caught, where they had picked and eaten wild strawberries until they were almost sick.

And he looked up the hill toward the house, where the big U-Haul trailer was parked, and then let his eyes drift down the rutted dirt lane to the main road. Across the road was the big yellow, black-trimmed mansion, owned by the people from whom he was renting this farm. There were memories all over this place.

And it was here he hoped the memory of Laura would remain. When he thought of her, the pain he had wanted to hide rushed to the surface, and he hung his head and fought back the tears that otherwise may have mercifully washed away all memory of Mrs. Coal Savage.

CHAPTER FIVE

Saturday, November 18

Coming home. Home to heaven—but transporting hell.

Katie Leigh had been nothing but a rotten stew of headache and heartache the vast majority of the twenty-three hundred-mile trip from Virginia. The only time she allowed any peace was when she was sleeping, and even then the heartaches persisted, because Coal was beginning to believe the conglomerate of nightmares his daughter was constructing was going to build her a house of isolation and self-destruction before her sixteenth birthday. He loved his girl, but for most of twenty-three hundred miles he had wanted to trade her in for a grasshopper and step on the grasshopper.

The boys were good. Virgil was quiet, keeping everything internal. Missing Mom. Sure—what kid wouldn't? In spite of the way Laura had become, she was still their mother. They still loved her, and she had loved them unconditionally.

Little Wyatt and Morgan, in spite of their obnoxious, "how much longers" and "are we almost theres", had been mostly nothing but pure joy. Coal liked to consider himself somewhat of a naturalist, something he had had ground into him by his own father from childhood. So all the way west, through pieces of eight states—maybe nine, he had lost count—they had talked about trees, and birds, even rocks, bushes and weeds. And the wildlife, that was the cream of the journey—whitetail deer, moose, raccoons, porcupines, rabbits, foxes, coyotes, then finally a few mule deer and elk, and even one black bear, spotted just after dawn. The boys seemed to love it, even Virgil, although he only showed his enjoyment with his eyes, never speaking more than a few words at a time.

With all of their worldly possessions now being pulled in a U-Haul trailer behind them, Coal drove his 1964 Chevy pickup, dark blue with white and chrome trim down the side of the cab and stock hub caps, white with the centered Chevy symbol in red. Opening the windows and the wing windows kept it cool—the opposite kept it warm. And it didn't hurt to wear his blanket-lined Wrangler coat or his leather jacket. The pickup was nearly new when he bought it, with forty-five hundred miles on the odometer and a full tank of gas, for seventeen hundred dollars. It was a solid piece of work, and he had never looked back. Thanks to his overseas military service and the use of his company car in D.C., it only had forty thousand on it even now.

Over the top of the pickup cab hovered the blunt nose of a cab-over camper, inside of which rode an angry young woman and a quiet young man, and that is where they stayed for most of the trip, Katie Leigh for pretty much the entire thing, unless she was going into some rest stop restroom or now and then if they stopped for a burger.

The wildly changing landscapes throughout the trip west were a miracle, from the hilly farms, rolling pastureland and deep hardwood forests of the East and Midwest, to the lakes of the North, and then to the windswept prairies and broken badlands of North Dakota and eastern Montana. At last, it was the greeting of the evergreen forests of home country that set Coal's heart thumping, and he had to choke back a lump in his throat. This was not just one of his every one to two year trips home to see his mother and to reconnect with a few friends. This was Coal Savage, coming home at last. To stay. And even the devil's spawn that Katie was pretending to be was not going to ruin this for him.

The rugged, towering beauty of mountain ranges around the grassland country of Bozeman, Montana, called to him, and the sunlight and cloud-shadows fought for supremacy. By three o'clock, around Butte, the clouds strung low and menacing, and cool wisps ghosted through the forests of pine, fir, and spruce.

They had to pull off in Butte to refuel, and as he coasted up to the pump, Coal swore and had to immediately apologize to the twins. Gas was up to thirty-eight cents a gallon! With pushing one hundred fifty miles to get back home, it was going to take nearly five dollars to finish out the trip. It was getting so a man could barely afford to live anymore.

Mumbling under his breath, he tried to act cordial when the station attendant came out to pump his gas, making the obligatory small talk. Coal settled down while the man talked about the cold weather and how hunting was going that year. The man cleaned the windows to a fine sheen, polishing them off with a rag from his back pocket, and Coal thumbed the demanded five dollars and seventy cents into his waiting palm.

"Well, I hope you get back home without gettin' dumped on, buddy," said the attendant. He had been able to get out of Coal that, in spite of the Virginia license plates, home was Salmon. "Careful on the pass. They had snow up there just last week, and there was a nasty wreck—a big rig and a station wagon. Might get snow again, if these clouds get any darker."

Coal nodded. He was still having to re-accustom himself to people being friendly. It wasn't that way in D.C. "Been in the snow and ice a time or two. I'll be okay. But thanks."

Before the man could say much more, he got back into the pickup and pulled to the far side of the parking lot so Katie and Virgil could finish making everyone sandwiches in the camper. Virgil brought him his when he was ready—peanut butter and jam on white Wonder bread. The stuff always stuck to the roof of his mouth, and he cursed the necessity of buying it. He sure did miss Laura's whole wheat.

Quickly saved from the melancholy of thinking about Laura by Morgan's long-awaited, "Are we almost there, Daddy?" Coal grinned and tousled the boy's brown hair. He was instantly ashamed to see he had rubbed a little peanut butter in it—but the boy sure wouldn't notice. It hadn't been washed for a week.

"Not yet, Morgan. A few more hours still."

Morgan hung his head, took a bite of his sandwich, and stared at the ground, dejected. He had never been on a cramped plane to Vietnam. None of his children had a clue what endless travel meant.

In twenty minutes, they pulled back onto the highway, bending north-northeast. The steel cloud ceiling eclipsed the mountain ridges now, and each succeeding mountain beyond the first one drifted fast into oblivion in its own cold sheet of gloom. But to Coal, it was only another aspect of paradise. He even opened his window for a while as they passed into the Beaverhead-Deerlodge National Forest, to catch scent of the wonderful bracing breezes of the woods, the musty, wet duff of the forest floor, where signs of the year's first snow were still seeping away into the black and spongy loam.

Deer lurked in the depths, and one time he pointed out to the twins a herd of bull elk, standing not three hundred yards out in a logged clearing, where the auburn grass stood tall and still. The elk were darker looking than normal because of being wet, made darker by the shadows and by the cold mist that swirled around them. Their antlers, from this distance, appeared black, and as they exhaled, clouds of steam puffed out, standing momentarily white against the deep green of the boughs of spruce and fir. The rut was over now, and the bulls had separated once more from the cows and calves. All they cared about today was pounding down enough nourishment to rebuild the strength lost while defending their herds from intruders during mating season—ironically, the very same intruders that were now their herd-mates. It was going to be a long, hard winter for them—in Montana, it always was.

The big tires of the Chevrolet hummed down the now-lonely highway, and blue darkness pooled along its edges from the shadow of the dense conifers. Morgan had fallen over in sleep against his side, and Coal eased the boy's head down onto his lap. It looked pretty uncomfortable, but the little guy slept on. Amazing what contortionists five-year-old children were, and what mauling they could sleep through without batting an eye.

Wyatt, on the other hand, was still staring out the window, fighting the sandman with chin tucked and both fists cocked. His eyelids would droop, and then his eyes would get really wide, and he would sit up straighter in his seat. He looked over at Coal once, caught himself being watched, and gave an impish grin.

"Might see a moose before long, if we watch careful," Coal said. Wyatt was his little game spotter, and even with his inexperienced eyes, sometimes he saw animals before Coal did—much to Coal's chagrin. He sort of fancied himself unmatched when it came to picking out hard-to-see game. Wyatt grinned, and his eyes got wider still. He scooted forward on the seat, unrestrained by any seatbelt. Those had been entombed in the depths of the crack between seat and seat back for as long as Coal could remember.

The forest was deep, and the sunlit road seemed like a ribbon of molten lava in comparison. Coal started quietly to sing an Eddy Arnold song from an album Virgil and the twins had just about worn out in Virginia. "Oklahoma Hills." Old Eddy. Quite a voice. Some said Coal had quite a voice too, but he always laughed at that. He was well aware that God had made him to legally harass the guilty citizens of his continent, and sometimes the world, not to entertain the populace with whimsical tunes.

Wyatt started singing along with him. Most of the songs Coal sang, his boys could sing with him, word for word. They had passed many miles that way.

It was hard picking up any radio stations out here in the forest, but after going through a few songs on his own, Coal clicked the radio on and spun the dial until he located Johnny Cash in the middle of piping out "Ring of Fire." He half-heartedly tried singing along, but his mind was elsewhere.

Coming home...

When his old friend, and his father's hunting partner, Jim Lockwood, had heard from Coal's mother that he was resigning under pressure from the FBI and called the same day to tell him Lemhi County would be looking for a new sheriff, Coal had been shocked. His old high school class mate, the current sheriff, K.T. Batterton, was a good man, tough and fair, and the people of the county loved and respected him. How did a man like that get ousted? But ousted he would be, Lockwood assured him. And Lockwood would know. He would of course also know why— but he kept that to himself. Lockwood was not a man plagued by the syndrome of loose lips.

Jim Lockwood had himself been the sheriff of Lemhi County, clear up until 1967, when age and a bad hip had finally forced him into retirement. Jim was a legend around Salmon and Leadore. Heck, clean up into Montana! Stories about him had grown to gargantuan proportions, and nothing anyone could say would ever shrink them now. Davy Crockett, to Tennessee, had nothing on Jim Lockwood, to Lemhi County.

Anyhow, when something happened in Lemhi County, Jim knew. Like that tired old fly on the wall, Jim knew *everything* that happened in the county where he had spent all but four years of his life. And Jim guaranteed Coal that he would walk into a job as county sheriff if he chose to ask.

Coal had been walking into jobs half his life, it seemed. Luck, he guessed. The same luck might even have gotten him out of his job with the FBI, although it had come too late to save his marriage. No matter. The fact was, he had a job. From forced resignation with five thousand dollars of "severance pay" in his wallet, to a reputable job in Lemhi County, his love and the home of his childhood—that was the stuff dreams were made of—for Coal Savage, at least.

Many names went through his memory, the names he had grown up with since first grade: Larry and Kathy MacAtee, K.T. and Jennifer Batterton, Trent Tuckett, Ken Parks, Tammy Hawley, Jay Castillo, Molly Erickson. There were many more, but those were the ones he had been best friends with and who had remained around Salmon after high school.

What were his old school mates going to think when it was Coal who had to pick them up for driving drunk? Or going too fast? Or running stop signs? How would he handle those times? Let them go? Show favoritism? He sure couldn't let *everyone* go.

He was turning south onto the Lewis and Clark Trail, the last stretch into home, when he heard it. The radio had turned scratchy, but he heard the voice, a faint mutter. The word Salmon. He keened an ear to the story. The words were broken, with holes in-between filled with static. Sheriff... Lockwood... murder... killer.... identified as...

And then the name, just before the station went out and his breathing seemed to come to a stop.

Larry MacAtee.

CHAPTER SIX

With a sick feeling in the pit of his stomach, Coal drove the last fifty miles toward Salmon. He had downshifted to second to let the gear compression check their speed on what would have been a hair-raising ride down the steep, winding road through Lost Trail Pass had there been ice or snow on it. He suddenly realized he was still holding onto the hard, round handle of the gear shift, and his hand was stiff and sore. Letting go, he flexed his fingers and watched the road.

The irony of life struck him hard when he realized now that reception was better, coming in from KSRA radio station in Salmon, that John Denver was crooning, "Take Me Home, Country Roads." Five or ten minutes earlier, he would have gotten a big chuckle out of that, and he would have been singing along. Now, after the pieces of the newscast he had heard, the words only left him cold.

The scenery outside the windows was breathtaking. The clouds had long since cleared away, and sunshine streamed over the mountain ridges to the right, throwing golden light over the treetops that stood like thousands of waiting soldiers and making the shadows seem ever deeper. The boys were both awake and watching, and thankfully both were too enthralled to ask if they were almost there yet. Coal may not have heard them at this moment, but if he had he might have lost his patience—which would have been a shame, after calmly answering that question at least a couple of hundred times since leaving Virginia.

They drove past Gibbtown—the locals' nickname for Gibbonsville—and now had thirty-three miles to go to hit the city limits of Salmon. But now Coal found he didn't want to be there. He wanted to be almost anywhere *but* there. In his head, he cursed. Had the twins not been here, he would have cursed out loud, then cursed himself again for not being able to control his language. His guts were in a turmoil. He had heard just enough of the newscast to know something bad had happened—a killing. And somehow it involved old Jim Lockwood, retired Lemhi sheriff and his father's friend and hunting partner, and Larry MacAtee, his best friend from high school. Larry was one of the few people in Salmon who had actually made any attempt to keep in touch with him, mostly by the mail, sometimes by phone. He was one of those Coal had most looked forward to reuniting with and visiting with over a cup of coffee down at the Salmon River Coffee Shop or Wally's.

His mind ran through the broken words of the newscast one more time, as closely as he could recall it. Lockwood. Murder. Identified as... Larry MacAtee.

The curves in this section of Highway 93, going through densely wooded forest, were too tight to be driving the pickup this fast with its camper on top and the trailer behind. Coal had to force himself several times to concentrate on slowing down. There was a good chance that a couple of the curves had already thrown Virgil and Katie around in the camper, which was going to turn an already angry young woman into a mountain lion in lipstick. But even more importantly, besides the tight curves themselves, at this time of year there was a chance around every corner that there were going to be elk or deer on the highway, maybe even a moose or some bighorn sheep. The last thing they needed was a wreck on the way into town, and no matter how soon they got there it probably wasn't going to help with whatever awaited them anyway.

But his foot kept prodding the gas pedal, and his teeth ground into each other almost hard enough to crack. Luckily, neither of the twins had yet sensed there was anything wrong. It was a benefit of being five years old.

They drove through North Fork, with some old farmer shaking his fist at them and yelling something about speed, and turned southeast, and now they were on the flats. The road was still winding, trying to mimic the run of the river, but nothing like coming down from the pass.

This was some of the most majestic country on earth. The north fork of the Salmon River—the River of No Return—snaked along on their right, with steep bluffs above it and along its shores cottonwood trees all pale gray and bare-branched now, already sleeping and awaiting the spring. Fields of grass and sawbuck fencerows, old weathered barns and log cabins, burned paintless and brown by decades of sun. Deer fed out in the meadows, and in one bend of the river there stood a huge bull moose, black as night.

They were going way faster than they should now, as fast as the pickup would go, and Coal found his hand locked on the gear shift handle again, his hand gone numb from the vibrations of the dense plastic.

The radio was loud and clear, as Coal wished it had been earlier. Buck Owens was singing "Bridge Over Troubled Water," and in spite of his country roots Coal frowned. Some songs should not be remade, and this was one. As much as he liked his country, it was impossible to best Simon and Garfunkel on their own turf.

Coal found himself grinning. The things a man can think of under stress.

They passed the Carmen post office, where a Riviera and a Cutlass sedan were stopped, side by side, and the drivers were chatting with each other through the windows.

Home. Almost.

But home to what?

Jim Lockwood. Man, he longed to see his face. Right now, this minute. Was Jim all right? And Larry. Good old Larry, always ready with a joke, and one of the few males Coal felt comfortable enough with to give a great big bear hug. His eyes would crinkle up into slits when he laughed, and his face would turn red, which was funny because it wasn't really the blush of embarrassment; no one on earth was more self-confident that Larry MacAtee.

Maybe he had heard the radio wrong. It had been pretty staticky. Maybe they were talking about old news. It wasn't like there had never been a killing in Lemhi County. It was one of the wildest places Coal had ever seen, outside of Vietnam. There were bar fights every night of the week, with the exception of Sunday, and then only because the "Blue Laws" had all the bars closed that one day of the week. Many men packed guns in the bars or at the least had one or two outside in their cars.

But his guts told him no. Whatever the newscaster had been talking about on the radio was current. He felt it. His first day back in town, and down deep he knew it was going to be a severely bittersweet homecoming. From what he had understood, piecing together the few words he caught, either Jim Lockwood had murdered Larry MacAtee, or vice versa. Neither seemed possible. Those two adored each other every bit as much as Coal did both of them.

They passed a hotel on the left that he had never seen before, built right on the access to the river. People just couldn't leave anything alone. There had been some great fishing right there, some big old cutthroat and even steelhead in those waters that hated dry flies so bad they wanted to tear them right off the steel leader, and take the line, and the rod and reel too, if given the chance, all the way back up the river.

It was Saturday evening, and it was very likely no one would be around, but instead of turning left toward his mom's, Cole turned right, heading up Courthouse Drive toward the elevated area above town that they called the Salmon Bar. Shortly after, he pulled in the wrong way in front of the huge rock and brick courthouse and slammed to a stop, jerking back the emergency brake. With whatever was on the news, maybe there was someone here, working late. He knew Jim Lockwood had done that a lot when he was sheriff and there was a big case brewing.

"You boys stay here," he ordered the twins. "Do *not* get out of this pickup."

With that, he leaped out and slammed the door. It made a loud metallic sound like an explosion, echoing up and down the narrow street. The main area of the courthouse was closed, and by now the hill was deep in shadow. The sun had long since gone down behind the mountains.

He hurried around to the back, and a huge relief washed over him when he saw private vehicles still parked there. He strode past a brown Chevrolet pickup and a dark blue Ford LTD he was sure belonged to the county and a black nineteen seventy Thunderbird that made him pause. Jim Lockwood had always been a fan of Ford Thunderbirds, but last time Coal had seen him he was driving a white sixty-four. Had he decided to upgrade? Rushing past the vehicles, Coal pounded on the door as loud as he could— almost as loud as his heart was pounding in his chest. Someone inside yelled something, and he pounded again, even louder.

The someone yelling back got perturbed this time, and the words, "Knock it off" were plain as day.

"Open the door!" he shouted back, and his voice was not that of a patient man.

The door flew wide, and a man who looked like he was about to berate him in anger instead let his jaw fall slack as he stared.

Two other men had walked up behind him, and both looked equally surprised.

One of the men standing back was Jeb Rowe, a local farmer who liked to drink too much Jack Daniels and seemed to enjoy the accommodations in the Lemhi County jail. The other one was ex-sheriff K.T. Batterton, Coal's old classmate and good friend.

But the one who mattered most was the man who had opened the door—the very one whose cranky old voice had told Coal to "knock it off."

There stood old Jim Lockwood.

CHAPTER SEVEN

When Coal thought back on it, the shock on his face must have been frightening, judging by Jim's face. Honestly, he hadn't known what to expect, but two things were strongest on his mind: either Jim Lockwood had been murdered, probably by some thug he had thrown in jail at one time or another, or that he had been implicated in a murder. The worst case scenario, of course, was that he had murdered Larry, or the other way around—both thoughts unfathomable. But here, as his mind finally registered, stood Jim, with no handcuffs on and not a sign in the world that he was in custody. In fact, he was wearing a belt gun on his hip— at a glance, his old service revolver.

Shock was the word of the day. Once Coal realized that Jim was not dead *or* in trouble, he leaped forward and threw his arms around the older man, and now it was Jim's turn to be shocked. Coal could see that when, embarrassed at his own impetuousness, he stepped back and let his old friend go. Jim just stood there, his mouth open beneath his bristly gun-metal gray horseshoe mustache.

"Damn, son!" the ex-sheriff finally stammered. "I don't even get that kind of reception from Betsy!"

Coal laughed out loud, and inwardly he cursed his misty eyes. What kind of an ex-soldier was he? And what kind of a future sheriff cried in front of other grown men?

Jim Lockwood was a solid fellow in his day, not more than medium height, not more than medium build, but with enough heart that he must have had to carry the extra in the trunk of his Thunderbird. Either that, or it was crammed into his chest under pressure and had probably squeezed past a very narrow waist and down into both legs. His sharp eyes were sky-blue, a touch cloudier than before. His jawline was softer, too, and his mostly gray hair rode a line above his ears now, having mostly deserted the dome of his head. Shoulders that had carried wounded soldiers off bloody hills in France were thinner now, and sixty-some years of age had creased, battered and spotted his tough old hands and his forehead too, although he could still boast the leanest hips in town. All in all, he was about the prettiest sight Coal had seen all day.

Trying to excuse his strange behavior and the dampness in his eyes, Coal said, "I heard pieces of a newscast on the radio, Jim. Hardly a story at all—just that there's been a killing, and they mentioned your name. And... They also said something about Larry."

Jim looked over at K.T. Batterton, and Coal's glance followed. K.T., standing five-foot-ten and weighing in at one eighty-five, was the "Prince of Pushups" among the Salmon Savages of Salmon High back in the day. The "day" was 1947 and 48—the year of their graduation. K.T., the handsomest boy in high school, had had to settle for "prince" because Coal was the crowned Salmon Savage king—but *only* of pushups.

It was K.T. Batterton the high school had crowned their homecoming king, and the student body president as well. As far as boys went, K.T. was the sweetheart of the school. But now most of his blond hair was gone, and his mustache and sideburns every bit as unimpressive as the day they graduated.

K.T. stood there in new blue jeans and faded red and brown plaid long-sleeve shirt, buttoned at the cuff. He met Coal's eyes, and a warmth flooded through his own as he stepped forward and grasped Coal's outstretched hand, pumping it hard. "No hug for *me*, buddy?"

Coal laughed. Any other time, he would have made some retort—some smart aleck remark about giving him a kiss instead, or something equally ribald. But his guts were knotted like a trussed up rodeo calf, and his cheeks tight with strain. He searched K.T.'s eyes for some sign, and those soft brown eyes gave him one. It was not good. It was a sign of pain. Staving off the bad news he knew was to come, Coal stepped closer and threw his arms around K.T. Maybe there was just no other way to say hello to old friends sometimes than a warm embrace.

They stepped apart, grabbing hold of each other's arms, and K.T. smiled. "Dang, you're still solid as a rock, Coal. I'm ashamed I let myself go to seed. How in the world do you still find the energy? I swear, every time I see you I think you're going to finally start looking like one of us humans, and instead I think you just keep packing more muscle on."

"The energy?" echoed Coal. "Well, K.T., that's a good question. It's called a fear of getting old, and sheer vanity. Between those two weaknesses, it's amazing what you can do in the gym."

K.T. chuckled, shaking his head. "Well, it's working out for you—no pun intended! How many pushups you up to now... *King?*"

Coal tried to put a light look on his face and grinned. "One hundred forty-five, buddy. No stop."

K.T. laughed. "Are you serious? Jeez, I think I'm down to five—if I'm full of Coca Cola." Then the smile and the laughter disappeared from his face. His eyes flitted over to Jim, then back to Coal, and moisture came into them that he tried forcefully to blink back.

Coal met his friend's eyes. It was strange what men found to talk about when they wanted to dodge a tough subject. What scared him most was the plain fact that no one wanted to talk about Larry.

"Coal, I sure was looking forward to you gettin' back here— until this morning. Now... I don't even know how to tell you what I've got to."

Coal swallowed. He felt his mouth twitch under his dark mustache when he looked back over at Jim. For a brief second, a thought raced through his mind, and he looked beyond the two lawmen to the farmer, Jeb Rowe. Rowe was a jovial sort of man who worked his farm like a demon, from spring until well after harvest, when all was back in order again. And then, for the winter, he drank like there was no tomorrow. November was pretty close to drinking season for Jeb. And when Jeb started drinking, he became something else—a *different* sort of demon.

A racing visual sweep showed Coal that there were no handcuffs on Rowe, either, and a bolt action Winchester rifle lay on the sheriff's desk, very much within the farmer's reach. Whatever reason they had him here, it was not for suspicion of a crime.

K.T. and Jim had both observed Coal's scan of Rowe. To negate the need for any questions, K.T. jerked a thumb at the granger. "Jeb, here, went out to see Larry this morning. Larry had said he needed five more ton of hay for his horses for the winter, but he never came to get it yesterday—and it was an ideal day for hay hauling. Never called to say why, either, and when Jeb tried to call, he didn't answer."

As K.T. spoke, Coal's chest constricted tighter and tighter. A tired feeling spread over him like a musty old blanket, bringing a need to fall into his mom's old brown La-Z-Boy and stare at the TV. Stare, and not think. He was exhausted. Weary of death. But words of death were about to be spoken. He knew it like he knew the hard, cold blue-gray color of his own eyes.

"So on the radio..." Coal broke in.

Jim's hands came up to stop his words. "Now, Coal, just—" He stopped and looked over at K.T. His chin had started shaking. Wearily, he sort of tipped his head and walked over to the parking lot-level window, leaving his back to the other three.

"Larry's the one they were talking about," Coal went on.

K.T. nodded, his cheeks looking drawn and pale.

"I didn't hear a lot of the broadcast, K.T., but I heard a word or two. One was murder."

Again, K.T. nodded. "Yeah."

"Who?"

"Oh, I don't know, Coal!" K.T. threw up his hands in frustration and turned and walked to the rifle rack. For no apparent reason, he raised a hand and set it on the forestock of a Model 70 Winchester chained in the rack, then he dropped his chin on his chest and just stood there for a moment.

Silence like a winter morning filled the room.

Jim, booted feet spread wide, stared out the window. K.T. had closed his eyes. Jeb Rowe was shifting his weight from one foot to the other and staring at the floor. Coal let his gaze range from one to another and waited. And then he could take the silence no more.

"I guess I just need to hear the words to make this real. Somebody has to say it. Anybody." He felt helpless and suddenly alone.

Rowe's eyes jumped to him. Jim started to turn from the window. K.T. was a moment faster. His tone sounded almost angry when he growled out the words, "All right, Coal. Yes, damn it—Larry's dead. Somebody shot him right at the door to his pickup. And nobody has a clue why."

Coal sucked in a deep breath. He let some of it seep out, feeling chills creep up his spine. Finally, his thoughts began to clarify, and he thought of Larry's family.

"What about Kathy? And the girls?"

"They were gone," K.T. replied. "Visiting her family in Utah. We had to send the Wasatch County sheriff to talk to them."

Coal bunched his jaws and gave a rapid nod. He pursed his lips. Shock was washing over him. Larry MacAtee was his very best friend. They had been like brothers since they were four years old, and until graduation had seldom been far apart. Coal knew Larry better than... Well, as it turned out, better than his own wife. Larry may as well have been a brother, and was in fact the brother Coal often wished he had. He had two brothers by birth, Collin and Nathan, and both as worthless as lips on a vulture. Larry had been everything to him that a brother should have been.

He thought of Kathy. And the girls. There had been one boy, Luke, but two years ago he had died in a rollover on his way to Idaho Falls, not too long after getting his driver's license. He should have been eighteen this year, Coal figured. The girls must all be between ten and seventeen. Too young to lose a father. And what a way to lose a father, or *anyone* they loved.

Jim had walked over and stood by Coal, and Coal's usual awareness must have gone south. Until Jim put his hand on the back of his arm, Coal didn't even know he was there. Startled, he jerked away and stepped back. He had embarrassed himself and now didn't know what to say.

"Shoot, Coal. Didn't mean to startle you."

"Sorry, Jim. Vietnam," replied Coal. "Never goes away. I guess not 'til you die."

"Kindred spirits, son. You don't need to tell me. Normandy and Omaha Beach have me by the short hairs still, and it's been near thirty years."

Coal just nodded, reaching up to squeeze the back of the older man's neck. Suddenly, a realization came out of nowhere and struck him hard. His eyes whipped up to look over at K.T., who happened to be watching him.

"Hey, K.T., what are you doing working this case anyway? I thought—"

"I asked for him."

Coal turned slowly to take in the man who had just walked out of the cell block and spoken. This man of five-foot-nine, narrow of shoulder but heavy in the belly, with reddish brown hair and bushy sideburns down to the line of his jaw, stared at Coal through dark eyes spread too wide apart in his face. His cheeks were heavy, the tip of his nose blunt, like in his youth someone had bitten it off.

There were very few people in Salmon Coal could think of off the top of his head that he truly disliked, that he had absolutely no respect for. This man, upon the chest of whose brown wool shirt Coal could not miss the golden sheen of a five-pointed sheriff's star, was one of the few.

Todd Mitchell.

CHAPTER EIGHT

In spite of the bile that rose in his throat at sight of Todd Mitchell, Coal kept his cool. He looked him up and down, allowing himself to take in a deep breath slowly enough so that no one noticed.

Finally, he tilted his chin up ever-so-slightly. "Hello, Todd. Shiny badge."

Mitchell's eyes hardened. "It's brand-new."

Coal's glance slid over to Jim Lockwood. "Something change since I talked to you on the phone, Jim?"

Jim quickly shook his head. "Not a bit, Coal. The commissioners and the county clerk wanted an interim sheriff, and since Todd was the only deputy, he was the natural choice."

Coal raised one shoulder, a half shrug. "And so... where does that leave us right now? Today."

Mitchell's voice was cold. "The job's yours, Coal. Looks pretty obvious that you have friends in all the right places. And after today, you can have it. So... the county clerk didn't know where my job would stand once you got here. As deputy, that is." It seemed to cause him great pain now to talk, and he didn't want to meet Coal's eyes until the last word was out of his mouth. "He told me I'd have to talk to you about that."

Coal's chest felt like a heavy old steel drum, with someone swinging a sledge hammer ponderously inside of it. He could feel all eyes on him. He knew Todd Mitchell had a wife, a woman by the name of Jan, if he remembered correctly—a slovenly woman with stringy blond hair, the hips of a fifteen year-old boy and, as a habit, too much lipstick. He believed they had two or three kids too. They came here from Shelley, one of the Salmon Savages' rival schools. However, none of that had anything to do with why Coal felt like he was being forced to eat someone else's spit every time he had to look at this man.

But even as much as he didn't like Mitchell, how did you flat-out tell a man to go look for another job? Houses weren't easy to sell in Salmon. And jobs here weren't easy to come by either. Could he just send this man packing, with a wife and kids? Many others would have. Hell, most people who knew what Coal knew would think it would be his first move. There was no secret that Coal and Mitchell loved each other like a lion and a hyena.

Coal drew in another deep breath. "Don't imagine you have any other job prospects, do you, Todd?"

Jaw muscles bunched—a fact barely visible beneath the padding of suet Mitchell carried around as extra insulation against the Lemhi County cold—he just shook his head. "Nobody hiring around here."

Coal managed a nod. "Don't anybody jump to conclusions, all right?" He was speaking to everyone, but he still centered his gaze on Mitchell. "Who knows what the county clerk will think of me after we have a talk? I doubt he'll just slide me into the job without an interview. And when elections come, I'll have to earn this position just like anybody. In a spot like that, I can't just go sending men packing off into the cold. Can I?"

The look Mitchell was giving Coal now was first one of simple confusion. But after a few moments, when the real meaning of Coal's words began to dawn on him, he straightened up a little bit, and his jaw slacked. "Did you say... You sayin' I can stay?"

"We'll work it out, Todd. Let's talk later."

To any passerby, the words might have seemed nonchalant, even cordial. But Jim and K.T. could not have missed the true feeling that shone in Coal's gaze. He did not want to have to greet this man every day, even in passing. He did not want to know Mitchell was the man who had his back in a bad fight. But he couldn't just put him out on the street—not without cause, anyway.

Todd Mitchell was going to have to earn the right to be fired.

"Talk to me about Larry, Todd. What have you got so far?"

"Hey, son," cut in Jim Lockwood, putting a hand on Coal's shoulder. "Don't go jumpin' here. We've got this for tonight, all right? Don't forget, I've been around the horn a time or two. I imagine you got four young'ns out in the truck who'd like to get home and settle in. Honest—this stuff can wait."

Coal started to protest. His mouth even opened to form the words. But Jim was right. The kids were waiting, and they had all had a long trip. It would have been long even without Katie, but she had managed to make it feel like they had driven the whole planet, with a few side-trips into hell thrown in.

Releasing a big sigh, Coal looked over at K.T., his good friend. His high school buddy, the Prince of Pushups. K.T. had this. Mitchell was wearing the sheriff's badge, for decorum's sake, but anybody could see what was going on behind the scenes here. K.T. was a good man. He knew his job. And if he didn't, and Mitchell didn't, then they had one of the most legendary lawmen in the state to back them up, in Jim Lockwood. As an ex-FBI agent, Coal wanted to mention fingerprints, bullets, ballistics, photographs and detailed drawings. He wanted to go over current findings, any rumors of bad dealings for Larry... The list went on. But there was no need. Not right now. It was time to go home.

"I don't know who makes the coffee here these days, but K.T., if you're still brewing that stuff that tastes like it has vinegar in it, I'd sure take it as a favor if you'd run upstairs in the morning and see if Cindy will come down and either make the coffee or teach you how." Cindy Hardlinger worked upstairs in the clerk's office.

Jim let out a laugh and pointed a finger at K.T. "What did I tell you? That's the worst damn coffee in the valley, K.T.!"

K.T. laughed, turning a little red. "Holy cow! Well, why didn't anybody tell me before?"

"I tell you every time I'm here," chided Coal. He laughed and slapped his old friend on the back.

"Your plan's all well and good," said Jim, "but in case you forgot, tomorrow's Sunday. You don't expect Cindy or anyone else to be upstairs on Sunday, do you?"

"Know what's funny?" cut in Todd Mitchell. "Cindy just got back from vacation a few days ago. I ran into her in the parking lot this afternoon, and she told me she has so much to catch up on that she'll be working the whole weekend."

"Then it's meant to be!" said Coal.

"You guys and your stinking coffee!" said K.T. good-naturedly.

Coal laughed. "Oh well, don't worry. Just have something hot. I'll be back at seven. Will any of you be in, with it being Sunday?"

"Sure, we'll be here if you are." K.T. seemed suddenly to re-member he was no longer sheriff, and he shot a glance over at Mitchell.

Mitchell forced a smile. "We'll be here. Seven o'clock."

"Yeah, we'll be in—to make sure there's some decent brew on," chimed in Jim.

And then Jeb Rowe, the farmer, looked around at the lawmen and said, "I won't be... will I?"

Coal gave a chuckle. "No, Jeb, we'll come by your place if we need anything. Go on home. But do me a favor, will you? Hold off on the hooch for at least a few more days. I don't want you fouling up any recollections we might be in need of."

*   *   *

Driving through downtown Salmon brought back a flood of memories. People Coal had known here. Places he had frequented. There was the Owl Club and Wally's cafe, on his right. And on his left the Smokehouse, Coffee Shop, and the Salmon River Inn. He had spent too many dollars watching Western movies at the Roxy Theater, and too many more regaining his strength on burgers and fries in the Coffee Shop and at Wally's, and even at the A & W, during summer months when it was open.

At the Texaco station, he remembered riding his old buckskin horse, Pepper, up and down the pavement, trying to rope the hats off his school buddies until Sheriff Jim—still just a deputy back then—sent him packing. It was there at the Texaco where beautiful Susan Lane had caught up to him and told him to go to hell because word had gotten around town that he had been telling people her prom dress had made her look like a big city hooker.

Susan. Prettiest redhead in Salmon, who would have graduated with the class of '49. She died in a fiery crash near Leadore two weeks after caving in to their first kiss. Perhaps the first girl he had ever thought he might fall in love with.

Coal drove on out of town, passing little farm and ranch houses in the gloom. He pulled out the headlight switch, which he should have done even in town, and it threw the rest of the outside world into an even deeper darkness, in comparison to the two beams that streamed silver along the highway in front of him.

Miles out of town, just after passing the Twenty-Eight Club, on the right, they turned left onto Savage Road, bumping along on washboard and gravel, with willow trees crowding them tight on both sides, just beyond the barbed wire. Less than a quarter mile to home...

Little Morgan was asleep again beside him, and this time Wyatt wasn't far off. His little cowboys. What was Salmon going to bring these boys? Good things, he hoped. But it was an isolated place, and if kids here didn't get into something good, and fast—they were sure as the moon going to get into something bad—and maybe faster.

He reached over and tousled Wyatt's hair, smiling at the glassy look in his little boy's eyes as he fought so hard against sleep. Wyatt was staring straight ahead when his eyes flew suddenly open, and Coal cringed.

He whipped his head forward in time to see the flash of darkness—right in front of his headlights.

CHAPTER NINE

There was no time to stop. There was barely any time to even hit the brakes. He was just driving along, bouncing on the ruts and gravel, and then it was there. Too fast, too dark to even recognize. In a move he had rehearsed hundreds of times in his head, he threw his right arm out in front of the boys just as the front of the Chevy struck the animal with a shattering crash.

He felt all of them thrown forward, and Wyatt passed beyond the tips of his fingers, hitting the dash. His own chest slammed against the steering wheel as the truck lurched to a stop. Dazed, he looked out the windshield, where one working headlight still lit the way ahead through the swirling dust. He watched a huge bull moose lurch up off the ground and limp crazily off beyond the side of the road, quickly disappearing from sight in the darkness.

With the metallic taste of blood in his mouth, he blinked to clear his vision and looked at the boys. Morgan was leaned back against the seat, crying, and Wyatt, much to Coal's relief, was sobbing and nursing what appeared only to be a bloody nose. As for Coal, his chest was already throbbing, but the pickup, due to the rutted road, probably hadn't been traveling more than twenty miles an hour. They had been lucky.

Thinking suddenly of Virgil and Katie, he threw open the door, which gave easily. Those Chevies were made like tanks. He ran around to the camper and jerked the door open.

Virgil came boiling out and almost fell as he hit the ground. The bewildered look in his eyes told Coal he had been asleep, like Morgan—and no kind of collision was a great way to wake up.

"You okay?" Coal asked, putting his hand on Virgil's shoulder and looking him up and down.

Like Coal had done, his son was blinking his eyes as if in a daze, trying to clear his vision. "Yeah, I think so. But Katie's not."

Coal's heart leaped, and he jumped up on the trailer hitch and into the camper, fumbling on the wall for the flashlight he kept clipped there. Fortunately, it was still there. Almost frantic, he snapped it on and flashed it around the tight space. Katie was sitting on the bottom bunk at the head of the camper, holding her face. Blood was oozing between her fingers.

A strange voice yelled from outside, and Coal caught the words, "Everybody okay? I called for an ambulance."

"We're okay. Everybody's okay." He caught the flash of Katie's eyes as she looked up at him, almost incredulous.

"Cancel the ambulance then?" the voice came back.

Coal, on a whim— "No, better keep 'em coming."

He didn't have words to say to Katie. He had never been afraid to talk to people, but he found he was now, with Katie. Had been for some time. No matter what he said, it would be wrong. At last, he mumbled, "Are you all right?"

"No!" the girl screamed, loud enough to be heard two football fields away. "Look at me!" She dropped her hands, and in the dim light he could see her eyes were already starting to swell, and her nose was misshapen. Broken. He had seen enough of them to know that—two or three times on his own face.

"Okay. The ambulance is coming."

"Marvelous," she snapped. "Just what I wanted." She sounded as if she had a serious cold.

"A moose ran in front of us, Katie," he said, stepping closer. Against his better judgment, he tried to lay a comforting hand on her shoulder, but she of course shook it off and jumped sideways on the bunk.

"Get your hands off me! Just get out of here!"

Stunned, feeling lost, Coal stumbled backward down the tiny hall and turned around, stepping out of the camper onto the hitch between the pickup and trailer, then down onto the ground.

Some man and woman he didn't recognize were standing there next to the U-Haul, fussing over the boys. They had gotten Wyatt's nosebleed stopped, and he looked fine, just shaken.

"Boys tell me you're Connie Savage's boy," the short, balding man said. He was a kind looking man, a little pinched around the eyes and wearing glasses.

"That I am. I'm Coal."

"I'm Walt Ledbetter," replied the man. "My wife Susan." He motioned toward her.

"Happy to meet you," replied Coal. Then, in a sheepish voice, "I wish it could have been under different circumstances, though."

"Well, sure," said the man in a southern drawl. "Anyhow, the ambulance won't be too far off. I think I'm hearing a siren already—unless that's an officer."

Perking his ears, Coal agreed. He could hear a siren.

Soon, the siren got loud, and he finally saw blue lights approaching from the direction of town. When they reached Savage Road, they pulled off and headed toward them.

The siren cut off a ways away, and with only the blues flashing, the car came on in, slowing down, probably to keep dust from rolling over the scene of the wreck. The car stopped, and he could see the door open and the shadow of a stocky man in a cowboy hat get out and hurry toward them.

"Everybody okay?"

Coal chuckled. "No. We're tired of that word."

The officer stopped, his lean form, cowboy hat, and the butt of his gun silhouetted against his own headlights. But Coal had them right in his face. "Hey! Coal Savage!"

It took a moment, after a year or so, to recognize the voice, but between the man's shape and the voice he recognized Bob Wilson. The two men closed together and shook hands warmly. Bob stood six feet tall, a dark-haired, warm-hearted man with a lean, friendly face and honest, dark brown eyes. He wore a thin slice of dark mustache. Coal and Bob had known each other only briefly, just since Coal's last trip home, when Coal had gone riding with him on his beat. But the two had instantly hit it off and become fast friends. Some things were just meant to be.

"Good to see you, buddy! I hear we'll be backing each other up around here, from time to time."

Coal let out a laugh. "Well, that's the rumor. Not sure after tonight, though. The county might decide they don't need any reckless drivers for sheriff. Why are you all the way out here? This is county stuff."

Bob looked a little sheepish. "Well, under the circumstances with what happened to K.T., they decided we'd have to back you up in the county at least until his spot's filled. What happened, anyway?" Bob asked, his eyes full of concern.

"Hit a moose."

"Oh man! One of them killed a guy over by Lone Pine a few weeks ago. Killed the moose, too. Where'd it go?"

Coal pointed in the general direction. "He was limping."

Bob pulled out his flashlight and let its beam ride out into the darkness, but other than a couple of horses that had wandered over to see what all the ruckus was about, and whose eyes sparked in the night, nothing else could be seen.

"So everyone's fine?" said Bob, dropping his flashlight back in the loop at his hip.

Coal winced, feeling guilty. "Well, my daughter, Katie... I think she might have broken her nose."

"Where is she?"

"In the camper. She isn't too happy-go-lucky right now, if you know what I mean."

"Did you get the bleeding stopped?"

"Bob..." He had been about to say too much with too many ears around. "Uh, no, I didn't. I wasn't very welcome in there with her."

Bob gave him an odd look. "Well, the ambulance will be here any minute. The dispatcher told me Maura responded right after the call came in."

"Maura?" Coal echoed.

"New EMT from Rapid City—moved here a few months ago. Whipping the ambulance service in shape, too. And on top of that, she could be a poster girl for the medical profession. You'll see what I mean."

As if in response to those words, the wail of another siren came over the trees and sagebrush from town, and red lights could be seen approaching, probably a mile out.

"Would Katie let me up in there?" asked Bob, a little cautious after catching the tone of Coal's voice.

"Maybe. I think it's just me she doesn't want near her."

Bob nodded and turned, but when he started to climb into the camper he saw Susan Ledbetter and her husband were already inside, fussing over the girl. He backed out and stepped onto the road again, relaying the news to Coal.

The subject of Katie had introduced an aura of awkwardness to the scene. Coal and Bob talked quietly, speaking of events in town after touching only briefly on the murder of Larry MacAtee. But Katie didn't come up again, and Coal was glad. That was a fox he was going to have to trap by himself—no one else's help was going to bring her around if Coal couldn't do it himself.

A few minutes later, the ambulance rumbled up, red overhead light revolving slowly. A man and a woman got out and came toward them, and Coal soon recognized his old friend, who owned the Coffee Shop, Jay Castillo. He had been a volunteer EMT for years now.

"Hi, Coal!" Jay greeted, in a soft, melodic voice, almost Castilian, although he was originally from Canada. The EMT had softly olive skin and thinning hair, but it was plain he had been quite handsome in his younger days. Still was, Coal reckoned—by a woman's thinking.

They shook hands, and Coal clapped his old friend on the shoulder. This night was like a reunion for him, it seemed.

Before they could ask, Coal said, "Jay, everybody's okay except Katie. I think she broke her nose."

"Tell that to Maura," Jay said. "She's the patient man tonight. I'm just her driver."

Coal turned for the first time to see a striking blonde, her long, wavy hair pulled back in a ponytail. She was taller than most women, no more than six or eight inches shorter than Coal himself. There was a tough, no-nonsense look about her, and more than that, a feeling—this woman was not one to be trifled with. Her voice, while polite, was not friendly.

"Hi, I'm Maura."

"Coal," he greeted. She didn't raise her hand to shake, so he didn't either. In the old school, if a woman wanted to shake hands, it was her place to extend the offer, and Coal was nothing if not old school.

"You said you think 'Katie' might have broken her nose? Where is Katie?"

"In the camper," Coal directed.

"And you are...?"

"Her father."

"Can we have her come outside?"

"Ask her. There's not much I could request from her that she would do."

Maura gave Coal a strange, appraising look, one eyebrow raised. Then, with her med kit in hand, she turned and walked to the camper. "Katie? Hi, I'm Maura. Can you come out here and see me?"

Coal could hear the Ledbetters inside, talking quietly to Katie Leigh. Finally, the three of them emerged, Walt first, then Susan, and last of all Katie. She came down the steps, holding a towel against her face.

"Hi, Katie." Maura's demeanor and voice had changed since talking to Coal. Now she seemed very warm and compassionate. "I'm Maura."

Katie nodded. She had already heard that, and Coal was well aware that his daughter had no patience for people who repeated things pointlessly.

"Can I see?"

With her nose already swelling up, Katie's eyes flashed toward Coal, and the look in them could be described as nothing more than pure malice. She lowered the towel, and in the glare of flashlights a slight sideways bend to her nose was obvious, along with the growth at the top of the bridge. Fresh blood was oozing out onto her upper lip.

"It looks like your father was right—you've broken your nose."

"*I* didn't break it," said the girl angrily. "*He* did!"

"Oh, why would he do that?" Bob Wilson cut in.

"Because he hates me. And I hate him!"

CHAPTER TEN

"All right. You men? Back off."

It was Maura speaking, and she had turned on Bob Wilson and Coal with fire in her eyes.

"Just back off, all of you. Susan can stay if she'd like. The rest of you make yourselves scarce. Better yet, make yourselves useful and go look for the moose. Maybe it has a broken leg. For hell's sake, kill something—that's what men do best."

Coal would be lying if he claimed this EMT, Maura, wasn't physically about the most attractive woman he had laid eyes on since leaving D.C. At least in the dark of night. But with an attitude like hers, he guessed she had a doctorate in making herself look ugly to men—a doctorate with honors. His opinion of her looks was quickly going south.

As the future sheriff of this county, he could ill afford to tell Maura what he thought of her. But he was having to chew his tongue into mush not to. Without a sound, he turned away and went back to the front of the pickup, carrying his flashlight.

He shone the light on the front bumper and grill. They were a little crumpled. Not horrible. Nothing a good body man couldn't fix. The nose of the hood was worse, and the right headlight was smashed. He swore. This was not a good way to start out his sojourn in his old home.

His mind went back to Maura. He realized he didn't know her last name. Didn't necessarily care, either. First glance at her marked her an attractive woman, though hard as a gun barrel. Her mouth was tight when she looked at him, and her eyes full of fire—a fire gained from years of unhappy living, he guessed. Or maybe she was simply born to be a witch. She would not have been the first, and like many another handsome woman, perhaps she felt like the world owed her a living, and the world did not agree. Either way, he wanted nothing more to do with her. He hoped she wouldn't be long in this county. In fact, he would have bet money on it. Salmon was a tight-knit community. They would not long tolerate an abrasive woman like Maura.

The twins had followed him to the front of the truck. "Hey, boys. You two doing okay?"

Neither boy was crying now. At a glance, it was obvious that Wyatt had put his long shirt sleeve to proper use to stop his nose bleed. As Coal had once heard his father say, to a man or a boy, having a long-sleeved shirt *and* a facial tissue or handkerchief was redundant.

He knelt down in front of the boys and crushed them both to him. They both squeezed him about as tight as little boys could. Oh, how he loved these little fellows! Neither could know it, but they were keeping him sane, when Katie's anger and Virgil's silence could easily have made him want to quit.

"We sure had a big scare, huh? I'm glad you two didn't get hurt. What would I do without you around?"

Wyatt giggled at that. He was quite a little man.

"Well, I'll tell you boys something. If you want to get up early tomorrow, I'm going to see if I can spot that old bull moose out in one of these fields. He was limping pretty good. Could be he got hurt bad enough to lie down somewhere and not be able to

get back up. You'd like a big bunch of moose meat for the winter, wouldn't you?"

"I've never had moose meat," said Morgan, and Wyatt
chimed, "Me either. What does it taste like?"

"Like big deer meat, I guess." Coal laughed. "Not saying I
can find him, but if you boys get dressed all warm and come with
me, it sure would be fun to try. Now let's get you back in the
pickup where it's warm. When the EMT's get done with Katie,
we'll see if Old Betsy will get us the rest of the way home without hitting anything else." He slapped the hood of the pickup for
emphasis and looked a ways up the road. The old home place was
already in sight, and not very far away.

Having gotten the boys back in the truck and snugged together in a wool blanket, he went back around to the rear. Bob Wilson
was sitting in the seat of his squad car, ostensibly writing a report. He thought about going to get in with him but didn't. Katie
didn't need him or want him here, but maybe Virgil did.

The look in his oldest son's eyes did not reassure him. Virgil's eyes weren't cold, they were simply... vacant. He stared at
the ground, shivering now and then, as Maura and Jay looked
Katie over and then as Maura stood there for a few minutes holding an ice pack on Katie's face.

At last, Coal heard Maura say, "Where did her father go?"

"I'm right here."

Maura cranked her head around, still holding the ice pack on
the girl's nose. "Katie needs her nose set. Do you want to go to
the hospital with us?"

"Yeah, and just leave my boys and the pickup in the road?"

"There isn't any need to be rude," retorted the woman. "A
simple no would be just fine. I wouldn't have expected you to go
anyway."

Coal glanced around at the others, then back at the woman.
"What makes you say that?" He tried to keep his voice calm.

"You're a man, aren't you? Most men would rather let somebody else take care of their children—at least their girl children. Just an observation I've made over the years."

Coal felt himself about ready to explode. He forced himself not to reply at that moment, but this was a bullet he was going to keep in his gun for some other time.

Walt Ledbetter cut in after a few moments of uncomfortable silence. "Mr. Savage, my wife and I can take your rig and the boys home for you if you want."

"Thanks, but no thanks. Apparently I'm just a man and wouldn't care to go to the hospital anyway. I'll take the truck. But I appreciate the offer."

Eyes flickering over toward Maura, the older man nodded. "Alrighty. Just wanted to throw it out there."

"Thanks."

Virgil's unexpected voice broke in. "Dad, I can go with Katie."

Coal looked at his boy for a moment, proud of him inside, but not willing to show a sign of it. "No, you need some sleep. Let's get you home."

Jay Castillo motioned for Coal to walk with him, and the two of them went into the shadows. "Your daughter's pretty mad, huh?"

"Is that what they call it? She pretty much hates my guts."

Jay laughed, obviously a little embarrassed. "Hey, buddy, I'm sure that isn't true. You really don't want to go with us to the hospital, huh?"

"Not right now."

"Somebody's got to fill out paperwork."

Coal stood there thinking. Finally, he shrugged, though it was too dark now for Jay to see it. "I'll come later. Let me get the boys settled first."

"Okay, sounds good." The EMT reached out and squeezed his arm. "Hey, I don't know what's going on between you, but I hope it works out. I went through some stuff with my boy too. Not fun. That's one thing, Coal—this Salmon country, it can eat kids alive if you don't stay right on top of it."

A chill ran up Coal's spine that was from more than just the brisk night air. "Yeah. I remember."

They walked back to the truck together, and Bob Wilson had joined the Ledbetters, Virgil, and Maura where Katie was standing and shivering.

"Hey, Virg, you want to hop up in the camper and get Katie Leigh a blanket?" Coal suggested.

"I don't want your blanket!" It was the first time the girl had raised her voice in quite some time, although she refused to look at him. Instead, she stared off into the shadows on the opposite side of the road. She would be wishing no one there could see her at all. Coal knew that feeling.

With his chin, Coal motioned for Virgil to get in the camper anyway, and the boy came back out with a blanket. He leaned close to his sister and whispered something in her ear as he gently laid the blanket across her shoulders. The girl only shuddered and closed her eyes. In the flash of the ambulance lights, Coal thought he caught the gleam of tears on her cheeks when she opened her eyes again.

"Well, we're taking off," said Maura, to everyone in general. "As soon as we can get backed around. Mr. Savage? If you'd like to send someone to pick up your daughter in an hour or so it would be nice." She glared at him for a moment, her eyes hard and full of spark. "Come on, Katie," she said, and they walked toward the ambulance, nothing more than a converted white Ford station wagon.

Jay walked over to Coal and patted his shoulder again, handing him a folded piece of paper. "Welcome home, buddy. You decide you need to talk, give me a call."

"Sure. Thanks, Jay."

Coal stood watching as Bob Wilson helped the ambulance back around and not run into the fence, then followed it with his eyes as it flipped off its emergency lights and went slowly down the road toward town.

Bob came over, and his face had a weird glow in the red taillights of the truck. He smiled. "Hey, Coal—Sheriff Coal, that is. Welcome home. It'll be good to work with you. Oh, and— I'm sorry about Larry. Let me know if I can help with anything."

"I will. Thanks, Bob."

He watched in silence as Bob got back in his patrol car, did a three-point turn, and headed back toward town behind the ambulance. It wasn't until then that he even gave another thought to a city squad car's being all the way out here in the county. It made him happy that the city fathers were willing to help out. Lemhi County hadn't changed. He would remember it when any city police officer ever sent out a plea for help.

The Ledbetters waited around until Coal started the pickup again. It started fine, so they said goodbye, and Coal limped it into the night with his one headlight staring defiantly up the road.

Welcome home, Coal thought. Inopportune moose, good-looking, man-despising EMT, busted headlight, and all.

CHAPTER ELEVEN

Other than his one headlight, there was no light on the driveway at home. Coal pulled up, and for a few moments just sat at the turn-in off Savage Road. It was hard to believe he was here at last. It seemed in some ways like he had been here just a month earlier, giving his mother a hug goodbye and whispering in her ear how much he loved her—something he seldom told *anyone*.

But the boys were almost five and a half years old now, and they had only been three then. He felt a surge of guilt. What kind of a son stayed clear across the country for that length of time making his mother watch her grandchildren grow up in pictures? His heart began to pound soddenly. Maybe Laura had been right about him after all.

He looked over at the boys. Both were wide awake now, but of course that wouldn't last long. An aching inside his chest began to gnaw at him. Had he done things wrong? Was he truly at fault for Laura's death? He felt a strange urge to be alone somewhere where he could think. And... And pray? It had been so long now. God didn't likely remember who he was.

He shook off that thought, and his eyes focused on the twins. They were both watching him, and he laughed when he heard Morgan utter those long-awaited words, "Are we almost there?"

"Yep, Morg, we are. This time we are almost there."

He had spent half the trip, it seemed, trying to teasingly convince these boys that there was technically no way to really ever be "there." Once you got to where you had been referring to as "there," it became "here." So the question, "Are we there yet?" he told them made no sense. He always laughed at the confused looks on their faces. Obviously, that concept was over their heads. But they must have grasped at least part of it, because they had started asking only, "Are we almost there?" and completely dropped "Are we there yet?" He probably should feel guilty for messing with childhood innocence.

With a big sigh, Coal turned the wheel at last, feathered the gas and eased off the clutch, and they turned into the driveway. The tires made a satisfying crunching noise as they came to a stop on the packed gravel.

Although the driveway had been dark, the yard itself was lit by two floodlights, and a lamp glowed in the front window. Grandma was welcoming them home.

"We're there," he stated.

Without a pause, he heard Wyatt exclaim, "No, Daddy, we're *here!*"

Coal let out a hearty laugh. "That's right, Wyatt. You learned well. We're here. Because we can't ever be 'there,' right?"

"No!" both boys agreed in unison.

A chorus of deep-throated barking emanated from inside the house—the voices of at least two very large, or at least very intimidating, dogs.

The boys were staring at him again. "Are those big dogs?"

"You'll see. Come on." He jerked back the brake and turned off the engine.

By now, there were lights coming on in the house, and soon a woman with silver hair that shone in the porch light threw open the front door and stepped out. With one hand, she was shielding what appeared to be a large Doberman pinscher that was trying its best to "shoot the gap" past her leg and into the yard.

Finally, she spoke firmly to the animal, and he backed up and sat down behind her.

The woman came down three concrete steps to a stretch of sidewalk that ran along the front of the house and out to a paved pad for parking. She crossed it in almost a run, her light-colored nightgown flowing back behind her at the bottom hem.

"Coal! Welcome home!"

They gave each other a huge hug, and Coal was happy to see his mother had lost none of her strength. She had always given the best hugs in the world.

Stepping away, Coal looked into the steel-blue eyes of Connie Savage, a woman sixty-eight years old, whose straight hair was kept long, and right now was tied at the back of her head. Although the hair had gone to silver, her eyebrows were still dark, and when angled just right they helped her eyes give the most severe gazes when she was angry, or even pretending to be.

His mother stood five-foot-six, with wide Germanic shoulders and cheekbones and eyes full of kindness.

Looking around, Connie's eyes found the twins, standing side by side watching the front door. There, through the glass of the storm door, the black Doberman still sat watching, and he had been joined by an even larger German shepherd that was going silver around the muzzle and eyes, its lower eyelids starting to droop.

"Don't you boys worry about those dogs, now. They're gentle as pussycats. Those are your daddy's dogs, Dobe and Shadow. And you boys must be Wyatt and Morgan. But I can't for the life of me tell which is which."

"I'm Wyatt. He's Morgan."

"Well, my, you've both gotten so big. The last time I saw you, you were just babies! Now look at you. You're little men."

Both boys beamed.

"Well, I'm your Grandma Connie. I don't suppose I could get a hug from my little men, could I?"

Coal didn't have to worry about coaxing the boys. They were both huggers, and both very respectful to their elders. Without hesitation, they stepped forward, and they hugged their grandmother as one.

When she stood up, her eyes went beyond Coal. "Hi, Grandma," came the voice of Virgil over Coal's shoulder. The thirteen-year-old walked forward, not as quick in his step as the twins, but he still hugged Connie with just as much vigor. She squeezed him hard, then held him away from her by the shoulders and looked him up and down.

"Be bigger than your dad in a couple years, Virgil! Look at you. I'm mighty proud of how you're turning out. Now where's that Katie Leigh?" she asked, whirling on Coal.

Coal took in the three of his boys with a nervous glance. "Uh, Ma—don't panic, but Katie's at the hospital." He jerked his thumb at the front of the pickup. "We had a little fender bender on the way in here. A moose ran out in front of us."

"Oh no!" Connie's hands flew to her mouth. "I heard the sirens. Is Katie okay?"

"Well, yeah, mostly. But she got her nose broken. They took her in the ambulance. She sure wasn't wanting any of me."

Connie frowned, searching her son's eyes. "Still hard, huh?"

"Yeah, Mom. Harder than when we talked."

"Okay, honey. It'll be okay."

"I know. It'll just take some time, I guess."

"Well, sure. These kids have been through quite a bit, you have to admit."

"Yeah. So... I really should get the boys settled and run down there."

"To the hospital?"

"I've got to, Mom. How would it look to them if I don't?"

This time a more serious frown came over Connie's face, turning the wrinkles around her mouth deep in the shadows. She put her hands on her hips. "Why, shame on you, Coal Garrett. Is that all you care about? Katie Leigh is your daughter!"

Coal's face flushed. "I know. I know. But you haven't seen how things are between us."

"No, that's right, Coal—you're right about that. But I can see how they're going to keep being if you don't get yourself down to that hospital and at least show her you care. Even if she's pretending she *doesn't* care right now, you are going to hurt her far worse than anything that's happened yet if you don't go see her."

"What? I *said* I was going!"

She cocked her head sideways. "That's not what I'm talking about. I'm talking about your *reasons* for going. If you're going down there to see Katie and check on her—for *you*—then Coal, I am darn proud of you. But if you're going just to make a show for the public, then you may as well just let me go and you stay here and take care of the boys. Which is it going to be?"

"I do care, Mama. I just... I said it wrong."

It was funny how no matter how high a man got in the world—Marine, Army MP, investigative agent for the FBI, and now sheriff of an entire county—his mother could still talk to him like a little boy and bring him right back down to earth. He wasn't so tough after all.

"I've got an idea," said Connie, her face softening. "Let us get these little men settled, and then you and I will just drive on down there together in my Chrysler. Maybe it won't be so harsh if I'm there. Come on, boys. Let's go introduce you to Dobe and Shadow."

*   *   *

After the boys were safely tucked in bed in the big old five-bedroom ranch house, and both dogs knew they were in charge of keeping them safe, Connie picked a handful of keys off a ring by the door and turned to Coal. "You wanna drive?"

"No, Mom. I just want to sit. I've been driving too long already. Besides, if Bullwinkle comes back into the road, I don't want to wreck your car too!"

Connie laughed, and then went out to the parking pad, where there sat a sleek pale aqua blue 1968 Chrysler Newport coupe with a bold white top, shining in the floodlight.

"You leave the yard lights on all night now?"

Connie grunted. "No, not all the time. But I do a lot, yes. We've been having bears come down and root around in stuff."

"Bears, down here?"

"I know. Seems pretty far from the mountains. Weird year, Son. All the way around."

They bumped down the lane toward the main highway. Coal wanted to talk, but he didn't. He couldn't get his mind off Katie. He loved his daughter. And he wanted to like her. He wanted it more than anything. But there was nothing left of his little girl for him to like. For weeks now she had vilified him, practically spat in his face. Not literally, for she knew that would bring on his true wrath. But she might as well have. It would have been no less hurtful than her vile words.

They hit Highway 28 and turned back toward town. Other than the softly humming tires, the car was silent now. Neither of them seemed to know what to say. They were almost all the way into town before Connie turned her eyes to him and laid her hand on his. "Son, I need to ask something, but I'm almost afraid to. Did you hear about Larry?"

"Yeah, Mom. On the way into town. I've already talked to Jim and K.T."

His mother let out a sigh of relief. "I'm glad. I just didn't know how to tell you. Are you going to be all right?"

"Sure." He felt like that was a lie. He would never get over losing a friend like Larry. "I went through a lot worse in Nam," he added.

She pulled into the hospital parking lot, on Daisy Street, and reached over to squeeze Coal's knee. "You and Katie are going to be all right, dear. It's just going to take some time."

"Too long," he replied. He wanted to say something about Laura. He wanted to say something about the pain that wracked his heart every day, every night. He wanted to talk—to *someone*. But he couldn't. He was Coal Savage, a man full-grown for more than twenty years. He would keep this inside until the day he died.

They climbed out of the car and walked into the lobby, which was dead quiet—a typical night for Salmon, because although there seemed to be fights daily in the bars in town, the men involved were generally too proud to seek medical attention. And the rest of the county kept pretty quiet and went to bed early.

Coal was expecting something of a confrontation in the hospital. Lately, there always was whenever he and Katie could not possibly avoid each other. But the confrontation he encountered was not the one he expected. Katie, in fact, was nowhere to be seen.

Instead, the first person he recognized made his guts tighten up instantly, and he unconsciously reached for a gun on his hip—which wasn't there.

Down the hall sat the largest man he had ever encountered. And one of the most ill-tempered and vile.

Paul Monahan—called Bigfoot by most people who knew him.

And Bigfoot Monahan, imprisoned for poaching and manslaughter, should not have been out for another five years.

Even as Coal spotted him and realized he was staring, Bigfoot's pale blue eyes pivoted, seeming to sense he was being watched. The moment they settled on Coal, they flattened out, like a snake setting itself to strike.

Bigfoot Monahan should not have been here. In sixty-seven, they had sentenced him to prison for a fixed sentence of ten years. But here he was, undeniable, big as day. He was here, he was a veritable mountain, and the one looming thought that punched Coal Savage in the guts like the kick of an angry cow was Monahan had sworn on the day they put him in the van to drive him to the penitentiary that one day he would be back.

And the first chance he had he was going to kill Coal Savage, Jim Lockwood, K.T. Batterton, and...

Larry MacAtee.

CHAPTER TWELVE

"Who in the name of creation is that?" Connie asked, standing next to her son.

Coal tried for the moment to pry his eyes away from the giant sitting far down the hall, outside one of the emergency examination rooms. Somehow, he couldn't. So when he replied to his mother he was still making eye contact with Bigfoot.

"His name's Bigfoot Monahan, Mom. Jim put him away back around sixty-seven—manslaughter."

Connie gasped. "Why is he looking at you like that?"

"Because I was there the night they took him down."

"You were there?"

"Yes, ma'am. In fact, I was the one who took him to the ground, then walked him back to Jim's car so he could cuff him." He laughed ruefully, trying to hide his expression from the other man. "I was on leave, just helping Jim out with a bad situation—a warrant he had to serve. In fact, it was me, K.T., Larry and Trent. Oh, yeah—and supposedly Todd Mitchell."

"Oh my land," his mother said, sucking in a hard breath. "You never whispered a word about that before. What do you think he'll do now? Why is he out?"

"I wish I knew. On both questions." He did not even dare tell her about the threats to his life—and to Larry's.

"Oh, Coal—he's getting up."

When Coal heard his mother's words, he whipped his eyes back to Bigfoot Monahan.

The man was sauntering their way, his six-foot-eight frame moving like a mixture between a proud longhorn bull and a lithe Siberian tiger.

Wherever Coal's daughter was at the moment no longer mattered. If he was not alive to check on her, *nothing* was going to matter.

The night they had taken Monahan down and handcuffed him, Coal had been lucky. Separated from everyone else on a search, after Monahan had fled when he heard Jim's car pull up at his house, Coal had caught the giant in the dark, unaware. Monahan was looking for a way through a tight neighborhood of trailer houses, and he had run up against a tall chain-link fence. It just so happened that the yard he was in when he met the fence was the same yard where he met Coal Savage. And neither man had the slightest clue where any of the other searchers were. Fortunately, Coal, who was unarmed, was crouched down by some bushes, and Bigfoot hadn't seen him.

Coal's stomach tightened when he thought of those next moments. Even the next minutes seemed to last forever. But worse than the memories was the present. Bigfoot Monahan, walking slow and sure, with huge hands swinging at ease along his thighs, was only ten feet away now. Connie was squeezing Coal's arm like a vise, yet he didn't even realize she was there.

"You be Coal Savage." The big man's voice was a crooning, deep growl in the quiet hall.

The wording used by the big man came out sounding odd. Coal wanted to say, *Okay. And you be Bigfoot Monahan.* But this wasn't the time to be a smart aleck. There would never be such a time with Bigfoot Monahan.

"I am." Coal stood ready to spring. He suddenly noticed his mother clinging to him and wished she were anywhere else.

"I got out of the pen."

Coal could not have taken his eyes from those shiny, almost white-blue ones of the bigger man if he had wanted to. He hoped he didn't seem to be making a challenge by refusing to avert his gaze.

He was aware of Monahan's bushy red beard, his deep reddish hair that framed his ruddy face. His shoulders seemed to go on forever beneath a black and red buffalo plaid shirt, endeavoring to creep out to both sides of the hallway.

"So I see."

What was Coal going to do? This was a fight he wondered if he could win. Sandan in karate or not. After all, last time it had been an easy takedown only thanks to sheer luck and the element of surprise. This was one huge, powerful man, and he was as mean as a fly-bitten bull. He had shown little pain years ago, after biting the ground on his back and after being led with an arm-bar back to the sheriff's squad car. Mostly, he had been taken into custody because in lunging up under his ribcage with a shoulder Coal had knocked the wind from him, not because he was hurt, and a man who can't breathe can't fight, no matter his size. Would Monahan feel any pain in a fight now?

"You threw me to the ground back in sixty-five, Savage. Only because you came up outta the dark, like a coward, and took me by surprise. But you can see I'm not surprised right now. Am I?"

"Don't appear to be."

"That arm-lock thing you put me in hurt my wrist for a good month."

Coal shrugged, feeling light on his feet. He kept his knees loose, ready to propel him in any direction.

Well, at least it was a good *month,* he thought snidely. "Yeah, it sometimes does."

"No apology?"

"Not really," Coal replied.

Bigfoot's eyebrows lowered a little more, narrowing his eyes so that the glow of them came eerily out from the shadowed depths of his hate. "Sometime I hope you want to try that again."

Coal shrugged once more. "Well... *I* don't."

The big man stared at him for a few seconds. By the confused look in his eyes, he seemed to be trying to digest Coal's meaning. Suddenly, he laughed, and the laugh was much louder than his speech. It was the roar of a lion, echoing through the nighttime hall.

"Sure is dark outside."

Without another word, Monahan raised one of his huge fists and gave it a little pump in front of him. It looked like he was contemplating striking Coal, but there was a glint in his eyes that appeared to be humor. He turned on his heel and strolled back the way he had come. He had to know Coal and his mother were watching him depart, staring at the incredible wide slope of his shoulders, his huge neck, and the spectacle of the great big bear paws some called hands. Not once did he look back. He just walked slowly, allowing them to take in the full, terrible picture, then slumped once again onto the tiny chair outside the door of the exam room. At least the chair *seemed* tiny. To most men it would have been just a normal chair.

Coal felt Connie let go of his arm, and a rush of blood came back into it. It actually felt a little numb. He looked down at his mother, who had breathed a big sigh.

"Dang, Mom, you haven't lost any of your bread-making grip. Trying to break my arm?"

"Hush." She gave him a smile of relief, and they both turned as one to search the emergency room. It was time to be out of Bigfoot Monahan's field of vision.

After a moment, Coal heard voices down the hall to the right, and they walked that way. Outside Room 4, they halted. Inside, a man was saying, "All right, this is going to really hurt, sweetie. But I have to do it, okay?"

The patient must have only nodded in response. Connie started to continue into the room, but Coal reached out and took her by the arm. "I think you should wait. She's pretty emotional, Mom. I'm afraid she might come undone if she sees you right now."

Connie nodded. "Yes, you're probably right. I'll wait."

No sooner had they both sat down than they looked far down the hall to see a door open, and two people came walking their way, both carrying coffee cups. It took but a moment to recognize Jay Castillo and his partner Maura.

"Oh, damnit."

Connie looked over sharply at her son. "Where did you learn to talk like that?"

"From you!" He let out with an uncomfortable laugh, knowing the EMT's were fast approaching. He was only remotely aware of Connie slapping his arm and saying something reproachful.

Jay came up and stopped. "Hello, Mrs. Savage. Sorry you had to come down here so late."

"Well, you don't tell Salmon's moose what to do, do you, Jay?" she said teasingly, standing up. "How are you?"

"Good. Just tired. You?"

"Oh, fine. Fine. Tired too, I guess. I'm not used to chasing ambulances in the middle of the night."

Coal smiled secretively. *Middle of the night.* It was maybe ten. Ten-thirty at the latest. He doubted his mother had a clue what the middle of the night meant. She was one of those who got up two hours before the sun to feed horses, go for a walk, brew coffee and watch the sun come up. Middle of the night!

Jay's eyes changed of a sudden, and he said, "I don't think you've met my partner, Mrs. Savage. Connie Savage, this is Maura PlentyWounds. She moved here a while back from Rapid City—South Dakota."

"Oh, it's a pleasure to meet you, Miss... PlentyWounds, is it? I've never heard that name."

"It's Sioux," Maura offered. "My father's father was a full-blood Lakota."

"Oh, how interesting! Sometime I'd like to hear more. So, I know Rapid City, a little," replied Connie. "It's a beautiful place."

"Thank you," replied Maura, her eyes showing no enthusiasm for her hometown. The friendly expression in those eyes for Connie, however, was nothing like what Coal had witnessed earlier. It was almost as if at the scene of the wreck he had been dealing with this woman's angry, disrespectful twin. With that happy look on her face, Coal realized that Maura PlentyWounds was indeed one of the prettiest women he had ever seen.

But when she looked back at Coal, her eyes took on a little bit of flint, a little of their look from earlier. The softness he had seen moments before was gone. Nope, there was no twin. This was a case, evidently, of EMT Jekyll and Miss Hyde.

"So did you find the moose, Mr. Savage?"

"No, ma'am, I didn't really look. He didn't seem inclined to hang around when he ran off. And he sure didn't send me out any invite." The moment he said it, Coal realized how much it sounded like he was trying to act out a part in some old Western.

Maura only tipped up her chin in reply, looking back at Connie. The haughty dismissal was the same as if she had slapped his face. "Well, Mrs. Savage, it sure was a big pleasure to meet you. I hope Katie will be okay. Dr. Bent is really great. He and Annie will give her the very best care—I promise."

"I know they will, dear," replied Connie, taking Maura's hand and patting it with her other hand. "It sure was nice to meet you too. You be careful out there now, you hear?"

"I will. We'd probably better get going, Jay."

Jay looked at Coal and shrugged. It was obvious there was a rub between his old friend and Maura. Nothing either could do about that. Must be a woman thing—at least a thing that Coal always seemed more than capable of finding in women. "Sure is good to see you, Mrs. Savage," said Jay. "Good night."

As Maura waved goodbye to Connie and walked off down the hall, looking far too good in low-heeled cowboy boots, snug-fitting jeans and a white cotton shirt that seemed tailor-made for all the curves of her torso, Jay stopped, holding a roll of bandages in one hand, and looked at Coal. "Sure is good to see you again, too, buddy. Maybe we can catch up more later. I'd better not leave Maura waiting. She gets a little impatient."

"Do tell," agreed Coal. "In more ways than one. All right, Jay, take care. Get some sleep, and don't let the bed bugs bite. Or maybe I should say don't let that woman bite."

Jay grinned, lighting up that face Coal had always thought a little too handsome for the man's own good, and hurried off down the hall after his partner.

After they were gone, Coal found himself contemplating Maura's last name and her supposed Sioux blood. The golden blond hair, even with its brown undertones, and the light-colored skin seemed more than passingly strange after such a revelation. He had known blond people of Indian blood before, but none that he could think of were as much as a fourth. He wondered offhandedly if her pale-faced look had made Maura somewhat of an outcast with her tribe. But it was no matter to him. Just another odd thing to think about.

By now, Coal was painfully aware that with all of the talking that had been done, Katie Leigh must know he and Connie were out here. "Maybe we should at least take a peek and see how things are progressing, huh?" he suggested to Connie.

"Well, you choose. If you think they're done."

"They're not building her a new face, right? Just setting a broken nose, and that doesn't even take a cast. Which come to think of it might be kind of funny, though. They could do a metal one—make her look like Kid Shelleen in *Cat Ballou.*" He couldn't help but laugh when he thought of Katie exchanging places with Lee Marvin in the comical Western that had been such a hit back in sixty-five.

"Why, shame on you, Coal! This is serious," chided Connie. But she had a little smile trying to twist at the corners of her mouth. "Now be nice."

Speaking those words, she leaned away from her son, edging an eye around the door frame to see into where the little operation was going. The operation, such as it was, had ended. Katie's face was swollen, especially around the nose, but at least her nose was straight. A nicely-built nurse with dark blond hair under-toned with brown was cleaning up the girl's face with a wet rag, a bottle of sterile water in one hand.

Katie, her jaw set so as not to reveal any pain, watched a short, balding man in a white coat, who was holding a bottle of aspirin and observing the nurse as she worked. Connie and Coal, viewing it all from the door, heard him speak.

"Okay, Katie. Just be careful washing around that area for a few days or a week, okay? Just to avoid reinjuring it. And, as much as you can, try to sleep on your back—or better yet, on your side—maybe with an old towel on your pillow. And I think a couple of Bayer or three will do you all right for the pain. But if you need something more, please don't hesitate to call and ask for me. You remember my name, right?" He gave her a searching look full of good humor.

"Yes. Doctor Bent," said Katie, and she smiled shyly. That was the smile of the old Katie Coal remembered, although it seemed so long since he had seen that girl. It certainly wasn't the old face he remembered, however: Her nose seemed twice its normal size, like a boil ready to lance. He winced at the thought.

"Go on in, Mom. I think she'll be happy to see you. I'm going to wait out here."

"No, Coal. You just settle yourself down and come on in there with me. Don't you be ridiculous. She's your daughter!"

Coal put his hand over his mother's, which had closed on his forearm. "Mom, do us both a favor. Go in there and say hi to your granddaughter, and get a hug that's probably much-needed for both of you. I'll go in afterward, but I can promise you the whole atmosphere of this hospital is going to change. Scout's honor."

"You don't know a thing about Scouts, Coal!" she said in a scolding voice. "You refused to go, remember?"

He laughed with the memory. "Yeah, I guess. I knew everything they pretended they were going to teach me. And they wouldn't let me just go off in the woods by myself and scout."

"Yes, and you've been a rebel ever since—and a loner, too. It's not good for you, Son. I don't know why you have to be like that."

"Mom, are we going to stand out here and talk all night, or do you want to see your granddaughter? It's a little late for me to sign up for Cub Scouts, you know."

Connie frowned. "Then fine. Stay out here and be stubborn."

"All right. I will."

He smiled at his mom as she went around the corner the rest of the way and presented herself in the doorway, standing there to stare at Katie for a moment while she waited, assumedly for the girl to spot her and for recognition to hit.

When it did, Coal felt a twinge of jealousy. "Grandma! Hi!" He heard his daughter jumping off the bed and her fast steps approaching, and soon he could see her hands close over Connie's back. It made a lump rise in his throat, and his vision dimmed. Blinking forcefully, he turned away. He was wiping at his eyes, so he couldn't see. When he opened them, Bigfoot Monahan was standing down at the corner of the admissions desk with a boy of nine or ten beside him in an arm cast.

The big man stared at Coal, and Coal stared back. The man had surely seen him wiping his eyes. He smirked, a derisive look coming over his face, and glanced toward the exit. He started to turn with the boy, then stopped and glanced back at Coal.

At the last second, he took the boy by the shoulder of his uninjured arm and spoke to him out of the corner of his mouth. And then, like a graceful bear—or, more aptly, the giant hominid from whom he had won his nickname—he started down the hall, right toward Coal. The boy marched stolidly beside him.

It was obvious they had no intentions of stopping before they reached him.

CHAPTER THIRTEEN

This time, Coal Savage stood alone. His mother had gone the rest of the way into the examination room with Katie, the doctor, and the nurse. There had to be a receptionist somewhere, or at least another nurse. *Someone* had surely released the boy to go with Bigfoot. But Coal had yet to see her. It was him, Bigfoot, and the boy. Alone.

Bigfoot Monahan and the boy stopped only three feet away. Well within range for Coal to deliver at least a good kick or two. Yet maybe a little *too* close.

"See this boy?" asked Monahan.

Coal looked down at the boy. He was looking up squarely into Coal's face with almost as much hatred as Monahan showed. Coal made no reply.

"His name's Danny, but we call him Butch. He's spent a long time growin' up without a pa."

"And hopefully learning something about poaching and speeding and running people off highways," Coal replied tersely.

"You got your mama in here with you tonight, Savage." The big man's gravelly voice was quiet. It was his pale blue eyes that were making all the noise right now.

"Not at the moment."

Bigfoot ignored the parry. "I always make it a point not to fight in front of a lady—if a woman that could drop a turd like you can be considered a lady. But she won't always be around."

Coal felt his spine stiffen. It was one thing to insult him, but now the man was getting dangerously close to insulting his mother. He forced himself to take a deep breath.

"Apparently Larry MacAtee's mother wasn't anywhere around."

Bigfoot's eyes drove coffin nails through Coal's face. "Nope, apparently she wasn't," said the big man at last. His voice had dropped a notch. "You remember that."

Coal waited for Monahan to make some move. *Anything.* So much as poking him in the chest with a finger. When he did, Coal was set to light up his Christmas tree. He was planning out every move in his head even now. Hadn't this man so much as admitted just now that he killed Larry? He had sworn he would, now he was out, and Larry was dead. And he didn't even try to deny it.

But Bigfoot Monahan made no move. He only stood there and stared, trying with his glare to drive Coal's eyes out the back of his head. But Coal had every bit the will this man did, even if he didn't have his size.

"I hear the bed bugs bite hard in Lemhi County, Savage. Hard enough to kill. You should let 'em work. There's some ways worse to die." Bigfoot flexed the fingers of his right hand, and two knuckles popped. "Come on, Butch. Ma's a-waitin'."

Danny kept staring at Coal. At last, he gave him a middle finger salute, and for a few seconds he held it, staring in defiance over his little finger into Coal's face. The boy could be pretty sure he was safe, with a man the size of Bigfoot standing beside him.

Finally, he turned with his father, they walked down the hall, and finally disappeared through the exit. Coal felt someone watching him and glanced over at the reception desk. There was a white-clad young brunette standing there, her eyes worried.

He just nodded and turned back to Katie's room. Steeling himself, he walked inside.

Coal forced a smile for Katie when she turned and looked into his eyes. She immediately looked away. As Coal had predicted, the atmosphere changed. A cold rush came over the room. The doctor and nurse, looking a bit confused, turned their eyes to Coal.

"And you are... Katie's father?" the doctor guessed.

"I reckon."

"Dr. Bent," the man said, reaching out his hand, which Coal shook. The man's fingers were long and soft and pink. It gave Coal a weird feeling to squeeze them, and he hurriedly dropped his hand.

"Coal Savage. Thanks, Doc. For all you did." He nodded at the nurse, suddenly realizing how striking she was. "Ma'am."

"Hi. I'm Annie Price." She held out her hand, and Coal took it as well. It was firmer than the doctor's, and her grip was solid but not demanding.

"Hello." Coal should not have held onto the woman's hand so long. He had no idea why he did, except perhaps subconsciously to erase the memory of shaking Dr. Bent's. Really, he didn't even know he was doing it. He just suddenly realized he was gazing into her smoky blue eyes, and there was something in the depths of them that spoke to him. Hers was perhaps not the beauty of a magazine model. In fact, he thought to himself, it was deeper, more pure. There was something readably strong and good and wholesome in this woman, and something mystical about the vaguely haunted look in her eyes. With her lips slightly parted, she met him gaze for gaze, searching for something, it seemed. He realized he was instantly attracted to her, and for that weakness he berated himself.

Coal felt Connie's touch on his arm, and he released Annie's hand, letting his own fall to his side. He had to force himself to drag his eyes away from hers.

"Your mother and Katie know everything to do, Dad," said Dr. Bent. *My name's Mr. Savage, or Coal,* he thought. "Just call if you have any questions. She'll have a little pain, but that will go away in a few days and she will only have the discoloration to deal with. Nothing we can do about that."

Coal nodded. "Okay. I've had my nose broken before. I know the routine."

The doctor nodded. "Your mother tells me you are to be the new sheriff of Lemhi County."

"If I live that long," Coal replied, his mind slipping back over his encounter with Bigfoot Monahan.

"We have heard good things about you. I'm sure the county will be glad to have you."

Coal just nodded. He was trying to ignore the derisive looks Katie Leigh was shooting at the wall by the door, and the disgusted shaking of her head.

When the three of them walked to the door, Coal couldn't help but turn to glance back—just for a moment. Nurse Annie was still watching him, her lips still parted, and a mixture of warmth and intrigue filled those eyes that seemed somehow to search the depths of his feeling. He would not soon forget the way she gazed at him. For hours, that strange, questioning look would haunt him.

Sunday, November 19

In the morning, Coal awoke early and stepped into his jeans. In spite of his six-foot-four, he was still wearing jeans that were thirty-six inches at the waist, and for a man of his age it seemed like some feat. He lotioned up his feet, because, in spite of how young his body felt, the old man-skin of his feet seemed to be turning into the cracked face of a desert. Then he pulled on a pair of cotton socks, another of wool, and then his brown work boots, lacing them up tight.

He walked to the hallway bath and flipped the light switch, and three globes above the sink illuminated the bulging muscle of his torso and his whiskered face. Echoing his name, his face seemed smudged with soot. Even freshly shaved, there was always a blue cast to it from the dark beard.

He sprayed shaving cream in a cone shape onto the fingers of his left hand, which he then began to bring to his jaw. He stopped partway and lowered his hand.

Who was this man staring back at him from the mirror? Hair that had been coal black at his birth, then gone nearly light brown, in his young childhood, had settled on this deep chocolate brown color at last, and was neatly trimmed to combat its desire to curl, which gave it its numerous cowlicks. His jaw had always been square, but somehow it seemed to be shrinking. And a neck that had been too large to let him button most store-bought shirts seemed smaller too—although he still could not button up the necks of most of his shirts. His face still had the overall square look, but he wasn't sure it was the hard, lean face he remembered. Wrinkles were starting to show at the corners of his eyes, and they creased his forehead deeply. His deep-set eyes showed not only his ancestry, which contained some Czechoslovakian, and, like Maura, a bit of Indian blood, although his was of the Cree tribe, but spoke of all the times he had been battered and scarred in battle. His mustache, even tightly trimmed, made his face seem somehow angry. He had heard that from others as well.

The torso, molded by years of martial arts and strenuous bodybuilding, seemed to be Coal's biggest link to his youth. The muscles of his abdomen, which were only slightly hidden under flesh, were sharply defined, his chest and shoulders large and rippling with power. His hands were thick and sinewy too. He had spent so much time in the gym keeping it all that way, and to build up those back muscles, his "lats," which could be seen even from this front view.

But why? Had it been so important? In the end, what did it mean? Did his wife even care that he was in that kind of shape, that he had the body of a weightlifter ten or fifteen years younger? Or was all of that bodybuilding only one more cinder block— a block in the wall he was building between himself and Laura? Did all that weight training, running, and eating special meals it seemed to take him forever to prepare only mean that many hours spent on less important things than his family?

There was another man than Coal inside the deep-set steel-blue eyes that peered back at him. That man was accusing him, telling him he might have done so much more. His vanity had taken its toll. It had taken so many hours away, hours he could never reclaim.

In the end, hadn't Laura proved that the bodybuilding didn't matter? That this physique was not what she cared about in the least? Yes, she had. In a great big way.

He raised his hand again and started dabbing the cream on his face, watching his eyes all the while. Finally, he had to look away. He did not like the accusing look that man gave back to him. He hated that man in the mirror some days. And, even sadder, that man seemed to hate him too.

CHAPTER FOURTEEN

Wearing a long john undershirt and blue-gray flannel shirt augmented by a thin, unlined Levi jacket, Coal was driving down to the Salmon highway, watching the bright eyes and dark bodies of deer bounce back and forth in the beam of his headlight, before he remembered: He had promised the twins he would take them looking for the misguided moose this morning!

Oh, they wouldn't remember, he told himself. They were only five. Another part of him said, Remember what Laura accused you of? Not spending enough time with your family. Making your job your number one priority, hunting your second. Your family is last.

He pulled the truck over to the side of the road. In the beam of the headlight, dust swirled as he saw the bright lights of a car on Highway 28 flash past at the end of the road. He watched a doe cautiously stick her head out of the willows, look for movement, then dive across the road in front of him and leap the barbed wire fence. Dumb-headed deer couldn't even wait ten seconds. No wonder they were always strewn all over the side of the highway.

What about the twins? Oh, they were sleeping! They wouldn't wake up for hours. The dust in his headlight beam was starting to settle. He looked in the rearview mirror, then thought, for what? Out here this morning it was black as... coal. Connie had been out with the horses—her morning routine. The rest of the world, any who had sense, were sleeping.

What time was it anyway? He leaned down and tried to see the horizon outside the window. The world was deep in sleep. And chilly. Cold as a refrigerator.

Coal leaned back against the seat. He let a long sigh escape him. Savage Road was too tight, but he thought about turning around at the highway and going back home to his boys. They would be warm in their beds, warm with sleep. But they would wake up quickly enough. The very thought of going on a hunt would wake them.

Or would it? Would they really care? Five years old? And then the name came flashing back to him: Larry MacAtee. And he knew he had to keep going to town. Larry was dead. Murdered. He could not just let that lie. He could not rest until his friend's killer was brought to bay. Besides, he had already arranged to meet Jim, K.T. and Mitchell. If they could sacrifice a Sunday morning, he sure could. It was for a friend, after all.

The boys could wait. The truth was, he knew kids well enough to know they weren't going to remember his suggestion when they woke up anyway. They would probably just want to get up and stay in the warm house playing with Dobe and Shadow or their Johnny West toys anyway.

Coal threw the truck back into second and started rolling again. At the highway, he turned right, and a satisfying chill ran up his spine as his bold-lugged tires started to whine on the asphalt. How he loved that sound! It was what had once made him want to be a long-haul trucker. Before the call of the Marines. Before two nasty Asian wars changed Coal Savage forever.

The sky behind him in the east was paling into silver, and the truck's heater was finally working, beating out the frost that had been coming out of his nose with every exhalation. When that heater started kicking out its waves, it was almost time to open windows. *Nobody* was ever going to freeze in this pickup!

Now Coal could see the dividing line between the dark, powerful, wild mountains and the sky. Those forests up there, in those folds and canyons of the peaks that loomed so ominously over the far end of town, were Coal's hunting country—some of it, at least. They called to him. They had been calling to him for years. But just like his family, those mountains had taken a back seat to his job—his drive to see justice done. He guessed it would continue to be that way. But at least now he could see them, on his way in to the courthouse. That was something. A far cry better than the roaring crowd of smoking, horn-blasting vehicles that cluttered the streets of Washington, D.C., and the low, heavily wooded hills between there and Broad Run, Virginia, that he had been forced into pretending were mountains.

On the far end of town, headlights veered off Highway 93 and entered Main, coming toward him. Otherwise, the town was still. A few cars were parked in front of the already lit-up Salmon River Coffee Shop and Wally's. He passed the oncoming vehicle, whose color, make and model old habit forced him to take note of, just before the Coffee Shop, where he leaned over and looked through the front windows. He didn't see Jay, but some teenage girl was pouring coffee for a table full of early-risers. He was sure going to miss that coffee if he got to the courthouse and found out K.T. had made his usual sour brew this morning.

In the block of the Coffee Shop, Coal noticed four pickups: a new Chevy, an earlier Chevy than his own, a beat-up Dodge, and a mid-sixties Ford. There was a red El Camino and a gold Chevy Caprice. By the time he was past, he had them all memorized by color and approximate year, as well as by any obvious damage viewable from a passing car.

Crossing the river, he started up the Salmon Bar, passed Redeemer Episcopal Church, and pulled beyond the courthouse to turn left into the driveway. He parked in the back. Besides the pickup, only Jim Lockwood's black Thunderbird and a green and white Nash he didn't recognize were there.

Just how early *was* he?

He had to stop when he got past the Thunderbird to the Nash. Dang, that had to be about the ugliest car ever made! He made a note to himself: If that car belonged to the night jailer, which it must, the county was obviously not paying him enough. Good thing there was parking in the back, out of sight of the public!

Jim Lockwood had left the door unlocked, so after a quick scan of the lot for anything out of the ordinary, Coal pushed his way inside. He led with his left side, for this morning he had his Model 27 Smith and Wesson strapped to his right hip.

"Mornin', son," greeted Jim, from the desk. He was sipping coffee from what appeared to be a rough clay mug the likes of which they used to force kids to make in art classes.

"You beat K.T. to the coffee!" Coal exclaimed. "Great."

Jim gave him a sort of facial shrug, "Well, in a way I did. Brought this from home."

"Oh." Coal was disappointed. "Thanks."

"Sorry. Thought you'd have sense enough to make your own or stop at the Coffee Shop on your way."

"My instincts told me to, but I was in a hurry."

"What have I always taught you out huntin', Coal?"

"Slow down and trust my instincts."

"But you didn't. What's worse, a man who don't know nothin' or a man who don't follow what he knows?"

Coal grinned sheepishly. "Yeah, yeah."

Jim stood up, stuffing one hand in the pocket of an overbearing sheepskin coat he had snugged about him. "Cold in here," he said. "Say, you recall this coffee mug?" He raised the mug.

Coal looked at it closer. "Should I?"

"Shoot, son. Those two wars really did mess you up, didn't they? You made this thing for me when you were in junior high."

Coal's mind immediately jumped back to his first thoughts at seeing the mug. "No way. Let me see that."

Jim pushed it closer, and Coal took it from him and studied it. The initials C.G.S. were etched in ungraceful letters on the mug body inside the handle. "Well, I'll be. You saved that all these years?"

"Why not? It's as tough as I am." Jim laughed. He stopped laughing when Coal put the mug to his lips and took a deep, scalding swallow.

"The coffee tastes like I made it for you in junior high, too," Coal said with a laugh, handing it back.

"Easy now, son. Betty made that, not me. You know how I am about people pickin' on my sweetheart."

In spite of the twinkle in Jim's eyes, Coal felt a twinge of shame. For one, he really *wouldn't* have said anything even jokingly derogatory about Jim's wonderful wife. Two, thinking back, he couldn't remember ever speaking about Laura like Jim had just spoken of his wife of so many years, at least not after the first year of their marriage. Not that he didn't ever think it. He just never talked like that about her, so no one could ever have known how he felt. But to Jim, Betty was always his sweetheart, his darling, or his beautiful gal. Sometimes he even still referred to her as his bride.

"It's good coffee, Jim," said Coal quietly, unable to meet his old friend's gaze.

"Hey, pard. I was funnin' you, you know."

There were a long few moments of uncomfortable silence, when Coal first noticed the *tock, tock,* of a huge clock in one corner. It was too big and too obnoxious to make the obligatory cliché *tick* in the language of its kind.

Jim pulled his hand from his coat pocket, walked over and threw an arm around Coal's shoulders. "How are you farin', boy? How are the kids?"

"It's rough. You know."

From the corner of his eye, he saw Jim nodding. "No, I don't know about that. Betty's still with me. Forty-two years now. I have no idea what you've been through, son. I wish I could."

Coal felt tears coming. He cleared his throat and stepped quickly to the gun rack, laying a hand on one of the shotguns, a twelve gauge Remington pump with disgracefully battered wood. He pretended to inspect it, running his fingers over the worst of its wounds.

"So tell me what we have on Larry, Jim." It still felt strange to be talking about his old buddy this way. Like he didn't exist anymore.

"We told you all of it last night. Need to go back to the house sometime today, try to see if we can tell whereabouts the shot was fired from. There's no evidence at the scene that we can find so far. Looks like maybe the killer never set foot on the place."

Forced now to think of Kathy and the girls, Coal asked, "Do we know yet when Kathy's going to be back?"

"Sometime today. She was pretty shaken up yesterday and didn't feel good to drive until afternoon. You'll need to go see her."

"Jim, I'm not sure I can."

"You're gonna be the sheriff now. It's going to get bad like this from time to time. Just like the war. You gotta just buck up and go."

"I know. I'll go. I just... How do you think of what to say?"

"Nobody ever knows what to say, son. Just don't feel forced into sayin' something foolish about God takin' him away because he needed him in heaven. Folks ain't stupid. God don't take people like Larry away. Killers and bad luck do. God just don't interfere when they do it. Heck, can you imagine how crowded this world would be if God saved everybody who didn't deserve to die?"

Coal stopped and gave his old friend a level look. "Right! It wouldn't be crowded at all, not if he took out all the ones who *did* deserve to die."

Before Jim could form a reply, a man came from the jail area at the same time that they heard a vehicle pull up outside, then shortly after, another. Coal looked first to the man coming from the jail—evidently the man with the hideous Nash out back. He was a big man, probably in his late twenties and built even leaner in the hips than Coal and beefy through the shoulders, although lacking Coal's heavy chest and back. His neck had maybe an inch in circumference on Coal's. His was the sleek build of one who knew his way around a gym and had been blessed with athletic genetics to get him on the right road.

Exuding an interesting mix of self-confidence and humility, the man walked to Coal. "Howdy. I'm Jordan Peterson. Your night jailer."

"Good to meet you. Coal Savage."

"I know. Everybody's heard about you."

Coal laughed as their hands melded together, further impressed by the firm grip that could have closed much harder had the young man wanted it to. "Well, I hope not all of it was bad."

"I'm pretty sure none of it was bad," said Peterson.

"Then the town's full of liars," Coal growled, and the younger man laughed. He made some reply, but Coal missed it as the door opened and Todd Mitchell came in, followed by K.T. Batterton.

"Mornin', Coal," said K.T. Mitchell just nodded.

"Mornin'."

"I'm smelling no coffee."

Coal shrugged and chuckled. "Yeah, that's exactly the same thing I smelled. No Cindy here yet when I got in. Maybe she got all her work done yesterday."

"I knew I should've stopped at the Coffee Shop."

"You should follow your instincts." Coal looked over slyly at Jim and winked. "Don't know what's worse, a man who doesn't know any better, or a man who knows and doesn't follow his instincts."

Mitchell looked up at Jordan Peterson. "What's wrong with you, you go to sleep on the job?"

"Huh?"

"Where's coffee?"

"I thought K.T. was going to make it."

"You don't drink coffee, do you, son?" asked Jim.

"Not very often."

"Easy to tell." All those who had tasted K.T.'s coffee laughed, even Mitchell.

Coal turned back to the jailer, not wanting him to feel like he was ignored by his new boss. "Looks like you spend some time throwing iron around the gym, Jordan."

"Yeah, a little. You too. In fact, that's the first thing I think they told me about you, and I've heard it several times since. You're pretty famous around here for your build."

Coal laughed. "Small towns sure don't have much meaningful to talk about, do they?"

Another car pulled into the parking lot. Coal went and peeked out the door. Cindy Hardlinger, a heavy-set mid-thirties woman with short brown hair running in a straight line across her forehead and dark eyebrows badly needing plucked was getting out of a beat-up red Jeep.

"Hey, Cindy!" Coal called, walking up the concrete steps to parking lot level.

Cindy turned and saw him as she was straightening her skirt. "Coal! Hey!" She hurried over and shook his hand, trying to hide a sudden rush of shyness. "Welcome home."

"Thanks, Cindy. Nice to see you. Say, I don't suppose you could come down here and show these yay-hoos how to make real coffee, could you? Can you spare a minute?"

She laughed. "You bet, Sheriff! Hang on while I go get my purse."

A minute later, Cindy came down the stairs and pushed inside. Coal stopped talking to the others instantly. "The coffee maker's right over there," he said and pointed.

There was a shiny new electric drip coffee maker sitting on a high, narrow table with a green tin can of Maxwell House coffee next to it. It was a powerful statement on the importance of coffee that although the sheriff's department couldn't keep well-cared-for weapons in their rack, the electric drip coffee maker had barely been invented, and they already had one.

Cindy walked over and started putting the coffee together, asking someone to bring her water. She looked over at Coal as she scooped out the grounds. "You must know first-off that if you would buy Folger's you would already be a step ahead in making good coffee. Who buys this Maxwell House stuff?"

"I confess," said K.T., raising his hand. "That was one of my last purchases."

"Take it easy, Cindy," cut in Jim. "I buy Maxwell House at home, too, and it tastes pretty good to me."

Cindy laughed. "Well, in general, I would—with all due respect—submit that men really have no taste. Take me, for example. I'm not even married yet, and I'm thirty-seven years old!"

Coal cringed. Why did people set themselves up like that? Cindy was a very sweet lady, but she was what some might call *un-beautiful*. It wasn't her fault, of course, and honestly, she would probably have made someone a wonderful wife. But still, how did a man even reply to a statement like that? The answer was, they didn't. The room, after her comment, went uncomfortably still until Cindy shoved her other leg into her mouth.

"Okay, well don't all of you reply at the same time!" She laughed, but this time Coal caught a rueful sound in it, and her face flushed. Poor woman. Who knew why life worked out the way it did sometimes? Truth be told, he really wasn't any better off than she was. And maybe worse.

When the coffee was brewed, and Cindy had taken her wounded pride and gone, Jordan Peterson shrugged into a jacket and took a ring of keys off his belt, setting it on the desk. "I guess I'm off, Todd. Or, uh... Coal." He blushed, realizing in mid-step that he was going to be answering to a new sheriff now.

"Go ahead and talk to Todd, Jordan. He knows more about running this place right now than I do."

Jordan nodded and smiled. "So, Todd, everything was pretty quiet. Jensen seems a little upset about something, but I couldn't get him to talk about it. I think he was trying to hide it from the other guys, but it looked like he was crying."

"Bawl baby," said Todd.

"Easy does it, Todd," Jim cut in. "I heard there's somethin' wrong with his daughter. She's in a hospital down in Salt Lake."

Todd stared dumbly at Jim. "Oh. Well, no reason to be crying in front of other men."

"You don't have kids of your own, do you, Todd?" asked Jim.

"Yeah, actually I do."

"You do? Why didn't I ever know that? Well, I'm surprised. Usually, a man's thinkin' changes when he has his own kids. Leastwise if he's a normal human being."

Coal quickly looked over at Jim. He found it odd that a man could be around another so much and not even know if he had children. It was a sad comment on how much Mitchell must care about those children, if he never even mentioned them. Also, Coal sensed a hidden meaning in Jim's sage words, but maybe it was only because of how he himself felt about Mitchell. The man really *wasn't* a *normal* human being.

Silence clutched the room for a while. Finally, Mitchell just nodded. "Okay. Sorry."

"Anyway," Peterson went on, "the other three were pretty quiet, other than Pepper talking in his sleep again."

Mitchell forced a quick grin. "All right. See you tonight maybe."

"Go get some sleep," Coal told the younger man as he opened the door going outside.

"Thanks. Sure was good to finally meet you, Mr. Savage."

Coal walked over to him with his cup of coffee in his left hand. He held out his hand and shook Peterson's again. "You called me Coal just a minute ago. We won't get along too well unless you keep calling me that. Or 'Sheriff,' if you want. Anything but 'sir' or 'Mr. Savage'." He finished his words with a wink.

"Sure thing, Sheriff. See you later."

"Oh, and one more thing," Coal stopped him. "Don't they pay you enough to sell off that ugly car and get a real set of wheels?"

Jordan laughed. "Well, it was a cheap buy. But no, not really. I make about enough to buy food and gas."

"We'll have to look into that."

After Peterson had gone, Coal sipped his coffee, walked over and stood in front of the others.

"So. No suspects, right?"

They all looked at each other. "I thought we rode that trail yesterday," said Jim.

"Okay. So you apparently haven't heard Bigfoot Monahan got out of the pen."

The room went deathly still. Jim Lockwood straightened up in his chair. "I... heard he was *going* to. Judge Sinclair said next month. Have you heard different?"

"Heard? Boys, I *saw*. If any of you had a radio on last night, that was me you heard about that got in the wreck. Katie's nose got broken, and I had to go down to the hospital. And guess who was there to greet me."

Jim's face was frozen. Part of it seemed to be anger, part of it hatred, which Jim rarely let cross his features. Another part, the part that disturbed Coal to his core, appeared to be pure fear.

CHAPTER FIFTEEN

"What happened?" K.T. Batterton finally asked.

"We exchanged words. He approached me twice, then backed off both times."

Coal told them of the two exchanges. Then he said, "He just talked pretty cryptic. Never outright threatened me, but the intent was there. Then his kid flipped me a birdie, and they left."

Todd Mitchell actually giggled. When everyone looked at him, none of them smiling, the smile disappeared from his face. "Sorry, just struck me funny at the moment."

One side of Coal's mouth came up in a smile. "It actually does seem sort of funny now."

Jim finally found his voice. "He promised to kill you, Coal. I don't know if you remember, but he promised to kill me too. And Larry."

Coal nodded. "Yeah, and K.T. and Trent Tuckett, too. I wasn't there when he made the threat to you, but I sure remember the day he was getting in the van and said it to me. What I'd like to know is how a man like that gets out of the pen and comes back home and not one lawman in the valley hears about it."

"Like Jim said, we knew he was getting out," cut in K.T. "They called and said he was a model prisoner and had even saved one of the guard's lives in a bad fight. Good behavior all the way. See what it can get you? But they said he'd be here in a month. In fact, I have nothing in writing, but I would swear they said they would call us the day he left."

"Larry sure should have been told," said Coal quietly. "Maybe he would have had some kind of chance to watch his back."

"So we have our suspect," said K.T. "Now what? We have no proof, do we? Do you think Sinclair will issue a warrant? Let us search his property for the murder weapon? I doubt it. He's pretty weak when it comes to handing out warrants."

"As a felon, Bigfoot owns *any* gun, he goes back to the pen to finish his time," Jim cut in.

Jim was right about that. The federal Gun Control Act of sixty-eight had made that a nationwide rule in every state: a convicted felon could never again own a weapon.

Jim went on: "So why not contact his parole officer? Should be able to walk in his house any time without a warrant and do a routine check. We find a gun—bam! Nailed."

"I don't know Bigfoot," said Coal. "I only know what I saw the night I took him down and when I came back to testify. But I have a feeling he's not dumb enough to keep a firearm right there on his property."

"If he's not, he's not. But it's still worth a try," Jim said.

"I agree. Just playing devil's advocate."

Jim looked around the room at the others. "Let's get something straight, boys. We all agree Bigfoot is our man—right?"

All agreed. There were too many coincidences.

"Then Coal, you, K.T. and me are gonna be his next targets. Or possibly Trent Tuckett. Do we agree on that too?"

"Seems to follow," said Coal.

"Then let's get his p.o. on the way. I mean to at least sort of enjoy my 'golden years,' not spend 'em dodgin' bullets."

"I'll make a call later," said Coal. "You'll have to dig up a number for me."

*   *   *

On the principle that four pairs of eyes were better than one or two, Jim drove out to Larry MacAtee's place with Todd Mitchell, while Coal drove the sheriff's car that Mitchell had been using, the dark blue 1971 Ford LTD. K.T. rode with him.

Before they reached the house, an aging, black-faced Border collie with a narrow white stripe straight up the middle of its forehead came running out to them, barking. Coal smiled. "Hey! It's Rowdy! Come here, boy."

The dog's ears perked up, and then, with tail whipping frantically, he ran to Coal and threw himself into him, squirming all over with delight. Two years gone, and this dog still remembered him! Coal rubbed the dog all over, speaking soft words. Rowdy took off and ran in a fast circle, then came straight back to Coal and fell on his side at his feet, immediately flipping over so his belly was exposed. Coal scratched the dog's chest, smiling. What a reception! Leave it to a dog to make a man feel adored.

While Coal was greeting the dog, the others walked off toward where a white fifty-eight Ford pickup stood, rusted spots and patches freckling its body. It was stationed next to a stack of straw some eight bales high. At last, Coal stood up and followed them, Rowdy running out ahead.

On the far side of the pickup from the straw stack, where the driver's door stood open, someone had spray-painted on the ground where Larry lay when Jeb Rowe found him. The pickup had not been moved, and a chain had been padlocked around the steering wheel to keep it in place until their return. They couldn't afford to pay anyone to stay here and watch the crime scene, so it had been left to the elements and to anyone who had come snooping. That was one drawback to a small agency like Lemhi County—among many.

Coal stared at the strange caricature on the ground as Rowdy came and leaned against his leg. That brought home to him the fact that the crime scene had not, indeed, been left unguarded. Larry's most faithful friend had stayed to watch.

Coal's heart pounded fast. It still seemed so strange to think of Larry being gone, and seeing this proof disturbed him beyond measure. The old dog stared at the mark on the ground, and at the dark place that had been a pool of blood, now soaked into the dirt and dry. He whined, looking up at his master's friend, and his. He seemed to be saying, *All right. Now you're here—show me where my buddy is.* So many times when the dog was young, Larry and he had taken him into the field, and while Coal held onto the dog, Larry went and hid somewhere, and Coal let Rowdy run off and find him. Rowdy looked up at Coal and whined again, then ran off a little ways, turning to see if Coal would follow. But the man could hardly see him to follow now.

Scrubbing at his eyes, Coal felt someone watching him and looked up to have old Jim meet his eyes.

"I'm sorry, Coal. I know it don't seem real. Not to me either, and I wasn't as close to Larry as you."

Coal just nodded.

"Let's talk about how the bullet went in, Coal," said K.T., who had also been friends with Larry but had had more time to digest the idea of his death and seemed to sense that Coal needed an immediate rescue from his thoughts. K.T. held up his hand, flattened, and made his fingers angle down. "It came in at an angle, maybe something like this."

Coal studied K.T.'s hand, then glanced around at the nearest hills, the high places from where a bullet coming at the angle indicated by K.T.'s hand would have had to be fired—also the only points from which a potential gunman who was not in the yard itself could have seen Larry. Most of the potential ambush spots seemed hard to access—or at least hard without someone spotting the shooter. There were several houses in the direction of the bluffs that were closer to them than Larry's was.

Finally, Coal looked back at K.T., who had dropped his hand to his side. "How'd you figure that angle, K.T.? Was there an exit wound?"

K.T. looked uncomfortably over at Jim, then at Mitchell. The look he gave Mitchell seemed almost apologetic.

Coal scanned them all. His jaw hardened. "Am I missing something?"

Jim put a hand on Coal's arm. "Easy does it here, Coal. Not sure how you'll feel about this. But you know how slow results for an autopsy can be coming back."

"Sure."

"Well, so do we."

"Yeah, and?"

"Coal, we hadn't really talked about it, but it sort of seemed like a good idea to figure as much of this out as we could before the coroner came. So we took a pen and pushed it into the bullet hole. That's how we came up with the angle."

"We?"

"Sorry, Sheriff—it was my doin'," cut in Todd Mitchell.

"I'm sorry if there's some highfalutin method of figuring the angle that's better," Jim said hurriedly, "and I hope we didn't risk messing up some other kind of evidence in doin' it. You're the one with all the big city training. We're just country bumpkins. Just figured if we knew at least that much now we could use that information to figure out where the shooter might have hid and start looking for spent casings or tracks, or *something*."

Coal looked at the three of them for just a few moments. "They would never have allowed it in one of our investigations.

You start sticking any old thing into bullet holes, there's an awful lot you can change—sometimes even the bullet path. But this isn't the FBI. This is rural Salmon, Idaho, and we're just not going to be able to do things like they do in the big city. I have no problem with it, boys. Actually, off the record, it was pretty good thinking." He was looking at Mitchell as he said that.

Mitchell seemed to stand a little straighter. He held Coal's glance for a moment but didn't say anything, only nodded.

"Did you get up on those bluffs yet? Look for sign?"

"Quite a while. Didn't find so much as a track," Jim replied. "Plus, the folks we talked to in those houses over there said they never saw any strange vehicles or heard a shot close by."

"Well, unless you think it's hopeless, we should do it again soon. Snow or rain may not be far off."

Jim nodded. "Good point."

"Here's another good point," said Coal. "So you estimated your angle figuring Larry was standing up straight—right?"

"Sure," said K.T. again.

"What if he wasn't?"

Mitchell stared. "Huh?"

"What if he was bent over?" Coal's voice was patient.

The others just stared at him, saying nothing.

"It would change quite a bit, wouldn't it? Maybe the killer wasn't on a hill at all. Maybe he was on even ground with Larry."

"You thinkin' he was right in the yard here?" asked Jim.

"How deep did the bullet penetrate?"

"No tellin'," replied K.T. "But it didn't come out. That's all we know for sure."

"Then he probably wasn't in the yard—unless we're talking about a pistol shot."

"We scoured pretty hard and didn't see any tracks in the yard," Jim reminded him. "So we had sort of ruled out pistols."

"Then how about on another hill, a higher one? Higher than the one you've been looking at. Tell me this: Where was the entrance wound on Larry?"

"His back," replied K.T. "Right between the shoulder blades."

"That could answer a lot then," said Coal. "He was bent over, the bullet hits him in the back at the angle you described... That gunman could have been at a point ten or even fifty feet higher than where you boys went looking for evidence—depending on how far he was bent over."

They all kept staring. The wheels inside were turning. Jim chewed mechanically on a match.

"There's also something else no one considered—or if you did you didn't say it."

Jim raised his brows. "What's that?"

"Where Larry was standing when he was shot."

"He was standing by the truck door," affirmed Todd Mitchell. "It was open, just like it still is, and it looked like he was about to get in."

"It 'looked like'. But what if he wasn't?"

"What do you mean? It was pretty obvious."

As Mitchell had pointed out, no one had moved the pickup, even to shut the door. The crime scene had been left as much intact as could be for Coal's sake. They knew he might have investigative methods of which they had never heard. But he was thinking now of two scenarios that *any* investigator should have thought of—not just someone from the FBI.

"All right," he said. "Let's suppose that Larry really was standing right there beside the truck. Do you all realize what kind of a rifle shot you're suggesting someone would have had to make to hit him at that angle?"

Jim looked over at the bluffs in question. "Yeah. It's a long shot, all right. It would be some incredible shooting."

"To say the least," Coal added. "My thought is that he was shot with a pistol from right here in the yard."

Jim looked hurt. "Come on, son. You've hunted with me. You really think I wouldn't have found some kind of sign?"

Coal looked an apology at his old friend. "You're one of the best, Jim. But Larry has walked all over this place, along with who knows who else. It would be pretty hard to sift a killer's tracks out of the mix. Besides, the ground's been frozen, hasn't it?"

Jim looked around the yard again and finally sighed and nodded. "Yeah, you're right."

Coal suddenly felt a twinge of guilt, looking at his friend's expression. "But what if you're right? What if the killer really wasn't in the yard, and it really was a rifle? It's not like that kind of shot has never been made before."

Without saying anything else, he pulled a pair of rubber gloves out of his jeans pocket, put them on, and went around to the tailgate. He climbed into the truck, where there was old straw, sand and bits of what appeared to be manure. He scanned the bed slowly as he walked forward, stepping lightly and raising his feet each step. He had almost reached the cab when he saw it, down among the straw and sand at the base of the cab: blood...

There were several drops, all dried now, of course. He stepped back and crouched down, lowering his head to try and get a different angle on the place where the blood was. In so doing, he saw something else: the straw and sand appeared to have been more disturbed where the blood was than any other place. Whereas it was pretty much evened out everywhere else, the way it would be after driving the truck around for a while at higher speeds, the disturbed place looked like it had been scuffed sideways, maybe by someone's feet.

Looking away from that scuffed place, he studied the rust spots on the rail of the truck bed. After a moment, he reached out and scrubbed one that was up near the cab with his finger. It came mostly clean, leaving the white of the truck's paint, with a thin, rusty-colored circle around it.

The other three were watching Coal, and when he stood up in the truck bed they all waited to make eye contact.

"Did any of you see the blood back here? And right there?"

"No, Coal," said Jim. "We didn't look in the back. And that other, no one looked at very close. The whole truck's spotted with rust. It just looked like more of the same."

Coal eased in closer to the straw and sand and pointed. "Look here, too. See those scuffs?"

"Sure." Jim looked back at Coal. "And I know what you're sayin'. Larry wasn't standing on the ground when he was shot. He was in the back of the truck, he got shot, and those scuffs are where his boots slipped sideways when he fell over the side."

Coal nodded. "Bingo."

"Okay," said Mitchell. "But does that change anything if he was up there?"

"It sure could," replied Coal. "There's another knoll just beyond the one you boys looked at. Not a lot higher, maybe, but it looks like Larry was up in this truck bed when he was shot, and that being the case, the killer could have shot from that other spot."

At this point, Jim walked all the way around the truck and looked beyond the bluff they had scouted out. "Damn! If he shot from there, Coal, that's gotta be pushin' seven hundred yards. You're givin' this killer a lot of credit."

"I may be. But we've both known men that could make a shot like that. I'm pretty confident I could—up to six, anyway. Anyone trained very extensively in the military as a marksman might be able to pull it off."

"Sure," agreed Jim as the other two stood there quiet and simply nodded agreement. "But it would still be a risky shot to take."

"Any shot would be risky," Coal pointed out. "Murder itself is risky."

"Well," cut in K.T., "let's get up there and poke around before the weather changes."

They drove together in Coal's car out to the main road and down a hundred yards to where another lane cut off, and here they drove into a yard that was in bad need of some loving care.

"This still Beebe's place?" Coal asked.

Jim nodded. "Yeah. Old coot should know he's getting too long in the tooth to be runnin' cows. Can't even take care of his property."

Coal laughed. "Some people just don't care."

As they were getting out of the car, an older man in rubber overshoes and an eared cap with the flaps tied up came walking around the barn. His nose, cheeks and ears were veined red, maybe from the cold. He stood at the corner and stared at them for a while, then raised a hand in recognition and greeting and came walking over, favoring a hip.

"Howdy, Don," greeted Jim, echoed by K.T. and Mitchell. "Say, you remember Coal Savage, don't you? Old Prince's boy?"

"Coal? Sure! Darn-tootin'. Best bull dogger that high school rodeo team ever had—even to this day. Howdy, son!"

"Hello, Mr. Beebe," replied Coal, stepping forward to shake the man's battered old hand, which was also red with the morning chill but had an undercast of old and sun-damaged gray.

"Coal's the sheriff now," Jim went on.

"Good!" said Don Beebe. "That's good. So what can I do for you gents? Must be important, you bein' out here on a Sunday mornin'."

Coal cleared his throat. "Well, you heard about Larry MacAtee getting shot."

"Sure," replied Beebe. "I already let Jim and K.T. go up on the hill there lookin' for empty bullets an' such."

Coal had to smile at the old man's terminology: bullets. Most folks didn't understand what part was a bullet and what part was a casing. The term "bullet" often covered every part of a loaded cartridge.

"And I appreciate your willingness to help," Coal said. "But we found something else that leads me to believe maybe the shooter was up on that farther hill there. Mind if we go look around on that one?"

"Shoot, no! Any way to help. It's pretty scary livin' out here and wonderin' if I'm gonna be the next one shot. There's no road up there, though—just a trail I drive my three-wheeler on sometimes. You'd have to hike, unless you want to take that." He pointed toward a blue Honda US90 three-wheeler that was splattered liberally with mud.

Coal looked at his old friend and motioned toward the three-wheeler. "Jim?"

"Hell, give me a horse any day! I'd just hurt myself tryin' to learn somethin' like that at my age."

Coal laughed. The idea of a hike appealed deeply to him after living every day in an office and in the streets of D.C. "Hiking will be fine, Mr. Beebe. We'll just go up there now. Thanks for your help."

"Any time, son. Just any time. Let me know if I can help again. And it sure would be good to know if you find anything up there."

Coal had no intentions of sharing any discovery with Beebe or anyone else not involved in the investigation, but there was no need to hurt his feelings. He just said he would keep him aware of anything they found, and then they started off.

With high hopes, the four of them climbed the bluff. Jim's years were telling on him, and he huffed all the way to the top, his breath coming out in ragged gasps. They had to wait for him a couple of times. When they got near the top, Coal finally looked back at Jim as he caught his own breath. It wasn't much more than forty degrees, and the air was chilly in his throat and lungs.

"So you wish you had taken that three-wheeler, you stubborn old dog?"

Jim swore. "Not on your life. These old sticks need all the exercise they can get."

Again, Coal laughed, and after another two minutes' rest, they meandered the remainder of the way up. The three-wheeler trail Beebe had mentioned ran across the top of the bluff from the southwest, then continued on down the back side of the hill and wound around to his corrals and some weathered loading chutes. What they saw on top, where their hopes had been highest, crashed their mood to the ground: fresh cattle and horse tracks. The top of the bluff was literally covered with them, all along the trail and to both sides.

With a little effort and a few grunts, Jim knelt down and touched a track. "Damn. These tracks are new."

"How new?" queried Coal.

"Not sure. Could be since Larry got shot."

Mitchell touched the side of one track and stood up. "I agree with Jim. They look brand new."

Coal was still irritated by Mitchell, in spite of feeling like he was really trying to give the deputy a chance. He somehow doubted that Mitchell knew much about sign and figured he was just agreeing with Jim to make himself look smart.

Turning away, Coal walked a ways closer to Larry's ranch. The top part of the truck was plain to see from here. With Larry standing in the back of the truck, an expert marksman could easily have made the shot. But from where he stood, which was the highest spot, it instantly started dropping down into a brushy crease before it rose again to the top of the shorter bluff that Jim and the others had previously scoured. To satisfy his own curiosity, he walked down the slope, and instantly the yard disappeared from his sight. He didn't see the truck again until he got to the far side of the other bluff, and from there he had a good view of the entire yard.

He walked back up to where the others were, now looking around in the brush. "Beebe couldn't have seen the killer if he was up on this hill," said Coal to Jim when the older man straightened up from his search. "But he could have from where you searched before. And so could his dogs. I don't know if you heard, but his heelers just now opened up on me when I was over there. One of them looked like it wanted to come up here and eat me."

"So you figure this is where he shot from then?"

"I think so, Jim. If he wasn't in the yard using a pistol, it's the only likely spot."

"Well, there aren't any tracks up here. Nothin' but cows and horses. And no casing we can find either."

Coal just shrugged. He looked bleakly around them at the sage and dirt. This hill was badly overgrazed. If the shooter had been up here, it should not have been hard to find some kind of sign. But now that cattle had been pushed across here, that was different.

That left them with a big fat goose egg. Larry MacAtee was dead, and other than the threat made by Bigfoot Monahan, there was not one single clue as to who might have killed him. Sadly, there was nothing in this case that any decent court in the country would convict Bigfoot on, either. If he had killed Larry, unless something turned up on a search of his house, there was a good chance he might get away with it.

CHAPTER SIXTEEN

Most of what Jim, K.T., and Mitchell knew to do had been done the day before, within hours of the body's discovery. They had canvassed the neighbors, asking about strange vehicles in the area, or if anyone had heard a shot. They had asked the usual questions—if anyone knew of arguments Larry had been in lately, or any legal hassles. Was he involved in any suits? Did he have any large gambling debts? Was he involved in any illicit affairs? Did they know one single reason, even a remote one, that anyone would want to harm Larry MacAtee?

Today, they visited with any neighbors, even ones who were one or two miles distant from his ranch, to whom they had not talked previously. They gleaned no new information. When they had done all they could, Coal sent K.T. back to town with Jim and Mitchell, and he remained behind at the MacAtees'. He had no way to make contact with Kathy, and he thought she would go to the courthouse first, but just in case she came here, he wanted to be here to meet her. He did not want her to greet this scene alone.

Once, he wished he had a cigarette. He had no idea where that craving came from, for he had only smoked for four months, in Vietnam, and he hadn't even liked it much then. It had just become an escape, something he did because everyone else did it whenever they took a break. After four months, one day he had lit up a Marlboro—the cigarette made famous to him by the so-called Marlboro Man ("come to Marlboro Country")—and the taste of it had suddenly turned his stomach. He glanced at his reflection in the mirror of his Army Jeep, looked at the others in the Jeep with him, all puffing away, and threw the cigarette out the window.

He had never looked back, and he couldn't remember a day until all the trouble and heartbreak with Laura began when smoking a cigarette had ever even crossed his mind. But now it did. He was just glad he had none with him and couldn't give in if he wanted to.

Reaching into his pocket, with the Border collie Rowdy watching his every move, he took out two sticks of Blackjack gum, unwrapped them absently and stuffed both of them whole into his mouth. Chewing as fast as a rabbit, he walked once again to the paint mark on the ground, the place where Larry's body had lain. It didn't seem big enough to represent his friend. And it seemed so cold there in the dirt. It was as if he were looking at a cartoon etching. Rowdy kept sniffing at the ground there, and finally he looked up at him and whined. It almost brought tears to Coal's eyes.

Coal walked to where the straw stack was down to only one level high and sat down, breathing deeply of the hint of grain. This stack had been here a little while and was aging. But it still had that homey ranch smell he had longed for so often in D.C. With Rowdy's head in his lap, scratching his ears, his eyes swept the vastness of the river valley and the mammoth Beaverhead Mountains to the east, along the Montana border. The snow that lay in those valleys and canyons now would stay there until late spring. He should be there. He should be hiking those draws, hearing the snap of brush beneath his boots. He should not be here waiting like a frozen bird for Kathy to come home—to come home and put him in one of the worst situations he had ever had to face: comforting an old friend—and a new widow.

And then he heard the crackle of his CB, and he went back to the car, leaning inside. He could feel Rowdy hugging the backs of his legs. Poor dog. He picked up the mic and said, "Dispatch, this is Savage. Was there traffic for me?"

The ensuing transmission was scratchy, barely audible, but he heard the unmistakable words: *...wanted you to know Mrs. MacAtee is just leaving the courthouse... on her way home.*

Coal took in a deep breath and pressed the mic button. "Roger. I'll be waiting. Out."

Dispatch out, came the distant reply.

Coal walked away from the car. He hurried past Larry's pickup and the picture of the body on the ground. He tried to put a smile on his face. He attempted a look of sympathy. Nothing seemed right. This was not his forte. If any man ever was out of his element, it was Coal Savage right now. He chewed his brick of gum furiously and swore, then liked the taste of it so much that he swore again. And again. Rowdy just gazed at him, head cocked to one side, still waiting for him to end the joke and produce their friend.

He squinted his eyes and looked toward town. He smoothed his mustache with the web of his hand. He wished he were a banker or a musician. He wished he were a cowboy. Or a long haul trucker. Someone who didn't have to comfort widows and orphans for a living.

Coal hunched his shoulders inside his loose Levi jacket. He stared at the ground, miserable with the gray, cloudy day and his own sad helplessness. He wanted to pray. But after what happened with Laura, God had no reason to listen. There could be no peace for him.

And then he saw the roof of a car appear out on the highway, a light blue roof that when it was nearly straight out from him looked long, like a station wagon. It slowed when it neared the MacAtees' lane, but not soon enough.

At the turn-off, the car's tires screeched, and it nearly slammed into the mailbox, missing it by inches and coming to a stop with dust swirling around its tires. The car sat idling for several seconds, then at last went into reverse for seven or eight feet before going forward again and making the sharp turn.

Coal walked toward the drive, and old Rowdy leaped up and followed him, his ears pricked toward the station wagon. Finally, Coal stopped, his hands in his pockets, his booted feet spread wide on the road. The car slowed down, and then finally it came to a stop, still twenty feet away. Rowdy stood out there ahead, nose pointed sharply forward, feet poised, ready to send him dashing.

Coal saw the woman driver, her dark hair worn in the page boy style, throw the car into park and just sit there for a moment. She looked down, like she was fiddling with something, and he saw her hands come up to her face and brush at it for a few moments. Then finally, she eased the door open and stepped out.

She stood there in wide-bottom jeans and a form-fitting, bright green turtle-neck sweater, and he could see the deep red of her lipstick even from twenty feet away.

Unaware of himself, only of Kathy MacAtee, Coal just stood there, glued in place—a statue. He watched Kathy start toward him. She was trying so hard to be in control of herself. In high heels, she walked slow on the rutted road, but it was not because of the high heels. She was moving slow because to speed up was to show her emotions, and to start showing her emotions now was to risk falling apart.

And then she was close enough to look into his eyes. And when she could see his, she knew he could see hers, and that they were wet with tears. The grown up woman vanished, and the little girl rushed in to take her place.

Before she reached him, she was crying out loud. She said, "Oh, Coal," and she fell into his arms, and in spite of himself he almost stumbled backward. He threw his arms about her and squeezed, almost fiercely. Her own strength seemed no less than his, and that was good. They were two people reaching inside of each other for every ounce of strength they could find.

He smelled the perfume of the shampoo in her hair, the hint of cologne on her neck. He held her, and she shook against him like it was all she could do not to explode into pieces. Coal heard the doors of the station wagon shutting, and he saw the three girls through blurry vision as they came close. It seemed like they were going to walk on by, but soon, first one, then the other two came over and surrounded their mom and their daddy's friend with hugs, and the five of them stood in the road while the girls wept, and only the mountains and the ranch and the Border collie were there to hear them.

Old Rowdy, after running around with his tail wagging and greeting all of them, finally let out one *yap,* looked back toward the last place he must have seen his pal alive, then went to his belly, laid his head on his paws, and, after one final thump of his tail, went still. In his own way, he was weeping too.

*   *   *

Forty miles away, wispy wet clouds hung low on the flanks of the mountains, and other clouds, clouds that were black with moisture, crowned the peaks.

He lit a Marlboro and smiled. In his mind, he could see the Marlboro Man riding wild, but sure in the saddle, in the deep powder snow, chasing Hereford cattle. At last, the winter drive out of the high country was over, and the Marlboro Man and his partners lit up smokes—Marlboros, of course, and the announcer, in a voice that was big and bold, said, "Come to where the flavor is. Come to Marlboro Country."

Damn, that was the life!

He drew deep on the cigarette and peered down the Unertl 8 power scope. The world through that scope was more real than the world outside of it. Everything inside it seemed so vibrant and alive. Yet so many things, when viewed through that scope, just begged to be shot at. Killed. Destroyed.

He sat on the ground, and as the legs of his bipod settled against the earth, he leaned into the rifle butt. He took another draw of the cigarette. There was his man. Big as life. Standing still. Waiting.

He felt the air seep out of his mouth softly, and the wind sprinkled him with tiny drops of rain, but his dark green baseball cap kept it out of his eyes.

He took up slack on the trigger, and the crosshairs settled and bit into the chest of the man and stayed as if they were glued in place.

The gun bucked and roared, and the long echo trailed away down the mountains and lost itself in canyons black with timber.

He had time to bring the bipod back to rest firm on the ground, and it was then, two seconds after the exploding sound of the shot, that he saw the man burst wide open, and blood—in this case water—spray through the frosty air.

The man, which was a half-gallon cardboard milk carton, rolled up against a clump of stunted sagebrush five feet away from where it had sat and lay still.

Again, he smiled, and he carefully worked the rifle's bolt so that the casing came out close to hand, and he picked it up. After sniffing the last of the acrid smoke out of its maw, he slid it into his shirt pocket.

Then he picked up his rifle, stood up to trudge back down the hill to his rig, and drove off the mountain. If this temperature kept plummeting, snow was not far off.

CHAPTER SEVENTEEN

Coal Savage sat at the MacAtees' dining room table and sipped coffee. Rowdy padded back and forth between his comforting hand and Kathy's, needing the reassurance of these people. He had spent two nights outside alone, sleeping in the straw, smelling the lifeblood of his pal so close by.

The girls sat on the sofa in the living room, with *The Wonderful World of Disney* playing on the TV. They alternated between crying out loud and laughing at the silliness of a young man named Dexter Riley, whose mind had turned into a computer. Every time one of them would cry, it would bring their mother back to tears as well, and Coal felt helpless to give her any comfort.

"He's gone, Coal," whispered Kathy after a long bout of crying. He patted her hand, which felt strangely cold. "Why? He never hurt anybody. He gave to everyone. He would have given up this whole ranch to save someone's life. Everybody loved him, Coal. How could anyone do this?"

"I wish I knew, Kathy." He almost told her not to worry, that they would find the killer. But those words were so cold and empty. Big deal. So they would find the killer. Finding him would serve the purpose of justice. It might give a tiny sense of closure. But Larry would still be gone. Every time Kathy or the girls saw one of his old shirts, his gloves, one of his saddles—in short, pretty much anything that could be associated with him—the memories of this most heart-breaking of days would come back. And likely for many years the tears would come too.

Daylight was growing dim out the sliding glass door that led from the dining room onto the patio that Larry and Coal had paved with tan flagstone one time when Coal was on leave. The bubbling fountain they had lovingly put together was a pipe dream, and it had quickly failed. Amateurs! Now it served as a planter, but the petunias that had survived the heat of summer and the crisp nights of middle autumn, in the wake of the ice-cold nights that had arrived now hung shriveled and dead. Death. Everything reminded Coal of it, it seemed.

"Coal," said Kathy suddenly, seeming to notice the gathering gloom outside for the first time, "I want to show you something. Come on. Come with me."

She got up, and Coal came to his feet to help her into a heavy, quilted blue winter coat, its polyester whispering loudly as she slid her arms into it and zipped it up. Coal shrugged back into his jacket and pressed his hat on his head.

Rowdy was already up, watching them expectantly. Which way would they go? Whichever way it was, by Rowdy's actions he must be thinking it would lead to wherever his buddy had been hiding. They had played a great joke on him this time, for sure! The one time he hadn't been able to find his friend. Rowdy was possibly a little ashamed of himself, but Coal could tell by the shine of his eyes that it was okay. As long as they took him there now—to Larry.

In spite of the stiff upper lip he had tried to keep for Kathy, sight of the dog's excitement, his happily wagging tail, almost made Coal break. He felt the tears coming, and he bit down hard on the insides of his cheeks. That stopped them.

Kathy picked up a flashlight from the countertop in the kitchen, and she took something else from a hook and stuck it into a rear pocket. She reached out, and Coal looked down at her outstretched hand. He looked up into her soft, wet eyes, then finally took her hand in his. Her skin was like ice. He was barely able, once again, to keep the tears back. She smiled at him, and a tear pinched out of one eye and rolled down her cheek. With her flashlight in one hand, and his hand in the other, she was helpless, so Coal reached up and brushed the tear away.

They went out the sliding glass door in the dining room and walked across the flagstone patio and toward a lonely shop that stood fifteen feet away, waiting humbly to be capped with new green shingles again and its sluffing coat of white paint refreshed. Winter was nearly upon them, and the shop looked so forlorn. Beside it, only partly covered by a tarp, sat the stack of shingles. Good intentions, frozen there in place.

Kathy read Coal's thoughts. "I know, the shop looks horrible, huh? All spring, then summer, he meant to paint it and put on new shingles. But you know Larry. He was always off helping someone else instead. I think he helped shingle two houses this summer—one of them almost totally by himself, for Alice Walters. She just doesn't have the money to pay anyone to do it anymore now that Clyde is gone. And he did enough plumbing for people to earn journeyman plumber. He even fixed a few cars, one of them Todd Mitchell's—and you know how much they despised each other. And he spent at least two weeks helping people get firewood."

"But you have enough too, right?" Coal's concern made him look toward the woodpile.

"Oh, of course! He got ours too, Coal. You know he'd never let me and the girls freeze."

"That's true. Sorry."

"No need to apologize, you sweetheart!" She squeezed his hand and leaned in against him with her shoulder, touching her head to him briefly.

They had reached the shop, and now Kathy took from the hip pocket of her flare-legged blue jeans the object she had put there, which was a key ring holding a couple of keys. She unlocked a padlock that guarded a hasp on a walk-in door into the side of the building.

"He was so excited to show you this, Coal. He could hardly wait until next time you came to visit."

The opening door whined, and Rowdy dashed into the building before them, running in with his ears perked and looking around with his mouth open wide. For all the world, he looked like he was smiling.

But Coal soon stopped noticing what Rowdy did. There before them, stationed in solemn silence in the gloaming, crouched a LeMans blue nineteen sixty-eight Camaro Z/28.

"Kathy!" Coal said in nearly a whisper. "Kathy," he spoke again, almost reverently. This was his dream car, and had been Larry's. The sixty-eight Camaro, the most beautiful automobile ever made, in Coal's estimation. And a Z/28 to boot! He walked to it and put his hand on the perfect white vinyl roof as Kathy went and threw up the overhead door, letting the last of the fast-dimming Lemhi Valley light stream inside, over the almost sparkling LeMans blue body and the bold white racing stripes on the hood and trunk, and flowing up over the spoiler on the back. He peered into the pristine blue interior of the car, at the four-speed gearshift handle, the wonderful, precise instrumentation of the dash.

He wasn't sure after a moment, but he thought he might have actually sworn out loud, in his admiration. He looked over at Kathy to see if she had heard, and she was watching him. Her eyes glistened.

"It's beautiful, isn't it? He knew you'd like it. It was supposed to be Luke's one day," she said, and that name made Coal's heart almost stop. Luke... The name reminded him how much pain this woman had already had to endure. No one who loves their children is left unscarred when one of them is gone, far too early. And Luke, even at sixteen, had been a fantastic young man—the finest of any Coal had ever known.

He had been far away in D.C. when Luke died, and he hadn't even been able to spare the time off to come home for the funeral. His condolence card had looked so pathetic to him and seemed so meaningless. He remembered shuddering as he heard it hit the bottom of the mail slot, on the first leg of its journey out to Salmon to try and comfort his very best friend.

Coal reached out, pulled Kathy to him and hugged her tight. She snuggled her face into the chest of his jacket and stood still, hardly breathing. But somehow, neither of them cried. "I'm sorry, Kathy. I wasn't here for Larry when Luke died. And I wasn't here to save Larry for you. I'm so sorry."

Kathy's voice was that of a woman gone numb. "You sweet man. We understood you had just been here and couldn't turn right around and come back. Larry never questioned that. We knew you loved Luke too. And with Larry—even if you had been here, there is nothing you could have done."

Coal simply nodded. His throat was too tight to make any words.

Kathy finally looked up at him, her arms still around his back and his around her. "You should sit behind the wheel, Coal. It feels wonderful. Just like your dream, and Larry's."

"No, I couldn't."

"*What?*" She leaned farther back from him. "Coal, come on. You've waited for this for four years. A sixty-eight Z/28!"

"I know, Kathy, but..."

"Coal, you just get your butt behind that wheel, right now. Larry would take a piece of your hide if you didn't."

"I'll sit in the passenger side," he finally said. "That wheel spot is Larry's." He let go of her and touched the shiny handle. "No dust," he remarked.

"Right!" Kathy laughed. "Dust? Larry was out here every morning with his little dust mop before he would do much to start his day, even before he would have coffee. It made him think of Luke. And you."

Coal fought the tears that surged up in him. Damn it, he was a Marine. A soldier! Military police. An investigator for the FBI. A sheriff of one of the wildest counties in Idaho. Such men did not cry!

Clenching his jaw, he opened the door, looking down at the sleek blue of the passenger seat. He eased down into it. It seemed to have been molded especially for him. He fingered the dash. The shifter. He laughed when he saw hanging by a chain from the rearview mirror a little cap gun. It was a Hubley Texan, beautifully chromed cast iron, complete with white plastic grips bearing the raised image of the head of a longhorn steer and an inset star. Coal remembered when he and Larry had both gotten these guns, back in forty-one, the Christmas just after the attack on Pearl Harbor had sent them into the middle of war with the infamous "Axis" powers. His mother still had his tucked away somewhere, safe in storage, but he had never dreamed Larry still had his too. He reached up and with his finger gave the old cap gun a swing. What memories. Memories of a simple, joyful time, Coal and Larry too young to even realize the magnitude of the life and death struggle their boys—and old Jim Lockwood—were engaged in overseas.

Coal looked to his left, to the place Larry would have sat if they had been riding together. Just for a moment, he saw his old buddy watching him, grinning, making those big dimples crevice his cheeks. Sure as shooting, Larry would have been making fun of his mustache, calling him a big city gigolo, telling him to stop drooling on his new seats. Coal smiled. And then he felt Kathy's hand lay gently on his shoulder as she crouched down outside the door.

"He would have been so happy to take you for a drive in it, Coal."

And those were the words it finally took. With his chin lowering to his chest, and Kathy leaning in to put her arm around him, Coal's tears began to flow, and his big chest to shake. There was no more damming this flood.

CHAPTER EIGHTEEN

Everyone was gone by the time Coal got back to the courthouse. Everyone, that is, except the early night guard, a young man by the name of Victor Yancey, not long out of high school and willing to work for minimum wage because he didn't want to leave his home place.

Young Yancey thought it was cool that his new boss bore the same last name as the mascot of the school from which he had graduated not very long ago. After talking to Yancey for a while, Coal realized the boy just liked the word "cool."

Coal sat at the desk and read through the reports K.T. and Mitchell had left for him. Jim, although retired and surely having much better things to do, had taken it upon himself to do at least as much work as the other two, and he had written his findings up in report form as well.

He smiled as he read over the reports, and as he thought back on the investigative techniques he had seen out at the MacAtee place. It was like watching *Gunsmoke*. Or, at best, the NBC *Mystery Movie,* with *Hec Ramsey*, starring Richard Boone. At least Hec Ramsey, in the series, had a rudimentary knowledge of turn-of-the-century forensics. Coal wasn't sure his boys had any.

But what they did know, they did well. He read all of the statements from nearby ranchers and farmers, all written in good form, all in fine order. They had covered all bases as far as personal relationships and also concerning whether or not anyone had heard a shot or seen any vehicles around that were unfamiliar. Nothing had turned up. No shot. No strange rig or person. No nothing. A ghost seemed to have killed Larry MacAtee.

In frustration, Coal thumped the bottom edges of the reports on the desk top, straightening them, then put them back in a folder and slid it in the bottom desk drawer. He leaned forward, elbow on his desk, and scrubbed his eyes with his thumb and forefinger. This had been a long day. A long day, with little accomplished.

He had heard a report come in while he was out at the MacAtees' of a possible poaching case up toward Gibbonsville. Something about a bull elk. With plenty on his mind, he had hardly listened to the call. Right now, that elk weighed pretty low on the scales compared to Larry. Other than that one call, the radio had been quiet.

But now Coal had something else to face. It was time to go home and see his family. And now that they were settled in, it was time to get them registered for school, too—in the morning. The whole mess of life, starting over again. He hoped it would be a lot different from back in Virginia. At least here he could understand the accents of the people who would be teaching his children.

In the parking lot, the brisk November air gnawed at his face. A fine sleet pelted his hat, and the asphalt was slick. Pine smoke drifted through the parking lot, a smell he loved, and one he had missed deeply. As he opened the door of the old pickup, he frowned at the camper that was still attached to it. He would have to get that off there tomorrow. He wasn't planning on moving anywhere any time soon, and with a job like this, he sure wasn't going to find any time to go camping. Besides, winter was coming on.

He sat down on the slick vinyl seat and let himself melt into it for a moment. It was ice-cold, but it felt good. He sat there, staring at the windshield, which was now iced over. With a sigh, he got out and scraped a hole to see through, then backed out and drove to the street. The Salmon Bar was quiet. Through the pattering sleet, street and house lights gleamed, and smoke puffed out of chimneys—the Salmon Bar, its own little community. The sky and the mountains beyond the Bar were black.

He turned and started down the hill, Salmon's downtown sprawled out below him. After passing the IGA grocery store, which was cold and dark looking inside, he paused on the river bridge and gazed at the sparkling lights in the water. Then on he drove, between the familiar old buildings, McPherson's store, the Salmon River Inn, a half dozen bars. Vehicles packed the curbs, mostly pickups, probably from the mining and logging camps in the mountains around town. Here and there, a few people walked the streets, but only, it seemed, in passing from one cafe to the next. The "Blue Laws" had all of the bars closed, as they did every Sunday.

At the Coffee Shop, he longed to turn in. Bright lights gleamed within, and the crowd there seemed jovial, untouched by the death of Larry MacAtee. Tomorrow, he would stop there early. It was a good place to ask about Larry, to learn the latest gossip. If anything bad had happened that concerned Larry, chances were good someone in the Coffee Shop would have heard about it—either there or at Wally's. But he was avoiding Wally's for the time because he hoped for his reunion with the owners, who were good friends, to be a happy one, and at the moment he didn't feel very inclined to happiness.

On the outskirts of town, he passed Ken's Automotive and Andy's Auto Body, and there were still lights on inside both. He thought about stopping and letting Andy look at the front of the truck. But he was bone-weary. He only wanted to sit down and stop thinking. Maybe when the camper was off he could take the truck in.

Down the old highway he went, up the dirt road, and soon he was sitting in the yard of his mom's house, and the dogs were barking inside.

The sleet still tapped on the roof and the hood and windshield, but in spite of it the front door opened, and Connie, a heavy coat wrapped around her shoulders and over her nightgown, came down the steps and met him as he got out of the cab.

"The twins sure were upset this morning when they woke up."

"Upset? What about?"

"Seems like somebody told them they were going moose hunting this morning?"

"What?"

"Moose hunting, Coal. You don't remember? Their memory of the details seemed pretty vivid."

"Well, sure, I remember saying something about it, Mom. But I didn't think they'd remember. Besides, I don't have a moose tag. I don't even have an Idaho hunting license."

"Then you shouldn't have told them that, should you?"

He tried to walk past her, his eye on the door, and she grasped his coat sleeve and turned him. "Coal. Stop and listen to me. If this wasn't important I sure wouldn't have come out in this weather to talk about it."

Coal took a deep breath. His friend was dead. Murdered. And now he had to listen to foolish talk about moose hunts? After a day like this, it was like a slap in the face.

"Talk to me, Mom. But don't expect me to change my mind. I told those boys last night *maybe* we could go look for that moose we hit. Dad used to tell me stuff like that all the time, just so I'd have something to be excited about."

"Yes, he did, Coal. I remember. Do you? Really?"

"What's that supposed to mean?"

"Do you remember the hurt of it? Remember when he told you he was going to come and get you out of school early and you were going to go to Panther Creek after elk? You waited all day, and when the last bell rang he still hadn't come. He went down the river to look for that stray bull of Neal Johnson's instead. You had to ride the bus home that day, and all the way here you had to hold in the hurt."

An old memory had clutched Coal's throat. He found that hurtful day still came back to him, too easily. "Okay, Mom, but I was twelve. I was old enough to hunt. Those boys are five! There's a big difference."

"Is there, Son? Does it hurt any less because of age? Because if you think it does, then I guess I won't mention the time when your father told you he was going to take you to Hamilton with him, and you were going to go shopping for your first cowboy hat. You wanted a big white one, if I recall. A lot like that one," she said, slapping his hat brim. "I think you were five that time— like the boys. Do you remember?"

Coal looked down at his hands for a long time. Moms were hard critters to get past. Damn hard critters. "Yes, ma'am. I remember. When I woke up you told me he tried to wake me up and I rolled back over and went to sleep. So he went without me. You said maybe he'd get me a hat anyway and bring it home and surprise me. But he didn't."

Connie reached up and put a knuckle under her son's chin, lifting his face up and meeting his eyes. She gazed into them for a long time. "I know you've been through a lot of hard life, Coal. A lot of killing. A lot of seeing friends die. A lot of pain that maybe other folks have never seen. And you've had a lot of responsibility resting on your shoulders, because you're the kind of man that people look to for leadership. But that little boy you used to be is still in there. So are all those hurts. Those memories don't go away easy. When you roll into bed tonight, you ought to spend some time thinking about what kind of memories these boys will have to look back on. And say your prayers, Son. You're not too old for that, either."

Coal reached out and hugged his mother to him. The old woman was a pain in the butt, but she sure was smart. He had to give her that.

They went in the house, and Dobe and Shadow came at him with what could only be called huge, silly grins on their faces. Shadow's tail wagged back and forth, and she wiggled her hind end with excitement. That was all Dobe could wiggle, because Coal had had his tail docked. He knelt down and met the dogs on their own ground, rubbing their necks and backs briskly and patting them on the head. He knew if he even tried to stop they would let him know in short order that this was *not* acceptable.

He wondered how his dogs would act when he was gone. Maybe they would just go on with life, for he was gone so often anyway. Looking at Shadow's sagging eyelids, all red-rimmed inside, and the gray on her muzzle and around her eyes, he knew he would be the one saying goodbye to his big girl, not the other way around.

Coal stood up and saw Connie still watching him. "Where are the boys?"

"In bed."

"In bed?" he echoed. "Why so early?"

"Coal," she said sternly. "It's twenty after ten."

The shock of those words hit him in the belly. *Twenty after ten?* How? It had just gotten dark. And... Surely she was wrong.

He looked over at the faithful grandfather clock ticking in the corner. His eyes in the dim light weren't what they had once been, but they were good enough. His mother was right.

He sighed. "Are they awake?"

"I reckon. Maybe. Wyatt probably is, anyway. He's been getting up every twenty minutes or so to see if you got home yet."

A lump rose in Coal's throat, and he looked at his mother, helpless. "What do I tell them?"

"Just tell them what you might have wished your daddy would tell you, Son. That's all they can ask for."

So he took off his hat and set it on a rack by the door, hung his jacket up beside it, and climbed the creaky stairs. He went in by the boys' bedside and clicked on a lamp.

Morgan's eyes were shut, and he was breathing soft and evenly. He never batted an eye. Coal went around to Wyatt's side of the bed. The covers were half off of him, and one leg was all the way out. But little Wyatt didn't seem to notice. He, too, was gone.

Coal wanted to reach out and ruffle their hair. He wanted to whisper that he loved them. He didn't remember ever having said those words to them before.

With a deep breath, he straightened back up and turned out the lamp, then went into the hall and closed the door behind him. He went more softly down the hall to Virgil's room. Through the inch that the door was ajar, he could see a light was already glowing. At least he could talk to one of his boys.

He eased the door open and looked. After a moment, he smiled a sad smile. Virgil lay there with his eyes shut, and an Ernest Haycox Western open across his chest, his fingers resting on top of it. Careful to make no noise, Coal went across the room and turned off the lamp, setting the book on the floor beside the bed.

One more room. One more child. A troubled child who wanted to be a woman and now had only her grandmother to show her
how. Coal took a deep breath. The door, downstairs off the same
hall as Connie's, was fully shut. No light came from under it. He
wondered if he could sneak in and at least watch his little girl
sleeping, the way he had done when she was small. But what if
she woke up? What if she woke and wanted a fight? His day had
already been too hard. That was not something he could take.
Katie Leigh was gone from him. If she came back, it would have
to be her doing. He couldn't bear to follow her any farther down
the road she had chosen.

That night, Coal had a dream. He dreamed of a beat-up white
pickup, a Border collie, and a straw stack. And he dreamed about
Larry MacAtee. In his dream, Larry was standing in front of his
Camaro, looking at him, and he suddenly held up a key. Then
Larry glanced upward, toward the top of the stack of straw,
which stood a good six feet higher than the cab of the truck.

Without warning, Larry jumped into the Camaro and drove as
fast as he could through the pasture and toward the hills. Although
there was no road there, the car ran as smooth as honey on toast.
And then it vanished. Larry and the Camaro were gone, just as if
they had never been.

Coal awoke with a start, soaked with sweat. For a moment, he
stared at the ceiling, reliving a part of the dream. But he didn't
think of Larry. His mind went straight to that stack of straw.

CHAPTER NINETEEN

Monday, November 20

Connie was quiet the next morning when Coal asked her to take the kids in and register them for school. To refuel after his early morning workout of sit-ups, pushups, and pull-ups, he sat at the table eating a huge helping of boiled eggs and mustard, home-made Polish-style sausage, and toast with cherry preserves Connie had put up herself.

Coal knew it was a big adventure for his mother each summer to drive toward the end of the road along the north fork of the Salmon River and stop at the Golden Boulder Orchard to pick the huge, juicy cherries grown there lovingly by a one-legged farmer named Warner Van Hoose. The preserves that came from that adventure were famous among all of Connie's friends.

Between bites, Coal pleaded quietly with his mom to help him out just one more time so he could drive out to Larry MacAtee's place and check on one more possible piece of evidence. He was too embarrassed to tell her this search would be based solely on a clue given to him in a dream.

With a red bandanna, Connie had tied back her soft, silver hair. She wore a green and black buffalo plaid shirt and tan canvas trousers rolled up at the bottom, and in spite of her beauty she looked every bit the tough ranch owner she was—at least they liked to call their place a ranch. She cut off a piece of the sausage she made with a mixture of ground pork, potatoes, and spices stuffed into washed lengths of intestine. She chewed on it for a while, then gave a grim smile to Coal.

"Son, I understand what you're doing. And I know it's your job. And Larry was your friend. Of course I'll go register the kids for you. I know if Laura were still alive that would be her job, and you wouldn't have to face it anyway.

"But you really need to start thinking about something: Those children need their father, too. Even Katie Leigh. She is full of anger right now. And Virgil is hurt too, although he demonstrates it by just not talking. But Katie will come around, Coal—if you let her. Just please... don't abandon these kids. They need you right now more than ever."

"I killed Katie's mother," said Coal as he sat up straight in his chair and laid his napkin on the table. "Mom, do you understand that? That girl is never going to forgive me for that."

"Stop it!" It was the hardest voice Coal had heard Connie use with him in years. "Just stop it. You did *not* kill her. Bad things happen, Coal Garrett. They happened to you and Laura. You have got to move on. You made mistakes, and so did she. She's gone now. That is *not* your fault." Her voice got very quiet now, and her teeth were clenched. "Don't you dare say that in my house again. It's over. You've got to get on with your life."

Coal stood up. His breakfast was half finished, but he didn't have any appetite for the rest. "Whatever you say, Mom. If you'd get them registered, I'd appreciate it."

With that, he walked to the door, put on his jacket and picked up his hat, clamped it on his head, grabbed the truck keys and walked out. He didn't say goodbye.

*   *   *

Driving the pickup down the rutted road, Coal tried to force thoughts of home out of his head. Thoughts of Connie, thoughts of the children, and thoughts of Laura. Anything was better to think about than that.

He made a mental note to take the truck in for a bid today. He had taken the camper off, and now it seemed much less ponderous on the rutted road, although he noticed a lot more bouncing on the washboard ruts. But he would feel better having the other headlight back in place and having the dent knocked out.

He went directly to the Coffee Shop, where Jay Castillo greeted him with his calm smile and a happy hello. Jay never seemed to get riled up about anything, unlike his wife, Carrie, who was a real spitfire—and one of Coal's favorite people in the world. They shook hands as Coal sat down at the counter and greeted several other early risers who hailed him from around the room.

"Say, Jay, has K.T. been in here since Larry got shot? Or Jim or Mitchell?"

Jay nodded. "Sure. Jim came in that day around noon and early the morning after, asking a lot of questions."

"Good. Thanks. I should have known he wouldn't leave this stone unturned. Hey, I'll just have a mug of coffee, all right? I already ate at home."

Jay nodded. "Sure, buddy." The proprietor of the Coffee Shop looked up to see one of his waitresses watching them. "Hey, Tammy, can you get Coal a cup of black coffee? No cream, no sugar."

Coal chuckled. "You don't forget much, do you?"

"Not much. You used to drink it like that in high school, and everybody but the rodeo crowd thought you were nuts."

"Maybe I was. All the rodeo crowd was nuts."

Jay sat down on the stool next to Coal. "How is the investigation coming?"

"All right, I hope. I'm going out there today to wrap things up."

"Word around town is Bigfoot Monahan might be gunning for you. Is that true?"

Coal shook his head. "You can't keep much a secret in Salmon, can you?"

"Not much."

"Well, we had words at the hospital the other night when I got into town. Twice. But I haven't heard a thing from him since."

"Did he really threaten to kill you and Larry when he got out of jail?"

Coal nodded. "He did."

Jay sat there thoughtfully. "You watch out for him, Coal. Man, that guy's big. And I'm not sure he's right in the head."

"Yeah, he's big enough to kill someone with his hands, if he wanted to. Do you know him very well?"

"I don't know if anyone does. He's been in here a few times. Acts real surly. Doesn't say much to anyone. Usually seems like he eats half a pig and a chicken coop full of eggs, then leaves. Likes his coffee just like you," Jay said with a smile. "Anyway, he always pays, and he leaves big tips—better than most of the people that have a lot more money than he must have."

"Really? He's only been out of the pen for a little while."

"Yeah, and he's only been in here three times since then. I guess a lot of what I'm saying is from memory—before he got sent up to prison."

"But he still tips good?"

"Yeah. I'm guessing twenty-five percent on his meals. Ask Tammy."

The waitress, a friendly looking lady with longish blond hair and bangs, gave him a big smile that brightened up her face like a spotlight. "You talking about Bigfoot?"

"Yeah, Tammy. He tips pretty good, doesn't he?"

Tammy raised her eyebrows as she was pouring Coal's cup full. "I should say so. Sometimes if he buys a three dollar meal he'll leave me two as a tip."

After the two of them went back about their work, Coal sat quietly and sipped at the nearly boiling coffee. Where was Bigfoot getting his money these days? What did his wife do for a living? And why was a man like that so loose with money? He thought about asking Kathy later if Larry would have carried much money on him. Jim and the others had averred there was no sign that anyone had come to the truck after the murder to rifle through things or obviously molest Larry in any way, but you never knew. Then he remembered it was a moot point: Larry hadn't been dead long enough for Bigfoot to be making himself noticed yet by spending anything he might have stolen off of him.

Coal chatted for ten minutes with others in the room, the ranchers and the loggers, and two miners, all getting ready to head outdoors for their day's work. When none of them seemed to know anything about Larry beyond the gossip Coal had already heard, he threw fifty cents on the counter for the coffee and dropped a dime into a payphone that hung on the wall near the door.

He dialed the jail, and Jordan Peterson, the muscular young jailer, answered: *Lemhi County Jail—Peterson here.*

Coal liked the professional tone of the jailer's voice. The young man impressed him all the way around.

"Jordan, this is Savage."

Oh, hi, Sheriff.

"Say, could you tell Mitchell when he comes in to meet me out at the MacAtees'? While you're at it, since I don't know the whole status on K.T., telephone him as well, would you? And Jim. I'd like to get them all rounded up again if they're willing. I'd sure appreciate it."

You bet, Sheriff. Anything else?

"Um... Yeah. Did you learn how to make coffee yet?"

He heard a laugh on the other end of the line. *Cindy's been down here already, and we made two pots and poured them in a*

*pitcher—just so she could teach me how to do it right. If you
don't mind my saying so, I think she's got a crush on you. She
sure seems interested in making sure I get your coffee right.*

Coal returned the laugh. "Maybe you aren't as smart as I
thought you were, Jordan. I've got four kids, and I'm forty-two
years old. If anybody, it's not *me* she's got her cap set on! See
you later, Rookie."

With that, Coal hung up the phone, and he heard a tinkling as
the dime fell. Out of curiosity, he pushed open the change return
door, and the dime was there. He slid it out with his finger and
turned to Jay. "Hey, amigo—this phone isn't going to make you
much money in that condition!" He spun the dime through the
air, and Jay caught it and laughed.

"Thanks, Coal. You always were too honest to make a dime!
I'll get it looked at."

*   *   *

Coal parked the Chevy in the MacAtees' yard after watching
the school bus pull away without picking up any of the girls. He
drew a deep breath. He didn't know if it was easier or harder having the girls here, but it would be what it would be. He couldn't
blame them for not being able to face school yet. Little Jen was
eleven years old, Sara was thirteen, and Milo sixteen. Any age
was rough to lose a parent you loved, but those ages... He knew
all too well how it must be for them. He was just glad they didn't
have him to blame as his own children did.

He stepped out of the truck and tried to shut the door softly,
but you couldn't latch one of those heavy steel doors without
some effort. It echoed through the icy cold yard. No sooner did
he hear the front door open than the first cold rain started misting
his hat.

Coal had dressed this morning in a gray and white shadow-
plaid cotton shirt, covered with his unlined Levi jacket. He wore
a pair of tan canvas Dickies pants and black cowboy boots, along

with his Stetson, which was silver belly in color, curving to a gentle V at the center of the brim, and boasted a cattlemen's crease. Even with the gold-plated five-point star on his coat and the modern Smith and Wesson .357 magnum on his hip, he knew he must not look much like a professional twentieth century lawman—more like an old-time Western sheriff straight out of a John Wayne movie.

Brushing self-consciously at his mustache, he started across the yard, where Kathy MacAtee waited inside the open front door with her brunette page boy haircut all in disarray, and wearing a plush fuchsia robe.

When he stepped up on the porch, she was smiling, but it was a sad smile. She hadn't applied any of her usual makeup, but it sure didn't look like she needed any. Only her puffy red eyes took away from her looks. He immediately felt guilty for thinking that, but he knew she would agree, even though it would hurt her feelings.

He pulled off his hat and gave her a hug, and she invited him in. The wood stove was going full force this morning, and that warmth that only a wood fire can give throbbed though Coal's body, giving him an immediate feeling of physical well-being. It seemed to penetrate every pore, even through his clothing.

"The girls are still sleeping," Kathy offered. "I didn't even wake them up for the bus."

Coal nodded. "They'll need a few days, I'm sure. I was seventeen when my dad died, and even at that age it was tough to go back to school and act like nothing happened."

"I remember. You tried to act so tough."

Coal tried to smile. "Sure. I guess I should have known you'd remember."

"Coffee's hot," she said.

Truth be told, that smell had struck him even as he came up on the porch. Something about the mixture of woodsmoke and

Kathy's coffee made this place feel mighty welcoming, in spite of his reason for being here. He thought about turning down the coffee. He had a cup in him from home, and the other from the Coffee Shop. But Kathy roasted and ground her own beans fresh every morning and brewed her coffee the old fashioned way, and that was something Coal just could not pass up. It reminded him so much of his father.

They sat and sipped on the steaming black brew while Coal told Kathy about his dream. She rubbed at her arms through her heavy robe as he talked, and when he finished, she said, "That gives me chills. I hope God will let me dream about him too." Tears filled her eyes, and he reached out and patted her hand, which lay on the mottled green Formica table top. Unlike the night before, it felt soft and warm. She sniffed. "So why do you think you dreamed that?"

He opened his mouth to speak, then sighed. After a moment looking into her eyes, he chuckled. "Well, I'm not sure. I just... Do you ever have dreams that seem like they're trying to tell you something?"

She shrugged. "I can't think of any right now."

"Oh. Well, this one seemed like that to me. I just can't figure out where it came from. But I've got to go out there again. And after today, I think we'll let you have your place back. If nothing pans out with this, I guess we're just going to have to wait and see if anything else turns up."

As the rain began a pattering noise on the roof, telling Coal it was picking up, and a brief spate of drops hit the window nearest him, he looked outside. The sky that had started the day with a tiny bit of blue in the west was all dim and gray now, and black bundles of cloud streamed low along the mountains.

"I called Jim and K.T., and they should be out soon," he told her. "Then we'll go take another look around that straw stack. Where's Rowdy?"

"He was already out once this morning. I think he's in sleeping with Jen. She's taking this so hard, Coal."

"I know, Kathy. I can only imagine."

"I guess we're in kind of the same boat, the two of us," she said. "We both lost someone we loved."

"Yeah. We sure did." He didn't say any more about that. He knew things weren't the same between Larry and Kathy as they had been between him and Laura. Not by a long sight. Someone had murdered Larry, probably for revenge. *He* had killed Laura. And damn whatever Connie wanted to think. She could not change God's truth, no matter how loudly she tried.

A vehicle pulled up outside, and Coal rose and looked out the glass of the front door. It was Jim and K.T. Not long after, Todd Mitchell pulled in. As the rain was coming down steady now, they all got out and made a dash for the house.

Coal met them at the door. "Jeez, looks like you pansies better get in here before you melt."

Jim, breathing hard, frowned at him. "Watch your mouth, sonny. You're sittin' in here nice and dry. You get an old goat like me all wet and see how you like the smell."

Coal laughed. Before he could say anything, the three men were greeting Kathy, giving her their condolences. Rowdy had become aware of newcomers in the house, and he was barking behind a closed door down the hall. Turning away without a by-your-leave, Coal invited himself down the hall, and before he reached Jen's room, the door cracked open, and the black and white Border collie came bounding down the hall.

"Hey, Rowdy!" Coal petted the dog's back briskly and let him get in one good lick across his nose. "Aw, come on! You've got dog breath!" He laughed.

Coal walked back to the others, the dog following and making his rounds. Coal noticed that the animal cut a wide swath around Mitchell. He almost grinned, but then he looked at the dog again, then at Mitchell. Was there something more to that than just instinct? He wondered. It wouldn't surprise him much if a man like Mitchell had given Rowdy a good reason to dislike him.

"Kathy, don't give these boys any coffee," he said, turning to the woman with a wink. "They taste that stuff once and you'll never get rid of them—especially K.T. He still doesn't know how to make his own!" He laughed and cuffed the former sheriff on the shoulder. Then he turned back to the woman. "Hey, it looks like the rain's slowing up, and if we're going to get this done we've got to get on it before it puts down much more water. We'll be outside, okay? And I need to borrow Rowdy."

They trooped out to the pickup, where on the ground Larry's outline was still grotesquely drawn. There was no longer any reason to have the door open, and Coal felt bad that he hadn't shut it sooner, before any vermin had a chance to make camp inside. He slammed the door.

"So what's new?" Jim asked when Coal turned to them. "You think of something else?"

Coal didn't dare tell any of them about the dream. "I did, Jim. Just a hunch."

He got into the back of the truck again and called Rowdy to him. After a couple of attempts to get in the truck, it was obvious the dog's age was pulling him down. Jim had to pick him up and hoist him over the side. Coal took him over and had him sniff around in the corner until Rowdy's nose stopped roaming and honed in. Excitement filled the dog as he started sniffing the area where Coal had seen the drops of blood. By the way he was acting, he might be smelling some that were so small Coal hadn't even seen them.

Coal knew this was a long shot, but if there was anything to his dream, he had to know. Now that Rowdy had that smell of his master's blood in his nose, he jumped out of the truck bed and lifted the dog down to the ground, then looked at Jim and the others, who stood staring at him a little like they thought he had lost his mind.

"Hey, just so we won't trample around on any evidence, why don't the three of you stay down here for a bit? We're going up on the straw."

He went around to where the straw bales were only one high, Rowdy happily running around with him. The straw bales went up somewhat like huge stairs, and he and the dog scaled the stack that way until they were on the uppermost tier, where the stack was five bales wide and three deep.

Lining up on the one straw bale that was directly above the place in the pickup bed where Larry's blood was, and where his outline was spray-painted on the ground, Coal pointed and encouraged Rowdy with an upbeat tone of voice to sniff around. It was mere seconds before the dog hit on something, and Coal grabbed his collar and pulled him back.

His heart was pounding against the inside of his chest, and a strange chill had come over him. Getting down on his knees and one hand, holding Rowdy back with the other, he stared at the place Rowdy had stopped, and where he was trying hard to fight his way back.

Coal's eyes weren't exactly those of a teenager anymore, but at last he saw it. His eyes that had been trained since a very young man to hunt and track in the mountains, and to trail a wounded animal by blood spots, served him well. He pulled out a little folding magnifying glass he had brought along in his shirt pocket for just this moment, opened it up, and got down close to peer through it. There on a stem of straw, looking almost invisible except to someone who had spent years looking for sign like this, glistened a tiny spot of blood, re-moistened by the rain. Coal's fingertip was wet from the straw, and when he wiped at the spot, it came off in the rainwater on his finger, and there was no longer any doubt. This was blood. Larry's blood.

Coal stood up with the other men watching him and scanned the landscape around the ranch again. At last, his eyes settled on the point of another bluff no one had even considered before—a bluff from which Larry could not have been seen, either standing on the ground or in the bed of the pickup. But he sure could have been seen if he were standing on top of this straw stack.

It was higher than the other two bluffs that had previously drawn their attention, but at the same time much farther away. Unlike the other two bluffs, there were no houses near the third one, and Coal could see a ranch road that ran along the bottom of it, then led who-knew-where. It disappeared on the far side of the bluff. A strange, eerie feeling came over Coal, for the scene looked an awful lot like what he had envisioned in his dream.

"You boys want to come up here?" Coal invited.

With excited curiosity, Jim, K.T. and Mitchell scaled the mountain of straw.

Three sets of eyes stared at Coal as he showed them the blood he had found on the straw, then pointed out the bluff that had drawn his attention.

"If Larry was standing on this straw stack when he was shot, and Todd, if your angle was right, the killer could easily have fired from that point right there. And it looks like he might have been able to get on that road from the main road and drive over there without alerting anyone around here, if he went up early enough in the day—or even the night before."

They all looked at the bluff, and Jim's mouth opened. "Do you know what you're sayin', Coal? That must be eight hundred yards distant."

Coal studied the spot for a moment longer, then looked at Jim.

"I'd say more. Maybe a thousand."

K.T. swallowed. "If Bigfoot Monahan can shoot like that, you and Jim better start driving armored trucks."

*   *   *

Coal and the others piled in his pickup, Mitchell and K.T. in the back, and drove out to the main road, then took it to where the ranch road turned off. They drove the road slowly over its ruts and potholes until they reached the base of the far bluff. The road continued on up its flank.

In spite of the new mud on the road, Coal headed up it, the truck tires sliding a little. Their big-lugged tread soon caught traction, and they worked their way upward. This was probably a road Larry used to haul salt blocks or hay up to his cattle. Coal parked at the closest place he could get the pickup to the top of the bluff without driving into the sagebrush, and they walked the rest of the way up.

From on top, where the bluff was flattest, they had a clear view of the top of the straw stack, and of the upper half of the house. But Larry's old pickup was completely hidden from view. From here, the killer would never have been offered a shot had Larry been standing beside the truck door or in the bed, as they had previously believed. Walking gently, they circled the hill, K.T. Batterton stopping to take photos with his personal Nikon camera every now and then of something that looked like it might be a scuff or part of a boot print. Coal was glad for that camera, as he had already learned the department only had a worthless Polaroid, which as far as Coal was concerned was good for little more than party photos.

Finally, old Jim yelled out. "Hey! Coal, come here. Everybody walk light now." He directed them to approach his location from the front edge of the bluff. At last, they stood beside him, and he indicated what appeared to be a set of tire tracks in the sage. Then he pointed at the ground.

"Now look at that."

Just the same as the other bluffs, this one had been trodden down and overgrazed by cattle, leaving patches of nothing but bare dirt between clumps of sage and rabbitbrush. In the dirt where he was pointing was a tiny mark made by some sharp object. Coal studied it, then got closer. There was another one, probably two feet away from it.

"That's bipod feet," said Coal, and from the marks in the dirt his eyes came up to look down toward the MacAtee ranch, and the yellow lump that was the mountain of straw.

K.T. swore. "This is it. This is where he killed Larry from. I'll be a— Can you imagine being cocky enough to take a shot like that?"

"Look around for brass," Jim suggested.

Coal looked over at his old friend. "We'll go ahead and look, just in case. But Jim, I'll bet you dinner this is over a thousand yards. If this boy can make a shot like this, he's a pro. There's no way in hell a sharpshooter this good would carelessly leave his brass lying around."

"You think?"

It was the voice of Todd Mitchell, and all eyes turned to him. He was pointing at the ground, a triumphant look on his face.

"Thirty-ought-six," he said. "Your killer uses a thirty-ought-six."

Coal stared for a moment, dumbfounded, and then a gust of air escaped him. He walked over and looked down, and there, not on top of the ground, but stuck down into it with its readable head poking up only a quarter of an inch, was a .30/06 casing with a spent primer.

"You're right. Thirty-ought-six. With a trajectory like a rainbow," he said. And then he let his eyes run back down to the straw stack. A chill ran throughout his entire body, and he felt the hair begin to rise on the back of his neck.

Coal had hunted for years in his younger days with the ubiquitous .30-06. He was well aware of the round's limitations. It was a good weapon for hunting anywhere up to about three, maybe four hundred yards. If a man was desperate, and very well practiced, he might take a shot at six hundred. After that? And at a thousand yards? Sure, a man could be killed with it. Old Carlos Hathcock, the famous Marine sniper they called White Feather, had made such shots in Nam, many of them even on men who were running.

But that was Carlos Hathcock, a living legend. Moses could also part the Red Sea.

Depending upon the particular load, a bullet coming out of a .30-06 was likely to drop somewhere between three hundred to over four hundred inches by the time it hit that stack of straw below. *Thirty-three feet!*

No one but a madman would attempt a shot at that distance with a cartridge like a .30/06.

And no one but a fool would make such a miraculous shot, then leave his brass lying about for anyone to find. At least not unless he *wanted* it to be found...

And yet, here the tracks of the bipod were, untouched by weather, and here was the cartridge casing, untarnished where exposed from the dirt—shiny and new.

Somewhere a madman was loose, and that madman might be the most expert marksman ever to set foot in Lemhi County.

CHAPTER TWENTY

It was only eleven in the morning, but the house was cold and empty when Coal walked in. To his surprise, even Dobe and Shadow were gone.

He almost took off his gunbelt and set it aside, but on a whim he decided not to. He couldn't shake the thought that someone could be out there wanting him dead. What if that someone came to visit him here? He would not be caught unprepared.

Cutting some sharp cheddar cheese, he threw together a grilled cheese sandwich and some Campbell's soup. He hated that stuff, but there was nothing else in the house. What he needed, unless he wanted to let go of bodybuilding altogether, was a big, juicy beef steak. Or some venison. And leaving behind the iron was not an option for Coal, not after more than twenty years of pursuing it. Some days, the gym was all that kept him alive.

The thought of venison made him think of the moose. Which made him think of the twins. He hadn't seen them since the night the moose ran out in front of the truck. At least not awake. Would they still be thinking about that moose? About his broken promise?

And what about Katie? Had she loosened up at all? Had Connie talked to her? No, Connie wouldn't. She would leave that stone for Coal to turn. It was his job. *Thanks, Mom,* he thought with a twinge of resentment. It wasn't a job he relished. Why was it that a man could go out in the world, be anything he wanted to be, do anything he wanted to do, talk to anyone he needed to, whether it be coaxing a confession from a killer or warning a drunken superior officer what was coming if he didn't step out of his car, but yet he had no way to talk to his own daughter?

Coal clicked on the radio and was in time to catch the hourly news. The day before, an airplane in Australia had been hijacked by a lone gunman—the first ever on that continent. And right there in the U.S.A., in the historically Negro Southern University, in Louisiana, a protest by one hundred or so students had ended up bringing down the wrath of the law. Fifty-five deputies and thirty state troopers had come in to quell the uprising, and two students had died by a shotgun blast. Not surprisingly, no one could identify the shooter.

At least that was what they claimed. Coal had a very hard time believing it. Sure as anything, his boys would never be able to solve the murder of Larry MacAtee, if the big guns couldn't solve a shooting committed in front of hundreds of eyewitnesses.

The grilled cheese was stiff, and the Campbell's tasted sour, as always. It filled his belly. Nothing more.

Sitting at the kitchen table, Coal fiddled with the badge on his shirt and stared out the window at the bleak day. It wasn't even going to reach forty degrees today, the weather report said, and the sleet had started pattering down again, more wet now than before. He got up and paced the house, stopping every minute or so to look out front for his mother and the kids.

Damnit, he had to have a steak! He also had to get back into a gym. He had been two weeks now without anything more than pushups, pull-ups, and sit-ups, and he was starting to feel it. His standard these days was two hundred pull-ups, three hundred pushups, and one hundred sit-ups—every other day. But it wasn't going to be enough to maintain what he had worked all those years to put on.

One more look out the window in the door. No Chrysler. Nothing but emptiness, and the sound of the sleet against the house.

Coal walked down the hall to his mother's bedroom and flipped on the light. It smelled like lilacs in here. Lilacs and horse manure. That made him smile. Neither scent was terrible. But the mixture of them? Interesting. But it was Connie—manure and hay on her worn-out Justins and lilac perfume on top of the jewelry box on her dresser, several drops of it dribbled onto a Kleenex and set there to scent the room—just like she had done every day as far back as Coal could remember.

Unabashed over his curiosity, Coal went to the closet and pushed things around on the top shelf. It didn't take long to find two of the things he was looking for: his dad's old Stetson, and a Colt Peacemaker .44-40 with checkered ivory grips.

He hefted the Colt, and suddenly he felt a grin cross his face, and he heard his own voice: "Hey, Dad."

The voice startled him. So did the tears that dimmed his eyes. He lifted the hat and looked at the sweat marks above the thin ribbon of band, on the lower part of the crown and also on the brim. "Guess you're still with us, Dad. Mom will never let you go."

He walked over and set the items on top of a patchwork quilt that gave him a great memory of its own. He remembered lying on the floor underneath the quilting frame while Connie and some friends from the church were making it. That was a magical time—in his own little cave with the sound of kind ladies' gossip lulling him.

He went back into the closet and dug past umbrellas and gun cases to find one in particular, made of black suede leather, with sheep's fleece showing at its mouth. Reaching down into it, he pulled out a lever action Winchester rifle, old as the hills—or at least as old as his daddy. Then he returned to the bed.

In the cold silence of the empty, lonely house, Coal sat on the edge of the bed and worked the action of the .40-40. He ran his hand over its smooth metal, felt every nick in the wood. The stories this rifle could tell! The deer, the elk, the rabbits and bears it had brought home to that very same chipped, sage-green table that still sat, solid as cinderblock, in their kitchen. His father had kept the Winchester and the Colt not only for the sake of nostalgia—they had been his own father's—but for the convenience of being able to use the same ammunition in them both. And old Prince's marksmanship overrode any downside to the lack of power in the rifle.

He flipped open the loading gate on the Colt and spun the cylinder. *Good for you, Mom.* It was loaded. Always loaded. He laughed, because it made him remember a line spoken by the Duke in his Academy Award-winning performance as Rooster Cogburn, in *True Grit:* "Well, a gun that's *unloaded* and cocked ain't good for nothin'."

What would his daddy have done if he were in Coal's shoes now? He asked the question of himself, then as soon pushed it aside. It was an impossible question, because Prince Savage would never have been in the situation his son was in now. Prince Savage had been as solid as a rock, and so was his marriage to Connie. He had his quibbles with his children, sure. But none of them were the same as what Coal and Katie were going through. Because Coal, unlike his father, was weak. And Laura, unlike Connie, had been weak too. And their two weaknesses culminated in a greater weakness—and in the end, perhaps, the downfall of a family.

*   *   *

It was raining outside when Coal got in the Chevy and drove down the road. On the way, he passed Connie and the children, and he feathered the brake, looking in the rearview mirror at their fading lights, headed home. He waited to see Connie's brake lights, but they never showed. She just kept driving, her speed unchecked. Didn't even stop to say hi. He guessed he should head home, too. At least say hi to Connie and the boys, even if he couldn't talk to Katie Leigh. Instead, after a moment's contemplation, he took his foot off the brake, put it back on the gas pedal, and drove on. If his mother didn't have any desire to say hi, then who was he to force it on her?

Sometime this week, Coal had to go have a talk with the county clerk, by whose say he guessed he either kept or lost the position as sheriff until next election. But no one so far had mentioned it to him. He had simply been shoved into the sheriff's seat, badge and all, and that was that. But what if the clerk, Nate Hanson, interviewed him, looked at his record, and the way he had been let go from the FBI, and decided he was not the man for the job? What if he wanted Mitchell back? Sooner or later, he was going to have to find out. But it was going to have to be later. He had no desire to talk to anyone right now—least of all to Hanson.

Salmon was drenched in rain when he drove up the street. Business lights were on, some of them reflecting out onto the ebony asphalt. Vehicles were parked up and down both curbs, but pedestrians were non-existent. When he passed the Coffee Shop and Wally's, he thought of stopping for a cup of coffee. But there were too many people inside. People were the last thing he wanted right now.

He drove past the Owl Club—thought of going in *there,* too. That was a place he remembered Bigfoot Monahan frequenting, and he needed to ask questions about Bigfoot—a *lot* of questions. Still, he drove on, and soon he was climbing up the Bar, passing the Episcopal Church of the Redeemer, then a wood house, and was at last at the courthouse. He pulled in and drove to the back. The Ford LTD was there, and he parked beside it and went in.

"No, now *that* I do know. He was too tall, he told me. And
-footed, too."

"Really. Where does he hang his hat, anyway?"

"Over towards Leadore, I believe. Ten, fifteen miles, maybe.
/er been to his place, though. Just his wife and boy there now,
ıess."

"Oh, you haven't heard? Bigfoot's out."

Jensen sat bolt upright in his seat. "Out? How?"

"Just out. Good behavior, I'm told."

Jensen whistled. "That could get interesting."

"Interesting why?"

"Word out and about was he swore to kill the sheriff and a
ple of other men for runnin' him in."

"I know," confirmed Coal. "I was one of them. One of the
rs was shot a few days ago—killed. From ambush."

Jensen's face paled, and he swore. "I'm real sorry, Sheriff.
t's not a good hand to play to."

"No, it's not. Hey, Howie, why don't you hang tight for a mi-
? I need to look at something." Saying this, Coal opened up a
ıle of drawers, found a file system in one, with tags sticking
ut of it. Thumbing through them, he was pleasantly surprised
e one that read, HOWARD GENE JENSEN. He pulled it out
started leafing through it, liking what he saw: Flight risk low;
of violence low; behavior good. One last note, scrawled on
ottom of the page: *Model prisoner.* Initialed at the bottom:
B.

Coal set the papers down and looked levelly at Jensen. "You
of this place, Howie?"

Sure am."

You a good worker? Got a trustworthy vehicle?"

Huh? Trustworthy vehicle? Well, sure. And yes, I'd say I'm
ɔd worker."

The smell of burned coffee was strong. He forbade himself
the dubious pleasure and simply turned off the burner. No one
was around. He stepped back into the jail, where there were only
six cells, and only five of them occupied.

Coal recognized three out of the five men in the cells. One
was Howard Jensen, about whom Jordan Peterson had been talking two mornings ago.

"Howdy, boys. Hi, Howard. Tim. Scott." He looked at the
other two. "I'm Coal Savage—the new sheriff."

The two men who were strange to him nodded, and one of
them said, "Adam Manetti, Sheriff. Good to meet you." The other
man just nodded and said his name was Brew Higgins.

Coal didn't know what was wrong with Howard Jensen's
daughter, only that Jim had said she was in a hospital in Salt Lake
City. He picked up the ring of keys by the door. "Hey, Jensen.
You mind stepping out here with me for a minute?"

"No sir, boss," replied Jensen, and when Coal unlocked the
door, he came out, and they went out into the office and shut the
door between it and the cellblock. Coal went over and turned the
deadbolt on the outside door, locking the world away from the
two of them.

He walked to his desk, then motioned to a chair. "Take a seat,
Jensen."

When Jensen complied, Coal plopped down in his chair behind the desk, but then he thought better of it and dragged it out
from behind the desk, so there was nothing between him and
Howard Jensen.

"How've you been?" Coal asked.

"Just fine, Sheriff. Just fine."

"Say, what are you in here for anyway?"

"You don't already know?"

Amused, Coal looked at him, drifting his hands briefly to the
sides—a shrug, but not a shrug.

"Ah, I was drunk one night. Run into Blake Shear's horse and killed it."

"Okay."

"Yeah. Then when he came out and yelled at me, I kind of hit him. Kinda knocked out a tooth."

"I see. You paying for all that?"

"Well, I guess, sorta," replied Jensen. "I got no money to speak of, boss. I'm payin' with jail time."

"That won't do Shear any good, will it?"

"Just the satisfaction of knowin' I'm in here, and he's out there, I suppose."

"Out there without a tooth and without a horse."

Jensen chuckled. "Yeah, I suppose. I told him I was sorry, but he kept yellin'. Just kept yellin'. Hurtin' my ears."

"Not a very good way to resurrect a horse, is it?" asked Coal with a smile.

"No sir. Didn't work so well."

"How long's your sentence?"

"Two months."

"How long have you been in?"

"Twenty-eight days. And a half."

Coal laughed. "But who's counting, right?"

"Yeah, right. Not me."

"Jensen—can I call you Howard?"

"Sure, boss. Howard or Howie's what I go by."

"All right, Howie. I need to know something. It's a family question, and if you don't want to, you don't have to answer. How's your daughter?"

"My daughter?" Howie looked immediately suspicious, but not angrily so.

"Jim told me your daughter's sick."

"Oh. He did? I don't like too many folks knowin' about it."

"Any reason?"

"Just don't want no pity."

"I understand. Well, Howie, if you don't have any fl who's paying for your daughter's treatment?"

"I don't know. Her ma's takin' care of all that. You k got sick after I came in here. The wife said she started and it got worse and worse with no let up. I ain't seen she got sick. They had to run her in to Idaho Falls first ' doctors here couldn't figure out what was wrong. Th Idaho Falls they flew her to Salt Lake, to the LDS Hospit

"I see. Say, you're a lumber man, aren't you, Howi asked.

"I was. Laid off now."

"Maybe we could change that."

"How?" Jensen scooted forward on his chair, suddenl ing very interested.

"I know a few people," Coal replied. "By the way, s of knowing people... You wouldn't happen to know old Monahan, would you? His real name's Paul."

Jensen laughed. "Paul? Hell, I could've never told y Why, sure I know Bigfoot. Who doesn't?"

"What do you think of him?"

"He can be a real nice guy—when he's sober."

"You ever work with him?"

"Sure. We was workin' together right before he got ser the state pen."

"You ever happen to go hunting with him?"

"Huntin'? Well, no. Lots of folks like to drink when t huntin'. Me included. I wasn't ever too interested in bein' him when he was drinkin'."

Coal chuckled. "No, I can't say I blame you there. We you ever hear about Bigfoot being a hunter?"

"Not as far as I can say."

"Was he ever in a war?"

"You an honest man?" Coal was still staring Jensen in the eye, and the man's eyes didn't flicker.

"I am."

"If you make me a promise, will you keep it?"

"Yes sir. I will."

"All right." Coal stood up out of his chair, and Jensen did the same. "I've got to have you sober, Howie. You've been in jail one month, and so far you haven't had to have a drink. So I know you can do it. If you promise me you'll stay sober, and work hard, I'm releasing you. As of today. You can come back in the evenings and serve your time after seven p.m., and we'll count it as a full day. I'm going to make a few phone calls and find you a job—either at a mechanic shop, a service station, or in the lumber yard. Maybe at the log mill—here or in Leadore."

"Why?" Jensen stammered. "Why would you do this for me?"

"I'm sending you down to Salt Lake to see your little girl."

Jensen was nearly in tears. "Wait... what do you mean?"

"Just what I said."

"I can't pay for that."

"I never said you were. I'm taking care of it."

Dumbfounded, Jensen stared at Coal for several seconds. Finally, he managed to say, "I sure do appreciate this, Sheriff, but... I really can't go all that way right now. My car works, but it doesn't have any gas in it. And like I said, I got no money."

Coal stepped closer. "Howie, if I get you a job, you'll start trying to make good on Blake Shear's horse, right? And his tooth?"

"I will. That I do promise."

"All right. I got some severance pay when I left Washington, D.C. I'm loaning you money to buy gas and food and lodging in Salt Lake. You'll pay that back to me, too, won't you?"

Tears had filled Howard Jensen's eyes now, so he could hardly see. He stared through them at the new sheriff. "But how can you trust me? How do you know I'll pay you back? How do you know I *can*?"

"Because you promised, Howie. You were looking me square in the eye, and you promised. I don't need anything more than that—and a handshake."

Jensen hastily raked the tears out of his eyes, and Coal walked away from him and pretended not to notice. He went to the coffee pot. "Hey, Howie, this coffee smells a little burned, but it's still pretty hot. You want a cup?"

He heard Jensen sniffle. "Sure. Sure, I'll have a cup, Sheriff. Thank you. Thanks a million."

Coal took his time pouring the cup of coffee, allowing Jensen a chance to get hold of himself. The whole time, his back was to the prisoner, and his .357 magnum was on his hip, where Jensen could have reached it—for all the good it would have done him.

Finally, Coal turned about and walked to Jensen, handing him the warm cup. "There you go, my friend. Drink that up and let's get you home."

CHAPTER TWENTY-ONE

The gray day persisted, and the mountains lost all form. Only the foothills could be seen clearly, a smeared watercolor mélange of grays and browns and smutty yellows. The wipers ran nonstop, sluicing the pouring rain off the windshield, and when Coal drew the pickup into the bank parking lot he was loath to get out. He leaned far forward and looked up at the sky, but the motion was pointless, for what he saw above only mimicked the downpour splattering on the glass in front of him.

Leaving Jensen in the truck, with the motor and the heat running, Coal dashed for the bank, withdrew two hundred and twenty dollars, and came back to feed two hundred of it off the stack of twenties into Jensen's hand.

"Two hundred dollars, Howie. Gas will be no more than forty cents a gallon, and hopefully down to thirty-five or less in some places. You should be able to get a nice room for less than ten bucks, as long as you don't head for the Hilton. And maybe seven bucks a day for food—if you make a pig of yourself."

Jensen got a laugh out of that. "I'm not a picky eater, Sheriff."

"Then two hundred should give you five days to a week in Salt Lake, easy. And food for your lady too."

Jensen just nodded this time. His emotions had put him beyond the ability to say any words.

They drove on through the rain to the west side of town, and Coal pulled up in front of a light green house on Idaho Avenue that was little more than a shack, with a fifty-five Buick parked in front. "When you get back, give me a holler, Howie. I should have work for you by then, and if you play your cards right you'll have enough out of this two hundred to get some groceries. Now what are you going to buy between here and Salt Lake?"

"A room, food and gas."

"Anything else?"

"No alcohol."

Coal laughed and nodded. "That goes without saying, because you gave your word. Anything else?"

Unsure what to say, Jensen shook his head.

"If you don't get some flowers for that girl and for that woman of yours, we'll have words when I catch wind of it."

Jensen laughed, and his eyes shone. "I'll never forget this, Sheriff. Not for the rest of my life." He put out his weathered, work-hardened hand, and Coal took it and held on.

"I'm expecting great things out of you, Howie. See you when you get home."

Howie smiled and pumped his hand one last time, tried to say something but failed, and got out of the truck with a wave, running through the rain for his front door.

Coal nodded with satisfaction as he watched Jensen disappear inside, then threw the truck in reverse and backed slowly out into the street. The neighborhood was dead. He could have sat across half the street for fifteen minutes without any fear of being run into. He took a deep breath and sighed. It was time to go check on Connie and the kids.

Down the highway, rainwater sluiced up off his tires. He eased onto Savage Road, and it turned into mud. With a few fish tails on the washboard surface, a few jarring descents into potholes filled with chocolate-brown water, he finally made it up to the driveway and turned in. Connie's Chrysler Newport was in the drive, but it didn't look so beautiful anymore. It looked like a mud wagon. Light woodsmoke huffed out the tin chimney pipe of the house, and amber lights glowed inside. He wished he could feel the same glow in his heart. And more than that, he wished his children would feel it when they saw him. But after what he had done to their mother, he guessed he couldn't really expect it. Not now, maybe never again.

Taking in another huge breath, Coal looked out at the sky again. *Well, it's now or never.* He threw open the door and dashed for the house and up the steps to the porch. He stepped inside, feeling pretty good about how dry he had stayed in spite of the storm. But then he swore, remembering he had left the last twenty dollars of his withdrawal on the seat. His mother looked at him questioningly as he ducked back outside, and Dobe flew out after him, the screen door banging shut behind them both.

Coal opened the door and reached in to grab the twenty off the seat, then turned and shut the door. Dobe was right at his feet, insistently sticking a paw in the air, wanting his master's attention. "Jeez, Dobe, can't you wait until I get inside?" Coal said with a laugh. But he was a sucker for a friendly paw, and he leaned forward to pet his friend.

The odd sound was a puzzle to Coal, just for a moment. Also strange was the feel of something pattering all over the back of his jacket, something bigger and more solid than just the rain, which was turning more into a drizzle.

Suddenly, the bellow of a high-powered rifle drifted to him through the afternoon gloom. He whirled as he grabbed at the snap on his holster, getting just one glimpse of the shattered window of the pickup as he spun and threw himself into the yard. He heard the *ping* of a bullet as it spat into the pavement, missing him once more only because of his sudden move. And then, two seconds later, the ensuing hollow echo of the report.

Frantically, like a retreating alligator, he scrambled on hands and knees across the yard, across the cold, drenched grass and through the mud of the vacated flower bed. As he turned, his back slammed up against the foundation of the house and nearly knocked the wind from him, and with a second attempt he was finally able to claw the Smith and Wesson out of its holster, blinking hard against the rain running into his eyes.

Looking out in the yard, he saw his hat, lying there against the grass, somewhat like a moon in a dim-lit sky. Dobe was fawning around next to him, trying to figure out if his master was playing. He didn't seem to find it odd in the least that his master was sitting in the mud and rain, and obviously, the distant sounds of the rifle shots hadn't bothered him whatsoever. They had come from too far away to sound dangerous, and could just as easily have seemed like distant thunder to him—which would have terrified Shadow, but which had never registered as any more dangerous than galloping horses to Dobe.

Coal heard the screen door open, and his mother hollered his name into the storm even before he saw her appear, first her extended arm, then the rest of her. She was about to yell again as she searched the yard for him when he barked at her to get back in the house.

Her eyes registered on him lying there in the mud. "What happened? Coal, get in here!" Her eyes flashed about the yard, mining the shadows for signs of danger. "Get up!" she insisted.

Never one not to obey his mother, Coal shoved up from his seat and leaped up onto the concrete porch, bursting inside on Connie's heels. Dobe darted through the door that was being held for him. The kids were all standing around the table, positioned as if ready to break for cover.

"What happened?" Connie demanded, voicing the same query in the eyes of the children, even Katie Leigh, who looked too startled to have yet marshaled her usual expression of despite.

"Someone shot at me!" Coal growled. "Did you hear the shots?"

"I heard something," Connie said. "In here, it didn't sound like shots."

"Get my rifle, Virgil!" Coal ordered, as with revolver still in hand he went to the drapes and parted them while standing off to one side of the picture window. At the very moment he looked out, he saw the Christmas glow of two bright red taillights on a dark vehicle that careened down off of Lemhi Road, which wyed onto Savage, and headed toward Highway 28.

That vehicle was going too fast simply to be traveling down to the highway to run errands. Coal whirled on the others, and as Virgil ran back into the room with his Winchester .30/06, he snatched it out of his hands and shoved the .357 back into its holster, not bothering to snap it in. "Turn off the lights! And stay away from the windows. Mom, call dispatch and tell them someone took a couple of rifle shots at me, and they're in a big, dark vehicle headed west. Call now! And don't *anybody* set foot outside this door or show yourselves until you hear from me!"

With that, he burst out into the murky light of the yard, running for the truck. He waited instinctively for the sound of another shot, for the feel of a large caliber rifle bullet taking him between the shoulder blades.

CHAPTER TWENTY-TWO

Coal drove the Chevy down the gravel and mud-lined road like a madman, the back end weaving dangerously back and forth. He managed to keep it on the road, and as he pulled onto Highway 28, he could see two distant red pricks of light headed toward town. No sooner had he seen them, however, than they turned left on a ranch road and rocketed out of sight behind a screen of huge willows. There was another set of red lights, much farther up the road, but instinctively, when he got to the ranch road, he took the turn, reaching over and pulling the Winchester closer to him.

He was still in his own pickup, and he cursed his stupidity for that. There was no radio in here, no way to call for backup, even if there had been anyone to help him. But such was the way of a small department like Lemhi County—Salmon, too, for that matter. A man had to rely on himself here. Rely on help coming, and you would wind up dead.

As he plowed on through the mud, Coal was aware that the storm was lifting, and the sky in the west growing pale gray. That was good, because his left side was already soaked from being exposed to the rain through the broken window.

He was glad for his canvas Dickies, because he could feel chunks of broken glass under his legs and butt. And thank heavens for tempered glass! Prior to these windows of tempered—or so-called *toughened*—glass, he would have been sliced to shreds on this seat.

Fresh tire tracks were visible in the muddy road before him, and the way the light struck them made them show up from quite a ways off. Besides, Coal could see no place to turn off. So he drove at a far higher speed than was prudent, fishtailing back and forth on the road, gunning his motor to catch up to the vehicle—a vehicle he was positive was being driven by Bigfoot Monahan.

This was too much of a coincidence to think any other way now. Bigfoot got out of jail, and within a month's time two of the men he had sworn to kill were either dead or had missed being that way by a tiny, very fortunate margin. It was time to put this dangerous criminal down forever. And the way Coal felt at the moment, he was not inclined to take the man prisoner. He had made that mistake once.

Ahead in the road, Coal saw a truck. His heart jumped, but he quickly realized it was pointing his way, and stopped. Furthermore, as he drew near it at upwards of thirty miles an hour he saw that it was light-colored, either white or pale yellow. No one seemed to be around it—probably broke down in it and deserted it before the storm.

With total abandon, Coal plowed through a huge pool of sloppy mud, right where the other pickup had come to a stop. He had the fleeting thought from looking at the size of that mud puddle that this truck, rather than breaking down, had probably gotten stuck in that mud, and he wasn't about to join them by slowing down.

Just as his pickup neared the back of the other, with a vaulting curtain of brown water and mud drops flying and coating the vehicle's body, something flashed. It was a face, appearing over the tailgate. Someone in a floppy straw hat, red plaid shirt and a dark green coat with a fur collar.

He had only time for one more thought to register on him before his wall of mud engulfed that person's face and the entire front of their body: It was a woman.

Cringing, Coal cursed, but rather than stop, he pressed down even deeper on the gas. There was nothing to be done for that woman now, and fortunately it wasn't anyone he recognized anyway. He just hoped she was gone before his business was finished, because he had been on this road before, and it was a dead-end. In spite of the fact that he seemed to have "escaped," he actually felt beads of sweat pop out on his forehead. Damn, how angry he would have been if he had been the one back there in her place!

It was light now, with the darkest of the cloud back behind him, and the sky ahead was a bright gray that almost hurt the eyes. There were no vehicles in sight in front of him, and when he realized that, he eased off the gas. There was no way that fleeing vehicle could have kept on going and left him behind—not by that far.

Coal eased the truck momentarily to a stop and worked the bolt of the Winchester five times, until he could see five shiny new cartridges on the seat beside him. *That's my mom! The only good gun is a loaded gun.*

Pressing the cartridges back inside, he put one in the chamber and set the rifle down carefully, then drove on, now going less than five miles an hour and scanning the willows alongside the road.

After a time, he saw a little cove beside the road, and several tall, furrowed cottonwoods anchoring the green meadow of an old homestead. There was a dilapidated, once-white house at the back of the meadow with windows still intact but a porch roof that leaned precariously.

The brakes protested against all the mud and water in them as Coal eased the pickup to a stop, the cold coming through his missing window just now starting to register on him through his muddy jacket. A dark-colored van, looking not much smaller than the homestead house, was parked on the far side of it, its lights out. Coal's heart started pounding harder, which was crazy because he had already thought it meant to come out through his nose.

But the car chase was over. It was time for gunplay. And from his blood-filled past, he knew there was nothing more terrible.

Easing out the door, he slid the Winchester along with him, leaving the door slightly ajar. What did it matter, anyway? It wasn't like he had to worry about anything getting wetter inside.

He looped the rifle sling around his left forearm, reached up and smoothed back his rain-wet hair, wishing he had his hat. *Wait a minute. Get your wits, Coal Savage. This* elk *can shoot back at you.* He drew a huge breath, then let it out slowly.

There was no obvious way to approach this house without being seen. But was the driver of the van in the house now, or still in the van? There was no way to know. A close look showed steam coming from the vehicle's tailpipe, so there was no doubt it had just parked. He couldn't have told anyone what kind of getaway car the shooter had used, but he could certainly swear this vehicle, big and dark like the one that had fled the scene, was the same one he had chased here. And the fact that they had chosen this remote place to stop was all the further proof he needed. No one in his right mind was out here taking a joy ride on a day like this, only to visit a deserted homestead.

"It's war, Coal," he said, this time in a whisper to himself, and with another deep breath he took off running for the near corner of the house.

As he ran, he dodged this way and that, creating a random zigzag that no one could possibly get any pattern from. He had learned a lot of lessons from hunting, and that was one the jackrabbit had taught him over and over in his youth: Keep them guessing. Never under any circumstances telegraph your movements before you make them.

Out of breath, he made it to the corner of the house and put his back to it. His eyes dodged this way and that, digging into shadowy brush and willows. The only movement was from a mule deer doe that stood switching her tail some two hundred feet beyond the house. She watched him intently but didn't break and run.

Coal put his ear to the wall of the house, listening for voices. Craning his ears for any sound of movement. It was eerily still. He looked out at the Chevy. Now that the light was better, it stood out on the road like a black sheep in a flock of swans. He cursed himself for getting so close. That wasn't what Daddy had taught him hunting—and it wasn't what the war had reinforced. But it was there now, and he was here. There was no changing that. Anyone looking out the front door of the house, or even the back window of the van, was going to see it.

Could this shooter possibly not know he had been chased here? It seemed unfathomable. Yet perhaps he believed his target so shaken by being fired upon that he was still back at his house, cowering in the shadows. Why else would he have stopped here? If he *did* know he had been followed, and that Coal was outside, how could he know there weren't others on their way? Unless he had a death wish, he must know that whatever he had to do here must be done fast, and then he must be gone.

And yet still there was no movement. Maybe Bigfoot Monahan *did* have a death wish. Maybe he was going to let his pursuers go down in a blaze of glory with him...

Coal looked toward the back of the house. Which way would the shooter expect him to approach, assuming he knew he was out here? It was the worst possible case of a fifty-fifty chance— to live, or to die. Taking another deep breath, and scanning the road back the way he had come, he saw only gray nothingness and muddy hills. He was alone. Just like a thousand hillsides of his young adulthood. Alone in the hunt...

Reaching down, Coal eased the .357 around in its holster, then started down the side of the house toward the back. He reached the back and had to skirt a cellar door that broke out away from the main part of the house, its own little section of roof protecting it from the weather.

At its corner, Coal peeked around. Again, all he saw was stillness and emptiness, only here in the back one of the windows had been shot out, and it opened on the gray world like a yawning mouth, or an eye, brooding upon his entrance to the scene, giving him no welcome.

The pale gray sky reflected harshly off the other windows, but through the hole Coal's gaze pierced, and there was no movement. It would be cold in there. He had been in deserted houses like that before, and often they seemed colder on the inside than out, perhaps because of their desperate loneliness.

After five minutes or so, minutes of deathly quiet, he crept on past the windows, moving smooth and fast. And now he was at the far corner, and there, just out of sight, was the van. Coal took a deep breath and raised the rifle butt to his shoulder. He came gingerly around the house, the rifle bearing on the front of the van. Now he could hear a faint sound, and he stopped, just for a moment.

Voices. Laughter. It seemed strange to ponder, but it was clear—someone laughing. Giggling. He squinched up his eyes, peering closer at the ugly gray monstrosity of a vehicle. *What the—?* Had whoever shot at him thought it was a joke? That made him madder than anything. He had barely escaped with his life. This was war, and a sane man didn't laugh at war.

With the anger rising in his chest, he set his rifle down against the corner of the house, drew his magnum, and advanced on the van. There was nothing the Winchester could do now that the fearsome .357 could not. Coal clamped his jaw hard and took four steps, reaching the side door of the van, not seeming to draw anyone's attention. Once more, he thought he heard a sound of laughter—a soft voice, not masculine at all.

With confusion filling his brain, something else tried to get in but failed. It was a warning to caution. But Coal was beyond caution. The adrenalin was squishing in his ears. And, in the famous words of Admiral Farragut, "Damn the torpedoes! Full speed ahead!"

With the pistol in his right fist, his left came out and touched the handle to the sliding door. He tried it, and it gave. It was not locked. Were they waiting for him?

With an inner oath, he threw down the handle and shoved the door back on its slide, going into combat stance but keeping the passenger door and the door post between him and the cargo area of the van for protection.

When he thought back on this moment in days, and years, to come, he would always realize how happy he was not to have had backup—just this once. And the young couple on the floor of the van would probably feel the same.

And, thought Coal wryly as he drove away later, he was not the one here who should be worried about protection. The first thing he saw was two people, a man and a woman, and the man was lying on top of the woman.

"Freeze!"

Coal's barked command was met by a horrendous scream. And then the young man's female companion let one out as well. Both people were fully clothed, but it was obvious by the glow of passion in the back of that van that in a matter of minutes they would not have been.

The young man whirled and practically fell back on top of the woman. "What the hell?" His voice was almost a scream again, but nothing to match the first sound he had uttered, which still rang in Coal's ears.

"Get your hands in the air!" Coal barked. "Both of you!"

The man slid off the woman, coming to his knees, and both obeyed. The woman realized her shoulder was bare, and she instinctively dropped her hand to pull up her sleeve.

"Stop moving!" Coal felt the heat in his face. The anger pulsed at his temples.

For several seconds, no one spoke or made a move. Finally, Coal dropped his left hand from the pistol, motioning at them with that hand. "All right. Both of you. Out of the van. Now!"

The couple scrambled to obey, and Coal saw that the young suitor had already managed to get his lady's shoes off, for she stood there in cute little socks getting soaked in the wet, yellow grass. She did not seem to notice.

"What are you doing out here?" Coal demanded.

The young man started to reply, then reddened. "Well... Nothing! Who are you?"

"I'm the sheriff, that's who."

The man swore. The girl belted her suitor in the back, and it made a serious thump that had to hurt. Her partner cringed.

"He told me this was public property," she stammered, doing a little dance.

Coal looked down at her feet and made a face. "Get in and get your shoes." The girl looked more than happy to comply, and when she had slipped them on, she stood again before him.

Looking at her more closely, Coal could see she was no more than a child, perhaps eighteen. Or perhaps less. "Maybe it is," said Coal. "I couldn't tell you that."

"Then... What did we do wrong?"

Coal sucked in a deep breath, keeping the revolver on them. "Anyone else in there with you?"

The young man looked confused. "No."

"Sure?"

"Yeah, I'm sure. We were..."

"I can see what you were doing," Coal cut him off. "How old are you?" he asked the girl.

"Eighteen."

Her gaze had faltered right before her reply. He went on a hunch. "Lie again and we'll go see your folks."

She paled. "Sixteen."

Coal looked at her male counterpart. "And you?"

"Seventeen."

Same flicker.

"You two can't seem to tell me *any* truth." He jiggled the gun barrel toward the boy's face, and the bore must have looked about the size of the back window of the house to him.

"Eighteen."

"Ever hear of statutory rape?"

A look of alarm sped across the young man's face. "What?"

"You heard me."

"But I didn't— I mean, she—"

"So the answer is no," Coal inserted. "I'm not talking about forcible rape. Boy, you're barely dry behind the ears, but the state of Idaho considers you to be a man once you turn eighteen. And they consider her to be still a girl. You have sex with her, that's rape in this state. Capiche?"

"Huh?"

"Do you understand. Capiche means do you understand. You were about to commit a felony, kid."

The young man's face was already white, but it got whiter. "I didn't know that."

"Did you get permission from this girl's parents to... take her to bed?"

"Well, no."

"Of course not. You must have figured there was something wrong about it then, huh?"

The young man only stood, hands still raised.

"What's your name, kid?"

"John."

"Okay, John. Sounds like a likely name. Any weapons in the van?"

"Uh, yeah. A rifle."

Coal didn't bat an eye. What young man in 1972 *didn't* have a gun in his car? "Get it. Real slow."

John, or whatever his real name was, complied, his hands shaking. He drew out a beat-up old Sears and Roebuck twenty-two.

"That's it?"

"Yeah."

"You didn't just take two shots at me, did you, John?" The rifle that had fired at Coal was high-powered, certainly no .22. It was more of a statement than a question, but to John it came across as a question, and he was more than adamant in his reply.

"No, *sir!* Hell, no! I promise."

"You don't have to. For once I can see you're telling me the truth. Put the gun away. Miss?" He turned to the scared-looking girl. "What's your name, please?"

"Cynthia."

"All right, Cynthia, my truck is missing a window, so it's probably not nearly as warm as that van—and especially not as warm as it was fixing to be. But you're coming back to town with me."

"To my house?" Coal thought she was going to faint.

"Afraid so."

Cynthia was fighting back tears. "Please don't tell my dad."

"Let's talk on the way back," said Coal. "John?"

The boy's attention snapped from the girl to Coal. "Yes sir?"

"I would suggest you figure out your real age and your real name. I'm going to be sheriff in this valley for a long time, son. And I don't appreciate being lied to. You know the old saying: I can be your best friend, or..."

"Or my worst enemy," John finished.

"Bingo."

John nodded, then put the lie to the name he had given. "My name's Lance."

"Really? And here I thought it was John. Last name?"

"Cooper."

"All right, Lance Cooper. Try to remember it, all right?" He turned to the girl. "Cynthia, my pickup's out front. Go get in it."

With a sick look on her face, and no look at all for her would-be lover, not even an accusing one, she turned and slogged past the house, headed for the road.

"For the record, Lance," said Coal. "You don't come across like a bad kid. But your hormones are making you head down a tricky road. You'd better find some reins for them while you can. What you were about to do can carry a hefty sentence—and that's if you live long enough to make it to trial. Some fathers in this valley can get pretty trigger happy."

Lance gave a nervous smile. "Yes sir."

"I'm not kidding, Lance."

"No sir."

"See you in town sometime."

Coal picked up his rifle and went back to the pickup, digging some gloves out of the glove box and dusting as much of the broken glass off the seat as he could.

The girl stared straight ahead, obviously very curious about the broken window, but too sick about her predicament to ask.

It took a few tries in the narrow road, but Coal finally got the truck turned around and headed back toward the highway. Looking back, he saw Lance's van sitting there looking lonely beside the house. It didn't appear that Lance had any interest in following them back out to the highway any time soon.

In spite of Cynthia being right beside him, he had stopped thinking about her and started thinking about what lay ahead of him. And that did not mean the attempted assassin. He had something in his near future he was much more worried about than some stranger who only wanted to kill him.

He had had time to think, and although sometimes his head was a little slow, what his thoughts had given him was a recollection. A recollection of just who it was up ahead in the road whom he had virtually bathed in mud. He hoped he was wrong. He almost wanted to *pray* he was wrong. But he knew he wasn't. Not this time. And Cynthia was about to see the big, tough sheriff eat crow—unless, of course, the truck had gotten out of its predicament and was gone.

But of course Coal's luck had never been that good. As they drove east, a huge, light-colored lump of vehicle partially obscured by mud appeared in the road ahead, and a dark, vertical line beside it that was the shape of a person.

And oh, what a person.

It was the angry EMT, Maura PlentyWounds.

CHAPTER TWENTY-THREE

Unconsciously, Coal slowed the truck. He wished he could have driven the opposite way, on past the homestead. No matter what could have awaited him that way—a mud hole fifty feet across, with molten lava on the other side; a pack of rabid werewolves; a gang of hoodlum grizzlies with Uzis. Whatever was there, it was a cinch it would be preferable to what lay ahead.

He thought about turning around and going back. He was a coward! It was something about women, he concluded. From fifteen up to a hundred. Woman messed him up, every time.

Not wanting to show yellow in front of Cynthia, Coal kept driving. But the truck was only traveling ten to fifteen miles an hour at best—half the speed with which he had gunned it past the broken down farm truck the first time.

"Who is that?" the girl beside him finally asked.

"What makes you think I'd know that?"

She sat silent for another five seconds, as the Chevy drew terrifyingly closer to the fury of a woman's scorn. "I can just tell."

Coal laughed. Maybe he was trying to set himself at ease. "Okay, I've met her. She's an EMT on the ambulance here in town. Goes by the name of Maura PlentyWounds."

"That's a weird name. What do you mean 'goes by'? You don't think it's her real name?"

"That I don't know, but it shouldn't be. Cynthia, in about half a minute you're going to see that her real name should be *Gives* PlentyWounds."

"She's mean?"

"She's mean, and she's mad."

Cynthia sat up straighter in her seat, her hair glistening in the light of the sun that had finally broken through the clouds in the west. "She's covered in mud!"

"Thus the reason she's mad," Coal admitted with a sigh. "So far, I can't explain the mean part."

To leave himself some cover he could duck behind, Coal eased the pickup to a stop some ten feet short of the woman's truck, a sixty-one International Harvester Travelette. It was a four door pickup, a rarity, once the color of cream, or perhaps a white made creamy by years of oxidation. It had enough rust spots to give a horse the term, "beautiful appaloosa." In a truck, "moth-eaten, rusty bucket of bolts" would be more common. It was ugly as sin, and apparently as broke down as a dead horse.

Coal sat in his seat for a second, feeling a sudden chill come back to the air, even with the sun's rays hitting the back of his neck. Then, as he sat, he sensed, more than saw, a gray gloom close over the sun again. Fitting.

Finally, he threw open the door and stepped out into the mud. He had to bite the insides of his cheeks to keep from actually laughing when he got close enough to get a good look at Maura PlentyWounds. In spite of the fury and deadly hatred in her face, he wanted to say, "Hello, Miss PlentyMud." He started to smile, the precursor to a belt of laughter that would be tantamount to throwing an armload of raccoons on a hot stove.

The woman didn't even ask the obvious, *What are you smiling at?* Like a professional wrestler, she went right for the throat with, "Who in the hell taught you how to drive, Mario?"

"Huh?" Coal was a little slow on the uptake. Mouth bullets were flying at him, and he had nothing to fight back with. He was also too dumb to duck.

"Mario? Andretti? I suppose a backwoods hick like you has never even heard of Indianapolis or Daytona, huh? So do you even have any speed limits in this county?"

Coal was quickly losing his lack of words. Only now his last bit of intelligence had clicked in and told him he would probably be well-advised not to use the words his mind was lighting upon as bullets in this particular gunfight.

"Look at me!" the woman almost screamed.

"Yes, ma'am. It's hard not to." Coal had to stop himself from laughing again. He was going back and forth between embarrassed, mad, and doped up with laughter, swapping positions faster than a career politician.

"My truck's broke down. I'm standing here hoping for help. And some idiot that wouldn't know how to drive more than a tricycle comes flying by and covers me from head to foot with mud. Now you came back to gloat over it, huh? You should have just kept going."

"You were kind of in the road."

"What?" A new light of war came into the woman's eyes.

"I wanted to keep driving back to the highway, but I couldn't get past you."

"Well, you sure have some nerve. I think you should take your little toy truck and leave me alone."

"Yes, ma'am."

Coal turned and went back to the Chevy. He climbed inside and threw it into second again, starting past the woman, whose head, had it been a cannon, would long since have exploded and blown them both into Custer County.

It was still somewhat funny to look at her. She looked like a chocolate rabbit—minus the ears and fluffy tail. But she was also about one of the rudest women he had ever run across. He didn't feel much like laughing anymore. That would probably come later, when he was alone in bed, or trying to relay the story to others.

He inched the Chevy toward the woman, who acted like she was going to refuse to give him the road, until the very last second, when she stepped back to the tailgate of her ugly truck. He had a surge of guilt when his door was passing her, and he started to say something, but she went into a tirade again. "Do you stare at everyone that way?"

That made his dam burst. "Just wondering if you taste like chocolate too."

And that was that. A well of anger, flooded too full, a tendency toward a biting sense of humor, and a rude woman covered from head to toe like a chocolate raisin, and what did she expect? He hadn't meant to say it. Hadn't even really thought about it. It just popped out. As his father once had told his mother, one of the times he got suspended from school, "You just gotta face it, Mother: Your son's greatest sense of humor comes out when somebody pushes him too far." That was shortly before Coal started fashioning the willow switch his father had demanded of him for telling his junior high principal he needed to move because his big butt was blocking the list of school rules he had been ranting about.

Maura PlentyWounds flew at the truck like a panther, slamming it with her fists, kicking at the door with her mud-covered cowboy boots. Coal slammed on the brakes. "Hey! I guess it's not hard to see how your truck ended up beat-up like that. Do you want a ride, or you going to walk back to town?"

"A ride with *you?* That's pretty ridiculous." The woman stared sharpened forks at him. "Go to hell. I'd rather ride a sheep back to town."

Coal just shrugged, his ire rising again, and let off the clutch, moving away from her. His tires spun a little in the mud, but soon they caught traction, and he drove off about twenty feet.

Suddenly, he heard the voice of the girl beside him. "Are you really going to leave her there? It's starting to rain again."

Coal, through his anger, looked at the windshield, blinking to clear his vision. Cynthia was right. Raindrops were spattering the windshield. "Good. She needs a bath. Besides, she wouldn't ride with me anyway."

"Well, maybe if you went back and apologized to her."

"*Me?* Apologize to *her!* Why me? What am I supposed to apologize for?"

"For being so mean."

Coal slammed on the brakes, making the truck slide sideways in the mud and come to a stop sitting quartered across the road.

"You have got to be kidding me. I did everything I could for her. I was chasing someone who had just taken two shots at me, little girl. Tried to kill me. And if it weren't for sheer luck, he would have, too. That's why this window's broken. And besides, when I passed her I had no idea she was even at the back of the truck. And one more thing you don't know: She was every bit as rude as this long before today, for absolutely no reason. I'm not the one who made her that way."

"Maybe she had a bad day that day."

"She didn't treat everyone else rude. Just me."

"Maybe she likes you."

"What the hell?"

"Sometimes girls are mean to boys they like."

"That's asinine."

"Well? It's true. And about today, she didn't even know you were chasing somebody."

"Huh?"

"I said I bet she didn't know you were chasing somebody. Maybe she just thought you always drive like that, and you were too rude to even stop and check on her."

Coal stared at her for a long moment. Finally, it hit him that he had never told Maura about the pursuit, and he looked down. The girl had a point.

He took a big breath. "You really think if I go back and tell her I'm sorry she'll take a ride with us?"

"You can try."

"Yeah, I can try. And she can tell me to go to H-E-double toothpicks again, too."

Cynthia thought about that for a moment, then giggled. "My daddy always says that. Well, I think you'd be the bigger person if you at least try. She could get hypothermia if she doesn't get out of all those wet clothes."

"Yeah, ha ha. I guarantee you won't catch me making *that* suggestion to her. You've been hanging around what's-his-name too long."

The girl realized the joke he had made and frowned. "That's not funny. Lance is nice."

"No. Nice boys take nice girls to the altar and get married to them *after* they have a good job to support them both. They don't jump on them in the back of a van out in Timbuktu."

Cynthia was silent for a moment, and they looked away from each other. She was looking down at her hands, which she had folded in her lap, when she said, "I'm glad you came when you did."

"What?"

"I'm glad you found me and Lance. I didn't want to be there."

A warm feeling came over Coal. "Serious?"

"Serious. He told me I could only prove I loved him by... doing it."

Coal scoffed. "Damn kids. He only proved he *doesn't* love you by using that old line on you."

"Well, thanks. I'm glad you were there."

Coal sighed. "You really think I should go back?"

"I really do. Look at her. She needs a friend."

A *friend!* What that woman needed was a willow switch, just like the ones his daddy used to have him make for use on his own rump roast.

He cranked around and looked at Maura PlentyWounds. She was sitting in the cab of the truck. Just *sitting* there. That truck wasn't going anywhere, and she knew it. Now it was raining, and dark was coming. By the look of the western sky, it was going to rain for a long stretch this time. Maybe the whole night, and surround her with a whole ocean of mud. She couldn't just sleep here. It was going to freeze tonight, sure as Santa's hind end. The rain might even turn to snow before the night was over. That was the Idaho highlands.

Coal grunted, blew a huge sigh out his nose, and avoiding Cynthia's eyes, he threw the truck in reverse and starting going backward through the November mud.

CHAPTER TWENTY-FOUR

Once again, when Coal's truck was just shy of Maura's, he stopped. But this time, he didn't pause, just threw open the door and hopped out. He had to do this fast if he was going to do it at all.

Maura PlentyWounds didn't move from her seat, just stationed herself behind the wheel and with bitter eyes watched him slogging toward her through the mud. He was darn glad he was wearing custom-made boots. Any old store-bought boot was bound to be ruined after a few walks like this.

Starting to get angry that the woman couldn't even get out and meet him halfway, he forced himself to take deep breaths all the way to her side of the cab. *Gotta get some O-2 to the brain.* Otherwise, he was going to come unglued on this stubborn ass of a so-called lady.

He stopped at her window, and she just looked at him. She didn't even have the courtesy to roll down the window. He stood there for a moment longer, staring at her, thinking of all that Cynthia had said. Just as he was about to turn around in disgust and walk back to his truck, he met Maura's eyes. Their gazes held. He stared at her, and she stared back, and just for the briefest of moments the anger he always saw in her eyes was gone. In its place was something more like sadness. Loneliness. He gulped another breath and went to jerk her door open. It was locked.

Now he *was* mad. What was wrong with this woman! He sighed and dropped his arms to his sides. Here she was, sitting in her truck cab staring at him, all but her eyes brown with mud that was starting to crack as it dried, the brim of her hat hanging down forlorn, her hair thick and clotted with mud. And here he was, stuck on the outside, looking in.

Unlike the mud, the woman's eyes were blue. It was a startling realization for Coal, for somehow he had thought because of her Indian blood they would be brown, and he had never been in the right light to see different. But they were blue—bluer than his own, which were more gray than blue. And hers were full of anger, toughness, hatred... and loss. A sense of aloneness that only a bad man can bring to a woman. That was something Coal had seen time and time again as an M.P.

Coal was tired of taking deep breaths. But he took another, and then he slowly walked around to the passenger side of her truck. As he reached for her door handle, he had a vision of her flying across the cab, trying to throw the handle down and lock him out. If she did, so help him, that was it, sad eyes or no sad eyes.

But she didn't. She turned her eyes back to the front, and actually leaned her head back against the seat. He opened the door and climbed in, slamming it solidly, then staying seated as far away from this Medusa as he could.

They sat in silence for ten or fifteen seconds, neither one so much as acknowledging the other. Then they sat for another second. And another. And soon, seconds were turning into half a minute, and the blast of Coal's heart against his eardrums was like the old grandfather clock in his mother's house.

"Miss PlentyWounds, that girl in my cab—Cynthia. She had some boy on top of her in a van when I just caught them. Both fully clothed, however. She tells me she didn't want to be there and thanked me for coming when I did. He told her she had to have... to *do it* with him if she wanted to prove she loved him."

Maura looked down at the steering wheel for a moment as he sat and pondered what in the world had prompted him to tell her that.

"So that's why you went tearing past me like a maniac? To save her from being defiled?" Her voice held a strong hint of sarcasm, but it was softer than any tone she had ever used against him before now.

"Well, no. That was incidental. When I was coming here to take over the sheriff's job, I had to hear on the radio that one of my best friends was dead. Murdered. I've been trying to prove who did it. And half an hour or so ago when I was just getting home and going in to see my mom and my kids, someone took a shot at me."

"Really?" She turned more toward him. "They took a shot at you? You mean to try and kill you?"

"I expect so. I bent over to pet my dog, and the bullet went over my head and through my truck window. A high-powered rifle."

She raised her head in understanding. "They actually shot at me twice," he went on. "I thought the vehicle they were in came up here, but it was the van those two kids were in. Whoever shot at me kept on going into Salmon, I guess."

"So maybe it was fate that made you turn there. And you saved that girl from something she didn't want. The spirits make us do things like that sometimes."

"The spirits?"

"Oh, sorry. You wouldn't understand."

He raised his chin a little, starting to voice the word, "Oh," but instead he said, without planning it, "I didn't mean to splash that mud on you. I didn't see you there until it was too late."

She frowned and nodded. "I know. I was bent down. I didn't know you were coming—at least not so fast." She gave a little laugh, glancing in her rearview mirror. "I look great, don't I? Like I'm wearing a mud pack."

She looked back in the mirror, and suddenly she started to laugh. He sat there watching her, watching the mud crack up all over her face as she laughed, then start to drop off in little pieces as she laughed harder. Suddenly, he found himself laughing too. Like it or not, she really did look funny. Funny, and incredible, all in spite of an eighth of an inch of mud.

"Let's get you out of here and get you warmed up. Get those clothes off you."

She stopped laughing and stared at him, then busted up laughing again, this time so hard that tears started to run down into her mud mask. It took her another minute before she could control her laughter enough to say, "You're a little forward, aren't you, Sheriff?"

He stopped laughing himself long enough to say, "I told Cynthia I wasn't about to say that to you. Sorry. You know what I meant."

"I know what you meant. But I've been needing to laugh for a long time. Almost anything could have set me off."

"I know the feeling. Sometimes everyone needs a good belly laugh."

"And a good heartfelt cry."

He looked at her, and she wouldn't meet his eyes. Her own, those sky blue orbs, shone bright with tears. She was watching the glowering eastern sky.

"I'll bet your truck isn't very warm," she said suddenly. He noticed she was starting to shiver.

"I'm big enough to block the wind. And they have these things called heaters now—invented since after you bought this old dinosaur."

"Hey! My old Ebenezer does just fine for me, thank you very much."

"Ebenezer? Yeah, sure, unless he dumps you in a mud puddle and leaves you in the middle of nowhere."

"I know. But I haven't been to a shop with this old guy in... two or three years, I bet. I don't even know any mechanics here."

"I do," said Coal. "A good one."

"Doesn't matter." She looked down again. "I can't afford to get it fixed anyway."

"Hurting for money?"

"Oh, that's not important," she said, throwing open her door and jumping out into the mud. "Let's go."

They walked side by side to his truck after she pulled a .30/30 Marlin rifle out of the back seat, and a Smith and Wesson .38 special from under her seat. Coal smiled at all the firepower but said nothing when she didn't mention it herself.

Maura stopped at the passenger side of the Chevrolet and looked in. The girl was sitting against the door. Maura then started around to the other side, and Coal's first thought was to stop her. It wasn't going to be comfortable for any of them if she felt forced to sit right next to him. But he couldn't think of a tactful way to tell her just to make Cynthia move over.

They walked around to the driver's side, and she paused, once again looking in. He threw open the door. "Better get in. It's not getting any warmer."

When she had climbed into the middle of the seat, Coal got a canteen out from under the seat, along with a wool blanket and a bandanna. He handed the bandanna to her. "I'm sorry this is a little dirty. It's been kicking around in here for a while. But it would probably be nice to get some of that mud off, especially around your eyes."

She silently agreed, took the bandanna, and while he poured water into it a bit at a time she began washing off her face. It didn't take long for her to start revealing the beautiful woman Coal had first laid his eyes on as she got out of her ambulance the night of his wreck. She was much worse for the wear this afternoon, but, in a rugged way, no less attractive.

When she had finished with her ablution, Coal stuffed the canteen back under the seat. He laid the blanket across her lap, and she hurriedly took it out of his hands to pull it up around her and pretended he had been of no help at all.

He couldn't help hitting her knees with his hand in shifting gears. Somehow, he found he didn't mind.

They had ridden for a while in silence before Maura seemed to become comfortable enough to talk to the girl. It was as if she had needed the truck's heater to warm her throat back up. "Hi! I know you."

"Hi. Yes, I'm Cynthia."

"Yes. Batterton, right?"

It was a good thing Coal wasn't chewing any gum—or even a turkey leg. Either one, he would have swallowed whole. He almost drove them off the road before swerving back into his lane.

"Batterton?" He looked at Cynthia incredulously.

The girl looked a little sick, like she had earlier. "Yes."

"K.T.'s your dad?"

"Yes."

"Why didn't you say something?"

"I was hoping it would go away."

Maura laughed. "Oh, Cynthia. They're good people."

Cynthia sat there for a long time, and Coal, even being one of those two-legged beings struck with the serious handicap of being male, realized that Cynthia was crying. Silently.

"Hey, it's okay," soothed Maura. She turned and wrapped her arms around Cynthia, pulling her close and patting her shoulder. "Come on. What's wrong?"

"Nothing."

"Was it something I said?"

"I guess, kind of."

"What?"

"About them being good people."

"They seem like great folks to me, Cynthia."

"That's just it. They are. And they have me for a daughter."

"Oh, hey. Don't say that. You're a great girl. I can tell!"

"She's right, Cynthia," cut in Coal, taking a chance by jumping into a woman's conversation, where no intelligent man's feet should ever trod—which perhaps was why it was okay for *him* to do so, he mused. "It doesn't take me very long to read people. I can tell you're a good girl. Hey, everybody makes mistakes. I could write you a book about it."

He cringed inside. Every time he or anyone else talked of mistakes, he thought about Laura. He thought about seeing her that last time, seeing the sheet pulled up over her face, knowing he would never again see that beautiful countenance the way it should have looked. It had changed forever that day, and all second chances had been stolen from him.

The cab was silent for a few minutes. They finally got to the place where Maura had told Coal to go, just off the main road, and he pulled up in front and watched two cow dogs—blue heelers—come running out to chase them off. The residence was a run-down trailer house, little to speak of for people to live in—but with great quarters for horses surrounding it. A lot of horse people lived that way, Coal knew—forsaking their own comforts to have a great horse property. He had once thought of doing it himself. Then came to his senses.

"Your dogs gonna eat me when I get out?"

She laughed and hollered out the window: "Chewy! Dart!" Then looked back at him. "You should be okay now."

Coal got out among the clamoring heelers so Maura could descend from the truck. His mother had taught him to help a lady out of a vehicle, but gut instinct told him not to offer a hand to this one. Instead, he took her rifle and pistol and held them as she got out, then started toward the door with her. Even that was too much.

"I can carry my own guns," she said, her voice a little tart.

"Oh. Sorry." He handed them to her.

Her voice was softer when she said, "I just don't need anybody's help."

When she had climbed a set of rickety, water-soaked steps to the front door, flanked all the way by Chewy and Dart, Coal could tell she was embarrassed. She had to turn around and find a place to lean the firearms so she could look for her key. He almost offered to hold them, then changed his mind. She had set those rules herself.

All of a sudden, she swore. She went from feeling one pocket, to the other, then the back pockets. At last, she almost frantically patted down the pockets of her green coat. Then she swore again.

"You don't hear me cussing around you," Coal said softly.

"What?" She looked up at him, confused.

"I said you don't hear me cussing around you."

"Oh wow, so you're Mr. Perfect!" Instantly after she spoke, her face softened. She sighed, obviously flustered. "I'm sorry. I forgot myself." She laughed, not a light-hearted sound. "This time I really am."

"It's all right. I'm just not used to hearing a lady cuss."

"Maybe I'm not a lady."

To that, Coal just gave a one-shoulder shrug. This was one time he knew not to reply.

"Well, thank you for bringing me home," Maura said.

"You're welcome. You going in?"

"Um... No, I need to feed the horses first."

Coal looked at her. No sane woman would go out to the horses as mud-soaked as she was, without at least trying to get something dry on first. She didn't meet his eyes. "You left your keys in the truck, didn't you?"

Maura laughed, again not a sound of joviality. "I think so."

"Do you have a spare?"

"No."

"You live alone?"

"Tonight I do. My boys are with their father."

"Close by?"

"No. In Mud Lake."

"Oh, great. How do we get you in? It'll be dark in an hour."

"I'll be all right."

"Not all wet like that, you won't be. Maura?"

"What?" she almost snapped at him.

"Easy does it, all right? Let me say something. I know you—or at least your type. You won't take charity. You won't take help from anybody. I know somebody else like that. That's why I understand. So listen—you either come with me easy, let me help you out. Or I'll go get my mom and bring her back. And believe me, she doesn't take no for an answer. Come on. Mom's about your size. We can get you some clean clothes. Then tomorrow we'll go get your truck and your keys and get a spare made for you. Mom's house is big enough for an army. What do you say?"

"I have to feed the horses."

"Fine. Cynthia and I will help you."

"I need to stay here." Her voice was firm, and her words were final. "Thanks anyway."

"Where are you going to sleep, under the deck? Some skunk will come along and change your perfume for you."

"I don't wear any perfume."

"Well, I guess you'll start."

"Just... go. I have things to do here that won't wait."

"Yeah, right. Like counting flowers on the wall, and watching Captain Kangaroo. I know." He was using a 1969 Statler Brothers hit as the basis for his dumb joke, but she didn't seem to get it.

"Go on," said Maura tersely. "You need to get Cynthia home to her parents."

"Okay. I'll be back in half an hour with Mom."

Maura laughed. A real laugh that made her eye corners crinkle and Coal's heart drop on the ground. "Men are such asses."

"Umm... Yep." He thought better of the comeback that came to mind for that one.

CHAPTER TWENTY-FIVE

Coal stopped the pickup down the street from the Batterton residence, on Hope Street. "This is still you, right?" He leaned forward so he could see past Maura.

Cynthia gave him an uneasy smile, and her voice was hesitant. "Yeah. We'll never move."

"Okay. Thanks for the fun afternoon."

It looked like the girl wanted to laugh but didn't dare, or didn't know if he was joking. "Why are you stopped back here? You're coming in with me, right? To see my dad?"

Coal studied the girl's face for a minute. She sure was a cute thing, and he could see why Lance was attracted to her. On top of that, she came across as a real lady, albeit a real *young* lady. "Hop out for a minute, Cynthia." He climbed out his side and met her on the outside of her door, putting one hand up against the truck, beside her head. "Cynthia, you seem like a sweet girl. Were you serious when you told me you were glad I stopped you today?"

She nodded and in a shy voice said, "Yeah."

"I've got a daughter just younger than you. She's had a rough time. Got into some bad stuff back in Virginia—which is one of the reasons I was so glad to get this opportunity to come back here. If you were my daughter, I would want someone to come and talk to me. I'll tell you that flat-out. But I don't think you're to that point. Do you?"

"The point of you talkin' to my dad?"

"Yeah."

"I'd rather you didn't."

"Then can we make a deal?"

"Sure, I guess."

"Cynthia, you know where I work. You know how to find me. We have a secret between us, right? You and me and Maura. If you feel like you're going to get in trouble—no matter what it is—you call me, okay?"

Tears came into the young woman's eyes. "Really?"

"Yeah, really. That's what I'm here for."

With a surge of emotion, Cynthia stepped forward and gave him a huge hug. He patted her back. "All right, now you get home. And don't worry about what happened today. I think someone was watching over you. You and me both."

"Okay, thanks, Mr. Savage. Thank you so much." He was looking in her eyes as she spoke the words, and he had no doubt of her sincerity.

The girl started to turn to her house, then turned back. "Can I say goodbye to Maura?"

He gave her a big smile. "I'm sure she'd feel bad if you didn't."

She turned and opened the door again. "Bye, ma'am. I'm glad I got to meet you."

Maura looked at her, her eyes warm. "Really?"

"Oh, yeah. You're real nice."

"Thank you, Cynthia. So are you. I'll bet Mr. Savage doesn't think that about me."

Cynthia gave a shy laugh. "But I bet he will. See you around, okay?"

"Sure. And if you ever need to talk to a woman about any-thing—besides your mom, I mean—you can get hold of me, right? You know where I live."

"Okay, thank you. Bye." With that, Cynthia turned, gave Coal one more look of pure gratitude, then turned, and he watched her run all the way back to her house.

For some time, he stood there, making sure she was safely inside. And thinking. A glow of happiness had come over him, had filled his chest to bursting. This was how a father should feel after helping his daughter with some big life problem. Instead, whenever he interacted with Katie Leigh, he was left feeling either cold and empty, or angry as hell. Why couldn't they talk? Why couldn't they be a real family? What would Cynthia think if she knew how he really was? It seemed so easy to get along with other people, and with other people's kids.

But as the saying went, *You always hurt the ones you love.* Seemed like there was a song that went like that.

With a suddenly heavy heart, he turned again and walked around the front of the truck, feeling Maura's eyes on him. He climbed in and slammed the door, and the metallic sound rang throughout the cab. He let out a long sigh, leaning his head back. In a moment, he became aware that Maura still sat in the center of the bench seat, and he glanced over at her. She was watching him, her cool, mysterious eyes gazing into his being. Or so it seemed.

He looked down at her leg, which was touching his, and it must have broken some kind of spell in her. She gasped. "Oh, sorry!" and scooted quickly over to the door. Now she seemed to hug up against it extra tight, like someone on a blind date gone awry.

He just looked at her, finding himself wishing she had not moved away so far. He was trying to think of something cute to say, but he couldn't. In utter silence, he pressed down the clutch, shifted into second gear, and drove back to Main, turning east, the direction from which they had originally come.

Neither of them spoke all the way there, but by the way Coal kept seeing Maura's face turn toward him, more frequently the farther they went, he knew she needed to say something. Finally, just short of his mother's driveway, he eased the truck to a stop on the muddy road. His hand still on the shifter knob, he turned his eyes and met Maura's. He hated himself for thinking she was so gorgeous, but no red-blooded man could have missed that fact. He had to remind himself how rude she had been to him, ever since their first meeting.

"What will Connie think of me for coming here? Sorry, I mean your mother."

He smiled, feeling his heart pound and hating that too. "It's okay, I knew who Connie was."

"Stop it! Seriously, what is she going to think? Why don't we just try to get a locksmith to get me in my own house? Or is it too late to go back to the truck?"

Coal's heart kept thudding heavily. Why didn't they go to a locksmith, she asked? Because it was hard to think rationally when Maura was close to him. But of course that was an admission no steam roller could squeeze out of him. And if Coal was completely honest with himself, it was suddenly very nice to think of having a woman like Maura at the house, if just for the night.

"Just don't worry about it. You met my mom. I could tell she liked you instantly."

"Mr. Savage, liking someone and letting them sleep in your house the second time you lay eyes on them are two completely different things."

"I used to bring home every stray in the valley," he said, proving the reality that not only could he not think rationally around this woman, but that he apparently couldn't think at all.

"Stray? Is that what I am, a stray?"

Frozen, he stared at her, trying to keep it cool. "A stray is something that isn't at its own home, right?"

It took a moment, but then she laughed again. "Yes, I suppose. So I'm a stray. It wouldn't be the first time."

"All right, stray, come on." He was happy to have dodged another bullet.

He started to put the truck back in gear when he heard a husky, "Hey." Turning, he couldn't help but notice her hand, partway across the vinyl seat, sitting there like a symbol of truce between his leg and hers. The heater was blowing out very warm, hypnotizing air, and the motor purred at their feet.

"That was pretty nice how you handled that little girl."

"Cynthia? You really think it was okay not to talk to her folks?"

"I think you did the best thing you could possibly have done. You made yourself a friend for life... Sheriff. I guess maybe you're not such a bad guy after all."

"I wish somebody would tell my daughter that," he said, perhaps too quickly. He had to say something to cover up the way this woman was making him feel. He had no right to even think of a woman, not after what happened with Laura.

"Let's don't go in yet."

Maura PlentyWounds's words were soft, made even softer because she was facing her window. For a moment, he wasn't even sure he had heard her right.

"Okay." He eased the stick back to neutral. Then he just sat. His heart kept pounding. Way back in his memory he recalled feeling like this with Laura. Women could make men feel like such fools.

A long string of seconds dragged by. Coal stared out the windshield. Now and then he stole a look toward her, but she was still looking out her window. Finally, from the corner of his eye, he saw her hand come up to her face. Wiping tears away? At last, she turned to him, and she scooted slightly closer on the seat.

"I don't know what's up with you and Katie. It's none of my business."

He looked down at her hand, still on the seat.

"Okay."

"But, Sheriff, I'm not really good for much. Not much at all. Except maybe cooking. And roping," she said, and laughed. "Okay, and I can use a mean black snake bull whip. And shoot the head off a match with a .22." She gave another laugh, then said a bit ruefully, "All the things a man really wants out of a woman."

"Cooking's good," he said.

She caught him smiling after he said it, and she giggled. "Okay, one good thing. But I want you to know something. If you ever want a wife, or a girlfriend, or even a date, you'd probably better look somewhere else. I'm beat down and worthless, and I'll never be a mate to a man again—not in any way, shape or form. But I'm a darn good listener, and I have boys of my own. Not girls—but it wasn't all that long ago, believe it or not, when I was one of those myself. And I think I kinda remember what makes their head go around. I'm pretty much good for nothing but listening, but I'll put my ears up to anyone's when it comes to that. Not that you want to talk. I'm just sayin' if ever."

He looked up and met her eyes, those incredible eyes, and somehow he found a smile. "I'll keep that in mind. Thanks for the offer."

"Okay." She gave a solid nod. "You're gonna freeze."

With a little smile, he threw the truck in gear and pulled on into the yard, knocking off the light before he got up to the concrete pad. Maura leaned forward and surveyed the house. "Wow, nice place."

"Thanks. Dad and I built it. With a tiny bit of help from a couple of brothers who just keep taking up breathing air in the world." He couldn't help a touch of bitterness to his tone and immediately regretted bringing them up.

"Okay. We won't talk about them then," the woman said with a teasing sound of concern in her voice. "Anyway, it's pretty. Just my kind of place. Nice car, too." She gave a sideways motion of her head toward the Chrysler.

"Yeah, Mom doesn't have cheap tastes. My daddy didn't either."

He caught her looking at him, and the look was a nice one, but she didn't say anything.

"Well, let's get inside. Looks like it could rain again any time. Or snow. I'll get you settled, and then I'd better get a tarp over this window. It's going to be cold enough in the morning without having to ride to work in a puddle."

The dogs had started barking, but Connie must have stopped them. Thanks to the gloomy afternoon, which was fast turning to evening, there were lights glowing in the house. He saw the curtain on the door part slightly, then close again. If it was his mom, she didn't come out.

He told Maura to go ahead of him, not just because it improved his view but because he was trying to be at least a little bit of a gentleman, then opened the door cautiously when they were both up together on the porch. With a last look and a grin at the mud that was still caked all over her hat and clothes, he stepped inside. The dogs were nowhere to be seen.

"Mom?"

"Yes, Son," came the reply from down the hall.

"We have company."

"Yes, I saw that. I'll be right in."

Coal was happy to see someone had picked up his hat out of the yard and hung it on its usual hook. He looked at Maura's. "You ready to dump that thing? That's pretty nasty."

"Yeah, I know. I had a run-in with Mario Andretti, remember?" With a teasingly accusing smile, she peeled off the hat, letting her long, mud-clotted hair fall loose around her face.

He took the hat from her, giving it a dubious glare, then hung it on a hook two rows down from his on the hat rack. He wasn't about to let that filthy thing contaminate his nearly white Stetson.

"Coat?" He looked down at it, then laughed. "Um, maybe we better step back outside before we try to take that off. I'm not in the mood for sweeping up mud."

They stepped out, and she took off the coat and shook it. Then they came back in, and Connie was standing there five feet away.

"Oh, my word! It's Maura. How nice to see you again!" In the dim light, she suddenly sensed, perhaps more than saw, that all was not right, and she gave the blond woman a look up and down. "Oh my word is right! What in the world happened to you?"

"It's a long story, Mom."

Connie's eyes flashed at her son, and there was a look of warning in them. "I guess it must be."

"The short part is, Miss PlentyWounds broke down on the road, and I gave her a ride home, but she left her keys in the ignition. I told her maybe you could loan her some clothes and we could let her clean up. And maybe stay in Virg's room for the night, and he can move in with the twins."

"Oh! Well that would be perfectly fine. Glad to have her. Maybe we can get Maura—or do you prefer Miss Plenty-Wounds?" She looked quickly at the woman.

"No, Maura is wonderful, thanks."

"All right. Maybe we can get Maura on her way to cleaning up, and get her some fresh clothes, and then perhaps you and I can have a little talk."

Coal swallowed and sighed. "All right, Mom." Immediately seeing the coming storm, he said, "I'm sorry I couldn't reach you sooner. I know you were worried. I'll start taking a rig with a radio in it."

Her face tried to remain stern, but he saw softness come over it, and moistness come into her eyes. "We'll talk about that when Maura's in a hot bath, Son."

*   *   *

The house seemed almost deathly still as the water in the bathtub ran, getting softer and softer sounding as the depth increased. Behind the bathroom door, Maura, like the house, was also deathly still. She must have been struggling not to make a noise, because Coal never even heard the sound of her boots hitting the floor.

"The children are at Margie's, Coal," Connie said after making him sit down on the cowhide sofa across from her La-Z-Boy recliner. She leaned closer to him, her elbows on her knees and her fingers laced together.

"Why?"

"Well, why do you think?"

He shrugged.

"Someone took two rifle shots at their father, Coal. Then their father ran off and left them in a state of panic, with no backup and without even a radio to call for help. I called the dispatcher, and they couldn't even find Todd Mitchell for fifteen minutes. He drove up and down the highway looking for you without one sign and finally came up here to apologize. He left just twenty minutes before you pulled up. And as soon as we're done here I think you'd better be calling your dispatcher, who's worried sick about you. And call Jim and K.T. as well. They've been killing themselves looking for you. And we'd better call the kids, too—or at least *you* had better."

Coal thought of K.T. and cringed. He was so glad his old friend hadn't found him when Cynthia was in his truck. There would have been no way out of telling him what happened then. He immediately chided himself: Once more, he was thinking of someone else ahead of his own family.

His boys must be sick with worry. That made him feel awful. As for Katie, he had no way to know anymore. He had no clue if she cared whether he lived or died. The way she treated him, he could take an educated guess.

"Anyway, the kids are waiting at Margie's. Honestly, I didn't want them to be here in case one of the men came back with the wrong news. I figured if that were the case I had better go tell them myself."

Coal nodded, put to silence and shame. Finally, he took a deep breath. "Mom, I wish I had had a way to get hold of you. Everything happened so fast."

"It's okay, Son." She spoke the words, and then tears came to her eyes. "I just couldn't stop thinking about losing your father." A tight throat made her voice sound broken. "I can't lose you too."

Coal got up, and she met him partway across the floor. He hugged her so tight he thought she might have to stomp on his foot. He whispered into her silver hair, "I'm sorry, Mom. I really am sorry I put you through that."

"I'm all right. I'm just worried about the kids. Maybe you should go get them."

"Me?"

She wiped hurriedly at her nose with the back of her hand. "Well, yes, you! Coal, they're your kids."

"Yeah, but I don't know what to say to them about something like this."

"Then it's high time you started learning. I'm not going to be around forever, you know. And if their own father can't even face them, then who can? Shame on you."

"You could at least come with me. What about Katie?"

"Now just what about her?"

"She would rather see me dead than alive. Can you imagine what's going to happen if I come to get her?"

"I wish you were small enough to take a switch to you." Connie's eyes flashed. "I'm not kidding, either. That is your daughter, Coal Garrett. Maybe if you had been acting like her father all along you wouldn't be in all this mess."

"I was working. Somebody had to earn a living." As he spoke those words, he couldn't keep eye contact with her.

"My keys are on the counter over there. I am *not* going to leave Maura alone here in a strange house. You know where Margie lives, now you get over there before I lose my temper. You're acting like you're no older than Katie."

Coal's jaw hardened, and he looked over at the keys. Finally, without a word, he walked over and picked them up. With a feeling of fatality, he went to the hat rack, put his hat on, and without another look at his mother he said, "Where are the dogs?"

After a pause, she replied, "I put them in the bedroom to keep them quiet so we could talk."

He went down the hall and opened the door, letting Dobe and Shadow out. He was taking the Doberman with him, refusing to go after Katie without some kind of distraction.

As for Shadow, he didn't want to make her feel bad, but she was getting very feeble, and he knew it would be hard for her to get in and out of the Chrysler. Besides, like most German shepherds she shed like a hail storm, and the Chrysler was just too nice. Telling the shepherd to sit and stay, and trying to ignore the disappointed, desperate look in her drooping eyes, he opened the door and called Dobe to his side, then stepped without a word into the night. The Doberman ran straight to the Chrysler and stood there jiggling his stub of a tail, looking back at him anxiously with his sharp ears pricked forward.

Coal stood on the porch for what seemed like five minutes, breathing in the crisp night air, before turning back around and easing open the front door and leaning in. Connie was still standing there. Her son was a lawman, no different than those of the wild Old West. She never knew, and he never knew, when would be the last time she would see him alive.

"Thanks, Mom. I love you."

Having said those words to Connie, when he shut the door again and turned to go to the Chrysler, it was good to feel like maybe he wasn't such a lost cause after all. With his life obviously on the line every bit as much as it had been at Long Binh Jail or in Washington, D.C., it was time he started telling his loved ones how he felt about them. But he had a long road ahead of him with Katie.

CHAPTER TWENTY-SIX

Margie and Wilber Rawson lived a little up the way, after the turn onto Lemhi Road, in a peaceful, green, little swell in the foothills. Trying to let Glen Campbell singing "Gentle On My Mind" on the radio calm his thoughts, Coal cut the lights and came in in the gathering darkness, feeling much like he was back in D.C. again, going in to serve a warrant in the still of the gloaming.

It was only perhaps six o'clock or so, but with the heavy black cloud cover it seemed much later. As the last notes of the song finally ended, he turned off the engine, got out of the car and gently pushed the door shut, then stood there staring at the house. His heart was ramming his rib cage, but it was not the kind of heartbeat he had felt around Maura. He hated to use the word on himself, as he had always thought himself a pretty courageous person—the first to get on a bad horse or bull, the first to go after a wounded bear, the one to pick the biggest bruiser in a fight—but the only word that fit how he was feeling now was scared. How were his children going to treat him? Especially Katie Leigh? And how would it look in front of Margie and Wilber?

Damn the torpedoes. Full speed ahead.

With a lung-filling breath, he walked up the sidewalk, onto the little concrete stoop in front of the humble white residence, and rapped on the door. A wrinkle-faced lady, short in stature with a haircut not much longer than his own, peeked out the door glass. A look of relief pushed the initial one of concern from her face, and she flung the door open.

"Coal Savage! It's very good to see you, young man."

"Hi, Margie. Good to see you too."

He couldn't say one more word, because out of the four pairs of eyes he had been aware of watching him, two of their owners rushed forward, yelling, "Daddy!" and threw their stubby arms around him in an embrace of love and relief.

"Hey, guys," he responded. He made them let go of him, then crouched down and gave them a real hug. He hadn't had a whole lot of time to think about it in the earlier excitement, but the one time he had, he honestly wondered if they would ever see him alive again.

"Hi, Dad," he heard Virgil say as he came up. The thirteen-year-old stood there awkwardly until Coal could untangle himself from Wyatt and Morgan and stand up. To Coal's surprise, in front of Margie and all, his big boy threw his arms around him and buried his face in the top of his chest. It was a feeling he hadn't had in... Coal was stunned. He realized he could not even remember the last time he and his big son had shared an embrace. It apparently took nearly losing his life to elicit one now.

Coal opened his eyes and looked across the top of Virgil's head to see Katie Leigh, her nose and around her eyes horribly purple from the accident, giving her otherwise strikingly beautiful face a distinctive raccoon-like flair. She was standing on the far side of the front room, her arms folded tight across her chest. Her eyes were on him, but he had no time to decide what kind of expression was in them. She realized he had looked up at her, and she skipped her eyes away from him.

There would be no embrace of happiness from his Katie Leigh. Coal's heart fell, but he would have been shocked if it had been different.

As they drove the eighth of a mile back down the road to home, Coal felt a sense of relief. Although Katie hadn't hugged him, hadn't even so much as said hello, at least she didn't look mad. And she was quiet, but it was not the kind of quiet he had felt with her in recent months—the type of quiet a man spends waiting for a bomb to go off, feeling the hatred from another person being in the room who would just as soon he were dead.

They pulled up at the house, and the twins squealed in delight to see a big, fat skunk with hair that seemed extra-long go waddling across the driveway and around the corner. Coal spoke softly to the trembling Doberman to keep him still. He remembered many evenings and nights in his younger days spent with a pillow over his face after some wayward polecat decided to gift the whole house through its inopportunely open windows with an aromatic spritz of potpourri, and because of that he felt none of the delight the twins expressed. But under the circumstances, he wouldn't let them know his negative thoughts on their salt and pepper visitor. They would learn the lesson soon enough. After the afternoon these little guys must have just passed, wondering if they were about to lose another parent, it was just good to see them happy and excited about something.

Coal wanted to get out and at least open the door for Katie, but she did that herself as soon as he threw it in park. She walked briskly past him and climbed the steps. She pushed inside the house before he and the boys even had their doors shut.

"Why's Katie so mad, Daddy?"

Coal looked down at Morgan. "I don't know, Son. I think she thinks I hurt your mom. You know I didn't, right?"

"I know, Daddy."

Coal looked over quickly at Virgil, who was watching them. These innocent little guys knew, but where did his older boy and his opinions sit? Virgil had always been quiet, but since Laura's death he was excruciatingly so. He was always polite, always courteous, but he never smiled anymore. And he never shared his thoughts. Then again, neither did Coal. They had both trapped their demons inside, seized them in a cage with a lock that had no key. Coal reached down and patted the solid, muscular side of his dog. At least he had two loyal friends, Dobe and Shadow.

When Coal entered the room, he and the boys interrupted what seemed to be a friendly conversation between Katie Leigh and Maura, her one-time caregiver. As soon as Coal came in, Katie's attitude changed, and she fled down the hall to her room. She didn't tell anyone so much as good night.

Coal was left standing there with Maura—standing stunned. The woman was dressed in one of his mom's blue and white plaid shirts and a pair of tight-fitting Levi's 501 jeans. Her feet were bare. In the low light of the room, her eyes looked deeper blue than before, and her yellow hair tumbled down and settled in tangled tresses against the blue and white squares of the shirt.

Even as he looked at the woman, she averted her eyes and raised a towel, with which she started caressing her hair, drying it from the roots out. Coal shouldn't have stared, but he did. He considered himself somewhat of an artist, so beauty had a way of calling to him. Sunsets, horses, sleek dogs, even an intricately engraved firearm. All had their special kind of grace and charm. But nothing was more heart-wrenching than a truly beautiful woman.

And Maura PlentyWounds was nothing if not that—a truly beautiful woman.

Her glossy hair cascaded to each side from a slight widow's peak to where her breasts mounded out the soft cotton of the shirt. Her mouth was full, her lips soft pink, her nose distinguished, her eyes as perfectly shaped as if painted by a master—large, yet not overpoweringly so. Even her face was sculpted, her cheeks full and her jawline finely curved inward. The one thing about her that might have been considered imperfect was a beauty spot of a mole just above the left corner of her lips, but as if by some magic, it made her seem even more alluring than she would otherwise have been.

Coal wanted to tell her how incredible she looked, but he couldn't. And besides, no woman who looked like that could possibly need to be told. So he forced his eyes to turn away from her and almost stumbled to the kitchen. *I'm sorry, Laura. I didn't mean to look at her like that.* And he sure didn't mean for his heart to beat this way. But Laura wasn't around to care anymore—if she ever had.

Half an hour later, Coal sipped hot chocolate. He didn't care if it kept him up all night. Most likely, his thoughts would anyway. The window of the Chevy was covered now. The kids were home. He had called the dispatcher and everyone else who had been out looking for him, to let them all know he was alive and well. There was nothing left that he needed to do.

Maura PlentyWounds sat wrapped in a blanket but still shivering. She had taken a seat on the black and white spotted cowhide sofa, so he stole his mother's brown fabric La-Z-Boy. Even if he had presumed to sit on the same sofa as the woman, he sure wasn't going to with his sons in the room.

Connie tried to make light conversation with Maura. Coal brooded. He thought first of his children—which might be a step in the right direction in his role as father—but soon had his mind drawn away by the afternoon's events. It was fine to play father, but someone had tried to kill him today. He could not forget that. No amount of pushing it aside and pretending everything was okay was going to make it so these kids could keep their father. He had to take down his enemy. Neutralize the threat. Take out the target. He had to be a soldier—and a soldier had no time to worry about a family. He had a job to do before he could enjoy having a family. Until that job was done, he had to put his heart on hold.

Maura, whenever Coal looked her way and made eye contact, seemed to have sunk back to her previous attitude toward him. Why? Had he said or done something wrong? She looked at him as if he were no better than a common thug. All tenderness, imagined or otherwise, seemed gone from her eyes, although she remained friendly and engaging with Connie, in spite of appearing to be overly chilled.

Whatever. She was a woman. No one could change that, and no one, not even God, could figure women out. Ever since Eve, it was a subspecies of absolute inscrutability.

Coal's mind drifted to tomorrow. What did he have to do? Who did he have to see? First off, he had to contact Bigfoot Monahan's parole officer. Second, he had to find out what kind of vehicle Bigfoot drove, and what color. He had no exact description of the getaway vehicle from the afternoon's shooting, only that it seemed large and darker in color. It was too far past when he saw it to get a good description of it.

While waiting for the p.o., he needed to find out where Bigfoot was working, talk to his co-workers and see if any of them had heard him make any statements that might be incriminating. If the man was working at all, that is. He had only been out a short time, and maybe he had no prospects for work whatsoever.

He needed to do some shuttling, get the Chevy in to the body shop and get Maura's truck towed to the mechanic. Ken Parks, an old buddy who had been two years behind him in school but had followed him around on the high school rodeo trail, was a good man, and an excellent mechanic. He could get the International running again—that is, if Maura even wanted his help tomorrow.

He also needed to have Todd Mitchell pick him up so he could commandeer the sheriff's LTD and from henceforth have a radio in his possession. He could not get caught in the toolies again with no backup and no communication with dispatch. There were plenty of times he didn't want dispatch to have any way of contacting him so he could be left in peace. But now, with the threat of death hovering over him, was not the time to be a loner.

Connie's voice of excitement suddenly cut in on Coal's thoughts. "Say, would you two like some cookies? I'll bet the kids would."

Maura paused for too long, and Connie was great at reading beneath hefty pauses. "Oh, I don't think I need any. They'd probably keep me awake all night."

"Nonsense!" Connie said, standing up. "Coal?"

He chuckled, "Mom, you know I have a weakness for your cookies, but it's sort of late, isn't it? That is, if you're talking about homemade cookies."

"What? Of course, homemade! I may buy some Almond Crescents once in a while, or those Keebler's sandwich cookies, but only out of sheer desperation. I can't believe you would think I've sunk low enough to offer store-bought cookies to company."

Coal's mother made him laugh. "Okay, Mom. I guess I've already had a cup of cocoa. Might as well send some cookies swimming in it, right?"

Connie went down the hall to Katie's room, and Coal heard her tap quietly on the door, and then Katie's muffled reply. She went inside and was gone for several minutes, then came back out and without a word went up to see the boys.

She came back down with a glowing smile. "Coal, the boys are getting in their p.j.'s and coming down to be part of the cookie making. And Wyatt is hoping you'll get out your guitar and play for us."

Coal frowned and squirmed in his chair. "Mom, I think the cold is getting my voice. I'd rather do it some other time."

"Oh, Coal—your voice sounds fine. How long has it been since you played and sang?"

"Since last time I was here, probably. Laura wasn't that into it."

His mother shook her head. "I never understood that. She seemed to like it when you were dating."

"Yeah, women seem to like a lot of things when they're dating, and trying to hook some poor guy."

"Coal! You should be ashamed of yourself. At least be a little upbeat when we have company in the house, will you?"

Coal felt heat rise under his collar and looked over at Maura. Predictably, she looked away.

"Well, you should think about playing and singing. Those boys aren't going to keep asking forever, you know."

Coal sank back in his chair. A part of him wanted to sing. But he was tired of putting himself out there in front of new people, taking a chance on whether they would care about his music or not. And besides, he had already taken a stand against it. It would be awkward to pick up the guitar now. He would feel like he lost a fight. And he was tired of losing fights with women, even if this one was his mom.

"Can I see your guitar?"

Surprised, Coal looked over at Maura. "You play?"

She laughed. "Well, a little. Not that great. But I love the feel of guitars."

"I'll go get it."

Coal got up and went upstairs. His room was quiet, and seemed somehow extra cold, and sparse. He wanted to get a bison robe and put it on his bed. For some reason that seemed like it would give the room a warm feeling, where now it was... austere.

From the far corner near the head of the bed, he pulled out his guitar and packed it downstairs. As he got it into better light, he saw that the case was filthy, and he apologized. "I guess that's what happens after a couple years of collecting dust."

"I'm used to dust," said Maura, as she watched him snap open the case. With loving, if unfamiliar, fingers, he pulled out the guitar and gave it a fond look before passing it to Maura.

"Gibson! Nice." The woman sat and stroked the wood for a moment. It was a tobacco sunburst pattern, with f holes, a little banged up from use, including years in elk and deer camps. But still beautiful. Still magical, in the right hands.

The boys came down in their pajamas, and Morgan ran into the kitchen. His tiny bare feet slapping on the dark walnut floor gave the house a suddenly homey feel. Virgil followed him, but Wyatt came over and stood by his dad, resting his hand on his shoulder. When Coal looked up, the boy was smiling at him, and the smile grew to its full limit. What a kid, thought Coal.

"Are you going to play a song?" Wyatt asked Maura.

"I don't know. What if I don't know any songs?"

"Daddy knows four hundred!" said the boy, beaming.

"What?" She looked at him doubtfully. "Four hundred? Really?" She turned her eyes to Coal, who shrugged.

"Last count."

"Wow. I'm impressed." She had a warm, glowing look on her face. But it was directed at Wyatt.

"Sing one," Wyatt said. In his innocence, he didn't believe she could possibly not know a single song.

"Okay, I will."

Maura started playing. Nothing fancy, just a key of D, three-quarter time. But nice, and without flaw. Two notes into the song, Coal recognized it. "Leaving On a Jet Plane." John Denver, *Rhymes and Reasons* album, 1969. Denver's debut. But who was keeping track?

It quickly became apparent to Coal that Maura was modest about her musical ability. Her voice was enchanting, a little husky, very on key, very alluring. Somehow, he wasn't surprised. He was inclined to sing along, but he didn't.

Wyatt did, however. They had sung this same song many times on the way out from Virginia.

When she was finished, Wyatt put his hands together and clapped loudly, and everyone else joined in. Even Connie put down her mixing spoon to applaud the newcomer.

"Very good, Maura! I am duly impressed."

"Thank you. I don't know four hundred, though."

Connie shook her head. "Oh, who does? But when Coal was growing up here there was nothing to do in the winter but drink and carouse or play the guitar and sing. We were fortunate that Coal chose to sing. His brothers drank enough for all three of them!"

"Hey, Mom, I'm sure she doesn't want to hear about our family. Especially those two."

"Fine. If someone were singing, I wouldn't be able to talk!"

Raising an eyebrow, Maura held the guitar toward Coal, who quickly shook his head, sinking back in the chair. "No, you do some more. Anything by J.D. these boys can probably sing along with."

So Maura, with a little coaxing, sang "Rhymes and Reasons" and "Country Roads." And then, in an act of sheer determination and woman's will, she got up and walked across the space between her and Coal, handing him the guitar.

"Now sing a song for your boys. You don't get a request like that every day." The look in her eyes told Coal there was going to be hell to pay if he didn't, and the boys and Connie would have joined right in.

With a sigh, Coal picked up the guitar, fiddled with the keys for a moment while he made sure it was tuned, and then started playing. Like riding a bicycle, it came back to him fast. He started singing, "On the Chisholm Trail, it was midnight..." and Maura cheered.

"Ooh, Billy Walker!"

Coal smiled, and Wyatt piped up, "'Cross the Brazos at Waco'!"

And Coal played and sang, and his heart, for a little while, felt good again.

Tuesday, November 21

Coal was not a skittish person by habit, but he jumped when the phone rang. He was lying on the couch, covered in wool blankets, and for a moment he stared around him disconcertedly. Finally, he threw off the blankets and rolled up off the couch, grabbing the phone from the coffee table on its fourth ring.

"Savages."

The voice on the other end was scratchy. *Coal?*

"Sure. Who's this?" His head was still swimming from lack of sleep and too much sugar the night before.

K.T.

"Hey. What time is it?"

Six-thirty. You need an alarm clock. Coal, I've got some bad news. It seems like you need a radio in your house, too.

Coal's head started ringing. "Why? What's up?"

We got an early morning fire call. Coal, Trent Tuckett's house went up in smoke. It was gone before the pumper could get there.

"No!" Coal exclaimed. "What about Trent?" He suddenly knew he didn't want the answer.

He's dead, Coal. He was lying just off his front porch when they found him.

Coal was silent, and shock rammed through his body. Trent Tuckett. The name was bouncing around in his head, but it didn't seem real. Coal, Larry, Trent, K.T. They had all made it through twenty-four years of hard living since graduation, and now, within one week, two of them were dead. And Coal had missed death only by a narrow margin. Coal couldn't help thinking that it was the same four friends, along with Jim Lockwood, who had been responsible for the arrest and incarceration of Bigfoot Monahan, back in '67.

Numb, Coal asked, "Where you at, K.T.?"

At the Pearsons', came the reply. *Next door to Trent's.*

"I'll be right there. Hey—K.T.?"

Yeah, boss?

Coal was feeling a sickness come into his stomach. "Did Trent die from the smoke?"

No, Coal. Gunshot to the chest.

For a long moment, Coal couldn't speak.

Boss?

"Yeah, I'm here. Were there any witnesses? Somebody had to hear the shot."

Nobody so far.

"It's right there in town, for hell's sake!"

Don't know, Coal. But we've asked everyone. Nobody heard a thing.

"So it was a long distance shot again? K.T., it's pitch black out there!"

It wasn't long distance. The shooter was in the yard.

"How do you know? He leave tracks?"

Sure, cowboy boots. Nothing worth seeing. But he also left the casing.

"What was it, K.T.?" He spoke the query in a dead sounding voice.

I'm guessing you already know. It was pushed down in the ground, exactly like the first one. Thirty-ought six.

CHAPTER TWENTY-SEVEN

They had finally put out the fire on Trent Tuckett's house, but not before it was a complete loss. The left wall and part of the rear still stood there, hovering over the smoking rubble in the light of early morning. The entire area on this part of South St. Charles Street smelled of wet ash and gasoline. Trent's Jeep and a blue sixty-six Impala were parked off to the side, and the paint on the side of the Jeep was blistered, but otherwise it appeared to be all right. The Impala was mostly protected by the Jeep, so suffered only minor paint damage.

However, anything Trent had owned was useless now, either burned, melted, or soaked with water. And in the grand scheme of things, it didn't matter, for there lay Trent's body, off to one side, covered in a sheet. Trent was an orphan, divorced, and had never had any children. Other than friends, there was no one even to mourn the loss of this sawmill worker who had spent all his time and money drinking and playing pool, or hunting and fishing during the season.

Although this part of St. Charles Street was pretty secluded and not very built up yet, bystanders stood all around the place, staring in shock at the covered body and at the burned rubble. It wasn't yet common knowledge that Trent had been murdered, but judging by the looks on some of their faces, Coal guessed the rumor was spreading. He always wondered how those things began.

There was a rough outline on the ground in front of the porch where Trent's body had been located before the firefighters dragged it away. Coal looked it over, but there was little to be gleaned from it.

"I tried to get a couple of photos, but the flames were pretty hot," said K.T. as he stood there shivering beside Coal. "And the lighting was hardly worth a photo."

"Who was here first?" asked Coal.

"I have a list of people. But as far as anyone official, it was Bob Wilson. And Chief George was here not much after that—both before the fire truck."

Coal didn't know Daniel George very well. He just remembered getting a good laugh out of his name when his mother had first told him who the new police chief was. Chief Dan George! A Salish Indian actor by the same name had made himself more or less famous with a part in the 1970 Dustin Hoffman Western, *Little Big Man*, so it was ironic when George had been appointed to the position by the mayor. Coal had a sneaking suspicion, knowing the strange sense of humor Salmon's citizens sometimes possessed, that George's being awarded the highest position in the local police department had to do more with his name than with any qualifications he might have as an officer. After all, how many police departments could boast of a "Chief Dan George"? But right now, a name that would have struck him as comical on another day didn't even make him crack a smile.

"Where are they?" Coal asked.

"I think the chief's in his car. Bob was wandering around earlier taking names of possible witnesses."

Coal nodded and walked away toward the pale blue Ford LTD K.T. had pointed out, sitting in the shelter of some trees farther south on the street, on the opposite side from the house. It had a blue and a red light on top of it, and on the door was the legend, "SALMON POLICE."

Coal knocked on the window, disturbing the police chief in the middle of writing something on a note pad by the light of a flashlight held in the crook of his neck. Startled, the policeman dropped the flashlight and looked up at Coal, annoyed. When it registered on him who he was looking at, he put down his paper and pencil and hurriedly rolled down the window.

"Sheriff! Good to see you again. It's been a couple years." He held out his hand, and they shook.

"Good to see you, Chief," said Coal. "What do you have so far on this?"

"Not a lot. No gas can, but you can smell gasoline all over the place."

"Yeah, I caught that."

"And they told you the victim has a bullet wound in his chest."

"Sure. Do you have the bullet?"

"Still have to look," replied George. "Went out the back, and if he had his back to that house the way it looks like he did, we may never find it."

"So I gather the exit wound is out his back?"

"Very obviously. Small hole in the front, dead center in the sternum. When it went out the back, it wasn't small. Mushroomed up pretty bad, and no matter how you want to look at it there probably wasn't a whole lot left to it, wherever it ended up."

"Where did it come out in the back?"

"Pretty much straight line from the front. Right through the middle of his spine. I'd guess it pretty much obliterated one of his vertebrae coming out."

Coal clenched his jaws. He didn't like thinking of that. But at least it sounded like Trent had gone quick. What was most painful of all was he hadn't even taken the time to visit his old friend when he got back to town. Things had gone crazy right away, and he had kept telling himself, *Maybe tomorrow.*

"Can we go look at it?" Coal asked.

The police chief's eyes widened. "Umm... Sure, if you want. Say, weren't you and Tuckett old high school buddies?"

"We were. He was on the football team."

"You going to be all right?"

Nodding, Coal said, "I was in Korea, and then in 'Nam. I've lost friends before—so many that after a while I stopped making friends on purpose."

Coal stepped back from the car door, and Chief George got out. Together, they walked to the body, where they had left a man standing to keep other onlookers back.

"You still need me, Chief?" asked the man, someone Coal didn't recognize, but a man who was big and tough-looking enough to discourage anyone wanting a closer look at the body.

"Yes, Pete, if you could hang around a little longer I'd sure appreciate it. Coroner's on his way."

Coal knelt down and lifted the sheet from the side, being careful not to expose Trent's face, because he wasn't quite ready to see him like that. Rather than tearing or cutting, at least the officers had unbuttoned Trent's shirt to expose the wound. The chief was right. The thirty caliber-sized hole was about dead center in the breast bone. They rolled the body on its side, and Coal drew an imaginary line between the entrance wound and the gaping one in the back, a ghastly wound that would have made him nauseous if he hadn't seen so much traumatic death in his life. If anything, the bullet had angled just slightly downward from chest to back.

Coal stood back up.

"Did he have any weapon around him?"

"Not that we found."

"Not a board, a pipe—nothing?"

The chief shook his head.

"Any sign of a struggle? Torn up spots in the yard near the body... Anything like that? No sign at all that he fought back?"

"No sir. And anything there might have been is mixed up with a lot of other tracks now."

"Sure. Firefighters are like a bunch of bull elephants when it comes to evidence preservation."

"Not to mention a bunch of do-gooders helping them drag fire hose around. We were lucky to get here and get a look at things before the body got dragged off."

"Well, we can only ask so much," Coal said. "At least they helped save the neighbors' houses. That's something. I guess we can't expect normal folks to know our job. They see a fire, they want to put it out. It could be worse—they could do nothing at all."

"I agree," said George. "Well, Sheriff, you're the one with the expertise. Do you want this one?"

"What expertise is that?"

"Well, I mean with the FBI. You're the investigator."

Coal chuckled. "Believe it or not, it's not exactly like in the movies."

"Oh? How do you mean?"

"Oh, just how they make the FBI out to be all-knowing, have a handle on everything about law enforcement. FBI agents are specialists, and my specialty wasn't really death investigations, although I did observe quite a few."

"Oh. Yeah, I didn't know that myself. What I get for believing Hollywood."

"Don't get me wrong, Chief. Like I said, I've picked up some things from being involved in a lot of murders and suicides, but I don't know how well any of it would hold up in court. I've taken a few classes, but I certainly wouldn't be subpoenaed as an expert witness, if it came down to that."

"Well, your choice, Sheriff," said Chief George. "I know Tuckett was a friend of yours. That could be positive or negative. I'll take it if you'd rather. After all, it's in city limits."

"Let's work together," Coal said with a nod. "I already have a very probable suspect in mind, and he lives in the county. Maybe we can help each other."

* * *

After taking his own notes at the crime scene, Coal bade farewell to K.T., the police chief, and Bob Wilson, then drove up the Bar to the jail.

Todd Mitchell had just come in, and he and Jordan Peterson were drinking coffee and talking about the fire. "I was just getting ready to head back down there," said Mitchell. "See if K.T. needed a hand."

"Yeah. Looks to me like you were drinking coffee," said Coal. He was not in a very good mood this morning.

"Just thought I should check on things here," said Mitchell, his eyes hardening.

"All right. Say, Todd, what's the status on K.T.?"

"Status?"

"Yeah. He's the one who called me this morning. And then down there at the murder scene he acted like he was actually working for the county. I don't think the county can afford to pay you both as full-time deputies, unless things have changed since I was here last."

"Oh, yeah. Well, there's a proviso for circumstances like this. I thought we could pay him from emergency funds."

"For Larry's investigation, you mean?"

"Sure."

"Okay, I agree. I'll take that to the county clerk. But now... He's pretty much helped with that all he can. I hate to do it, but I think we're going to have to cut him loose. And what about Jim?"

"Oh, Jim's just been helping as a friend. He doesn't expect pay."

"All right. Well, first things first, I need you to follow me down to the body shop. I've got to get my truck in. Then I'll have you bring me back up here so I can start using the Ford. I can't be caught without a radio again like yesterday. Say, do we have a line on anything with four-wheel-drive? You can't get far up in these mountains without it."

Mitchell shook his head. "Nope. We've been pretty much stuck to the road. There's that old brown Chevy, but it's two-wheel."

"All right," Coal replied. "We're going to have to change that. I'm not even sure why any county in its right mind would buy a two-wheel drive pickup in this country. Politicians." His voice had a derogatory tone.

Saying goodbye to Jordan Peterson, they drove down to Andy's Auto Body, which was attached to Ken's Automotive. The shop was run by Andy Holmes, who rented his space from Parks. Andy, a good looking, amiable young man who kept his head shaved bald, promised Coal he could have the Chevrolet looking like new in under a week.

Then Coal went to talk to Ken, grabbing hold of the big bear paw the mechanic called a hand. "You've got a better grip now than you did from dogging steers, Ken," he said with a chuckle.

"Hauling around big blocks," said Ken with a shrug. "What's new, buddy?"

"You know half of it."

"Yeah. Sorry to hear about Larry. And now Trent, too."

"Did you go on the fire?" he asked, knowing Ken worked as a volunteer firefighter.

"Yeah, for an hour or so. It was pretty much over before we got there. Did you see Ruel?"

"No," Coal admitted. "I'm not too much in the mood for greeting old friends this morning." Coal felt bad for not stopping to greet Ruel Arrington, the man who still acted as chief of the volunteer fire department. He wondered how Ruel could still carry on that kind of work, which he had been at off and on for as far back as he could remember. Although ten years or so younger, Ruel had been pretty good hunting buddies with Coal's father, Prince.

They talked for a while, and Coal got Ken's first impressions of the fire scene, taking down notes on paper. Ken was no more an investigator than most of the others at the scene, but sometimes people saw things differently, and anyone's input might end up being the piece of the puzzle that could solve a crime. The most important thing he wanted to know from Ken, like everyone else at the fire scene, was if there were any suspicious onlookers there, seeming overly interested in the goings-on. Like everyone else Coal had asked, the answer was a fat negative.

Before Coal left, he said, "Hey, I need you to do me a favor, Ken. One of the medics broke down out on the first ranch road coming this way from Savage, but on the south side. Maybe a quarter mile in. Her rig's still sitting out there, and I told her I'd have you tow it in and fix it. She's not doing super great on money, so cut her a break if you can."

"Her? You talking about that new gal, Maura Plenty-Wounds?"

"Yeah, that's her."

"Ain't she a looker?"

"I suppose she's pretty enough," admitted Coal carefully. No one was going to get more than that out of him.

"Pretty enough? Yeah!" Ken laughed, seemed about to go further in ribbing his old friend, then stopped. "Hey, Coal—I forgot to say how sorry I was to hear about Laura. It seemed like things were going so good with the two of you."

Coal just shrugged. "One thing you learn in law enforcement is things usually aren't what they seem on the surface. So... How about Maura's truck?"

Ken studied his friend for a moment, seeming not to be finished talking about Laura. Finally, he shrugged it off. "It's not one of those damn Dodges, is it?"

Coal laughed. "No, it's an International Harvester. A Travelette."

"Not a whole lot better," Ken said with a laugh. "All right, I'll go get it in a minute."

"Just give me a holler when it's done, all right?"

"All right. I'm pretty strapped, though."

"Yeah, as usual. Just remember, she doesn't have anything to drive until you fix it."

"Why don't you bring her by? I have an ugly Ford station wagon out back that I just got on a trade. It's not much, but it runs."

"You renting cars now too?"

"Heck no! Too much paperwork. No, if she's a friend of yours, she can just use it until I get her truck done. Side benefit is she might make it smell better!"

Coal laughed. "Well, thanks. And by the way, she's not really a friend of mine. I just owe her. I kind of gave her a mud bath."

"You gave her a bath?" repeated Ken, a sly smile on his face.

"Very funny. A different kind of bath. Say—I almost forgot. I have a fellow who'll be getting back to town in a few days and really needs a job. Howie Jensen's his name. You wouldn't happen to have anything he could do, would you?"

"Is he a mechanic?"

"How do I know?"

Laughing, Ken said, "I don't know how, but you're the one looking for a job for him. If he's a baker or a candlestick maker, I don't know how I could use him. Jeez. Find out what he can do, would you? You might want to ask Andy, too. Maybe he could have him sand out some of his body work. That wouldn't take much skill."

Coal thanked his friend, and he and Todd Mitchell drove back to the jail, where Coal had another cup of coffee, sent Mitchell home to get some sleep, and then paid a visit to his old friend Rick Cheatum, who was on the county commission. It was getting about time, after three days, to find out if he was even going to keep the sheriff's job.

CHAPTER TWENTY-EIGHT

Coal knew Rick Cheatum to be as honest as the preacher in the glass house. He had to be, with a last name like Cheatum: He was the president of the Salmon First National Bank.

He was also a bigtime gun collector, knew about as much as anyone in town about guns with the possible exception of local self-proclaimed celebrity gun writer Elmer Keith, and on top of all that was a first-rate friend.

Cheatum, a man in his late fifties with heavy black-framed glasses and dark hair streaked with silver, gave Coal the biggest and most genuine smile he had seen all day and came almost on a run from his office to greet him when he saw him come through the front door. "Coal! When did you get back in town?"

"I'm ashamed to say, Rick. A few days ago. Sorry I haven't been by to see you sooner. I thought the county clerk would be calling me in for my obligatory interview by now, but he hasn't."

Cheatum quickly waved that off. "Aww, Coal! Shoot, with everything that's been happening around here, I don't think *anyone* expected you to have extra time on your hands for such foolishness as visits. So... Rumors are flying, but I was running late on my way in this morning and didn't get to talk to anyone. Is it true about Trent Tuckett?"

"It's true, Rick. He's dead, and his house is a total loss."

"What is going on with this town?" Cheatum asked, shaking his head. "I'll be damned if I can make heads or tails of it. I know you went to school with old Larry MacAtee. Trent too, right?"

"That's right."

"Sorry, pal. I wish there were something I could do. What *can* I do for you, anyway? Hey, first off, let's get into my office. This bank has ears!"

Coal followed his old friend into his plush office, and at his invitation fell into a heavy old leather chair that sat kitty corner to a highly polished mahogany desk with two statues on it, one of a mule deer buck, the other of a huge caribou bull. On the ornately paneled wall behind Rick's head posed a mule deer with antlers every bit as imposing as the crown worn by the bronze on the desk, and a spread of no less than thirty-five inches. The bases of his antlers looked almost as big around as Coal's wrists. Next to it was the full body mount of a bristly, menacing javelina, with nasty tusks exposed and eyes flashing, standing on a fake slab of red sandstone.

Other than that mount and two paintings by Charles Russell, the walls were tastefully bare, and the thick carpet on the floor was as high quality as Coal had ever seen.

Rick Cheatum sank onto a walnut chair behind his desk, where a few papers were neatly laid, along with an expensive looking pen. "What's up, Coal?" he said, crossing his hands on his midriff and leaning back a little in the chair. "Is everything okay? You regretting taking this job yet?"

Coal shrugged. "Other than the fact that these are friends of mine, which makes it all kind of personal, it's not a lot different from my Washington job. As for the job... Have I actually 'taken' it? No one has said a word to me. I haven't had to fill out any forms, haven't been sworn in officially, haven't really been lined out on my job. It's all pretty strange. I'm not used to things being so informal."

Cheatum laughed, both his voice and his eyes spewing forth joviality and warmth that could not be feigned. "Coal, don't forget: This is Salmon, Idaho, buddy! It's not like you're taking over Scotland Yard!"

Coal laughed in return, although with Trent on his mind he felt more ill-humored than good-humored. "I'm just not used to it yet, Rick. You try living in the bureaucracy of D.C. for four years!"

"Well, just relax," Cheatum rejoined. "Danny Shea and Bill Taylor are both friends of mine, and we okayed your being interim sheriff. And the county clerk is Nate Hanson. I don't know him super well, but he seems like a pretty decent guy—some carrot top that just waltzed in here, bought the Smokehouse, and walked through the election like he owned the place. Anyway, from the few contacts I've had with him, he seems all right. So what do you have to worry about?"

Coal thought about Shea and Taylor for a moment, the other two members of the board of commissioners. He didn't know either of them very well, but he did know Rick was a man who understood people and had great judgment of those he could trust. If he said the two men were all right, then they were fine with Coal—at least until they proved themselves otherwise. He had been alive long enough to know people could change like a breath of wind when it came to self-preservation.

It sounded like the county clerk, Nate Hanson, would be the wild card.

"So when can the four of us meet with this Nate Hanson and talk about the county?" Coal asked.

"Wow, buddy, you're like a bulldog! I really don't think we need to sit and talk, but if you really want to, I can set it up. The earliest in the day possible would be best, I think. Even eight o'clock."

"I'd be all right with that."

"Then I'll make some calls. Tomorrow? How about we meet at the Smokehouse?"

Coal chuckled. "You make me laugh."

"What?"

"You really *do* want this to be informal, don't you?"

"Don't you?"

Coal gave him a serious regard. "Rick, I've been hurt by shaking hands with official people and forgetting to have them sign on the dotted line. That may work for the layman, but these guys are politicians, all right? Sorry to sound mistrusting, but I need to know my legal limitations in this job. I don't want to end up like K.T., getting removed from office for something Jim Lockwood says was pretty minor."

Cheatum blushed. "Well, there was a lot of pressure on that one, Coal. Don't jump to conclusions. You know I'm not at liberty to discuss what led to it, but the powers that be wanted K.T. out. And sometimes there's just no choice. He stepped on the wrong toes, to be honest with you."

Coal studied his old friend. "Okay, I'll have to trust you on that one. I just hope politics don't ever come between you and me."

Cheatum scoffed good-naturedly. "Right! Not you and me, Coal. Never!"

The two shook hands, and Coal looked up at the big buck on the wall. "We need to get up to Alaska and get a bull caribou to match your other statue sometime."

"We will, buddy. You just name the time."

*   *   *

It was Coal's aim to get back to the house and be waiting for the bus to drop off the kids. But the county of Lemhi had other goals for him. He had to do some pavement pounding trying to pull strings and get a job for Howard Jensen before he got back from visiting his daughter in Salt Lake. He had to contact Bigfoot Monahan's parole officer, in the city of Pocatello, and get him pinned down to come up and scour Bigfoot's property for violations—particularly the ownership of an illegal .30-06—before anyone else died. Namely, him or K.T. Or Jim Lockwood. For all Coal knew, maybe Judge Wiley Sinclair was also on the big lumberjack's list. He was obviously insane enough to do anything. It seemed pretty obvious that he had shot Trent Tuckett right in his own front yard.

Coal had called the house around ten o'clock and talked to his mother. She told him she had taken Maura out to her place earlier, and they had fed her four horses together, and the blue heelers she kept there to harass the horses mercilessly. Then she had taken her back to the house with her. The first chance Coal got, which was around noon, he drove back out in the LTD.

He pulled up in the driveway and parked next to the Chrysler. There was a thin haze of cloud over most of the sky, broken only by occasional patches of blue, but most of the rain water had soaked into the ground, which was not yet frozen enough to make the water puddle for long. The scent of decaying grass and leaves filled the air, along with that crisp something that infuses late fall with magic and brings on thoughts of Thanksgiving dinner and impending sleigh rides. He was kind of surprised there wasn't any snow on the ground yet. It seemed kind of late in the year for things to still be brown.

Coal took a deep breath as he stood beside the LTD, looking at the windows of the house, which for the most part only glowed back at him with reflected pieces of pale gray sky. He wasn't sure if he was ready for any more of Maura PlentyWounds yet. He had yet to figure her out—as if that would ever be possible. He didn't necessarily wish her to be too friendly toward him, but he also wasn't looking forward to the sullen side she seemed to save up special just for him.

Going up to the door, he was greeted by Shadow and Dobe, running around demonstrating their happiness with their tails, Shadow's wagging, Dobe's wiggling. They both liked to have the top of their rumps scratched—one of the few places they couldn't reach, and Shadow, in spite of her age, would bow her front end clear to the ground to make sure he understood her request.

No one was in the house, but it was only a couple of minutes before the back door opened, and Connie and Maura came in stomping their feet. Their cheeks were rosy red, their hair wind-blown. They took off hats and gloves, and Maura's blond hair tumbled again over her shoulders and made Coal curse himself inside. He didn't want that to stir him like it did.

Coal expected an onslaught of accusations about leaving home in a hurry, not saying goodbye to the children, etc. He got none.

When the women saw him, their eyes softened. Maura stayed back in the kitchen as Connie came close to Coal. "Son, are you all right? We heard about Trent."

"I'm all right, Mom. You get used to this after a while."

"Sure you do. But you must have expected to come back home and find a little peace from what you had in Vietnam and Washington."

He nodded. "Yeah. I did that. Sometimes I think it follows me."

His mother reached out and rubbed his shoulder through his denim coat. She must have decided not to embarrass him with a motherly hug in front of the other woman. "If you need to talk later, you know I'm a listening ear. Hey, want some soup? I brought some out of the freezer and heated it up in the pot. Beef barley—your favorite, right?"

"Sure," he said with a smile. "As long as it's not Campbell's Condensed. Any bread left?"

"There is. I saved a big piece just for you—with a half cube of butter, just the way you like it." She laughed. "You know that's not good for you, right?"

"Yeah, right! Someday they're going to find out they were wrong about butter, and that disgusting margarine is what's really bad for you. Mark my words."

"Okay, Son, have it your way. I think all the doctors and scientists have been saying how bad for you the saturated fat in butter is since clear back in sixty-five. But don't listen to them—they're just doctors!"

"That's right, Mom. They *are* just doctors—not gods. You just give me my butter, all right? If it kills me early, then I'll die happy. But I still say it's the rest of you who are in for a surprise."

The three of them sat quietly and ate. Maura and Connie smelled of horses. Not the good scent of their faces and their musky scent, but of old, dirty hair, and of manure decaying in the pasture and tracked in on their boots. The stale scent of it was even in their hair. It turned Coal's stomach and actually served to counter Maura's attractiveness, so in the end it was a good thing.

"Your mom has nice horses," said Maura when Connie went down the hall to the bathroom.

"Yeah, she does. She dotes on them."

"We don't have to hate each other."

Startled, Coal looked up from his soup. "Huh?"

"You don't have to treat me like the enemy."

He raised his eyebrows, sitting back from her. "What're you talking about? The 'enemy'?"

"Yes. I'm just trying to make conversation."

"I agreed!"

"It was the tone of voice you agreed in," she countered.

"I'm not even sure what's going on here. Last night you would hardly even look at me. Now I agree with something you say and *I'm* treating *you* like the enemy?"

The bathroom door opened, and Connie came walking down the hall, her boot heels clicking. Maura looked at Coal and just shrugged, both with her eyebrows and with her shoulders. She looked down and finished her soup, and he knew the conversation was over, at least as long as his mother was in the room.

"Let me make a phone call," said Coal as he finished his soup and set the spoon carefully in the bowl.

He dialed up Ken Parks, down at the automotive shop. "Hey. Did you get that truck yet?"

I did, said the voice on the other end of the line. *I can fix this in a day. Does she want the station wagon?*

"Hold on." Coal put his hand over the receiver. "This is my mechanic friend. He's got your truck and your keys. Wants to know if you want to borrow a station wagon he has down there until your rig's done."

"Oh." The woman looked surprised. "Wow. Sure. I thought I was just going to be grounded."

"She says yes," Coal said into the receiver.

All right. Come get it then—as long as you promise she'll make it smell good. Ken's rollicking laugh came over the receiver into the room.

"Well, I can't promise you that, especially not right now." He was still very conscious of the stale horse-stink.

Okay, I'll take your word for that. Anyway, her keys are here—including her house keys, I think. Or does she have spares?

"No, but I'll bet she will now."

Oh, really? So... Where'd she sleep last night?

"I don't know what you're getting at," Coal shot back good-naturedly. "See you in a minute." Before Ken could come back with anything else, he dropped the receiver back on the base. Maura was looking at him expectantly, as if to hear him relate what Ken had said. "Funny guy," was all he said.

They got in the Ford and drove back downtown, and that was the end of Coal's plan to be waiting at the bus stop for his kids.

It came across the radio that somebody down past North Fork had busted a huge ram, right on the side of the highway, and some legal hunters had caught him red-handed at the scene of the crime, trying to hoist the ram into the back of his pickup. Coal was needed right away.

As Coal pulled up to the mechanic shop to drop off his charge, Maura said, "Just go! I'll ride with you."

And thus began one of the longest rides of Coal's life. Nothing like the feeling of a woman's scorn to make an easy jaunt down the highway into a roller coaster ride through hell.

CHAPTER TWENTY-NINE

Just after crossing the Salmon River bridge, Coal veered right onto Highway 93. It took all of thirty seconds to get all the way from Ken's Automotive and out of town, and only one additional second for Maura to thrust her nose and even her entire fat head into Coal's affairs.

"How far are we going?"

"North Fork is just over twenty-one miles. It sounds like they're not far beyond that."

"Good. You're going sixty-five. That gives me twenty minutes."

He glanced sidelong at her. "And then you self-destruct?"

"Funny. Maybe *you* will. Sheriff, you want some advice?"

"I'm not sure. Would it make a difference if I said no?"

"Probably not. You're a captive audience."

He sensed that she smiled, but he didn't sense that it was amicable. He was looking straight forward at the road, so he couldn't be sure of either.

"Then... what?"

"It's about your daughter, Katie."

"As opposed to my other daughters...." He was trying to lighten a mood he sensed was about to get heavy. It lightened it something like dropping a bar of lead into a cup of cocoa.

"Do you often talk just to hear your voice?"

"Huh?"

"Will you just clam up and listen to what I'm going to tell you? You don't have to follow up everything I say with a smart aleck comment."

"Sorry." And he truly was—sorry he hadn't thrown her out at Ken's.

"Do you know that your daughter should be one of the most physically beautiful girls in Salmon High? At least to judge by what I can see and by the photos your mom has on the wall. In fact, she should be incredibly gorgeous."

"And?"

"And she's not. She has a broken, swollen nose, raccoon eyes, and it seems to her like every kid in school is making fun of her. She feels like a total outcast."

"Okay. So? Welcome to life."

"You know what? You're a bastard."

"Whoa! You can watch your mouth in my car or you can get out and walk home."

She stared at him. He was trying to be a responsible lawman and watch the road—with the added benefit of not having to meet the woman's blazing eyes.

"Okay, I'm sorry I swore. Only because that word pulls your mother into this. Do you want to hear this, or not?"

"What do you think?"

"No, of course not. But you need to."

"Okay. Shoot." *Why did this woman think she had a right to tell him about his children?* But the question would be moot.

"Shoot? That might be the best," she said tartly. "All right. I know you had a friend get killed before you even got to town. I know you've had another one killed since. But you can't tell me for one second that there haven't been a few minutes here and there that you couldn't have at least asked your children how they are. How school went. Anything. Something to show you give a damn about them."

"All right. Maura, I think maybe this conversation needs to stop. I got rid of one wife. I didn't sign up for another."

"You really are pretty much an egotistical pig, aren't you? There were a few moments I thought I had judged you wrong at the scene of your accident, but you're really proving me right now."

"What am I supposed to do?" he growled, taking his eyes off the road too long and letting them pierce hers. "Just let the murderer go?"

"For a little while, maybe."

"Sure. And then when he kills his next victim, I wait on that one too. For how long, Maura? He's already shown us he's not done, and he's capable of anything."

That silenced her for a moment. Finally, she raised her hands, took a deep breath, and exhaled as she set them both down slowly on her thighs. "Okay. Okay, I do understand. You do have to catch this man. I'm not arguing that. Maybe I'm coming across too harsh."

"Maybe?" he echoed.

"Will you just *stop?* Can't you even see when someone's trying to make peace?"

Mimicking the woman, Coal took a deep breath in, easing back a little on the throttle to curve around a place in the road that hugged the river, which sprawled out on their left, gray to match the gloomy sky. "Maura, those are my kids. I'm trying to do the best I can. I don't know what else to do. My wife is dead. Katie blames me for it. I think Virgil does too, at least to a certain extent. The little guys are made out of rubber. They'll bounce back from anything. The older two? Especially Katie? There would only be a fight if I even tried to talk to her. I couldn't say I liked how her hair looked without ending up in a fight."

"What happened, Coal?"

He looked over at her, hoping to find some sign what the question referred to without having to ask. She just looked at him, solemn, her big, honest, blue eyes searching his soul.

"What happened? With what?"

"Your wife."

He let out a big gust of air. *Nobody* asked about something like that. Nobody! He turned his eyes back to the road. He stared over the wheel for a while, unmoved by the wonderful country flying past. Ten more miles to North Fork. This woman made it seem like a hundred.

He took in a huge breath, which made a little sobbing noise as his lungs filled to capacity. He let it out slowly through his nose. "No one's ever asked me that."

"Why?" she demanded softly.

"Because I don't think anyone thought I would want to discuss it."

"Do you? Because if you don't, you don't have to. You can forget I ever asked. But I think it must hide a lot of things that would make all of this make so much more sense to me."

Coal drove. He drove and drove, and suddenly the poached ram didn't seem so important. Here was a chance to spill his guts. It would be the first time, because although the FBI had offered him a chance to talk to a psychiatrist, he had turned it down, telling them he had no need of anyone playing mind games with him. But he couldn't take this opportunity. At least not now. In the first place, there just wasn't time.

"You're not ready," she said at last.

"I'm sorry. Some other time, maybe."

"I understand. In my case, I could only *wish* my husband had died. In your case, you have to live with it."

He jerked his eyes sharply over at her. He thought she would be watching him, but she wasn't. Her eyes were concentrated on her hands, which were folded in her lap.

There was a part of him, way down deep where no one could touch it, not even God, he hoped, that Maura seemed to have read. And oh, how he hated himself to know it was there. And he hated that Maura had found a probe that somehow reached into that place where no one else had ever gone, or even tried to go.

Without thinking about it, Coal pressed down harder on the throttle, until Maura was hanging on tightly to her arm rest. He saw some old man flip him the bird as he flew through North Fork too fast and turned left, and finally, up ahead, several parked trucks appeared along the road, making it look like a parking lot.

Easing to a stop some twenty feet back from the closest pickup, Coal reached into the glove box and grabbed a set of handcuffs, snugged his gunbelt down on his hips, then picked up his radio mic with his right hand. "Dispatch, I've arrived at the scene." He read off the license plate numbers of the vehicles he could see, along with a brief description, then stepped out of the car. He was going to tell Maura she could stay inside, but she was already getting out.

"If you're coming with me, pop the trunk and get out the shotgun. Bring it with you." Without waiting for a response, he started toward the cluster of men who stood around the back of one old brown Dodge pickup.

"Howdy, boys."

All eyes that hadn't already looked at him turned now. There were some average-sized men in this group, but also two that were big and burly, neither of whom Coal recognized. He did take note of one important thing: None of them was bigger than he. However, all in all there were seven of them—with one skinny one, legs drawn up toward his chest, lying on his side on an open tailgate. Below that tailgate was one of the most majestic full curl bighorn rams Coal had ever seen.

"This fellow just taking a nap? Or you boys holding him there for a reason?"

A couple of the men smirked. "We're down here steelhead fishin', Sheriff," said one man with a beard to his collarbone and reddish brown hair. He wore the stereotypical red buffalo plaid hunter's shirt made famous in much of Charlie Russell's art. "We come around the corner, and this here jack was tryin' to hoist this ram in his truck. Fresh blood everywhere."

"It's a nice ram," observed Coal. He studied the red marks on the face of the man who lay on the tailgate, and the dried blood on one side of his mouth and in his mustache below one nostril. "That ram do all that damage to your face, mister?"

The man's eyes flickered around at those who towered over him. He didn't seem particularly scared, but certainly wary. "Yeah, he must have," said a blond fellow with a butch and a big mustache. "You know how tough those big ones can be."

"Yeah. So I hear. But some of them aren't as tough as they think they are." He stared the blond man down, not trying to hide a challenge in his eyes. At last, he turned to the poacher with a show of boredom.

"What's your name?"

"Miley. Roger Miley." The voice was scratchy and weak.

"From around here?"

"Challis. Well, Clayton."

"You know the season on bighorns?"

"No."

"You draw a tag?"

"No."

"I see. Guess knowing the season wouldn't really matter then. This your truck?"

"Yeah."

"A fifty-eight?"

"Fifty-nine."

"Shame to lose it."

"Huh?"

"Ram like this, you not even a local boy? Wiley Sinclair's our judge, and he doesn't take kindly to poachers from outside coming in here killing our game. Stand up. Can you?"

Miley tried to stand up and almost fell as his feet touched the ground. He grabbed the edge of the tailgate and stood leaning to one side, trying not to make eye contact with any of his captors.

"Let's turn you around and put these cuffs on you."

Those words had no more than left Coal's mouth before Miley swore and stood up straighter, pulling back his shoulders. "No way! I'm not getting in no handcuffs!" His face was belligerent, but this time his eyes had taken on a look of fear.

Suddenly, the man with the red-brown beard came out of nowhere, slamming the man in the side of the head with his fist. Coal lunged against the man, knocking him back and putting his hand out toward his chest as he took a step forward.

"Back off! You boys have done enough." His gaze was not pleasant. He had no intention for it to be.

The big man was shaking, in his anger, and he and Coal stared each other down. Four of the other men had started edging closer, as if to form a half circle around Coal. Suddenly, the jacking of a shotgun shattered the icy feeling in the canyon.

"All of you just back off. I hate seeing what shotguns do to human flesh."

The captors of the poacher all turned to Maura PlentyWounds, their eyes open wide. Coal shot his look of surprise at her too. There was no mercy in this woman's eyes.

"Do me a favor, Maura, and hang onto that. Boys, let me take down your names, and then I want all of you out of here. Go catch some fish or something, but don't stay here. You first." Coal pinned the man with the red-brown beard with his eyes. "What's your name?"

"Runnigan."

"First?"

"Drew."

He took down his address and phone number.

"All right, Runnigan. Who's with you?"

When Runnigan pointed out two other men, he made note of their information. Then he looked at the big man again, the one he decided was the ringleader. "Runnigan, this gent poached a bighorn ram. Highly illegal taking a prized ram from Lemhi County."

Runnigan stared him down, silent.

"But so is beating up people. I don't know what kind of medical treatment Miley might need, but you may be answering for it before this is all over."

Drew Runnigan was incredulous. "What did you say?"

"I said, if he's hurt very bad you may be paying for it. Just keep it in mind."

"Well, I'll be damned," Runnigan growled. "I stop to be a public-minded citizen, and this is how I'm treated. Don't worry—next time I won't help. I'll just let him take your game. No skin off my nose."

Coal just watched the man. When he was finished, he said calmly, "It wasn't the roughing up I'm talking about as much as that last blow. You can tell he's already hurt."

"Whatever." Sullen blue eyes sliced into Coal's face. "Come on, boys," he said to his two cohorts. They backed up, went to one of the pickups, and drove off down the river.

Left behind were five men who looked tough but didn't seem inclined to take any bulls by the horns, other than perhaps the blond one, a man by the name of John Huskie. He hailed from Gibbonsville, since just one year ago, he told Coal. Coal took down his information last, when there were only him and his younger brother left behind.

"You know, Runnigan was right. It seems like you would thank us for stoppin' this man, not treat us like criminals."

"I'm taking names," said Coal. "It's all part of the reporting process. If you feel I'm treating you like a criminal, you should call the county commission, or the clerk. But just remember, there will be photographs of Miley and a doctor's report on his injuries. And honestly? I doubt this one man struggled hard enough against all eight of you to deserve looking like this. I've seen men stomped to death in my time, Huskie. A few more minutes and it looks like Miley might have been among them."

The entire time of the questioning and taking names, Maura had stood watch with Coal's shotgun, and Roger Miley leaned against the tailgate, trying to look like he wasn't hurt. But he *was* hurt, and pretty badly. He breathed in wheezes, and now and then, in spite of himself, a breath that was too deep would cause him to clutch at his midriff.

When John Huskie and his brother drove away and left just Coal's LTD and the Dodge pickup there on the road, Coal turned his full attention to Miley. "You going to be all right?"

"Hell, mister, I was in the Marines. I've fought all-day battles in worse shape than this." The effort of speaking set Miley to wheezing and sucking for air. He suddenly started to double over, but he caught himself and straightened up. His face had turned pallid.

"I was a Marine too, Miley, and Marine or not, I know serious damage when I see it." Coal thought about the handcuffs in his hip pocket. Should he take them out again? Just what kind of a threat was this man right now? "How are you going to go to jail?"

Miley stared at Coal. "Please don't take me to jail."

"It's too late to beg."

"Please, mister. I can't go in a cage."

"You're going to the hospital first, not a cage."

"I can't go there either."

"We don't have a choice, Miley. You took that away from yourself and you took it away from me."

"I ain't going with you."

"I'm afraid you are."

Without warning, Miley whipped a hand up under the back of his jacket. Before his hand could come all the way back around, Coal saw the flash of metal. With years of training and experience behind him, Coal drove into him, grabbing his right wrist with his left hand even as he drove a knee into his groin. He came around with a knife-edge palm to the side of Miley's neck, feeling the man instantly slump against him. Whirling to the left, he threw him down face-first on the freezing asphalt, his arm locked up tight behind him. A snub-nosed Smith and Wesson filled his fist.

Wrenching the uncocked weapon from Miley's grip, Coal threw it to one side, hearing it hit the pavement and grind as it skipped several feet away. Reaching behind him, he whipped out his handcuffs and applied them to the arm-barred wrist, then yanked the other arm out from under him and cuffed that one too. Breathing a little heavier from the exertion, he double-locked the cuffs so they wouldn't tighten up even more when sat on, then got to his feet, yanking Miley up with him.

"I can't go to jail! Don't take me! Please!" Miley was screaming all the way to the car. In spite of the man's pleas, Coal deposited him in the back seat and slammed the door. Then, huffing, he turned and started back toward the pickup.

Maura walked in stride with him, and they stopped where the bighorn lay. Coal contemplated the back of the pickup, then turned and looked at his sedan. Finally, he went and got in the Ford, leaving Maura with the truck, and turned his car around, backing it up close to the sheep. He got out and popped the trunk with intentions of throwing the three hundred-plus pound ram into the vehicle alone, but as he bent to the task, Maura positioned herself at the back legs. He straightened back up.

"Don't hurt yourself. Lemhi can't afford the insurance."

"Sure, tough guy. You try throwing this thing in there on your own and we'll see who needs insurance."

Coal just chuckled and shook his head. He bent down again and took the front feet. "All right, get a hold. When I say three, we'll lift."

He counted three, and as he started to lift the bruiser up, he was amazed how much lighter this woman made it feel. Using his knee to shove it a little higher and keep its momentum going, he leaned against the ram and let it fall partway into the trunk. A little maneuvering got it most of the way in, but it was obvious the trunk would have to stay ajar all the way back to Salmon.

"You wanna drive the truck back?" He eyed the woman.

She stared him down. "You're welcome."

Coal had to chuckle once more, taking a deep breath to catch his wind. "Oh, yeah. Thanks for the hand."

"Uh-huh. You don't need to try and show off for me, Sheriff. There's no way you would have gotten that in there by yourself. You would have just ended up making a fool of yourself and gotten bloody to boot."

"I said thanks." Her words were getting under his skin. "Do you want to drive the truck, or not?"

"Not really."

"What?" He was taken aback.

"Send someone else out to get it. I want to ride back with you."

He couldn't believe his ears. For a second, he had been over-joyed at the thought of some freedom on the way back to town. "Why? You haven't jabbed enough darts in me yet?"

She glared at him, her eyes on fire. "Fine. I *will* take the truck."

He grunted. "Thank you."

He was standing there beside his door, watching Maura go to the driver's side of the Dodge. He needed to make sure it would start before he took off—although it might have been nice to learn later that he had stranded her out there by herself. As she threw open the door, he saw a look of shock come over her face.

"Well, hi there!"

Coal stared at her, squinting his eyes.

"No, honey, don't be scared. I promise I won't hurt you."

Just for a moment, Coal thought the woman was playing with him. But there was no look of a game about her face. Urgently, he strode to her, pushing her gently aside as he came up to the truck.

There, her back glued up against the passenger door, was a brown-haired little girl, staring at Maura and Coal with the horri-fied eyes of fear itself.

CHAPTER THIRTY

The little girl's face became even more terrified as this huge man came into focus at the door. She pressed her feet against the seat, crushing her back against the door. If she had been any stronger, she might have pushed herself right outside. And if Coal hadn't known any better, he would have thought someone had put a "Creature from the Black Lagoon" mask on him when he wasn't looking.

Maura, seizing the moment, put her hand on Coal's arm and eased him aside, gazing at the girl. "It's okay, sweetheart. This man is the sheriff—the good guy. His name is Coal. I promise you we won't hurt you. We just want to be friends. We're here to help."

The girl's eyes sped to the woman, but she didn't speak, and her gaze flashed back to Coal, the more imposing of these two strangers who had suddenly appeared in her little world.

"I'll just be over here for a minute," said Coal in as soft a voice as he could muster. He realized the girl's terror was not going to diminish while he was within her view. He went to stand by the tailgate, watching Maura smile and try to ease the girl's fear.

"My name is Maura. Can you say that?"

No sound from the cab.

"I'm an EMT. It's like a nurse, only I work outside of the hospital and bring sick and hurt people to the doctor."

Still no response.

"Do you have a name, sweetheart?" A long pause. "What does your daddy call you?"

After a moment, Maura threw a sidelong glance at Coal. He was just a man, but he wasn't completely dense, and he got her drift. He walked back to the Ford and opened the back door, leaning in to look at Roger Miley and getting a powerful whiff of the scent of a man who had been living far too long out of the cab of his pickup. The man was ashen, but with a purple cast to his bruised and bloody face. He was leaned forward out of necessity because of his hands being cuffed behind his back. But he looked like he might have sat that way regardless. Coal had never seen anyone who looked more ready to throw up.

"You doing okay?"

The man looked over, his eyes dull, and shook his head. "Hurtin'. My head is achin' powerful bad."

"Sorry, buddy. I'll get you to the hospital as soon as I can. But before then, it looks like we got a problem. I know why you didn't want to be arrested."

The man simply nodded, sickness in his eyes.

"Is that your daughter?"

"Niece."

"Niece, huh? Why's she with you?"

"Folks died... in a car wreck."

Coal didn't reply for a moment, as a wave of sickness washed over Miley's face and he appeared about ready to heave.

"You going to puke? You need to get out?"

"No. I haven't had a thing to eat in two days."

Coal's mind went to the bighorn. Was there something more to the poaching than simply the drive to possess the massive, battered horns?

"Two days? Does that go for that little girl, too?"

"I made her a sandwich. But the bread was moldy, and I only had a little bit of salad dressing to put on it."

Coal cringed. He had tasted moldy bread before, and the thought made his stomach turn. "When was that?"

"Yesterday morning for breakfast. It was an end piece, folded in half."

"Why didn't you tell me she was in there?"

"Please don't take my girl," Miley pleaded suddenly. "I don't have nobody else. She don't either."

"Mister, I wasn't planning on taking her. Why didn't you tell me she was there?"

Fear made orbs of the man's eyes. He stared at Coal, his face paler gray than ever. "They say I'm not fit to raise her. The sheriff in Challis—he's tryin' to take her from me. Mister, I don't got another soul in the world who needs me."

Compassion filled Coal's chest. There wasn't any doubt about this man's real fear of losing the girl. But he also wondered if Paul Matthews, the sheriff in Custer County, wasn't right. How could a man like this care for a little child? He couldn't even feed her—or himself.

"You got a house in Clayton?"

"I did."

"Did?"

"The bank took it."

"So... You're living in your pickup?"

"Only temporary, Sheriff—honest. I'll get a job soon. My last one just recently run out."

"Doing what?"

"Uh..." Fear flashed across Miley's face. "Just, uh... delivering messages for a guy."

"A guy?"

"Yeah."

"Who?"

"Don't know his name."

Suddenly, Miley cringed and leaned farther forward, squeezing his eyes shut and holding a grimace on his face. Coal waited until whatever pain had come over him released him enough to open his eyes. He decided it was pointless to question him any further about his last job. Miley, for some reason, was clamming up.

"Meanwhile, Miley, how does that girl eat? Not to mention you."

"I'll make do. I will. That's why I wanted that sheep."

Coal nodded. By now, he had figured as much. This man wasn't poaching to put a trophy on his wall. He was fighting for survival.

"What's her name, Miley?"

"Her real name is Clarissa. But she mostly answers to Sissy."

"How old is she?"

"One more month and she'll be four. December the nineteenth."

"Do you feel well enough to walk to the truck with me?"

"Huh?" Miley looked confused.

"Can you get out?"

"Sure, I think so."

"Maura's having trouble getting Sissy to talk. Maybe you can help."

"Okay." A huge look of relief had washed over Miley's face. In spite of obvious physical torment, he scooted himself to the end of the seat, and Coal helped him get his feet out on the ground. For a long moment, Miley sat there bent over. Finally, he took a deep breath and struggled to a standing position, Coal steadying him by the filthy sleeve of one arm.

They moved slowly to the pickup, where Maura was now sitting behind the steering wheel. Coal spoke the woman's name softly as they got close, but he startled her anyway.

"Sorry to scare you. Hey, I brought Mr. Miley over to talk to his niece. He says her name is Sissy, and she will be four years old in a month."

Looking over at Miley, Maura caught the sadness and relief mixed in his face. She looked back at little Sissy and laid her hand on the seat between them. The girl gave it a leery look, but otherwise she didn't react.

"Sissy, your uncle came to talk to you now, okay?"

The girl stared, nothing more than a flicker in her eyes to show that she understood. But the moment Maura climbed out of the truck, and Miley appeared in the girl's line of sight, she scrambled up and across the cab as fast as she could. She threw herself against her uncle, and only because Coal had his hand on the man's back did he manage not to fall over backward. The first sound Coal had heard out of Sissy was now, the sound of her wailing with relief.

Maura laid a hand on Coal's shoulder, and he turned to look at her. She gave him what he could only refer to as the evil eye. "I am *not* sitting on that disgusting seat again, and I am *not* driving that truck back to Salmon. If you have to have it back there, you can drive it yourself."

Coal had been around some filthy houses and nasty back alleys, and perhaps his senses were dulled to it. But now that Maura mentioned it, it seemed like a waft of stench came out of the cab that he hadn't noticed before. It was like a mixture of bodily fluids and cigarette smoke, perhaps mingled with spilled beer and very stale food—much like the stench coming off Miley inside the back seat of his own car. He leaned a little closer to Maura and sniffed, then made a face. "Well, it's all over you now too." He couldn't help but start to laugh, and he had to choke it back quickly. *Not the time, Coal!*

"Go ahead and laugh. We'll see how you like it yourself. It'll take three washings to get that smell out," she hissed.

By now, Miley must have been over his relief at seeing his little charge. He heard Maura whispering and looked over at her, with Sissy standing on the truck seat and pressing up close to his chest. He stared, almost dumbly, and Coal hoped he hadn't understood what the woman was talking about.

"I'm sorry about the truck, ma'am," Miley said, his face humble. "I been livin' there. No place to wash up this time of year."

Maura tried to smile. A sick look had come over her face. Again, Coal held back a laugh. It was rough to be caught!

"I'm going to lock your truck up, Miley," Coal decided out loud. "We'll send a wrecker back for it."

"No! I can't afford to get it out of impoundment."

"Let's worry about that later. I've got to get you to the hospital and have you checked out, and we need to get Sissy cleaned up and get some food in her."

Obviously numb, Miley nodded agreement. "Can you uncuff me? I can't carry her like this."

Coal frowned doubtfully. "Miley, you couldn't carry her anyway. You can barely stand yourself."

Again, Miley nodded. He was smart enough to agree.

Sissy clung so tightly to Miley that to see into her eyes they would have had to pry them apart. He lowered his chin to whisper into her ear. "Hey, Sis? Can you listen to me for a second, honey?" No response. "Sissy, I need you to do something for me, okay? This woman and man are the good guys. They'll do anything they can to help you. I promise you from the bottom of my heart. But your papa is really sick, hon. I'm not going to be able to carry you over to their car so we can drive to town and get some food. Do you think one of them could carry you?"

There was a long pause, and no one moved. It seemed like all of them held their breath while they listened to the sobs of recovery from the girl. Finally, she nodded her head. She immediately sought someone out, and it was Maura. She let go of Miley and let him step back, and then, like a forlorn statue, resigned to her fate, she stood there on the edge of the seat and waited in silence.

Maura stepped to her and said in a quiet voice, "Hi, Sissy. You can call me Maura. I promise I'll be your friend. Do you want to get some food?"

The girl raised her eyes, which looked extra dark brown against the red and swollen look from crying. She only nodded. When Maura slowly put her arms out, the girl simply stepped toward her, tired and beaten. She sagged into Maura's grasp, resting her face against her shoulder. Maura's nose twitched, and she fought back a grimace as the smell of the girl's hair reached her senses. But bravely, she pressed the little body to her own, and they walked to the Ford.

When Coal got Miley once more into the back seat of the Ford, Maura let Sissy slide in next to him and lie down across his lap. Then she got into the passenger side and leaned back her head. Coal was looking at the woman when an uncontrollable sadness swept over her face, and tears filled her eyes. She whipped her head the other way, so her eyes could only be seen from the other window.

Embarrassed for having seen the woman's wave of emotion, Coal went and pulled the pickup off the road, then took the keys, locking the doors by shoving down the handle of the passenger side and turning the key in the driver's door. He returned to the Ford and took one last look around, trying to give Maura a little more time. It was in that moment that he saw the handgun he had taken from Roger Miley, and he went over, bent down and picked it up. Old habit made him flip open the cylinder. There wasn't even one cartridge in the cylinder.

Holding the revolver in his open palm, Coal looked over at the car, trying to see Miley. The reflection on the back window only let him see a silhouette.

When Coal finally climbed in the car, Maura's face was still turned away from him. He watched her for a moment, just long enough to see her shoulders shaking and hear the wetness in the sound of her breathing. Without a word, he laid the empty gun down on the seat between them, with the cylinder opened so she would see it wasn't loaded. Then he turned the key in the ignition, wishing he had done it sooner, for a damp coldness had permeated the car from top to bottom, and little Sissy must be dying back there. There had been no coats in the pickup cab, and only one blanket, but it was so filthy and gray that he wasn't about to bring it with them. He made a mental note to himself to put some blankets in the trunk as soon as they got back to town.

With a deep breath, he looked over at Maura. Damn women. So emotional. He saw her shudder again, fighting hard to weep in silence. The sight and his thoughts brought tears to his own eyes now, and he had to clench his jaw and blink forcefully to fight the feeling away.

He reached out, his own hand uncertain, to where her hands were folded in her lap. He softly laid his hand over hers and gave it a couple of comforting pats. At least he hoped they would be comforting. But if they were, it wasn't obvious. He was watching her face, and as his hand settled on hers, he saw her jaw bunch up, and her eyes closed hard. Then she bowed her head, and her torso began to shake. Women.

He put the car into drive, took a deep breath, and started rolling toward North Fork.

CHAPTER THIRTY-ONE

The first stop once they made it back to Salmon was the hospital, on Daisy and Main. Coal left Maura with little Sissy in frightened tears in the waiting room while he went back with Miley to have him checked out.

Coal felt a strange flutter in his chest when nurse Annie Price came around the corner. He hadn't been consciously thinking of her, but some part inside him evidently was. After a necessarily quick hello, Annie took Miley back into an exam room. The quintessential nurse outfit of the day was the stereotypical white dress that ended just above her knees, with white panty hose, white patent leather shoes, and a white cap. None of the outfit did anything to take away from Annie's curves or her attractiveness as Coal watched her walk away, supporting Miley.

Now Coal was stuck. He had to wait through all of Miley's medical procedures, keeping guard not far from his room, while Maura and Sissy stayed in the waiting room and tried to occupy their time.

When they escorted Miley off to x-ray, Coal took the opportunity and went to find the EMT and her little charge. He found Maura reading *Where the Wild Things Are*, by Maurice Sendak. He had to smile. Sadly, he didn't remember much about his kids' childhoods, but he did recall Laura sitting with them, wrapped up in a comforter, and reading this book. Because the wonderful drawings in another book called *Little Bear* were done by the same artist, the imaginative Sendak, he remembered them both fondly. Did that mean he was not heartless after all? It would have been hard to convince Laura of that.

Coal stood watching Maura and the girl for a moment, even after Maura had realized he was there, looked up at him for just a second, then looked back down to continue reading. The moist look of her warm blue eyes stayed with him for some time.

Finally, he chose to sit near Maura, away from the girl. He had a feeling that being next to a strange man, besides feeling "surrounded," was not in the girl's list of favorite things right now.

"Good book?" he asked when finally the last page had been turned.

Maura laughed. "I always loved this book. My boys grew up on it."

"Me too—loved it, that is."

"Yeah, I was going to say I didn't think you were quite that young."

"Not quite. *Not hardly,* as the Duke would say," he added with a chuckle.

"It figures you're a fan of the Duke."

"What? You mean you're not?"

"I didn't say that." Which left Coal wondering exactly what she meant by the cryptic comment in the first place.

"Did you find anything to eat? I'll bet our little friend is starving."

Sissy didn't look up at him from silently turning the pages of the book, but Coal saw her perk up her ears. She seemed almost like the cat that pretends to be aloof, not caring one whit about its master's pet bird outwardly, when in reality that bird is *all* it's interested in.

"No, but I'm sure you're right. We were waiting for you." The look in Maura's eyes seemed almost hopeful, which took Coal aback a little.

"Well, thanks. But it looks like I could be here a while yet. Miley just went in to x-ray."

"Oh." Maura shrugged and looked down at Sissy. "Okay then. Hey, sweetie—do you want to get some food?"

Sissy looked up at Maura. Coal could see a connection had developed between them. She gazed at her for just a moment, her lips pursed, then nodded once. But it was a big enough nod for three.

Maura's eyes turned to Coal, and she smiled. "Well, I guess that's a big yes. I suppose we'll head down to the cafeteria."

"You don't have to," Coal countered. "Take the Ford, if you want. I'll bet Jay would be happy to feed you like a couple of princesses at the Coffee Shop."

"Really? Your car? What if you get a call and have to leave?"

Coal dug the keys out of his pocket. "Listen, I'm pretty much stuck here with Miley until they're done with him. If somebody else needs me that horribly bad, I'll just run over to the Coffee Shop and grab it from you. Deal?"

"Deal." Maura actually gave him a smile. At least what for her was a smile. Not that she never smiled, because he had seen that beautiful expression light up her face plenty of times. Just not normally for him.

After Maura and Sissy left, Coal wandered back to where Annie Price was working the desk. "What do you think of our friend Miley?" he asked her.

Annie stopped rocking a yellow number two pencil between her fingers. She gave Coal a long and searching gaze. Unlike the other night, this time that gaze came through a pair of eyeglasses that in some unexplainable way made her seem more sophisticated than before, perhaps even magnified her attractiveness—something he had not thought possible.

Annie didn't give him a huge smile, just a contemplative look and a sort of quizzical upturn of her lip corners. It was like she did not want to commit herself to looking happy quite yet.

"Oh, he's all right. Sort of. He smells bad, though."

Coal chuckled. "Yes he does. Sorry. He rode all the way back from the other side of North Fork in my back seat, and believe me, I was tempted to throw him in the Salmon a time or two. We had to crack the windows."

"I'm sure life's been rough for him, living in his truck."

"Sure. Tough to keep clean."

Annie got a distant look in her eyes, then suddenly giggled. "My mom would have taken him in and fed him, then given him one of our bedrooms. She would take anyone in who needed help."

"Sounds like a nice lady."

Mist came over Annie's eyes. "Yeah. She really was. I miss her."

"Has she been gone long?"

"Two years." Annie's gaze was locked on a stack of papers on her desk. All of a sudden, she drew a deep, chattering breath. She looked up at him and smiled. "You would have liked her. And she would have liked you."

Coal wasn't sure where that comment had come from. He and Annie Price had exchanged very few words in their short acquaintance, and most of them on a professional basis. She caught his consternation and rescued him. "Oh, I can just tell."

"Tell what?"

"What kind of a man you are."

He laughed to cover his discomfort. "I hope you're right. But as for Miley, what do you think of his medical condition?"

The pencil rocked back and forth a couple more times, as if being used as a crank to get her mental capacity up and running, and, Coal sensed, away from her mind-reading thoughts about him. She pumped one shoulder. "Somebody beat him up pretty bad. I don't think I've ever seen him here before, so I have nothing to compare to, but... He seems a little slow to me. You know—" She tapped the pencil to her temple a couple of times.

"Seems that way to me too. Didn't know if it might partly be the lack of food."

"I guess it might be," Annie conceded. "Who knows? I wish we knew someone who could say what he is normally like."

Dr. Bent, wearing a white lab coat and his balding head shining in the hallway lights, came in massaging lotion into his hands and stopped near Annie. "When the x-rays come back, we'll know more, but his motor skills seem all right so far, and his pupils—equal and reactive. I don't see anything obvious beyond the surface. But as far as the surface... Wow. Somebody really worked him over, didn't they?"

"They did," agreed Coal. "He shot a bighorn down by North Fork. Poached it. But I think these guys got pretty over-zealous in dealing with it. I'm thinking about bringing them in on charges."

"Nice to be a civic-minded citizen," said Dr. Bent. "But at what cost?"

The doctor spoke with Coal and Annie for a while longer, then wandered off. During the conversation, Coal had noticed Annie's lack of jewelry, other than the stud earrings that he guessed were the most that hospital policy would allow. That was standard. But the lack of ornament he noticed most was on her left ring finger. Annie wasn't the type of woman who would appear as a model in a catalog. That was a false kind of beauty, at least to Coal. No, this woman's kind of beauty went way deeper than that, and her eyes held a kind of softness, yet at the same time a sense of mystery. They seemed to search a man's soul, digging for answers to questions she had not been bold enough yet to ask. The thing he noticed most, like he had the first night, was the feeling that something haunted this woman, tormented her down deep, in a place beyond where any human being would ever tread again.

A corner of Coal's mouth turned up under his mustache. Annie smiled, showing her teeth this time, where usually her smiles were with closed lips. "What's that devious smile?" she asked.

"Smile? Me?" How could he tell this woman he barely knew that his almost-smile was his conscience, chiding him for digging so deep into the personality of a woman he knew absolutely nothing about? What did he think he was anyway, a shrink?

"Yes, you," Annie said, her smile and narrowing eyes sort of accusing him, in a teasing way.

"Honestly, I don't even know."

"You do too!" This was the lightest their conversation had gotten. The soft, wondering look in her face made Coal swallow hard.

"I was just thinking how cute you look in those glasses."

After a moment of surprise, her lips parted wetly, making Coal wonder what it would be like to kiss her, and simultaneously chiding himself for the untoward thought. Annie slapped her hand on her desk, causing the pencil to make a loud click. "Stop that. You're going to make me blush."

"Sorry. But no, really, they do look good on you."

"Well, thank you. You just made my day. I have been hating them."

"Don't. I promise—I don't lie about things like that."

She smiled shyly. "I have a feeling you don't say much at all about things like that."

You got that right, he thought. And he wondered what had goaded him into saying it in the first place.

*   *   *

Doctor Bent signed off on Roger Miley shortly after Maura and Sissy's return. Other than stitches for a cut by his eyebrow and some ointment for some of his worst abrasions, there seemed to be nothing out of the ordinary. Apparently, there was an area under the left side of his scalp that seemed to have fluid collected in it, indicative of the kind of blows he had taken from his captors, but it was nothing to give the doctor major concern. So he was free—at least of medical personnel.

Because the doctor had spoken to Coal and Miley far down the hall from Annie Price, he didn't really get a chance to say goodbye to her. As he was reapplying the cuffs to the man's wrists, he looked toward the desk, catching a look that seemed to be of disappointment from the nurse. She hurried a little wave his way. Then she turned and rushed down the hall to some important task, and he couldn't help but watch her go.

Back at the courthouse, Coal found it hard locking in jail a man who was the sole caregiver of a three-year-old girl. His one saving grace was the fact that Maura had come to the jail with him—as if she had any choice—and she was doing her best to get on the good side of little Sissy.

Actually, he had given Maura the option of being dropped off at Ken's Automotive to pick up the station wagon he was going to loan her, but mercifully she chose to stay with him. Sissy was her excuse.

"Miley, I have to put you in a cell until the hearing," Coal said. "Sorry. And I'm going to need to search you first."

He had Miley empty out his pockets, which consisted of half a stick of gum that appeared by the grime on it to have been saved for quite some time for "an emergency," a movie ticket, a couple of folded slips of paper, a worn-out business card for a bail bondsman, and ten cents in pennies, a dime and two nickels. He took off his beat-up plastic Casio watch and pulled a paper-thin wallet from his torn back pocket. Such were the worldly goods of Roger Miley, besides his rifle, his revolver, and his truck.

After writing down everything he had gotten off the man's person and slipping it all into a manila envelope, Coal slid the receipt across the desk to Miley. "Sign right here. We'll get your stuff back to you when you go."

Miley signed his name with painstaking care, but even so it was a horrible scrawl. Coal felt bad for him. He was amazed that a man like Miley could survive so long out in this hard world alone.

"Take off your shoes and socks and put them in that plastic bag," Coal said. "I'm going to get you back to the shower and have you clean up, and then we'll issue you some coveralls and clean underwear and socks. We'll get this stuff cleaned up for you." That was going to be on Coal's own dime, back at the house. But he just couldn't see having to hand that garbage back to Miley as filthy as it was. Besides, he told himself, he didn't want it to stink up the office while Miley was in jail. But the truth was that with the clothes tied tightly in a plastic bag, the smell could not escape.

While Miley was cleaning up, Coal laid out some underwear, socks and coveralls on a chair outside the shower.

"Are you supposed to stay with him?" Maura asked when Coal came out and sat down at his desk.

"Probably, by regulations. You want to?"

"No!" Maura shot back indignantly. "You're sick."

Coal laughed. "Sorry."

Maura's face softened, and she tilted her head toward Sissy. "So... What about her?"

Coal took a deep breath. "I have no idea what about her, Maura. What am I supposed to do?"

Maura shook her head. "Put her in jail too?"

"Right. I've been knocking my head on the wall since we picked them up. I don't know what to do."

"Yes you do."

"Huh?"

"I think she trusts me, Sheriff. I have a big bed in my trailer. Too big just for me."

Coal felt emotional, and he quickly looked away from Maura. His eyes landed on the little girl, bedraggled, scared, and worn-out. At least now her belly was full. What was going through the mind of that little thing? Her whole world had just fallen apart—what little world it had been.

"You'd take her in?"

"Well, of course only temporarily." She looked at him for a long time. "Sure. I'll take her."

"You're a lifesaver, lady."

"Lady?" she echoed. "Wow. Is there someone else in the room?"

Coal stood up and didn't reply. He walked to Sissy, and Maura followed. He crouched down, trying to stay back far enough not to frighten the girl. "Hi, Sissy."

The girl shot a look up at Maura, who just nodded and smiled. "It's okay, hon. I'm here." Sissy looked back at Coal, her eyes wide and worried.

"Sweetheart, your uncle has to stay with us for a while."

The girl gave him a confused look, and Maura knelt down by him. "She calls him 'Papa'."

"Oh, sorry. Your papa has to stay here for a while. Okay? He has some things he needs to do. But he thinks it would be all right if you went to be with Maura for a little while. How does that sound?"

The girl looked at Maura, who crawled toward her on her knees and held out her hand. Sissy took it instantly, and the other thumb she inserted in her mouth before looking back at Coal.

"Maura has horses," said Coal. "And dogs."

The girl's eyes grew wider, and she looked at Maura.

"How about it, Sissy? Just for a few days, until we straighten things out with your papa."

The little girl tilted her head to one side, looking at Coal. At last, she nodded. And so, at least for now, Sissy had herself a home, a bed, and a woman who genuinely cared for her. The thought of it warmed Coal's heart.

*   *   *

Jordan Peterson came in a bit later, after Miley had gotten out of the shower, smelling, and looking, somewhat like a new man. Miley said a tear-filled goodbye to his little niece, after being told where she was going. He looked at Maura and held out a trembling hand. "Please keep my little girl safe. We only have each other."

"She'll be fine, Mr. Miley," said Maura with a warm smile— a smile that made Coal a little jealous, since he seemed always to be the one in line for her frowns and her not-so-warm smiles.

"I'm done for the day," Coal told Jordan. "Put Mr. Miley in Jensen's old cell, and I guess I'll see you in the morning. I'm going to take Maura and Sissy home."

With that, the odd threesome trooped out the door and up the steps, leaving behind the smell of overcooked coffee and the warmth of the dingy cinderblock office and entering into an outside world of icy air perfumed with the smoke of evergreen wood. It was well toward dark, and probably crowding twenty degrees.

At Ken's Automotive, the light was still glowing, and Coal got out with Maura and Sissy. They all hurried inside out of the cold, where Parks was using a big salamander heater to try and heat a space that was almost too large for it.

Coal introduced the woman and child and got the keys from Parks, then went outside to get the car running and starting to heat up. He came back in for a while, and they shot the breeze with Ken, then finally the three of them went out back to the station wagon.

"Not what I'm used to," said Maura, looking over the low riding vehicle. "But it's free, right?"

"Sure," said Coal. "Who can complain?"

"Well, me for one," Maura replied. "But it never did any good before. People just called me a whiner."

"All right, Whiner, you two had better get home before it gets totally dark. And watch out for deer."

"Yes, Dad," said Maura, dropping down onto the bench seat and then letting the girl crawl over her to the other side.

"See you later, Sissy," said Coal. "Have fun with Maura, okay?"

The girl looked at Coal, put her gaze on Maura, then hurriedly pushed her thumb into her mouth and turned to face the opposite door. Maura reached up and patted the hand Coal had rested on top of the door panel. She winked at him and gave him a smile, nodding reassuringly. This time, to his surprise, the smile was warm.

"See ya, Sheriff."

"I'll see you," he replied. He wished he could have told Maura how much he appreciated what she was doing for that little girl. He stood and watched the station wagon all the way out of the lot, onto the street, then onto Main, heading in the direction of Leadore. Until the car was completely out of sight, he stood there in the now very lonely lot and watched it.

Instead of cutting through Ken's, he skirted around the building to get back to the LTD, then drove over to K.T. and Jennifer Batterton's place on Hope Street, a few blocks south of Main. He wanted to check on young Cynthia and see how she was doing. And it was time to tell K.T., if he hadn't already been told by Mitchell or figured it out for himself, that they would have no more use for his services. He had not looked forward to this moment, not when, truth be told, he would one hundred times rather have K.T. working as his deputy than the sniveling, dull and cowardly Todd Mitchell.

Cynthia was out when Coal called, and she had not yet returned when he gave K.T. the news. It turned out to be no big deal. K.T. had known it was coming the day Mitchell asked him to help out.

But it was opportune that Coal had come by anyway, because K.T. had some information for him. A strange vehicle, a red and white station wagon, possibly a late fifties or early sixties Chevrolet, had been parked down the street from his place two days in a row. The driver had stayed inside, and the vehicle had remained there for sometimes up to an hour each time. The first day, K.T. had gone out to do some work at his parents' ranch west of town, and he couldn't say for a fact, but he thought he had seen the vehicle following him out that direction.

Later, the vehicle was back again, and K.T. went out to see if he could talk to the driver. The moment he started walking toward the car, it sped past him, nearly clipping him as it went by.

"What does Bigfoot Monahan drive?" asked Coal.

"I'm not sure. None of us even knew he was back in town, remember?"

Coal nodded. "Okay, well watch out for yourself, will you? I've got an appointment set up with Kevin Wilhelm, a parole officer from Pocatello. He's supposed to be coming out this way to go pay a visit to Bigfoot with me and see if we can get any violations on him. I'll do some checking around his place for a vehicle like that while we're there. But like I said, for heaven's sake, keep your eyes open. Anything suspicious happens, you call me at home. And I mean *anything.*"

"Will do, buddy," said K.T. "And thanks. Hey, Coal," he said as Coal bade goodbye to K.T.'s wife, Jennifer, and turned to go. "I'm sorry I messed up and lost that job, but I'm sure glad they've got you now. I feel a lot safer with you running the show."

Coal looked at K.T. long and levelly. He started to ask him point-blank why he had been let go, but then he changed his mind. However, the question was in his eyes just long enough.

"It was stupid, Coal. It stemmed from an arrest I made on Phil Harringer three months ago for driving drunk. And man, Coal, I mean he was *drunk*. And mouthy, too. I'll admit I probably would have just taken him home, but he was such an ass."

Coal remembered Harringer. He was one of the wealthiest ranchers in the valley, and his sway on the county's affairs was frightening. "So?"

"Well, you know how low the pay is here. You saw what Jordan Peterson drives, right? That ugly Nash?"

Coal chuckled. "Yeah, I know. Pathetic."

"So I tried to get the county to swing for a little raise. Enough for gas money, that's all. I don't want to lose a jailer like Jordan."

Coal nodded.

"They turned me down. Flat. Told me any monkey could do that job for a lot less. Okay, so I lost my head a little. I took two hundred dollars out of petty cash and gave it to him. Kind of a bonus is how I was looking at it. For hard work well done. I didn't think it was all that criminal."

"I would have done the same, K.T."

"You would?"

"You're damn right I would. It's a crime what they pay all of us, especially when there are men like Harringer out there raking in the cash left and right."

"Well, the county didn't see it like you and I. They found out, and the commission and clerk told me they had to let me go— with the backing of the governor, I might add. Just like that. And that Mitchell was taking over until someone else was found."

"That being me," Coal put in. "How'd they find out? There wouldn't have been a paper trail."

"I'm not sure, Coal. That's the sad thing. I have no idea how. Jordan and I were the only ones who knew. But the thing is it was Harringer who was really pushing for me to be fired. I found that out from Rick Cheatum."

Coal stared at K.T. for a moment, then shook his head, denying something in his own thoughts. "Rick admitted that?"

"Yeah."

"Did he try to stick up for you?"

"I think so. He says he did, and I've never had any reason to doubt him before."

Coal thought a moment longer. "Well, Jordan didn't give you up, I'll wager on that."

"No. I'd never believe that."

Coal's thoughts were dubious. He decided not to voice them.

"Well, my friend, for the record? You should still be sheriff. That was a low blow if I ever heard of one. Politics tick me off more than most anything else I can think of."

"Get used to it, buddy," said K.T. "That's the biggest part of this job, and if you pee in the wrong punch bowl you're down the road."

Coal couldn't even laugh. *Someone* had peed in the wrong punch bowl, and he was not going to rest until he found out how the county had learned about K.T.'s misstep and how the news had reached the ears of rancher Phil Harringer.

CHAPTER THIRTY-TWO

Thinking about Sissy made Coal inevitably think about his own little girl. After he drove away from the Battertons', he pulled up to the curb on South Daisy, in front of the hospital. One more turn to the right would put him onto Main, and then headed home, but instead, he just sat there for a while. He thought about Annie Price, possibly still on shift inside, and if so, only feet away from him. He had a feeling he could talk to her about Katie, that she would understand what he was going through without all the criticism he got from his mother and from Maura. But he couldn't go in there. He hardly knew her. And he was supposed to be the county sheriff, and thus invincible. What man such as that would dump his cares on the first innocent woman who would listen?

In the gloaming, his headlights streamed like beacons out across the bleak darkness of Main. He pulled off his cowboy hat and set it on the seat beside him, running his fingers back through his hair. Taking a deep breath, he held it for a moment and closed his eyes, remembering...

Katie. Little Katie. At Marine base Calvin B. Matthews, in La Jolla, California, she had come writhing into the world after nineteen excruciating hours of labor on Laura's part, looking something like an alien buttered with cream cheese. For a few seconds, Coal waited for the midwife to tell him their baby was dead. It wasn't customary for a man to be in the birthing room at the hospital, which was why Coal and Laura had chosen to have Katie at home. But after his first view of the lifeless creature he sort of regretted their decision.

Then it began to move.

When the midwife had cleaned the little thing off, and Katie was warm and pink and sleeping soundly, cuddled up in his strong arms, he thought he had gone to heaven. And for all the years of her young childhood, he had—at least as far as his relationship with Katie Leigh went.

With Laura, however, it was different. Life in military bases was not easy, whether he was serving in the police or as a pistol shooting instructor. Either way, he had many occasions to run into women, either enlisted in the military or married to officers. That would not have been an issue, for Coal had no interest in any woman but his beautiful wife as anything other than a friend. But he was friendly and outgoing by nature, apparently gave out too many hugs and too many pats on the back and too many smiles, and Laura proved early in their marriage that her jealousy was of the over-the-top variety.

There were constant fights, long stretches of the silent treatment, and not nearly enough making up. There were longer bouts of Coal going out to be with the boys, whether it be at the range, out driving their pickups, or at the bars. Although Coal didn't drink very often or smoke, and he never had for any length of time, he had come to relish in the atmosphere of a smoky bar. And although Coal could honestly say he had never picked a fight, neither had he ever run from one. He was good at boxing, at martial arts, and at steer wrestling, and all three often came in handy in a bar fight. He was also very strong and very fast, and perhaps a little overly proud of both.

But Laura wasn't. The two of them didn't drift apart; they exploded apart. The only moments when they seemed to truly still be as in love as when they were dating were either when he was leaving for a long stretch of time, or coming back after being gone. The rest of it, as far back as he could remember, was some mixture of arguing, yelling or awkward silence.

And then came the day, after all of those years Laura had endured the military and at least been a virtuous, if not an overly happy, wife, when she took the job as a substitute teacher in Warrenton, Virginia. The day that began her downward spiral. The day Coal would always think of as Black Monday.

Coal took a deep breath as he found his vision blurred. He leaned back against the seat and blinked forcefully a couple of times. The streets were growing ever darker, and traffic was slow. A heavily weighed-down lumber semi loomed up out of the darkness, coming from the west, its wheels whining on the pavement. Coal gazed at the huge links of the chains that held the logs in place. He looked at the massive tires. He thought of the days when he had watched those wheels and dreamed of a career in the driver's seat of rigs like that.

So long ago...

Long before Laura's drug abuse began, and then Katie's. Back when at least in front of the children they were still able to pretend to be a functioning family.

Drawing another deep breath, and with Katie on his mind, he put the car back in drive, eased onto the throttle, and pulled away from the curb. He paused just for a moment at Main, looking both ways, at the dancing, semi-blurry beams of headlights swimming in his moistened eyes. He worked his jaws, wishing he had a stick of his Blackjack gum. Anything to occupy him so he didn't have to think.

But he *did* have to think. He had to think about talking to Katie Leigh. They had a new chance to be friends, here in this little community. Some place, sometime, somehow, that had to begin. And he, as her father, had to begin it.

He pulled onto Main and headed southeast, moving slowly without thinking about it. He had made up his mind. This was the night. Hell or high water. If he and Katie were not to be friends, it wasn't going to be because he didn't try.

The front windows of the house were solemnly aglow only with lamplight when Coal pulled into the drive. He heard the dogs bark a couple of times, a deep-throated sound that gave him little wonder so many thugs had their hearts spill over with fear at its eruption. When a Doberman or a German shepherd opened up, and the listener was not familiar with dogs, it must surely sound like the gates of hell had fallen over. Even if the dogs belonged to you, it was still a sobering noise, akin to the roar of a lion in the night.

The dogs had ceased barking, so either Connie or the boys must be with them. Coal rubbed the stubble of his jaw and leaned forward to look at the front door. A fine dusting of frozen rain had started to pelt the windshield. He put his hat back on and stepped out, shutting the door quietly behind him. *Okay, Coal, this is it. You're the man of this house. Act like it for once. You killed Laura. Don't kill Katie too.*

He went up the steps slowly and pulled open the screen door, then put his fingers to the inner knob. He took another big breath, looking through the front window. The twins were sitting on the couch, watching TV. They must know he was home, but perhaps he was just a stranger to them. They didn't even get up.

Easing the door open, he was greeted by a barrage of attention from Shadow and Dobe. Thank heavens for dogs, often the only being in an otherwise cold and lonely house to ever let a man feel like he had been missed. He managed to fend them off enough to shut the door, then rubbed them all over as they practically fawned over him, vying for his attention. When he had had enough, he pushed them away and looked at the boys. They were watching NBC network's *The Flip Wilson Show,* and when Coal realized that, he cringed. Where had the evening gone? It didn't even air until seven.

"Hi, boys. Good show?"

Wyatt turned his head, just now seeming to notice him there. "Daddy!" He jumped up and ran to him, nearly tripping over Shadow's feet before she could retreat out of the way. Morgan wasn't far behind his brother, and they both laid into their father with mighty hugs—and gave him a mighty warm heart. It wasn't that his boys hadn't missed him—he guessed they just tended to get too engrossed in the antics of Flip Wilson.

He held onto the boys an extra-long time before noticing Connie standing in the entry to the kitchen, watching them. "Hi, Mom," he greeted. She just lifted a hand and gave him a little wave, and he was sensitive enough to realize that the scene before her had rendered her temporarily unable to speak.

Finally, he gave the boys a good pat on the back and said, "All right, you two, don't miss your show." He stood up, and they hurried back to their warm spots on the couch.

The homey smell of pine smoke wafted through the front room from the Franklin stove, and somewhere in the middle it mingled with the scent of dinner—pot roast, by the aroma of it. Coal walked to his mother and gave her a huge, affectionate hug. After fifteen seconds or so, she said into the shoulder of his jacket. "Wow. That's like a homecoming hug, Coal."

He laughed. "Well, I just came home, Ma."

"You should save some for Virg. And Katie, too."

He pulled away and took her shoulders, looking down into her gray, misty eyes. "You know what? That's exactly what I was planning on."

"Good, Son. Good. Good luck." She pumped her fist happily as he stepped away from her and started up the stairs.

He tapped lightly on Virgil's door. His young man sat at a desk his father had built out of logs he sawed in the hills and had milled into boards at the local sawmill. Coal had fancied at one time that he had helped his father build it, and he had told all his visiting friends that was the case. But a closer inspection of those vague memories told him he may have mostly just watched, and maybe pretended to sand it a little and paint on shellac. Either way, the old thing had served him and his brothers for many years, all the way through junior high and high school. It was heart-warming to see his own boy making use of it now.

"Hi, Dad."

"Virg." Coal stood in the doorway for a few more seconds, vainly hoping for a hug. He guessed his big boy was just that—too big. He waited, but a hug never came. Coal swallowed and stepped closer, pulling up a chair that his father had also made—although without the same success as the desk. One leg was a little short, and it always rocked, and, before the brown shag carpet got laid on the floor, irritated whomever was trying to concentrate on whatever they needed to concentrate on in the rooms down below.

"How was school?"

Virgil stared at his book, taking shelter there. "Fine."

"Anything happen?"

"Uh-uh."

Strike two. Last pitch. "Make any friends?"

"No, not really."

You're out, Coal Savage. Silently, he swore. How did a man talk to a son he loved? He was one of the best investigators he knew of in D.C. The man other agents sought out, even some supervisors, when serious interrogation skills were needed. But he couldn't wring one item of value from his own son.

"Well... How's your schedule?"

"Fine."

Coal nodded. Virgil didn't see it. His face was in his book. Coal sneaked a peak. Algebra. What were they doing teaching algebra to a thirteen-year-old? Or was Virgil fourteen? He cursed himself. Some father he was. Well, he was going to make his escape while he could, because if Virgil asked him for help with an assignment in algebra, he was about to be reminded how imperfect his father truly was.

"I'm proud of you for working hard on your homework, Son," said Coal, standing up. The only reply was a slight giggle.

Coal's children had never been taught the rudiments of politesse. Or else *thank you's* and *pleases* just seemed too highfalutin for them. He seldom coaxed either from any of them, and that knowledge shamed him. But he wasn't the one who had always been home with them. That had been Laura's purview. And she had failed.

Coal felt his face grow suddenly hot as he stood like a carving in stone and watched his boy read, or at least pretend to read so he wouldn't be forced into talking. It was true that Laura was the one who had always been home with them. Because for Coal, work had taken over his life, and his family had come second. Now he would pay the price. Laura had been home with the children, and she had failed. Coal had simply failed to be home.

He backed out of the room in awkward silence and pulled the door shut quietly, as if trying to pretend he had never been in there. He looked down the stairs. The one child he was most afraid to see was the one he needed most to see. Coal Savage could wade into a room full of drunken brawlers with no fear and fight his way back out victorious. But even the thought that he could get the worst of it gave him little fear. However, it was different with his own daughter. Walking into her room was akin to another man, a herpetophobe, falling into a den of snakes.

But it was time. *Walk into your snake den, you coward.* Coal started down the stairs, walking as if to avoid stepping on newborn hamsters. He got to the bottom of the stairs, turned and walked down the hall, stopping at the last door on the left. He knocked without waiting. To wait was to cower away.

"Uh-huh?" came the answer to his knock. His heart was already pounding. Now it seemed to double in power and speed.

"Katie, it's me."

Long silence. Deathly silence. Eternal silence.

"Can I come in?"

"Why?"

Pause. Take a deep breath. "I'd like to talk to you."

"I'd rather not."

Coal tried the door knob, and it turned. Should he walk in? Did he risk everything by doing that? And what if she weren't even decent at the moment? That would compound all of their issues. A hundredfold.

Another deep breath, trying to still his nerves. *Don't let Laura happen all over again,* he prayed.

"Katie, I need to come in."

If she had not been dressed, she would have said something. In fact, if she had even thought of the excuse she would have said something. Instead, silence. Silence as deafening as the still of the great north woods.

Coal had not released the knob. Now he simply pushed, and the door came open. Daniel in the lion's den? Somehow it was the first image that came to his fevered mind. What was he doing? What in the world was he going to say? What could *anyone* say to a young lady who had been so damaged?

Katie sat on her bed, staring laser beams through the dark window that fell upon the side yard. She had been holding a stuffed toy bear. It was *the* bear, he realized. *Little Bear,* the one from the children's book, but in the flesh. So to speak. He remembered the bear. He recalled the very day he had picked it off the shelf at Toys R Us. The day he had bought it. *He* had picked it out. *He* had bought it. A fleeting moment of sentimentality, perhaps. But he remembered well standing in dim shadows watching Laura read the book to Katie and Virgil. He remembered the rapture in their eyes. So when he saw Little Bear in the toy store... He couldn't *not* buy it.

He had picked it. He had purchased it. Laura had carried his purchase from the store, and it was she who had come home all excited and presented Katie with that gift. Never had she told their daughter that her father had picked Little Bear for her. Without a word concerning Coal, she had given the gift as if it had all been her idea. "Look, Katie. Little Bear!" And that was that.

Katie had just been hugging Little Bear to her body. Instinctively, Coal knew that. Now he was on the bedspread, being pressed down, compressed by the weight of Katie's hand. There were shiny places on Katie's cheeks, places from which even an insensitive father knew she had just wiped tears.

That was my Little Bear, Katie, thought Coal. But he could never say it, never in a million years. All these years later, it would be seen only as a struggle to win affection from this girl who had decided to hate him. This girl who knew without a doubt he had killed her mother. Had put the noose around her neck himself.

Coal cringed and blinked his eyes hard. He stared, frozen in place. *Katie...*

His daughter was beautiful. So incredibly beautiful. Even with the bruising around her eyes and nose, now turned to an ugly purplish red. Anyone could see how lovely she was. Any boy would have been proud to have her on his arm. If she was catching grief in school, the cause of it was jealous girls, not boys.

Dull-voiced, Coal stood there with his hands in his pockets and said, "I'm really sorry about your nose, Katie. It looks a lot better."

She cranked her head farther the other way. One more turn and it would snap off like the stem of an apple.

"I hear some kids are giving you a hard time in school." *It's because you are so beautiful, and you scare them.* Should he say that? It would sound pretty stupid. That wasn't the kind of thing a man said to his daughter. "Kids can be cruel." And he was savvy enough to know she was thinking, *So can some dads.*

"I'll go in tomorrow, Katie. I'll go fix it and make them stop."

Wrong! Those were the wrong words, and it took less than a millisecond to figure it out. "Don't you dare go to my school. You'll make it worse! Stay away from my school. Stay away from *me!*"

"Hey," he tried to soothe. "I'm sorry. I was just trying to help."

Katie scrambled off the bed, Little Bear dangling from her right hand. She pierced him with lances that had once masqueraded as eyes. "Just leave me alone!" Even double earplugs and shooting ear muffs could not have blocked that sound from all ears in the house. Or anywhere on the Savage property, for that matter.

His daughter whirled and ran past him out the door, and Coal stood and stared at the empty place where she had been. The image of his little girl lingered there, a fading shade of the angel he used to know. Then she was gone, and he was left with a dank cave, empty of love, filled with hate and anger.

Coal heard Connie yell, "Katie, wait!" and then the slamming of the front door.

With feet like blocks of dead wood, he walked from the room, mechanically flipping the light switch down. He went down the hall. His mother stood staring at the front door, where both dogs turned around and around in nervous circles and started to whine.

Connie turned shocked eyes on her son. "What happened?"

"I guess you heard."

"No, Coal. I heard the last part. That tells me nothing."

"I apologized for bruising up her face. I told her it didn't look that bad."

"That's all?"

"Just drop it, Mom. Let's face it: I was right, and you were wrong."

Connie put her hands on her hips, running her tongue across her upper lip. "All right, Son, let's have it. What else did you say?"

"It doesn't matter. Obviously, it really doesn't. I told her I'd go to school and make them stop. I said I'd fix it. Okay?"

"You did not say that, Coal. You can't be serious."

"What?"

"You can't go in and just *fix* high school social problems, honey. Those kids have to fix them on their own. That's part of growing up, finding their way."

"What was I supposed to say?"

Connie stood there and gazed at her boy, her one boy who seemed to be making anything of his life. A vastly sad and sorrowful look came over her face, her eyes reddened, and she tilted her head to one side and brought a self-comforting hand up to hide her mouth.

"You poor boy," she said, and putting both arms out, she hurried to him and hugged him. "I'm sorry. I'm so sorry."

They held each other, and the twins remained silent. Only this time they were certainly well aware of the mood in the house. Flip Wilson was long forgotten.

Connie sniffled after a minute. She still had not let go, and neither had her son. "Coal, do you remember in the first grade? When those girls chased you all over the playground for days and days?"

Coal chuckled. Hell, how could a man forget something like that? Carlena Robbins and Teresa Hanley. The two female bigwigs of the first grade kingdom of Mrs. Black's class, in through the school entryway, first door on the right. The room that smelled like crisp autumn and dirty hands and sweaty playground runners and school books and Elmer's paste and Playdough. Carlena and Teresa had big plans of kissing poor little Coal, a boy who had never been around kids in his life, other than his own brothers. They had chased him every recess. He had begged Mrs. Black to let him stay in the classroom during recess. No dice. She only told him to stop teasing the girls.

So, with all hope lost, he went to his fate, and one warm spring day they found him, as they had sworn to. They cornered him in a cul-de-sac, and there, in front of what seemed like a hundred other girls, they kissed him—right on the mouth.

He went home crying, and Connie went to school and chewed the girls out in front of everyone. Coal swore he would never share anything traumatic with his mother again. And he had stayed true to that word.

But now he had been ready to do the same thing to his own daughter. How easily a parent forgot those days of scary, sensitive childhood.

"Yeah, Mom. I remember. You gave them what for."

"Yeah, we sure did... And I have kicked myself ever since. What I put you through, and you just trying to find your little way. You tried to do the same thing, you know. And to a woman nearly grown."

"You're right. I just wanted her to know I'd protect her."

"That girl is full of more pain than I've ever seen, buddy. She is going to need some help that maybe none of us can give her."

He pulled back from her but didn't let go. "You mean we take her to a shrink?"

"Well, that makes it sound pretty bad," said Connie, frowning. "But a psychiatrist, yes. She has been damaged, Coal. Nobody can walk into something like that and come out normal. Nobody can even imagine what she has been through."

Coal shuddered, thinking of Laura, imagining her still form, her face turned deep purple, her eyes still open, vacant, staring.

"No, Mama—I can imagine. I'll always be able to imagine."

CHAPTER THIRTY-THREE

"Give her some time."

The words rang in his head.

"Give her some time."

His mother was usually very wise, but tonight Coal was no longer sure. Yes, Connie said his girl had grabbed a coat on her way out the door—which just happened to be his Wrangler jacket—but still, it couldn't be much over fifteen degrees out there, and that jacket, although it had a blanket liner, was still just a jacket. Where was she? What in the world was she doing?

She could have gone to the barn. That would be the obvious first place of refuge—if Katie were her grandmother. But Katie, for the most part, was a born and raised city girl. Although the hay and straw would serve to keep her warm, and those big old horses would put off enough body heat in the closeness of the barn to heat it up a degree or two as well, it was likely that their quiet munching of feed, blowing and nervous stamping in the dark would frighten Katie more than comfort her. Even in the daylight, Connie had told him she had tried to get Katie out there with the horses, and the girl always had something else she would rather be doing. So Coal's gut told him it would not be Katie's first choice.

Maybe Margie and Wilber Rawson's? That was a possibility. But a discreet phone call by Connie disproved it.

Well, wherever Katie had gone, the Dean Martin show had been on for quite a while now, and it would be over in a few minutes. Jack Benny and Lynn Anderson were guest starring this evening. Jack's dry humor that usually tickled Coal's funny bone could not penetrate his crust now, and even Lynn's voice fell flat. All he wanted to know was if his daughter was someplace safe and warm.

The boys were all in bed now. Normally, he was not responsible enough to have made them hit the hay, but fortunately Connie was. His little buddies were going to miss out on an awful lot of great entertainment thanks to their grandmother's sense of responsibility. Besides *The Dean Martin Show,* on Monday nights there was *The New Bill Cosby Show,* and on Sunday, *Night Gallery,* which he guessed was a little over their heads anyway and would cause them to have nightmares he wasn't equipped to deal with. But then there were some great dramas: *Cannon, Gunsmoke, Mission Impossible,* and *Owen Marshall.* And one of the channels had a movie playing every night, which was the only chance his boys were generally going to have of seeing the Duke or Clint Eastwood. Then, although he wouldn't have let them watch it anyway, there was *Love, American Style,* where once, in a few minutes of boredom, Coal had sat glued to the TV screen watching how true love was supposed to be and how it never was.

Coal couldn't take another minute of Dean Martin's glued-on smirk. He looked over at Connie, who sat on her "easy" chair about as *un*-easy as a wet doggie biscuit in a room full of Great Danes. "Mom, I gave her some time. Where is she?"

Connie needed the sound of his voice to release her. She had been waiting on the edge of a knife. "Come on, let's go look." And she was up as if catapulted by springs, grabbing her stall-mucking coat from beside the door, her keys already in her hand.

Coal got a tan, insulated Dickies coat out of the closet and got his own set of keys to the Ford. "I'll drive toward town and then start back this way. You start knocking on doors along the highway."

"Wouldn't someone call?" asked his mom.

"You and I would have. But I can't speak for anyone else. Some people might be concerned only with keeping her safe and not want to upset her."

"You're right. Then meet back here in... half an hour?"

Coal nodded as they turned and headed out into the cold night. *Half an hour.* It was long enough for just about anything to happen. The entire attack on Pearl Harbor only took ninety minutes.

With a sick feeling of dread in his chest, he sat on the icy cold car seat and cranked the engine over. He backed around in the tight driveway, then pulled out into the lane, driving too fast over the creek, down the alleyway of willows and finally to the main highway. He drove northwest, wondering why his daughter would come this way. She was a city girl! He imagined her being totally calm and intrepid in a room full of teenage boozers, drug addicts and potential rapists, but the Salmon highway at almost ten o'clock at night? With deer and moose on the loose, and horses, cattle and sheep making strange noises out in the dark? It hardly seemed probable, especially with seven miles to go just to get to the edge of town. Yet where else could she have gone? He swore, helpless. He forced himself to slow down. Any place was as likely as the next to spot his wayward daughter walking along the shoulder, coming home.

The only business on the way to town was on the left side of the road, not far from his own lane: the Twenty-Eight Club. He pulled into the parking lot and went in, but a query there proved that they had not seen a girl fitting her description.

He finally cruised into the quiet streets of town with never a sight of anyone. Seven miles. This was ridiculous. The street, like the highway, was slick with the earlier sleet, slick and shiny in the dim glow of the street lights. A quarter of a mile into the town limits, a red fox darted across the road in front of him, making its rounds of the town as brazen as a New York City hooker. Coal slowed down in the busiest section of town, where lumberjacks, miners and ne'er-do-wells stumbled up and down the sidewalks from bar to bar. Now that daytime's steady stream of lumber trucks had ceased, it was replaced with roving miner and logger vehicles, mostly pickups.

Now and then, he saw a face he recognized, and three times he stopped and asked about a lonely, scared looking fifteen-year-old girl. Each time, the half-drunk look on the men's faces darted away into an instant look of sober worry. Even as rough as these men were, they were all soft toward the plight of the father and his missing daughter, and all of them swore to be on the lookout and to call dispatch if they saw her.

Coal went up to the sheriff's office after a fruitless search of town and stepped into the jail. Jordan Peterson was surprised to see him.

"Hey, boss! What's up?" Jordan glanced at his wristwatch, then almost immediately at the clock on the wall.

"My daughter took off, Jordan. Have you had any phone calls?"

"No sir." Jordan had the typical instant look of worry in his eyes.

Somewhat absently, Coal asked, "How's the new guy? Miley?"

"Seems pretty sick. Sleeps a lot, won't hardly wake up to eat."

Something sparked deep in the recesses of Coal's mind, and he took the keys to the cell block and went back, flipping on the lights and garnering several complaints, which he ignored.

He looked into Miley's cell. The man had his blanket drawn up tightly around him. He hardly seemed to be breathing. Coal opened the cell and went to look down at the scrawny looking poacher. His features were twisted strangely, but it was only a moment before he drew a breath. A moment later, another. Coal would have thought as skinny as he was he could see him breathe from out in the hall. He put a hand lightly on his forehead, but his temperature seemed normal too.

Going out, he locked the cell behind him and said good night to the other inmates. A couple of them even said it back, then rolled back into their blankets.

"At least he's breathing," he answered Jordan's questioning look. "But check on him every now and again anyway."

Without saying anything else, he went to the phone, picked it up, and spun the dial. The number to his house was 756-1776, but he dialed only 6-1776. Almost every outside prefix was long distance and required the area code, so the first two digits were superfluous when dialing a number within the same prefix.

The phone rang five times, and then he hung up. Just like he would have been at the boys' age, they were obviously unaware or unconcerned about their sister's welfare enough that no one answered. They were probably delved deeply into the world of their boyhood dreams—or maybe nightmares, if anything like their sister.

No sooner had Coal hung up than the phone rang, and he jerked it back off the hook. "Hello. Sheriff's office."

Yes, who am I speaking with?

"The sheriff," Coal replied crisply. "Savage."

Oh. Hi! This is Nadene, one of the night dispatchers. I'm happy you're there. We've just received a call from Sheriff Batterton. Sorry, I mean Mister *Batterton. Your daughter Katie is at his house.*

Coal jerked the phone away from his ear and looked at it, as if he would see Nadene's expression there. He pressed it back to his ear. "Come again? You said she's at the Battertons'? That's a good eight miles from our house! And how would she even know them?"

A long pause. *I'm sorry, sir, I don't know that.*

"Of course. No, I'm sorry. Thanks for calling, Nadene."

Without waiting for her reply, he dropped the phone back onto the bed, making the bell clang.

Jordan looked down at it, then back up at his boss. "Found her?"

"She's at Battertons'," Coal replied, knowing he had a confused look on his face and not taking the time to hide it. "See you later, Jordan."

He was out the door before the jailer could reply, bounding up the steps, and almost to the car when he slipped on the icy pavement and nearly fell. Cursing the ice and the cold and the woodsmoke smell he normally loved, he fell into the front seat and backed around, then spun his tires out of the lot. Once more, he had to remind himself of the slick pavement.

Driving across the river, Coal turned onto S. St. Charles, and a few blocks later left onto Hope, where he pulled past a Catholic church and the residence next to it and parked at the dark curb in front of the second house. He didn't want to get out. He was too mad. And too relieved. He didn't want actually laying eyes on his daughter to make the first emotion override the second.

Forcing himself to take several deep breaths, he closed his eyes, flexing and then loosening his fingers on the steering wheel. At last, he got out and went up to the door, knocking four times.

It opened promptly to the face of the once-pretty, now over-weight and dour-looking Jennifer Batterton. Wrinkles creased the sides of her mouth, around her eyes, and especially the loose skin gathering at her throat, but looking into her quizzical blue eyes Coal could still pick out the pretty girl of their teenage years, when she was a Salmon Savage cheerleader and one of the most sought after dates at Salmon High. She smiled at him uncertainly, then motioned behind her with her eyes, a kind of warning.

Coal smiled back at her, nervous, and let his eyes slip beyond her shoulder. On the sofa sat Katie, with Cynthia beside her. They were both sitting as sideways on the couch as possible, and Katie's eyes were turned toward the wall. She knew who was at the door.

From the corner of his eye, Coal saw another dark figure and looked over to see K.T. leaning against the side of the doorway that led into the kitchen. Dressed in dark jeans and dark blue shirt, he blended into the unlit room behind him. His friend gave him a sympathetic look as Jennifer stood aside and he started slowly toward his daughter.

"Hi, Katie."

No reply—no surprise.

"Grandma's been pretty worried about you." No sense mentioning that he had been too. He knew it would only set her off again. "She should be getting back home within a few minutes, if you'd rather have her come and get you."

Cynthia looked up and gave Coal a little smile, tilting her head to one side. He didn't know if he should acknowledge the fact that they had already met, and immediately decided better of it. He could have no idea what she might have told her parents about the other day, and he wasn't going to be the one getting her in a tight spot with them.

All of a sudden, Coal heard a toilet flush down the hall, and then tap water running. In another minute, a door opened, and down the hall came a shadowy form. It hesitated as it drew near the front room, and Coal guessed whoever it was had just become aware of his presence.

For a moment, the form stopped, and Coal actually thought he—it was obvious now from the shape that it was a man—was going to turn around and retreat back down the hall.

Finally, however, he came on into the light. Coal's stomach tightened up, and his heart fell. It was Lance, the young man from the van incident. He had been so caught up in the moment that if his van was outside Coal hadn't even noticed it.

"Hi, Sheriff," greeted Lance, his face reddening.

"Lance. I'm surprised to see you here."

"Yeah. I was just about to head out." The young man looked toward the girls on the sofa, and both of them were staring at him. Perhaps it was the protective father in him, but the look Katie gave Lance took him aback. Maybe he had only imagined it. But it seemed like there was a lot of familiarity there, a feeling he couldn't shake. He looked instantly at Cynthia. The look in her eyes for Lance seemed to be one of nothing but disdain. But Coal didn't know her enough to truly judge that.

"Katie?" Coal turned back to the girls. "Will you ride with me?"

A long moment of silence, and then Jennifer laid a soft hand on Coal's shoulder. "She'll go with you, Coal. But just drive, okay? Don't try to talk." Her long gaze into his eyes was one of an all-knowing mother, protective of a child on the verge of being lost.

Coal nodded and tried to wink at Jennifer. "No talking, Katie. I'll just drive you back home. I'm sure Grandma's there by now, and she is dying to know you're safe."

Katie and Cynthia's eyes met, and Cynthia reached out and gave his daughter's hand a squeeze. He was dumbfounded. They had barely moved to this town. How did two girls who had been strangers to each other two days ago get to the stage of being able to comfort each other in that length of time?

"Sorry about all this, K.T." Coal looked over at his old school mate.

"Don't be, buddy. What are friends for? I'm just glad Cynthia saw her."

Coal peered closer at his friend. A dozen questions surfaced, but with Katie right there, how could he ask any of them? "If you want to wait in the car, Katie, I'll be right out."

Katie didn't reply. She just looked for a while longer at Cynthia, finally giving her a little sober nod. Her eyes went to Lance, and Coal's followed. The boy was stoic.

Katie got up and went to the door, looking last at Jennifer and trying to smile. "Thank you, Mrs. Batterton."

Jennifer smiled and gave the girl a little wave. "Any time, sweetheart. You are always welcome here."

"Goodbye, Mr. and Mrs. Batterton," said Lance, and Coal couldn't make a scene by following him and Katie outside. His eyes shot to Cynthia, but he also didn't dare look at her too long and let her parents see the familiarity.

"I was driving home from Lance's when I saw a girl walking alone down the side of the highway," said Cynthia before Coal could say anything else.

"Okay...?"

"I met her at school. She seemed kind of lonely, and some of the girls were treating her bad. I didn't like it."

"You helped her?"

"I told them to go away," said Cynthia. "I hate bullies. Your daughter is way prettier than they are, too. They're just jealous."

"This is our daughter, Cynthia," said Jennifer.

"You remember Cynthia, don't you?" interjected K.T.

Coal looked back at the pretty young lady. It wasn't something he had given much thought to, but he did remember a much younger K.T. with a grinning little girl walking beside him. Years had passed, and the memory was faded.

"I think I do. She was just a *little* princess back then—knee-high to a grasshopper, my dad used to say."

K.T. laughed. "I remember that! He used to say it about me!"

"He sure did. Or knee-high to a short sheep."

Again, K.T. laughed. Suddenly, he looked over at Cynthia again, and he held up a scroungy-looking orange-brown Teddy bear so it was facing her. "Oh, and hey, *princess,* you left your bear in the bathroom again this morning."

Cynthia's eyes darted over to Coal, then back to her father. "Oh, stop it!"

"Stop it? Maybe I should throw this ratty old thing in the trash. You're too big for Teddy bears anyway, right?"

With a spunky face, she retorted, "That's not just any Teddy bear, Daddy! That's Buddy. You and Mom got him for me when I was three, and I'm never giving him up!"

K.T. laughed and threw her the bear. "Oh, all right. Just keep him out of my bathroom. He probably has fleas."

Cynthia giggled and stroked her bear's worn-out little forehead, giving her father a mock look of reproval.

Coal looked from the girl back to K.T. and Jennifer. "Hey, guys, thank you for looking out for Katie."

"The least I could do," said his friend. "Since you named her after me and all."

Coal just stared for a few seconds. "Huh?"

K.T. looked at him uncertainly. "You named her after me?" His friend's eyes flickered to Jennifer, who gave him a bewildered look.

Uncomfortable and feeling something strange in the pit of his stomach, Coal chuckled. He tried to put on his best face. "So... Who told you?" he asked casually.

"Well, Laura—who else!" K.T. laughed. "She said never to mention it to you, that you'd be embarrassed. But I thought since..."

Coal smiled, composing himself. "It's okay. I'm not embarrassed. Just glad to know you already knew. I always meant to find a way to tell you. Named my daughter after the Prince of Pushups," he said, pumping his fist.

His eyes slid past the paunch sticking out over K.T.'s belt, and without looking at her he thought again of how Jennifer had gone to seed. When he looked in the mirror at himself, it seemed he had hardly aged. And Laura, too, had looked like a twenty-five year-old—right up until she started into the heavy drugs. But the day was not so long ago when these two were the most beautiful people at Salmon High. He smiled again, but there was a melancholy behind it.

"Well, guys, I'd better get going. It's cold outside."

K.T. came forward and held out his hand. Coal, feeling numb inside, shook it and then tipped the brim of his hat at Jennifer.

He stepped outside. Katie and Lance were standing too close to each other for comfort on the sidewalk. The second the door opened, Lance took a couple of steps away.

Coal walked down the steps and stopped by Lance. Katie had already moved away toward the Ford. "I'll be talking to Cynthia again, Lance. Soon. I hope nothing she says upsets me."

Lance's eyes jumped toward the front door of the house. "Oh! No, don't worry. I promised her I was okay with us being over. No, it's totally fine."

"I'm a little worried about her being at your house tonight."

"Yeah, don't be." Lance's voice sounded a little sullen now. "She broke up with me the next day. Tonight she just came out to get a Zane Grey book back that she had loaned me, and I came into town to bring her a scarf she had given me that I thought she would want back. She's safe with me, I guarantee you."

A huge feeling of relief washed over Coal. *Good girl!* he thought.

"You make sure of it. Jail doesn't do good things for green kids, Lance."

He heard the car door shut and looked over to see that Katie was inside the LTD. "I'd love to not see you back at this house. Or anywhere with that girl. She and I have a deal."

"Okay."

"Okay?"

"I'll leave her alone, sir. She doesn't want anything to do with me, thanks to..."

"Thanks to what?"

"Nothin'."

"Thanks to me?" Coal's ire was instantly rising, in spite of his knowing he had to watch his temper like a skunk in the hen house—it was that untrustworthy. "You ought to thank me, Lance. At least you're not going to jail. Now go home before either of us says something we'll regret."

Coal didn't shake the young man's hand. Normally, he would have—a way to gage him. But he just didn't like Lance that much. He didn't feel like touching his skin.

He hadn't quite reached the car when suddenly he realized why Lance no longer cared if Cynthia was attached to him, and the realization struck him like a mule kick to the guts. Lance had found himself a new girlfriend!

Goose bumps ran over Coal, and he had to calm himself before he opened the car door to get in with Katie. He took a breath and climbed in, trying to act like nothing was wrong, when inside his stomach was doing flip flops.

The long drive back to the house was quiet. Coal had promised there would be no talk, and that promise was easy to keep. He had something else on his mind, even besides anything that was going on between Katie and Lance. The revelation that *they*—he and Laura—had named their only daughter after the Prince of Pushups. And until tonight, Coal had never had a clue that he had taken part in that decision.

Laura, he thought, *I know I wasn't the greatest husband who ever lived. I was a provider, but I wasn't there all the times when you and the children needed me. I lost myself in my job. But what kind of a woman were you? What kind of person did I really marry?*

Were there others, besides Robert Laine? What kind of a fool had Coal been all these years anyway? He had never been there for Laura. But gangly, scrawny Robert Laine had, with his bulging Adam's apple and all.

And now, he couldn't help but think, maybe K.T. Batterton had been too—the surprise namesake of his daughter.

CHAPTER THIRTY-FOUR

When Coal and Katie got home, she jumped out of the car and hustled into the house almost before Coal had even opened his door.

As Coal walked in, he saw Connie with the olive green phone pressed to her ear, and she looked at him and motioned him over. "He's here now, K.T. Hang on." She held the receiver toward Coal. "K.T."

"Hi, K.T." Coal still felt a little numb saying the name.

Hey, buddy. I called for a couple of reasons.

"Shoot."

Listen, man, I'm pretty thick-headed. I knew something was kind of off earlier, but Jennifer was really the one who kicked me in the butt. I don't know how to say this for sure, so I'll just say it. I'm sorry I sprung the name thing on you. I mean about Katie being named after me. I'm guessing Laura just did it on her own and never told you, huh?

"No, you're right. I wish I could say we did that together. I probably would have been happy to go along with it if she had just bothered to ask me. Sorry."

Hey, don't apologize! I named my girl Cynthia, remember? Not Coalette or something. You weren't obligated to name anyone after me. Shoot, man! Everyone knew Larry was your best friend. I'm just sorry I caught you off-guard. So... Why would Laura do that?"

Coal laughed a little ruefully. "Come on, Mister Prince of Pushups. Captain of the football team. Homecoming King. Most Wanted to Date. Most Handsome. You're kidding, right? Laura always had a crush on you, from way back in junior high. Heck, what Salmon girl didn't?"

Aw, cut it out. You can feel me blushing now, right? That's all a bunch of crap now, though. Look at me, and look at you! I went to seed, going bald, got a belly, getting wrinkly. And you? Heck, man, you look like you did when you were thirty! Still built like a German tank, got all your hair. Looks like you found the Fountain of Youth. Laura should have known how lucky she was.

For a long time, Coal was quiet. Finally, he said, "Yeah, K.T. She was real lucky. There are a lot more important things than any of that."

Well, I know I would marry you, buddy, if I was a girl! K.T. laughed, and Coal heard Jennifer tell him to hush.

Coal laughed too. "So the air is clear on that, right? Laura just had a crush on you."

I suppose. Still don't understand it, but you knew her better than me.

"What was the other thing you wanted?"

Oh, yeah! I forgot to tell you I saw that red and white station wagon again. I think it could be an Impala.

Coal perked up. A bad feeling came into his guts. "When was that?"

Eight-thirty, maybe. Not long after Cynthia and Katie came in. He came cruising down the street, real slow. I didn't even go out, just opened the curtain, and he zipped off down the street.

"What's the driver look like?"

Couldn't tell you. He was moving too fast. Dark hair, kind of thick.

"Could be your brother," said Coal.

Funny! I mean his hair was thick, not his belly!

"Well next time you see him, call dispatch, would you? And if you can get a plate number I'd sure like to have it."

Sure thing, buddy. Hey—no hard feelings about the name thing, right? No telling what a woman will do.

"Of course there aren't hard feelings. Nothing you did. Besides, I'm proud to have my oldest kid named after you."

All right, Coal. Thanks for saying that. Have a good night, my friend. And thanks for watching out for us, too. I'm still glad you took the job.

"Cram it, K.T. What are you trying to do, get out of a ticket?"

Laughing, K.T. hung up the phone.

"What was that all about?" asked Connie.

"Oh, some car keeps casing the Battertons' house. Weird."

She stared at him for a long time and finally gave up, knowing he was not going to say more. "Yeah? It's always something, huh? Hey, the roast is done, I think. Do you want a plate?"

"I'm not real hungry, Mom."

"What did you do, stop off for a burger?"

"No way! I'd much rather eat here."

"Just not hungry, huh?"

"Not really."

"How'd you like to go for a walk, Son?"

Coal eyed her, his guard coming up. "A walk? Why, what's up?"

"Why don't you leave your coat on for a while, okay? Let's get some fresh air."

Not again. She wants to talk. I'm damn tired of people talking and expecting me to listen. Why did God have to come up with so many words? Not to mention such strong tongue muscles?

"Sure, Mom," he said. "Grab your coat." What the heck? She was his mother. How could he turn her down?

They walked up the lane for no more than twenty or thirty yards before Connie reached out and hooked her gloved hands in the crook of his arm. "I love you, Son."

He reached over and patted her hand. "What's up, Mom?"

"I love you," she insisted.

"Sorry. Mom, you know that's not my favorite thing to say. Love you too."

Connie grunted. "Hmm... Coal, did you ever wonder how much Laura loved you?"

"Huh?"

"Would you stop that? You heard every word I said."

"Okay, you're right."

"And?"

"And... I'm sorry?"

"And?"

"Yeah, Mom, I wonder how much she loved me. And I keep getting more and more reasons to wonder, it seems like. Did you know the reason Laura chose Katie's name was because of K.T.?"

"I did."

"Why the hell didn't you tell me?"

"You watch your language, Coal. I may not be able to force soap in your mouth when you're awake, but you have to sleep sometime."

"Funny. But I think I deserve an answer."

"What purpose would it have served?"

"What purpose? How about avoiding what happened tonight, for one?"

"That's a good point. But no one ever saw that possibility. She asked him not to tell you he knew."

"Great. Makes me feel a lot better."

"Coal, she came and asked me when she was pregnant if I thought it would be okay to name her that. She said K.T. was such a good man, and he was kind to everyone. Smart, funny. She wanted to give him a tribute."

"That's swell. What about me? I'm kind of her father, after all. Or Larry, my best friend."

"Sure, Son. That would be great. What would you suggest? Coaleen? Larella?"

Coal pulled in a deep breath of the crisp night air and sighed it out. "Yeah. Okay. Then how about Laurena? Or how about just plain Hannah? Or Emma? She didn't have to name our daughter after *anyone*."

"You're being pretty silly," she said, dropping her hands from his arm and shoving them in her coat pockets. "It's done, isn't it? And don't you like the name Katie?"

He thought about that for a long moment. Sure, he liked it. It was one of his first choices when Laura had shown him her list. But... Sure. He liked it. Maybe he *was* just being silly.

"Does she know?"

"Who, Katie?"

"Uh-huh."

"No, I wouldn't suppose so. Should she?"

"I... I don't know. I haven't thought about it."

"I'll let you in on a little secret, Coal. I think it's time."

"I suppose I'm adopted."

Connie laughed. "No, Son, that is a *big* secret. Or at least it *was!*"

He returned the laugh, feeling suddenly lighter. His mother was good at doing that. "So what's the secret?"

"I guess this is kind of a big secret too, but here goes... I once loved a boy named Coal Garrett. In Dillon." Dillon, Montana, was where she had grown up, where Prince Savage had found her his freshman year in college.

"Mom, you're pulling my leg now." He stopped and turned to fully face her.

"Nope. I'm not."

"Did Daddy know?"

"Heavens, no! But he wanted to name you boys weird things. Like Ralph and Stanley and Ronald. Names from his family I didn't think sounded much like Western names. I wouldn't have it. I went through the pain to bring you boys here. Naming you was my right."

"Hmm...." Coal's only immediate response. He turned and held out his hand to her, and she took it. They walked farther along the road, their feet scuffing in the loose gravel. "What happened to him, Ma? This Coal Garrett of yours?"

"When I was a freshman at Beaverhead County High, he was a big junior. Wow, Coal, he was the best boxer in the whole school! I was so in love with that boy. He had black hair, like you had when you were born, but the darkest brown eyes." She sighed, and for several seconds she looked off over the dark pasture to their right. She filled her lungs with ice-chipped air and turned back to the front, walking and holding his hand. Her grip grew tighter. "He and his daddy used to fly their plane into the Bitterroots. That boy loved to fly, more than anything. He thought he must be reincarnated from an eagle." She let out a little, nostalgic laugh. "I think he really did. Well, anyway, they flew back in there for a whole week. Coal, he was so proud! His first big hunt. A brand-new Winchester .30/06. He was going to get the biggest elk ever killed in Idaho and have it stuffed on his wall. They tell me he got it, too."

There was a little shudder in her voice as she said that. "They found it in the wreckage of the plane, two days after they were supposed to be home. I had made him a silk tie. Painted the head of an elk on it and everything. I couldn't wait to see him when he got back. I just knew he was working up to kiss me."

She stopped and tried to laugh, but it didn't work out too well. He let go of her hand and put his arm around her shoulders, drawing her in tight to him. She leaned her head against his shoulder, and he tried to walk more smoothly to keep from rocking her head around. "I cried for two whole weeks. I don't think I slept for three days. And I sure couldn't go back to school. Finally, Grandma made me."

"Hey, Ma." Coal stopped in the middle of the road and turned to her, taking her in his arms and holding her against his chest. "Sounds to me like my *last* name could have been Garrett instead of my middle one." For a long time, she didn't speak. Finally, he heard her sniffling. "You still love Coal Garrett, huh, Mom?"

"I guess I still do. But if he were alive today I wouldn't even know him."

"I know you loved Dad too."

"More than anyone ever loved another person."

"I guess it's all right, naming a child in someone else's memory." But inside, he couldn't help holding onto the knowledge that K.T. was not a memory to Laura. When she chose Katie's name, he was still very much alive.

"Want to walk back home?" Coal asked. "It's got to be pushing ten degrees out here."

"Sure. I'm ready if you are."

They turned around and walked back, and Coal was thinking about K.T. Even now, in his forties, and in spite of the fact that he had let himself go and had lost a lot of hair, which was a third gray, his old friend was still a decent looking man. And Laura was right. K.T. was one of the nicest guys around. Even as the captain of the football team, he was humble, and kind to everyone. He took the homeliest girl in the whole valley out to Junior Prom when he found out no one else would do it. And his girlfriend at the time was all for it, or at least she said she was, the night he came to her and begged out of their date—asked for a rain check.

K.T.'s girlfriend in their junior year was a gorgeous little sophomore, a girl whose ash brown hair fell to the middle of her back in glossy luxuriousness, and whose blue eyes could break a boy in two or tell him how much she adored him, with a single blink. Her name was Laura Hutchinson, the daughter of the local jeweler.

In the middle of July, 1947, those incredible eyes turned to a local high school rodeo star and boxer by the name of Coal Savage.

One side of Coal's mouth came up in a smile full of memories. Laura. Oh, how he had loved that girl. She could sit a horse prettier than anyone he had ever laid eyes on. And she could fill out a white satin wedding gown like a goddess. K.T. had been one of Coal's groomsmen that night, and when she hugged and kissed them all, Coal's oldest brother, Larry, Trent and K.T., K.T.'s kiss was right on the lips. His memory of it, even all these years later, was how it seemed to linger.

But after all, Laura had loved K.T. first. And he had no doubt—K.T. Batterton, the Prince of Pushups and football captain, would be a hard young man to get over.

And what's more, K.T. was his friend, and one good man.

Wednesday, November 22

In the morning, Coal and Connie let the kids sleep in for half an hour. It was Friday. Coal had decided to drop them off at school himself. He sat by the front window sipping coffee and watched the big yellow bus draw up, sit for a moment, then roll on by.

A warm fire crackled in the stove. A good fire, of Idaho pine and fir. Its aroma filled the room, mingling with bacon and eggs, maple syrup and pancakes. The parole officer from Pocatello was planning on coming up to meet him today, to go pay a visit to Bigfoot Monahan. He prayed they would find a rifle. Hopefully a .30/06. He hoped that beyond all hope. He wanted the mystery over. He wanted the killer in jail. He could not stand the idea of losing anyone else in his county.

The kids came in and gathered at the table. Calming sunlight was breaking over the Beaverheads, washing like a sheet over the valley of gold. Connie carried in the food and set it on the table, then called him over, and he stood. The phone rang just as he was taking his seat, and he groaned. The kids were going to be late if they waited to eat.

"Say the prayer, Mom, would you? I'll be right back."

He picked up the phone, trying to speak quietly so as not to disturb the prayer.

The prayer wasn't strong enough.

The prayer wasn't soon enough.

Nor was it truly the food that needed to be blessed.

The voice on the other end of the line was Deputy Todd Mitchell. It was not strong. It was not cocky. *Sheriff Savage? You gotta come meet me, right away. I got Jim Lockwood here with me.*

Coal raised his voice a touch. "Meet you? Todd? Where are you? Where's 'here'?"

You gotta come out to the Batterton place. Sorry! I mean the Erickson place.

Something seemed to ring in the back of Coal's head. It seemed like he was floating in another reality. His head started to swim. The Ericksons, Leo and Sharleen, were the parents of Molly Erickson, one of Coal's core group of close friends in high school, and for a little while K.T. Batterton's sweetheart. Leo and Sharleen were like second parents to Coal, but even more so to K.T., who had loved going out in all his spare time to help them on their ranch. They used to joke about how they were going to adopt K.T. as their own.

"The Erickson place?" Coal repeated. "Why, what happened? Are Leo and Sharleen okay?"

Uhh... Well...

Suddenly, another voice came on the phone. *Coal? Jim here. Coal, maybe I should come get you.*

"Why, Jim?" Coal's voice sounded hollow in his own ears. "Jim, where are you? Todd first said the Battertons', and then he changed it to Ericksons'. What's going on?"

A pregnant pause. *Uh, no, we're out at Ericksons', all right. Coal, you hang tight. I'll drive over and pick you up.*

"Jim!" Coal practically yelled into the receiver. "Don't you hang up on me." Luckily, the prayer over breakfast had just ended. Coal felt many sets of eyes drilling through him.

Son, please. The voice on the other end of the line had a pleading tone. *I'll be there in five minutes.*

"The hell you will, Jim. I'll be *there.*" With that, he hung up the phone and looked at Connie, at the spread of food laid out there before his family, and then, one by one in a fast sweep, all of the kids.

Connie didn't speak. Neither did Coal. He just walked to his jacket and shrugged into it. He snugged his hat over his hair and slid his holstered Smith and Wesson onto his pants belt, settling it on his hip.

He looked again at Connie. His eyes felt dead. "You'll have to take the kids, Mom. I have to go to the Ericksons'. I don't have any idea when I'll be back."

Dobe and Shadow nuzzled his legs as he opened the door. He felt their faces against him, but he was too numb, too scared, to think about acknowledging or returning the affection.

Starting the Ford, he backed around and drove away from his mother's home, his heart in a vise. He didn't even feel the icy grip of the vinyl seat against his backside.

To be continued...

LAW OF THE LEMHI, PART TWO

Coming February 2017

Author's note

When my good friend Brad Dennison first presented me with the original idea for this book, it was to be a stand-alone novel of a small town sheriff dealing with a troublesome daughter and an assassin from out of his past. In typical Kirby Jonas form, it soon became a massive undertaking with many complex characters and a list of subplots as long as my arm. It also turned into the premier book of a series, *Savage Law.*

My first thought when reading over Brad's premise was that it would be a huge side-road from the Westerns I have written my entire life. My second thought was: This is exactly what I needed to break me out of the writing depression I was suffering at the time.

My third thought was: Salmon, Idaho, is *the* perfect remote town, and Lemhi the perfect county, to be the setting of such a book. And the 1970's the ideal decade in which to set it. With the Vietnam War looming large in the background, and many strange, mysterious, and fascinating characters coming and going through Salmon, no stage could have been better set.

And so, with pen and notebook, recorder and camera in hand, I set out to the "civilized wilds" of Salmon, where I started out my wildland fire fighting career, to re-create the county, the city, and the people of 1972.

This will also serve as my acknowledgments page, as I thank profusely those who have helped me along the way, both in learning Salmon more intimately, and in the in-depth research needed to recapture a decade so far removed from our own.

First, Paul Prochko, both for providing me with a wealth of information on snipers, their firearms and equipment, and for his glimpses of 1970's Salmon. It was also Paul who introduced me to a man who has since become like a brother to me, Bob Wilson, and in whose company I have spent many hours listening to the history of Salmon's police force and the town itself.

Thank you to Michael Moats, Richard Sellick, Dan Rufe, Danny Kovoch, to Julie Barbarick, Keri Burley, Vandee DeCora, Steve Beller, and all of the incidental people I ran into in Salmon but whose names I either never heard or I forgot to jot down. Thank you to the Armstrong and Ottonello families, who feel like a part of my heart. To Debbie, for her endless hours of being my listening ear, and to the memory of Elmer Keith, firearms aficionado extraordinaire, and also the memory of Bill Baker, arguably the most famous lawman Salmon ever had, at least in modern times.

Thanks to all of those who have allowed me to use their names and perhaps even a few of their personal characteristics to give life to some of the characters who populate these books: Maura Romero, Bob Wilson, Jordan Peterson, Ken Parks, Andy Holmes, Jay and Carrie Castillo, Tammy (Hawley) Pfeifer, Rick Cheatum, Joshua Olschewski, Kevin Wilhelm, Robert and Dennis Pratt, and Bobbie Lynn Williams, and to those whose faces will also appear on books under assumed character names:

Ashley Bullock, Dina Gardner, and Warren Webber. As an important note, none of the things done within these pages by any of these characters reflects in any way upon anything they have done in real life and should not be construed in any way as being a factual account of any moment in their lives.

And thank you to the town of Salmon and the county of Lemhi, for lending me their wonderful setting, their warmth, and their small-town charm.

About the Author

Kirby Frank Jonas was born in 1965 in Bozeman, Montana. His earliest memories are of living seven miles outside of town in a wide crack in the mountains known as Bear Canyon. At that time it was a remote and lonely place, but a place where a boy with an imagination could grow and nurture his mind, body and soul.

From Montana, the Jonas family moved almost as far across the country as they could go, to Broad Run, Virginia, a place that, although not as deep in the timbered mountains as Bear Canyon, was every bit as remote—Roland Farm. Once again, young Jonas spent his time mostly alone, or with his older brother, if he was not in school. Jonas learned to hike with his mother, fish with his father, and to dodge an unruly horse.

Jonas moved to Shelley, Idaho, in 1971, and from that time forth, with the exception of a couple of short sojourns elsewhere, he became an Idahoan. Jonas attended all twelve years of school in Shelley, graduating in 1983. In the sixth grade, he penned his first novel, *The Tumbleweed,* and in high school he wrote his second, *The Vigilante.* It was also during this time that he first became acquainted with Salmon, Idaho, staying toward the end of the Salmon River Road at the Golden Boulder Orchard and taking his first steps to manhood.

Jonas has lived in six cities in France, in Mesa, Arizona, and explored the United States extensively. He has fought fires for the Bureau of Land Management in five western states and carried a gun in three different jobs, as a Wells Fargo armed guard, a security officer for federal governmental facilities, and as a police officer.

In 1987, Jonas met his wife-to-be, Debbie Chatterton, and in 1989 took her to the altar. Over some rough and rocky roads they have traveled, and across some raging rivers that have at times threatened to draw them under, but they survived, and with four beautiful children to show for it: Cheyenne, Jacob, Clay and Matthew.

Jonas is currently employed both as a municipal firefighter for the city of Pocatello, Idaho, and as an armed security officer for local federal facilities not allowed to be named.

Books by Kirby Jonas

Season of the Vigilante, Book One: The Bloody Season
Season of the Vigilante, Book Two: Season's End
The Dansing Star
Death of an Eagle
Legend of the Tumbleweed
Lady Winchester
The Devil's Blood (combination of the *Season of the Vigilante* novels)
The Secret of Two Hawks
Knight of the Ribbons
Drygulch to Destiny
Samuel's Angel
The Night of My Hanging (And Other Short Stories)

Savage Law series
Law of the Lemhi, part one
Law of the Lemhi, part two
River of Death

The Badlands series
Yaqui Gold (co-author Clint Walker)
Canyon of the Haunted Shadows

Legends West series
Disciples of the Wind (co-author Jamie Jonas)
Reapers of the Wind (co-author Jamie Jonas)

Lehi's Dream series
Nephi Was My Friend
The Faith of a Man
A Land Called Bountiful
Shores of Promise (forthcoming)

Books on audio tape

The Dansing Star, narrated by James Drury, *"The Virginian"*
Death of an Eagle, narrated by James Drury
Legend of the Tumbleweed, narrated by James Drury
Lady Winchester, narrated by James Drury
Yaqui Gold, narrated by Gene Engene
The Secret of Two Hawks, narrated by Kevin Foley
Knight of the Ribbons, narrated by Rusty Nelson
Drygulch to Destiny, narrated by Kirby Jonas (forthcoming)

Available through the author at www.kirbyjonas.com

To order books, go to www.kirbyjonas.com or write to:

Howling Wolf Publishing
1611 City Creek Road
Pocatello ID 83204

Or send email to: kirby@kirbyjonas.com